Speechless

Mike Johnson

Speechless

LASAVIA
PUBLISHING

Published by Lasavia Publishing Ltd.
Auckland, New Zealand
www.lasaviapublishing.com

Copyright © Mike Johnson, 2025
Cover/Design: Daniela Gast

ISBN: 978-1-991083-36-4

So here I am, speechless before eternity.

Wolfgang Hilbig, *The Tidings of the Trees*

Literature, for me, is the only place that accepts silence.

Adania Shibli

The Little Mute Boy

The little boy was looking for his voice.
(the king of the crickets had it.)
In a drop of water
the little boy was looking for his voice.

I do not want it for speaking with;
I will make a ring of it
so that he may wear my silence
on his little finger.

In a drop of water
the little boy was looking for his voice.

(The captive voice, far away,
put on a cricket's clothes.)

Federico García Lorca

If you think that the Truth can be known from words
if you think that the Sun and the Ocean can pass through
that tiny opening called the mouth O someone should start laughing!

Hafez

I cannot remember another time when words themselves
have felt under such threat'

Margaret Atwood.

Part One
The Word Bringer

Cedric

My first memory is of a teddy bear called Cedric. I thought the name must be important, for my mother repeated it often while shaking the bear back and forth in front of my eyes.

Cedric. Cedric the bear.

I learned that word before any other.

Cedric was a soft toy with a stitched smile, but had, deep within the stuffing of his belly, a mechanism to give him a muffled, cow-like voice. I didn't have such a mechanism inside me. When I was turned over no sound automatically emerged. I had to make the sounds, and couldn't always make them.

Sometimes when I turned Cedric over, my mother would come as if I had called her. Cedric had my voice. He could say his first word before I could say mine. Sometimes she would ask if Cedric needed anything.

I don't know what happened to Cedric; he disappeared into the years. As he got older his head got wobbly, his fur thinned to patches, his eyeballs came loose and stuck out with a downcast look, his grin unravelled. Impossible to say at what point he vanished, taking his one word with him. That's what struck me about Cedric: he had only one word. One single word.

Mama.

He would never learn another.

Before the word

From the beginning, words were difficult for me. As a child, I would lose my way among them. Words couldn't escape my body. They would get stuck in my chest and throat. I would stutter. Words were legion, but none exactly fitted my tongue. My body was expected to carry the burden of that precision. What should have been the right words sounded strange to my young ears. I couldn't always see the relationship they bore to the world. They were like an ocean that went dark just as I was setting out upon it. I would dip my net into that ocean and come up with nothing. The right words were always over the horizon. I could hear them in my head as elongated sound shapes, but the task of forming them with my breath and mouth seemed hopeless. Meaning attached itself to sounds by the most fragile of threads.

Pitfalls would open up when there should have been an easy word or two. I would ready my mouth to speak only to find words had fled, leaving me vacant. I would laugh or make some noise to cover up. I played the fool to be the fool.

Where were the sounds I needed, utterances which came so naturally to people? Why did my body feel so hollow, my chest like an empty drum, silence reverberating through me? I quivered. I cast around for something to hold onto, to keep me connected to the world, but those sounds hovered beyond my grasp, silvery and elusive. They seemed to exist in their own world, mirroring each other as echoes. They were no longer real words but ghost sounds, suggestive of form but in essence formless. They had no concrete existence.

This made me afraid. I was fearful I would be cut off from the human race, isolated in my little pod of silence, forever trapped in the amber of speechlessness. Struck dumb by the word. And I would never grow up, because it was words that brought time into existence, sentences that strung time into chronology. Without them, I would be trapped forever in a child's body.

That panic would last only a moment or two, like a brief breathlessness. Then, once I was away from people, I felt liberated by silence. Where there had been a clutter of words trying to get out of my mouth, there was a marvellous, untenanted space into which I could expand. There were no words to hedge me in. No need to pick my way through sounds and their slippery meanings. The field was clear. I could run away to my whispering place where no adults could follow. I could curl up under the tent of the sky and listen for the sounds of birds. I could turn bird sounds into speech, imitate those sounds. Bird speech came easily to me. The vast silence of the sky was my natural playground; words dissolved in its formless blue. The song of the sky is pitched beyond human hearing. Birds can navigate that song, but I was in a human body and had to try to shape the awkward, clumsy sounds our bodies make.

That didn't satisfy people, of course. They became worried, angry, insulted, dismissive and uncertain, just as they are now.

My present speechlessness feels like a reversion to my fundamental condition, a state I knew before Cedric with his one precious word, before you, the word bringer, arrived, before I pushed through the stutter, before the circus procession of meanings began; an open, empty country into which I could grow, and find in silence the true ground of my being.

The Molesworth boys

There was a river, wide and stony, where I found further opportunities to be alone and far from the troublesome sound of human voices. This river had a name which you, word bringer, taught me but I didn't like to use it, not to begin with. For me it was The River and not just one among many. Sometimes it was restrained and chattery. Often it was boisterous and fast, roaring out of the mountains with a rough, gravelly voice. When in spate, it could roll huge boulders before it in a terrifying demonstration of power. Even in more settled conditions, it bustled along, full of eloquence, vigour and sparkle.

Its incessant, busy prattle didn't bother me. I would wander upstream to a bend where willow trees overhung a dark, swirling pool, my favourite spot for sitting and watching the world around me in a mute daze, enjoying the feeling of the water bubbling through my head, carrying childish thoughts and terrors away with it. Shadows from the willows would come and go on the water, shift and reform, just the way thoughts did. Peering into its depths, I would sometimes see sleek trout holding themselves steady in the fast current with periodic flicks of their tails, seemingly suspended in another medium.

Time would loosen its grip on me and the sun would pass from one part of the sky to another without me noticing except for the changing shapes of the shadows on the water. I learned that a word-bound world was a time-bound world, and if I left the first behind, the second would follow. Sometimes I would sing to myself, not words as such but sounds that issued from my body and modulated themselves to the air around me. They were conversations in blue and green.

Returning from these expeditions, I would sit quietly in the tumult of everyday activity and slowly adjust to human time. Sounds would settle into words, people would speak to me and I would try to formulate words in return, words I wouldn't stumble over.

As well as the river we had Conical Hill. That was one of the first place-names I learned to say. One day it went from being The Hill to assuming its name and becoming its individual self. I liked the way it repeated the 'k' sounds; I could say it over and over, just enjoying the sound of it. I'd voice it as a bird chirp. That way I wouldn't stutter at those 'k' sounds. The name made me think of a tall dunce's hat, not so pointy but complete with comical cone. The name of that hill gave me my first taste for the feel of syllables, how syllables can bang up against each other like stones in the river, and there was a pleasure to be taken in the rough or velvety feel of them.

My mother would take me up the hill's winding loop track when I was too small to make it without being carried at least some of the way. She sometimes did this to 'get out of the house,' as she put it. I gathered that getting out of the house was something very important to her. I could join her and we could both get out of the house. After Frank was born he could come too, perched in a backpack.

There was a lookout at the top. She would stand beside it and point to distant ranges, saying that over there was the Molesworth Station. She sounded deeply impressed when she spoke of Molesworth Station, as if larger-than-life things happened there. And they did. One of those larger-than-life things was called mustering, which called for physical strength and endurance. Men on horseback rounding up cattle and bringing them in from the outreaches to winter pastures. I have early memories of these men riding into town after the mustering, whooping and hollering, their horses whinnying and snorting. Kegs of beer sprouted on street corners, and for a few days our largely dry town was awash with booze and brouhaha.

These celebrations excited my mother, and she and Dad would join the revellers on the street where there would be singing and dancing, while the girls of the town received lots of special attention. It was a source of pride to Mum that these roughneck cowboys treated her with perfect respect, offering her a place to sit down, running to pour her a drink and calling her 'Mrs'. She would sit among them, drink in hand, looking flushed and pretty, while Dad got drunk with the cowboys and sawmill workers.

I enjoyed these street parties as I could team up with my friend, Cargill, passing among the adults unseen, stealing sips from unattended glasses and spying out kissing couples. I was quick to notice that drunk people had as much trouble talking as I did, struggling to find and stumbling over their words. Although I learned to keep out of their way, I was delighted to observe adults battling sounds the way I had to. Cargill and I would follow the cowboys when they took the girls up Conical Hill into the giggling shadows, but those sharp-eyed musterers soon spotted us and shooed us away.

Being around drinkers helped train me to talk. I learned how to articulate carefully, like a drunk trying to sound sober. The shapes of the words felt too big in my mouth, like river stones, and I had to proceed with great care. If I didn't, mixed up sounds would pour from my mouth like vomit. When that happened, Mum would look away. To her I didn't sound like someone trying to imitate a drunk person, just a kid who sounded stupid.

As soon as I was able – I can't have been more than four years old – I would treddle up to the top of Conical Hill on my own, beneath the cedar and cypress trees, breathing in the odours of that airy forest, wearing the hush of it like a cloak. Getting out of the house suited me too. When I reached the lookout, I was on the threshold of a huge and unknown world. I could survey the valleys and peaks of the alps vanishing in the distance and the border world of the sky. Awareness of time would fade as the shadows around me came alive, and moments turned into sing-song. I would sing myself into the sky where I could see more and more of the world. Beneath me the river wove its way through the valleys in a silver thread, coming down from Molesworth where the cowboys reigned.

I had to be careful to begin my return journey before the shadows grew too long under the trees. Fairy-tale worlds blossomed in those shadows along with the snuffling of wild pigs. Real wild pigs. Somehow, I would always make it home just before dark. Sometimes my mother would be waiting at the back door for me, her eyes grown big with searching, but she didn't once offer any word of reproof or attempt to issue me with instructions on what to do next time. She would simply put her hand on my shoulder and guide me to the warmly lit kitchen for stew and potatoes. And sometimes she wouldn't be waiting and I would find her on the couch or in the bedroom, crying, and there was no stew and potatoes.

The dancing pig

Those post-mustering parties would go on all night, and get wilder as the night progressed, with shouting and singing to the accompaniment of breaking glass. On such nights my little brother, Frank, and I would find it difficult to sleep, no matter how exhausted we were. Frank would shut his eyes tightly, as if that would keep out the sound, while I would lie on my back looking up at the ceiling and the passing parade of shadows that cavorted there. The shadows would sway this way and that as if compelled by the raucous music.

On one particular night our house became party central. Loud big-band dance music, Louis Armstrong and Woody Herman bounced off the walls. The saints came marching in as well as the big butter and egg man from the west. They shook the timbers while the heavy stamping tumbled my teddies off their shelf. My father was a big man. He carried too much weight, but his laughter was soft and light. Not when he was drunk. That night he was shouting in a brutal, slurring voice. My mother's laugh had turned into a screech.

Suddenly the door opened and the noise from the party came billowing in. I looked up and saw my mother standing by my bedside. She gathered me up in her arms, held me tightly to her chest and began to dance. She was a skinny, intense woman and I could feel the bones of her chest pushing into me. She danced clumsily around the room with me, her movements growing increasingly wild. I was swung this way and that, and yet her face was concentrated and grim. As she danced, she turned into a large, pink pig, moving upright, her back trotters clacking on the floorboards like a tap dancer. The more I struggled to get away, the tighter she held me. Her eyes were dull and heavy, but full of hunger. That hunger terrified me because she was getting ready to eat me, to snuffle her snout into my flesh and suck up my blood.

I screamed and woke up. Frank had come to my bed and was lying beside me, looking up at me with frightened eyes. The music was still pounding through the house, but our door was shut and Mum wasn't in the room. I searched out the shadows to make sure she wasn't lurking somewhere. Then I heard her. She was squealing the way a pig does when a hunting knife goes into it.

Frank and I hid under the blankets.

The coming of the word bringer

One of my first memories is of standing in tall grass, taller than me, singing both out loud and in my head, feeling you coming into being around me, feeling that the world itself must have come into being that way, through the agency of song, the resonance of voice.

I didn't know who you were. To me you were the keeper of secrets, and the secrets lay inside the words. I thought of you as a Father Christmas of words, hauling them through the sky in a huge sack and riding a cowboy horse. All the words I would ever need were in that sack, and I could have them on condition that I clearly understood one day you would leave me and take them all away with you back to the sky, for, unlike Father Christmas who comes only once a year, you would come and go as you pleased.

I felt you most strongly when crouching in the secret little cave I would make in the soft muehlenbeckia with its tangled zig-zagging branches and small heart-shaped leaves, where nobody could find us and I could hide for hours until my mother's voice came floating through the air calling my name, seeking me out, calling me home. Recalling me. In that little cave no one could see me. I had a pleasing invisibility. I had refuge from the intimidating sounds of human speech. Once my mother went right past me, so close I could have touched her, looking for me, not even seeing me.

In that cave you would talk to me and gift me the words I needed to talk back to you, and eventually to other people. You taught me that words are more than just complicated air flow through the throat, that words take body, and that the word's meaning is its body. Every word has flesh, and if that flesh is stripped away nothing is left but the hollow sound, meaning no more than an echo. When I sang them, my voice became flesh too.

You made it easy for me to talk to you. I told you all my stories, some made of stone, some made of water, some made of sky and some made of fire, and when no one else was listening you were there, and you heard everything, whether I spoke it out loud or not. My stories took shape in your invisible ears. You let the whispers run through the muehlenbeckia like scuttling insects. You let them play. You let them discover themselves. You let them procreate. At the same time you fashioned a home for silence to know itself after the whispers had all scuttled away or faded into the rustle of leaves. You taught me that words arise from the theatre of silence and sink back into it again, that silence is the womb of speech, and that while words can be noisy, even clamouring creatures, full of their own self-importance and drama, they cannot escape the silence from which they came and which permeates their beings. They are of flesh but also of dust.

This was most evident in the whispering place in the muehlenbeckia, for whispered words are full of secrets and silences. Full of breathing. In their hush they belong as much to mind as to air. I used the whispering place to practice my speaking, bringing words from your Father Christmas sack into the world, giving flesh to the word.

While the muehlenbeckia has gone, the whispering place is still there, like a memory banging in the wind, our singular space, a locus of awfulness and beauty. As we turn our attention to it, it pushes back the boundaries of words, makes a secret place for us to hide.

I cannot, however, escape a particular urgency. You have put me on notice. Soon this whispering place itself will be gone. The word bringer will steal away, taking all the words, leaving a brief susurration of leaves, before silence.

In the shadows of my name

There was another me, waiting in the shadows of my name, hiding in the mirror on Mum's dresser. An articulate me. A me that could talk with all the words you brought me in your sack. A me that you cultivated. A master of words, or at least a lover of them. Another me that was beginning to emerge from the world of reflections. It started with me giving names to my soft toys which I could murmur out loud. They weren't real names, just sounds that seemed right. I had Wurzle and Burzle and Swingle and Bingle. And their names were not necessarily fixed but could change from day to day. It didn't matter because they were just made-up sounds with no stable or final form, and maybe because of that I had no trouble getting my tongue around them.

I had three teddies that I did give names to: Cedric, always crying for his mama, a middle-sized one I simply called Ted, a small one I called Little Ted, one rabbit with tall ears who had many names, and a grey mouse-like creature who refused to be named. They had no need for speech, and no capacity for it either, as their mouths were all sewn shut with bright thread. We got along fine without words. Only as I got older did I learn that, unlike my soft toys, humans need to constantly talk to one another, even if they don't have much to say. I came to appreciate that words were the medium in which people live. If I were to be considered a real person, I too would have to enter that medium and find my way among words like all the other chatterers.

That was not easy. It felt like climbing a Conical Hill without end on a pathway that kept getting steeper. Some kids took to words naturally, as if they had been born full of them and it was only a matter of time before they ripened in their mouths. I used to envy those kids. My friend Cargill was the same age as me and he talked all the time. He talked about everything and nothing, it didn't seem to matter as long as he could keep generating words. He loved the sound of his own voice. We were friends because he could talk and I didn't have to, and because he rarely stopped talking, he didn't notice my silence or care about my stuttering. I could nod and mumble and that's all he seemed to need. When I was with him, I could hide the fact that I found words difficult, difficult to find and when found, difficult to give sound to. It was as if the words themselves did not want to leave my body, be thrust into the air where they would, after a momentary existence, dissolve. I learned that time sweeps words away as soon as they are uttered, which made it seem strange to me that people spent so much time producing them. All that effort to make sounds which are gone in an instant.

I welcomed the slow emergence of the other me from the shadows of my name. Slow and fitful. Sometimes I would feel him in command and a sentence or two would flow from my mouth without hinderance, other times he would desert me halfway through a word and I would lose track, unable to find a way forward. Consonants bubbled in my mouth, vowels became elongated, words would twist up before I could get them out. Then came the gut-wrenching realisation that a particular word wasn't coming out of my mouth no matter how I strained. It was as if the words wanted to go inwards, back into my body rather than outwards, into the world. My mind would go blank. Blood would rush to my cheeks and my ears would burn. My breath would come in short gasps, my palms would get sweaty. Sometimes I would feel light-headed, as if about to faint, and my heart would thud uselessly in my chest. I wanted to run away and never come back. I dreamed of running to catch a bus, only to have it pull away just as I arrived. I dreamed of falling and never touching the ground. I dreamed of swelling up inside until ready to burst.

My parents had little sympathy for my affliction, not because they were cruel or indifferent, but they were working people and had little time for a kid who couldn't articulate. Also, they had another child, my brother Frank who quickly learned that one prolonged yowl was all he needed to capture his parents' attention. They would brusquely finish my sentences for me, making assumptions about what I wanted to say. I hardly had a chance to correct them if they got it wrong. This left me feeling bereft, robbed of the words that might have been mine to say.

I had to be patient, let the other me move at his own pace. The world was strange and enormous and it was easy to get frightened.

The tale of Midnight the cat

I acted out the enticement of the new, articulate me, in the taming of a wild cat. I first noticed the cat out the window one night. I'd heard a strange yowl, like the cry of a wraith or a child in pain. At first I could see nothing in the glass but the ghost of my own reflection, then the dark hue of grass and a shadow moving against a moonless night sky. The shadow had leapt from the ground to the gatepost and seemed to be facing me, looking back at me.

I was spooked and got Frank to have a look. Frank said he saw a cat, but he was very little and I wasn't sure that he even knew where to look.

When I looked back after talking to Frank, the shadow had moved from the gatepost and try as I might I saw no further sign of any mysterious feline.

That was my introduction to Midnight the cat.

It was soon established that there was in fact a cat lurking around in our vicinity, a black cat that didn't like to be seen and usually only got about at night. It didn't belong to any of our neighbours so had to be a wild cat, a feral cat, a cat that could never be tamed. I vowed to tame it, and came up with a plan. I started by leaving a plate of rabbit meat out by the gate, our gate to the road, at the bottom of the gatepost. Frank and I would cluster at the window to see if we could see the cat come for the food. Very rarely did we see it, but in the morning the meat would be gone.

I shifted the plate closer to the house, on our roughhouse of a lawn, and soon that meat began disappearing too. Progressively, I moved the plate closer to the house, drawing the wary animal in. When we got close enough to the house, Frank and I could see it, a shadow among shadows crouching at the plate.

I told Frank stories I made up about the cat, who I christened Midnight and who became the slinky hero of my stories. My stuttering faded when I told Frank these stories, how Midnight was attacked by magpies and had to take refuge in thick gorse, how Midnight battled Old Tom, the crusty ginger cat from down the road with a half bitten-off ear, how Midnight saved a kitten from being eaten by a nasty, hump-backed rat. Of course Midnight always came out on top, outwitting the magpies, jumping away from Old Tom's claws while scratching his nose, and chasing the hump-back rat halfway up Conical Hill before leaping upon it and devouring it.

Eventually, we left the plate inside the porch to the back door and Midnight would come right up and eat. We learned that 'it' was a she.

I'm not saying I tamed her. You could never tame a cat like Midnight. She would come into the house but only on her own terms, and would disappear for days on end. She was never comfortable with being picked up and would lie tensely in my arms ready to leap away at the first opportunity. Once I did succeed in picking her up, stroking her to keep her calm, and out of curiosity took her to my mother's dresser to let her see herself in its tall mirror. Her fur flew up along her back and she dug her claws into my arm before leaping away.

It was that incident that prompted me to associate the other, articulate me with Midnight. I had to be patient. I had to entice the other me out of the mirror a bit at a time, draw him forth, for he did want to come – he was looking for a world in which he could speak freely without impediment.

'n' before the 'm'

Just as I didn't like to say the name of our river, I took every opportunity to avoid having to say the name of our town. The river was The River, the town was The Town, the mountains were The Mountains; these were referents I did not want to relativise by giving them names, names that would have to take their places among other names.

It wasn't always possible to avoid names, however; names kept coming up. I found when I tried, with all the will I could summon, I couldn't pronounce the name of our town, which was the same name as the river: Hanmer. It looks easy enough, but saying it even now I have to stop and think, getting my humming sounds in the right order. I had trouble putting the 'n' before the 'm' and would slur them over, making it sound like Hammer, or, when I tried hard, Hamner. I noticed I wasn't the only one who said Hamner and nobody seemed to care too much. If I couldn't avoid the word, I wanted to get it right. The more difficult I found a word, the more I wanted to get it right, and the more I struggled, the less able I was to do so.

The word Han-mer was everywhere. There was the Han-mer town, the Han-mer River, the Han-mer Road, the Han-mer Primary School, the Han-mer Springs and the Han-mer Hospital. I practised saying the word in front of the mirror so that my articulate self could get it right and say it without hesitation. Once my other self got it right I could take it out into the world. I could run down the main street shouting it, flourish it before my friends and present it to my teacher. Han-mer was my prize, the first difficult word over which I triumphed, the first sign of the emergence of the other me.

The sounds of gunfire

I learned to sing with my feet. That happened when I ran. The faster I ran the louder my feet sang. I was sure that if I ran fast enough, the song of my feet would carry me right around the world, maybe lift me off the ground to run through the sky. I'd heard that if you ran in a straight line you'd end up back in the same place. I thought that was a fairy-tale, but worth trying out. There was a dirt road that passed along the back of the sawmill I liked to run. It was a short cut home from the river. It was uneven and I had to jump across the ruts left by the logging trucks that used the road. When I jumped, and was flying through mid-air, I could feel the seconds stretching out before my feet re-connected with the earth. In those seconds my feet learned how to sing and my body was in harmony with the air. I didn't end up back where I started, but rather deep in the forest of European larch and Corsican pine.

On one of these runs, following the dirt road away from the town, I reached the outer edges of the world I inhabited. The silence was deeper there than anywhere, even Conical Hill. Hanmer seemed very far away. I paused as if I had reached an invisible wall. Beyond this point I had never ventured. This wall, I imagined, encircled the town. I had only gone so far in any direction. Beyond the wall lay the rest of the world.

Pausing there, uncertain as to whether or not to take another step, I heard the sound of gunfire. This was not the quick snap of the .22s used to hunt rabbits, or even the louder crack of the .303s used to hunt deer and pigs, but steady, heavy fire, and it seemed to be coming from all around me. I could hear men shouting hoarsely, although I couldn't make out what they were saying, and people screaming. I thought I caught glimpses of faces in the trees but couldn't be sure, appearing only in the corner of my eye. When I focused there was nothing to see but the trees themselves seeming to bend back and forth as if buffeted by high winds. I could feel the world swirling around me as if I were still moving. Several magpies shrieked as they swooped over me, too low for comfort. A deer gave me a startled look as it raced across the road, bouncing high in the air. Then I saw the boy, no older than me, standing on the road up ahead of me, facing me, unmoving. All I knew was, he wasn't a kid from Hanmer. He wore only a pair of tatty shorts. His arms hung by his side, palms facing forward towards me. We stared at each other in mutual fright. I turned and ran back the way I came as if the hordes of hell were at my heels. I was too scared to look back. As I ran past the sawmill, a worker shouted 'Look at that kid run!' and the other workers laughed.

I didn't stop running until their laughter was far behind me.

The boy who flew

While on one of our Sunday drives, which allowed Mum another opportunity to 'get out of the house,' which was the true purpose of these drives, I opened the back door of the car and allowed the wind to take me. For a moment I sank through the air, gently, the air buoying me up. I was like a stone sinking quietly through water. Like a hawk sinking through the wind. I barely felt it when I touched the rough gravel of the road.

My parents later said that I was very lucky to be alive. Lucky because they were driving quite slowly on the gravel road, and because of the quick reactions of the driver of an empty logging truck following behind. He slammed on the brakes and the truck slewed across the road, coming to a halt moments before running me over. And lucky because somehow I was unhurt. Hardly a scratch on me. I got up and walked away. Mum said that was because I had not stiffened my body. She saw me in the rear-vision mirror. She said I looked completely relaxed. That stunned her.

'Why did you do that?' Mum asked, her voice crackling with fear and anxiety. What a worry I was to her. You never knew what I would do next.

I had no answer. I was still learning to distinguish the elements into which I had been born, still learning the way words connected with the world, the way my body connected to the air and the earth. The way time could stretch and compress. On the logging road, running from the sound of gunfire and the apparition of a strange boy, I had learned to fly, at least for those moments before my feet hit the ground. I had no fear.

Not long after that, something similar happened. We drove to visit Mum's parents who ran a petrol station in Scargill, an hour or so's drive from Hanmer. They lived in a two-storey house I loved because of the stairs, which were made of dark, polished wood with a strip of well-worn red carpet running down the middle. An orange and yellow glass window at the top threw a mellow light over them, but as that was the only light the mellowness edged into gloom. Standing at the top, I could look down at a landing below where the stairs turned before continuing their descent.

I liked to stand at the top and imagine that, after they turned, the stairs led not into my grandparents' ground floor but another world that existed in its own medium. Creatures that lived there could swim through the air. That made the stairs magical, which made me think that if I jumped off the top, I would float to the landing below and come to no harm. The air would hold me up. I would have no more weight than a dandelion floating in the wind. As I stood there, this feeling grew into a certainty. Opening the car door and flying out was done on impulse, but in the case of flying down the stairs, that was a conscious decision. I knew it could be done. I had no doubts. I stepped back a few feet, ran, and leapt off, aiming for the landing.

I floated.

It was a distinct and unmistakable feeling, much stronger than I'd felt when leaving the car. I landed on my feet without even going off-balance. It felt so natural I didn't see it as something remarkable. I didn't do it a second time. I had no need to. I was satisfied that I had understood something about the world in which I lived, which was not always what it appeared to be.

The mistake I made was trying to tell the adults about it. At first they didn't grasp what I was saying, but when they did, silence fell at the table where they were drinking coffee and nattering. Dad gave me a squinty look and shifted his bulk uncomfortably in his kitchen chair, as if he couldn't quite get a fix on me. Mum's face creased with concern.

'Bloody death trap those stairs,' my grandfather said. His voice was as wizened as his body, which formed a question mark against the back of his chair.

My grandmother, a tall stately woman, offered me a buttered scone with raspberry jam she'd made herself.

The new girl under the sycamore tree

I first noticed the new girl on the day Cargill and I got into trouble. One of the unique features of our town was a hospital dedicated to drunks who came to dry out. Like lizards they would sit in the sun on benches that ran along the front of the main building, stare at things and murmur to one another in broken voices. The hospital ground boasted a large artificial pond in which lilies floated on top of a rather scummy dream. Cargill and I discovered that this pond was shallow, reaching just over our knees, and we would wade in looking for frogs or tadpoles despite this being strictly forbidden and likely to draw the wrath of the groundsman who had special words he kept for naughty children. 'You pipsqueaks!' he would shout, 'You brattish small fry! You carrion birds!' Later, I came to identify him as Captain Haddock of the Tintin series, full of big words and bluster, although he was taller and skinnier than Haddock.

The drunks took little notice of us, or would laugh, shout encouragement and rub their gums with grimy hands.

On this day, the day I noticed the new girl, we found a plug, just like the plug in a bath with a ring on top for pulling, only much bigger. We immediately applied ourselves to pulling it up. We didn't have to discuss this, we simply did it. After a brief struggle we met with success.

The plug came out and all the water drained away, leaving the lilies limp and stranded, the tadpoles and cockabullies wriggling and jumping in the slime, and us, the culprits, exposed.

The groundsman came around the corner of the building at full tilt, flourishing a fist, imprecations and threats already filling the air. He would skin us alive like a couple of rabbits, he said. The lizards croaked and hooted and pointed. Seems we'd made their day.

Just as we were making a run for the street, I saw a girl standing under the sycamore tree outside the gate, watching us. She had dark, curly hair, which mingled with the shadows of the sycamore, and wore a long, pleated skirt in greens and ambers, very different from the short, brightly coloured print skirts and frocks the other girls wore. That was the first time I saw Olga and I wasn't sure she was real. She looked like a construction of shadows from the branches of the sycamore tree. When she saw us charging towards her, the angry groundsman galloping along behind us, she retreated and disappeared. Once we were through the gate, the groundsman gave up the chase. He had other things to do, like refill the pond with water before the lilies and the fish died. I looked up and down the street but she was nowhere to be seen.

Cargill hadn't seen her and was not convinced she existed. After all, we knew all the girls in Hanmer, and had little time for any of them. There was Mary with the straight black hair, freckles and a nasty tongue. It wasn't her. And there was Leda, whose parents were from Holland, with a fuzz of blonde hair and a sugary voice. It wasn't her. Or any of their backbiting friends. I must have imagined it.

Cargill ran off home. He was afraid of getting into trouble for the pond incident. 'They'll find out, you wait and see,' he said. Cargill was frightened of his dad.

I stood by the gate in the shadows of the sycamore, exactly where the girl had been standing, and watched the groundsman unroll a hose. I felt protected and invisible. The groundsman glanced towards the gate a few times, checking maybe to see if we had the nerve to come back, but he didn't see me. There was a faint leathery smell, laced with a trace of sweetness. I wasn't sure. It could have been the smell of the tree, but I'd never noticed it before.

I was thinking of the girl who maybe I'd just imagined, when in front of my eyes a sycamore seed did its tight, single-winged spiral to the earth, fluttering like a living creature.

Spare the rod

Cargill was right. We did get into trouble. Later, when I got home, my parents were waiting for me.

'Didn't we tell you never to go into the hospital grounds?' Dad said. Of course Dad knew the hospital groundsman; everybody knew everybody in Hanmer. A fly couldn't get in or out without the gossips noticing.

'Y-Y-Y, Yes,' I said miserably.

I looked to Mum but her mouth had turned into a thin line. Her thin face looked small and pinched.

'Go into the bathroom,' Dad said.

He lumbered behind me.

The bathroom was where punishment was administered, I'm not sure why.

I needed words then, to make my protest, but couldn't speak, not a word for my own defence.

In the bathroom Dad took off his belt, ordered me to drop my shorts, and administered two decent welts across my backside.

He didn't say anything. Presumably, I had learned my lesson.

It stung, but all was not lost. I had my vision of the girl under the sycamore tree, her face turned towards me. I kept seeing her in my mind's eye.

Later, Cargill told me that his parents had locked him in a wardrobe in the dark for an hour. I preferred the belt any day.

Olga in bright sunlight

The next day, at school, I saw the girl again. I pointed her out to Cargill who had to agree that she was not imaginary, although he had to rub his eyes a couple of times as if he doubted what they showed him.

It was a new entrants' class, so we must have been five years old. I'd grown up with most of the kids and knew them all, although because of my speech impediment I remained on the outside of their little gangs. This girl was new. Nobody knew her. She hadn't made friends with anyone before school started. She wore the same autumn-coloured, pleated skirt and the same dark curly hair behind which she could hide her face, this time not mingling with the shadows of the sycamore tree but shining bright in the sunlight. She was very quiet and shy and didn't screech and yell like the other girls. When I heard the teacher use her name, Olga, something happened to me. In some way, her name came in from the world and entered me. In that moment I learned that names were secret things full of power. Saying them was like chanting a spell. Her name was full of a mysterious potency I couldn't fathom. I could say her name without difficulty. It rose up from the back of my throat sounding dark and rich in my mouth, round and full, anchored in the world by the guttural 'g'. A two-toned word: Ol-ga.

Like me, she was quiet and observant. Because of that we noticed each other, observed each other being quiet and observant, recognised that we were marked out somehow from the others. I soon learned that her quietness was largely a result of not knowing English; we both had our language problems. She was not only new to the town but to our country, and all she spoke at first was Russian. Sometimes she would blurt out some Russian, forgetting that no one would understand her. She sat apart from the other kids to have her lunch, not only because she couldn't join in the talk, but because her lunch was different from ours, not sandwiches with butter and Marmite or jam, as we often had, but potatoes and dumplings.

One day I approached her because I felt sorry for her sitting alone. I asked if I could sit with her by gesturing to the empty bench beside her. I could tell by the way she nodded that she was pleased, even though she could hardly look at me. We didn't try to speak but sat silently in mutual embarrassment, totally alive to each other's presence. Some of the other kids were looking at us but I was used to ignoring them. Then she pushed her mass of curls back off her face and smiled at me, and I saw how pretty she was. I'd never seen a girl as pretty as that. Leda, with the fuzz of blonde hair, was considered the prettiest girl in the class, but she couldn't hold a candle to Olga.

'Hell oo' she said.

'H-H-Hell oo' I said back to her. I sounded like a wounded owl.

We laughed together. It was a start. We'd take it from there. The sky was our oyster.

Our first efforts at conversation were halting and mutually humiliating. We got through it by laughing and making a joke of it. That's how the first sounds of what was to become our own made-up language started, silly mispronunciations of English, adopted and given a meaning. When she heard me stuttering she became very quiet and attentive, and would never interrupt or imitate me for fun the way other kids did. She would watch my mouth as if encouraging the words to come forth. It seemed easier to find words with her eyes on my lips.

She accepted me, took my stutter quite naturally as if it were nothing at all, and just required a little patience. It was with Olga that my stuttering began to fade as the other, articulate me gained in confidence. I was grateful to you, word bringer, for your bag of words, but more grateful to Olga for her gentle forbearance.

I didn't care if we talked or not. Just sitting beside her made me happy in a way that was new to me. My body felt light, as if I could float up into the air. I was giddy with her presence. She seemed to be constantly surrounded by a nimbus of light. When I walked with her, it felt like the ground was made of soft cushions.

After we became friends, she would babble away to me in Russian, quite happy just to be able to talk freely and not in her tortured English. I would listen with great fascination to the sounds streaming unhindered from her mouth, accompanied by animated facial gestures. To her the sounds were full of meaning, but what I enjoyed was their meaninglessness, their shapes and patterns, and the contours her pouty red lips made when she spoke.

I discovered, in the way of the magic of names, that Olga sounds like Volga, the name of a river in Russia, a river that flowed south and eventually flowed into the Caspian Sea. After that, I always thought of her talking as a great word river, one which flowed into other word rivers and eventually into a great word ocean where all the words that ever were get joined and mixed up. Sometimes I would dream of swimming in that ocean, all the while having to keep my mouth shut in case all those mixed-up words were sucked into my body and drowned me. I would learn to swim in that ocean however, I knew I could. I would find in words my medium.

I introduced her to my favourite spot on the riverbank where the willows grew. Until then, I hadn't shared this spot with anybody else, even Cargill who would have got bored with it. We'd sit on the bank in the shade, Olga would talk and I'd happily listen to those turbulent sounds so full of mystery and fascination. When we thought nobody was around, we'd hold hands. We'd stop talking then, and the world became hushed and special. We watched a magpie flying overhead as if it were a miracle. Felt the river bubble with consciousness. The sky rained blue. Everything fitted into everything else seamlessly.

I started to dream about Olga, and to think of her all the time. I dreamed of her under the sycamore tree. She had grown tall and full of deep magic. I couldn't get her name out of my mind. It rolled through my head over and over, like Orthodox priests chanting. It lost its meaning as words will with constant repetition, and became pure sound, an outward breath in two steps, Ollll-gaaaa, and that sound was one with the flesh and the blood of the girl. In the morning, after a night of restless Olga dreams, I would eat my Weet-Bix and sugar with my heart moving lumpishly in my chest, and a peculiar emptiness in my abdomen as if I were about to come apart, squirming with the anticipation of seeing her again at school, perhaps her skipping through the gate, perhaps sitting at her desk with her hair over her face. When the time came for us to part and return to our homes, a great loneliness would descend upon me. I was bereft. A whole night lay between then and seeing her again, a night only made tolerable by fantasies of all the things we could do together.

I fell in love with Olga as much for that mysterious and wonderful flow of Russian as the mass of dark curls, her lustrous brown eyes and ruby lips, or the way the sun got tangled in her hair. I told my parents that when I grew up I would marry her and they laughed, perhaps at my great seriousness. I was hurt by their amusement. This was the moment I learned that when we finally get our words into the world, across our stumble tongues, we have no control over how they will be received. Some things, I learned, were better left unsaid. Even tolerant, loving laughter can be cruel.

The other girls were not kind to Olga. They couldn't get the measure of her, and looked askance at our friendship. Mary of the straight black hair and freckles was particularly nasty, and orchestrated attacks on Olga, calling her that 'slutty Russian,' hair pulling and arm-scratching, the other girls and some of the boys egging her on. The attacks on Olga brought Leda and Mary, previously rivals, to an alliance. Leda didn't like being upstaged and no longer the prettiest girl in the class, and said she hated Olga for her 'stupid face.' The two of them would shriek and laugh together like a couple of cackling witches.

They gave Olga no peace.

The first lies

It came as a shock to me to realise that not all the kids in our town were as charmed by Olga's strangeness as I was. I couldn't believe they didn't see the sweet person I saw, or admire the way her hair shone in the sun or her smile brought the world to life.

Some seemed to be scared of her, or offended by her. They called her horrible names like 'ruskie' and 'rushbag' and 'rushface' or just 'Russian pig' or plain 'slut.' They hurled these at her as if the words were rocks that might bruise her skin or make her bleed. That didn't happen, yet the insults hurt her just the same. When the kids saw this, they redoubled their efforts to hurt her even more, going about it with fiendish glee, following her around shouting and yelling and discussing what they would do to her in excited voices until she ran home crying her eyes out. They took every opportunity to make her life miserable.

When I stood up for her and tried to tell them to leave her alone, they'd turn on me and mock my stutter. 'L-l-l-l leave h-h-h-h-her a-a-a-a-l-l-lone' they'd chant at me. 'Why don't you go and kiss the Russian pig? You kiss her, don't you? Ewww, kissy-k-k-k-kissy.' And they'd smack their lips with a wet sound, dig each other in the ribs with their elbows and giggle hysterically.

Sometimes they would surround us, make a circle we couldn't escape and chant 'kiss her kiss her kiss her kiss her,' until both of us were reduced to tears. When we tried to break out of the circle they would push us back, shove us until we bumped against each other and then scream with delight. 'Kiss kiss kiss, go on, kiss kiss kiss.'

Mary was in the forefront of these tormenters and would whip the others into a frenzy, jabbing Olga with her fingers and looking at me to see what I was going to do about it. I wanted to hit her, but that's what she wanted so she could run off and tell on me and get me into trouble.

At first the boys ignored all this, or watched from a distance, but eventually got drawn in, insulting me, throwing all kinds of words at me like 'freak' and 'Rusho-lover' and 'pigface' and 'doggie-doggie.' My friendship with Olga marked me as being 'peculiar' not just because she was Russian, but because she was a girl. Girls and boys didn't become friends because they didn't have much to say to each other, spoke a different kind of language. The boys jeered at me for having a 'girlfriend,' which was beyond their comprehension. So they started calling me a girl, as if that were the worst thing you could possibly be, and would ask me when I was going to start wearing a skirt to school.

The chief tormenter among the boys was a florid-faced, overweight kid called Terry who would punch Olga viciously on her upper arm whenever he passed her. Once, when we were alone in one of our hiding places, she showed me the black and brown bruises on her arm and I kissed them to make them go away. Mum said that if you kiss bruises and wounds they would vanish away. 'Kissy-kissy-k-k-kissy,' I would whisper as I kissed her arm, briefly tasting her sweet fragrance. The bruises did not go away and faded only in their own time. I'd been told a lie and began to realise that adults couldn't be trusted, and would say all sorts of things just to make us feel better. I began to see that words could be two-faced.

I nourished a hatred for Terry and was always on the lookout for him. Once, when he wasn't around, I defaced his schoolbook by scribbling all over it, getting him in trouble with the teacher. He guessed who had done it, but instead of coming at me, because he was scared of me, he redoubled his attacks on Olga. One of his favourite torments was to shout in her face unexpectedly, giving her a horrible fright.

Even Cargill joined in this bullying, although not as enthusiastically as some of them. He didn't understand why I didn't want to play with him after school and preferred to spend my time with Olga.

When I told my parents about this, their reaction was muted. They didn't say much but gave each other a look I couldn't interpret. Later my mother gently suggested that while it was fine for me to have Olga as a friend, I should make other friends as well. What happened to that nice little boy, Cargill? They seemed to forget that the nice little boy and I got into a lot of trouble, were little 'hellions' in fact – my mother's word – and that Olga and I would make ourselves scarce and didn't cause any trouble to anyone. I got tangled up with my words when I tried to explain that I didn't want to be friends with kids who seemed, for no good reason, to hate such a sweet person as Olga.

One afternoon, when my mother saw I'd been crying because of the kids' cruelty to both Olga and me, she taught me this adage:

Sticks and stones may break my bones, but words will never hurt me.

I chanted these words when the kids were insulting us until I realised that they were yet another lie. A big adult lie. Words *can* hurt a person, if not break their bones. Words can bruise us. We can be broken inside. Often, Olga's face was puffy from crying. She didn't have to understand all the horrible words kids called her to know that they were horrible. I put my arm around her shoulders as my father would do with my mother when she was upset. I made my voice as soft as I could so she would know I was on her side, and she would bravely try to smile. We had each other and that's all that mattered.

I taught Olga the same adage my mother taught me but it didn't work any better for her than for me. Cruel words kept on hurting her, hurting both of us. Afterwards, I felt sad and guilty that I had tried to reassure her with a lie. I became so upset I told the teacher that Terry was thumping Olga on the arm, that she had the bruises to show for it, and that it wasn't fair. The teacher took Terry aside and gave him a good talking to, and afterwards spoke to the class, but that just made the kids sneakier and more vicious in their attacks. Terry would pretend to stumble and just happen to push Olga over. The girls would cheer when she hit the ground, grazing a knee or elbow.

After school we would escape up the river and hide among the willows in our favourite spot where we would hold hands, our fingers laced together, or go up Conical Hill and hide among the tall trees. The kids, the girls mostly, would try to follow us but wouldn't get too far before giving up and turning back. From this I learned that most of the kids were afraid of being too far from home without adults around, afraid of the rough-voiced river or the tall trees which sighed and creaked in the wind. They were scaredy cats. We got good at hiding, finding places where we could huddle together, feeling the comforting presence of each other's bodies, waiting until the pursuit faded away and we could breathe easy.

I further questioned my parents as to why the kids hated Olga so much. They weren't able to give me a straight answer. I was persistent with my questioning, and in the end my father said something about people resenting foreigners who were coming to our town and taking people's jobs. That didn't make sense to me. Olga wasn't taking anybody's job, and her father established a general store that employed two local boys. One of those boys was the older brother of the bully boy Terry. To make it even stranger, Terry's own family had come from a faraway place called Ireland, and Terry curled his sounds in a peculiar way.

Since this didn't make sense, I decided that my father had lied, just as my mother with her little rhyme had lied. That made me sad. I discovered that there was no truth in words, not in themselves. Words can be a lie in one case and true in another, which was confusing.

I kept on asking why? why? why? until my mother taught me another little rhyme:

Ask no questions and I'll tell you no lies
keep your trap shut and you'll catch no flies.

I don't think my mother realised that by saying this she was admitting that she and my father were lying to me. When I saw that, I stopped asking questions.

One day, after Terry told Olga that her mother was a pig who had given birth to a little piggy-wiggy, and that one day he would stick a knife in her guts which was what happened to little piggy-wiggies, I smacked him in the face and made his nose bleed. He went running off to the adults, crying and bleating that I had attacked him. That caused a big kerfuffle, and I was told off by both the teacher and my parents who said they were very disappointed in me. They said I wasn't allowed to hit people. If that was the case, I said, how come Terry could hit Olga and get away with it? How come Dad could send me to the bathroom for a taste of his belt?

Nobody had a straight answer for me.

A secret language

The slow emergence of the other, more articulate me who came out of the shadows of my name did not put an end to my problems with words, but rather signalled a whole new round of them. It meant I could answer back without losing the effect by too much stuttering, if I could get the words out quick enough, and annoy adults in authority. I could trade insults with bully boys in the playground, and after bashing Terry in the nose, those boys steered clear of me, and Olga too, at least when I was around. Olga was under my protection and that suddenly made me ten feet tall. A quick, sharp word was normally all I needed.

But I also had the knack of blurting out the wrong thing at the wrong time. 'You have to learn how to hold your tongue,' my mother said after one occasion when she had friends over for morning tea to sample the scones she'd baked, and I told them about how Midnight had pooed under my parents' bed and my mother had got so angry she'd rubbed the cat's nose in it. Everybody except my mother found that amusing. 'It's the best way to teach them,' one of her friends said, perhaps wanting to ease the situation for me.

Those gaffes, however, were nothing compared to the difficulty of writing. I had as much difficulty writing my letters as I'd had speaking them, getting the b and the d facing in the right direction, deciding what the letters were and getting them in the right order. I didn't know how to cluster letters into words, and my early efforts at writing produced a scattering of letters across the page with no clear gaps to indicate separate words. It was writing only I could read. It took me a long time to understand that words are sounds with a shape. Rather than being broken into disparate clusters, I saw language as a continual stream, like the sounds from Olga's mouth, and that's the way I tried to write it.

Only much later, as an adult, did I learn that the earliest form of written English had no gaps between words, rather a continuous text. Gaps were added later. Discovering that, I didn't feel so bad about having run my words together as a child; I was enacting the evolution of writing.

Spelling was equally beyond me. I learned the alphabet by chanting it, but there is no natural way to write down words, and words never seemed to have the order of letters that I expected. I was struck by the fact that the word spell is the same word we use for talking about magic. Each word has a magic spell of its own. I had to learn it, to say it and write it down many times until the sound of the word and the look of the word came together in my mind. I had to do this with every word. I had to learn to crack the spell.

Looking at my first attempts at writing, my parents would exchange grins. At the same time there was a touch of worry in their faces. A stutterer who can't write isn't going to have an easy time of it, they figured.

I had trouble talking to others, but not to Olga. With her my stuttering would disappear almost entirely, at least in patches. Forgetting myself, I would babble away just as she did. Perhaps it was easier because she didn't understand me very well, and I didn't have to turn sounds into sense. I could say anything, any old nonsense. She liked hearing my voice just as I liked hearing hers. We could both babble away to each other without understanding anything. She wouldn't laugh if I said something silly, or judge me, or ask questions I couldn't answer, or stop the words in my mouth before I could get them out.

At first, when real words were still difficult for me, I would just make up words out of sounds the way I had with my soft toys, thinking Olga wouldn't know any different. That was how I eventually learned to talk without stuttering too much, not by trying to form real words, which seemed beyond my reach, but nonsense words which were easy to say and carried no burden of meaning.

Olga figured out what I was up to and began to do the same. We created our own language made up of bits of Russian, English, and lots of made-up words of neither language but sounding a bit like one or the other. We did this mostly as a game, for fun, but also as a secret language we could use. We called it Rushish, and it was spoken by our little nation of two. It took us to a place where words could mean whatever you wanted them to mean. A place far from the everyday world.

It wasn't long before Olga's English began to improve. Her first efforts produced broken sounds that hardly resembled any language at all, more like my stuttered attempts, but soon words began to emerge. Watching her mouth twist about trying to shape unfamiliar phonemes would make me laugh. You might think it made me happy to be able to communicate with my friend, that we could finally understand one another, but instead I became uneasy and oddly disappointed, perhaps because I could no longer make up what she was saying rather than understand her. I loved that voluble stream of Russian I could listen to forever, like listening to water passing over rocks when the river was high. But all the wonderful, magical things I thought she might be saying turned into very ordinary, mundane things. What she had for breakfast. How she needed a new skirt. How she hated getting stones in her shoes. How her mother would shout at her in the mornings to get her up.

I hid my disappointment from her quite successfully. Sometimes, however, I would ask her to speak to me in Russian so that I could recapture that sense of strangeness and mystery, the enchantment of sound freed from everyday meaning. It was not the same, however, and she found it odd. It was her Russian that was starting to become halting and unfamiliar in her mouth

We used our made-up language less. I would have kept it going, but Olga had a powerful drive to master English and wanted me to speak it. After a while I didn't mind. The way she spoke English started to have its own enchantment.

A meal at Olga's place

One day Olga invited me to her place for an early evening meal. Her father spoke some English, her mother very little, and most communication was done with gestures and facial expressions. I was quite happy to do away with words and communicate that way. It was fun waving my arms about and making my face into different shapes. And no one would notice any stuttering.

Olga's mother proudly presented me with a dish they called a pelmeni, which was mince mixed with sour cream, raisins and other stuff and made into dumplings. They all had big smiles on their faces as I took the first mouthful. The taste was new and strange and I wasn't sure I liked it. My parents would sometimes make mince on toast, but this tasted nothing like that.

This was an important moment to them; Olga bringing a friend home from school was a big deal, more important than I understood. I understood enough, however, to smile and make mm-mmm sounds, and that satisfied them. Olga glowed with pleasure.

After the pelmeni, they served another dish they called syrniki, which was like a cheese pancake with sugar added. They laughed good-naturedly when I tried to pronounce syrniki, and I wasn't too embarrassed. I didn't have to pretend to like the syrniki, and the three of them beamed at me when I looked for a second helping.

After the meal Olga's father, whose name was Mikhail, produced a map of Russia which he spread out on the table and showed me where they had come from. A town called Balashikha close to Moscow. They were very proud of this town and obviously missed it very much. Olga's mother, whose name was Varvara, brought out some photographs showing buildings and people in a street. She pointed to one of the buildings and I gathered that this was their home. Olga said she'd like to take me there one day, which made her parents laugh.

'I have story about Balashikha,' Mikhail said. 'A very true story.' Varvara gave her husband a warning look, but Olga clapped her hands and nodded furiously. Mikhail looked from one to the other. 'A very true story,' he repeated. Varvara gave a theatrical shrug, and Olga let forth a stream of breathless Russian. I didn't have to understand Russian to know that she was egging him on. 'A very very true story with little boy and his mama.'

In his broken English, and with help from Olga, Mikhail related how, not so long ago but likely once upon a time, a boy and his mother woke up one morning to find the city emptied of people. Not a soul anywhere, just empty streets and silent buildings and trees that sighed in the wind. No voices on the radio, no children singing, no military parades with brass bands, no aeroplanes streaking the sky, no dark-haired mothers pushing prams with loaves of bread under their arms.

They lived alone there for fifty years. They couldn't leave the city because there was a seemingly unbreakable mirror wall, about twice the height of a human being, surrounding it. They could see trees and sky beyond, but were cut off from the world.

'Why didn't they get a ladder and climb over it?' I asked.

Varvara nodded as if that were a very good idea, something they should certainly have done, but Mikhail shook his head sadly. Like Olga, he had a shock of dark curls and they swung from side to side. He, and his shaking curls, suggested that my question was one that shouldn't be asked or that the mother and her son just didn't think of it or couldn't do it. I understood, in my own child's way, that you don't ask those sorts of questions of fairy-tales, which have their own logic. It was like asking what they ate.

One day the boy woke up to find that his mother had died, Balashikha had come alive with people and dogs and loud noises, and that he was no longer a boy but a fifty-year-old. He told his story, but nobody believed him. People assumed he'd left the country and returned. He learned not to talk about it in case somebody reported him and the authorities questioned his sanity. He knew the truth and had to be content with that.

I was intrigued by that story and dreamed about it afterwards. Mostly I was alone and wandered around the empty city looking for food. When I came to the mirror wall I would stare at myself. In my dream I found that words were useless to me, that a person living on their own had no need of them. Words would just bounce back at me off the mirror. It's no use talking to things that can't talk back. In one dream I had a cat and talked to him, and his silence became unnerving.

The magic of names

My parents told me that Mikhail was the Russian version of Michael, which was my name too. I found it curious that even my name would change in another language. I felt that my name should stay the same everywhere. I wondered if I had a different name, would I be a different person? After all, names are not fixed to people the way the colour of their hair or eyes are. If I were a Charles I would be a Charles. If I were a Manu I'd be a Manu. I wouldn't be a Michael. If I changed my name to Manu, where would Michael go? If I were Michael and Manu at the same time, the rapid movement between the two would turn me into a blur. Later I was to discover that people do change their names in the hope that they can leave their old selves behind along with their old names. Maybe they can, or maybe that's just a superstition, their old selves still inside them like an image frozen in a window. When we outgrow our old selves, we cannot leave them behind the way a snake can shed its old skin, but carry them around in the graveyards of our memories.

Later, too, I would learn that meanings are not fixed to words either, and can slip and slide according to our desires.

At the time, however, I found some names I liked and which fascinated me. I didn't stutter so much if I whispered these names under my breath. I liked the sound of the name Balashikha, especially when Olga said it, and found it wasn't too hard to pronounce if I just went with the vowels, the double 'a' and the 'i'. I was very proud that eventually I could say it without stuttering at all. It sounded good in my mouth. Say names like Balashikha over and over and they will become something else, a word from some other strange language altogether.

When I got home after the meal at Olga's place, my parents quizzed me on all aspects of my visit. What was their house like? Was it clean and tidy? What was the food like? Did it taste funny? What were they wearing? Was their house warm enough? They were avidly interested in every detail. Because I was so young I didn't notice the things they wanted me to notice. I noticed how thick Mikhail's fingers were as he held the ladle to dish up the pelmeni, how Varvara clucked as she served the syrniki, and how happy Olga looked. I don't think I ever saw her happier than on that night.

I grew weary of my parents' questioning and quoted my mother back to them both:

Ask no questions and I'll tell you no lies
keep your trap shut and you'll catch no flies

My mother was not amused and told me to hold my tongue. My father was impressed. 'He's not silly, whatever else he might be,' he said to her as if I was not present.

The mirror world

I was not supposed to go into my parents' bedroom, especially when they weren't there. It was adult territory. 'You have the whole outside to play in,' my mother would say. But it was in that bedroom I found the most fascinating object in the world – my mother's dresser. It was the oldest object in the house, made of dark wood, maybe mahogany, had sets of drawers on either side and a scalloped curved centre-piece with a drawer beneath. Of most interest to me, however, were the three mirrors, the centre one fixed while two flanking side mirrors swung on hinges.

It was the only piece of furniture in the house possessed of any aspirations towards style. Hanmer was a little country town, serving farmers, loggers and the men who worked the hill country stations, and any style was accidental, usually something inherited. This, I believe, was the case with my mother's dresser, which had belonged to her grandmother and was either imported from Europe, where style still counted, or made to look that way. The dresser, and the oblong backless chair that went with it, were my mother's indisputable territory, the nearest she had to a private space. Approaching it I always felt that I was trespassing, crossing a boundary I was not supposed to cross, entering a world of mysterious and forbidden objects such as her red satin jewellery box, which contained a solitary pearl necklace, a round box with a colourful inlaid lid containing fragrant talcum powder, and some tubes of lipstick which, when turned, caused the red lipstick itself to come sliding suggestively out of its cylinder like a soft tongue. I had no business being there, and always felt guilty, but the lure of the mirrors was overpowering.

My first thought on seeing my image was that if I could walk into the mirror I could meet myself, that secret self that had been incubating there as I grew. I discovered that when I sat in a certain position, leaning forward, and manipulating the two side mirrors, I could create multiple images of myself, images I could move in and out of existence by swinging the side mirrors back and forth. I was able to play peek-a-boo with those images of myself while the image on the centre mirror remained stable. That centre mirror showed me my secret, articulate self, the self that you with your bag of words were bringing into being.

Could there really be so many of me, I wondered, able to appear and disappear at will, and was there really a stable me at the centre? What if the centre mirror wasn't fixed and could be moved back and forth? Then I could make myself completely disappear. Then there would be no words at all.

Furthermore, I found that if I put the side mirrors in a certain position, where they mirrored each other, I could create, or discover, a corridor of faces curving off into the distance. I was nothing more than an image reflected to infinity in a pair of facing mirrors. I tried to see to the end of that endless corridor by leaning forward a little further, but then my view was blocked by multiple editions of the back of my own head. It seemed there were some things that couldn't be seen, that space itself was a curved tunnel down which I receded from view. Time too might be seen in the same light, bending away from the eye, I thought.

I was a three-dimensional creature looking into a four-dimensional space.

All the while I would be listening for my mother's footfall. After all, I shouldn't have been there, and the insights I gained in front of those mirrors had a prohibited feel to them; I'd had to break a taboo to get them. They took their place with the jewellery box, the powder box and the cylinders of lipstick.

In my dreams of Balashikha, my dream-self discovered that the mirrors, or the one continuous mirror, created infinite numbers of Balashikhas. My dream-self could fly into the mirror and find itself there, in the same streets under the same sky, with multiple images of itself fading into the distance. When my dream-self spoke, the same thing happened to my words; the syllables multiplied indefinitely into a fading echo. As they receded, the words got pulled apart until there were only overlapping, dwindling sounds.

After these dreams I found it almost impossible to talk, and stayed as quiet as I could at school, marvelling at the ease and fluency with which those around me wielded words. I began to see words as physical entities over which, unlike most people, I had uncertain control.

The DeSoto Firedome Sedan

Eventually Olga's parents sold their general store and moved out of our town to the city. I'd heard talk of 'The City' but had never been there. It was another world, beyond the stand of pines that marked the threshold to Hanmer.

It was a solemn moment, watching them leave. I was the only one who turned up to bid them farewell. I stood on the street watching Mikhail loading the last boxes into the deep boot of their DeSoto Firedome Sedan while Olga dashed about not knowing where to put herself. I kept repeating the name of the car under my breath. *DeSoto Firedome Sedan* rolled sonorously through my mind full of its own majesty. (I think 'majesty' is an amalgam of magic and mystery.) It was a fancy chariot, a monster coloured deep-red with a white roof come to sweep Olga away to a far-off place.

Olga's mother was all smiles. She was pregnant and glad to get out of Hanmer where she'd been treated as an outsider and where her generosity had gone unacknowledged.

Mikhail had a thing for big, old American cars, and his was the only DeSoto in town. Every weekend he polished and waxed it, the envy of many, especially the young blokes in thrall to their flashy Zephyr Sixes. They would make disparaging comments about it – there was never a generous word for anything the Ruskie did – while giving it avid glances. One young fellow who worked at the timber mill plucked up the courage to ask Mikhail if he could give it a drive. All the young blokes gathered to watch their mate drive up and down the main street in the Ruskie's DeSoto.

None of those young blokes turned up to watch the DeSoto take its last trip out of Hanmer, down on its springs at the back from the weight, roaring defiantly and blasting blue smoke from the exhaust as it disappeared beyond the pines.

Olga waved to me from the back window for as long as she could still see me.

When I turned back to the ordinary, quiet streets of Hanmer, the town felt empty, hollow as a forty-four gallon drum with a dead rat at the bottom. It seemed that Olga had taken all the best words away with her.

Cat got your tongue?

I had my first experiment with not talking shortly after Olga left. It was what prompted the duck-shooting expedition. I came back from one of my walks one day and felt no need to pick up words again. I couldn't trust them, or trust myself to say them, so I would stay away from them. My parents didn't notice until dinner time. Mum was the first to grow suspicious of my silence and asked me some direct question. I didn't answer and she grew angry. 'Cat got your tongue?' she said. Dad looked confused. A child who didn't talk was a new one to him; most kids talked far too much. Like Frank. Frank was happy to fill in my silence with his chatter. Everybody kept eating but my mother was fuming.

They waited patiently for two days and then started to get worried, and talked in low voices to each other about it. To me, they spoke slowly and carefully, loudly enunciating every word as if I were deaf. They wrote me a note asking if I could hear them, and I nodded in reply. I didn't want them to get upset, it's just that words were very far away and I had no desire to search them out.

I did learn however that in this mute state there lay a certain power. My mother was both fearful and angry at the same time. At one point she shouted at me and raised her fists as if to beat me. I cringed away but still didn't talk.

They took me to a doctor. He had lots of words, mostly big ones. His words were important. They had an important sound to them. My parents hung on to them avidly. I'd never seen words used this way, with such terrifying authority. A word was produced to fit my wordlessness, which was considered a condition: autism, autistic. This word frightened my parents. On our journey home from the doctor's, they didn't say much to each other. They hardly looked at each other. They were locked inside their own thoughts.

Not talking placed me at one remove from everything. School was especially difficult as teachers demand a certain amount of participation, answering questions in particular. When I didn't answer the questions put to me by the sincere young woman who was my teacher, she assumed that I was being disobedient and non-cooperative. Once she'd assured herself that there was nothing physically wrong with me, she put me out of the classroom. I had to stand outside the door in shame; I wasn't allowed to go and sit on the benches in the sun.

Only my friend Cargill, who came back into my life somewhat after Olga left, didn't seem to mind my muteness. He was always the talker. We would walk up Conical Hill together playing various games with him talking ninety to the dozen. On one occasion he said something so silly that I had to correct him. I opened my mouth to speak but there were no words. Cargill blathered on and there was no way I could stop him or the bullshit he was spouting.

I became frightened then that I would never find words again, that I had banished them to such a far place they would never return, so I decided to talk again. The scary thing was that at first I couldn't. There were no words in my body, although I could hear them in my mind. To avoid embarrassment I practised on Frank, at first imitating his sounds, real and pretend words, remembering the shared language Olga and I had evolved, and finally found spoken language again.

Decoy

I never saw her again. I got a letter from her, however, not long after they'd left. Olga's letter was on coloured paper decorated with flowers. Her words were large and roundy and sloping forward, as if leaning into the future. I wrote back, but because I couldn't form my letters as well as she could, I mixed up my words with little pictures, stick figures of me and her. I hoped they would make her laugh.

My mother was sympathetic. She said encouraging things about my efforts. 'One picture is worth a thousand words,' she said. Now that Olga and her family had gone, my mother was very nice about them.

I posted the letter but I didn't hear back from her. I was disappointed. I learned that you can send words out into the world and get nothing back. Your words go to some empty place and die there. Frank had just learned to talk and he talked all the time with none of the problems I had, often saying the same things again and again. We shared a bedroom so I couldn't escape his voice. He would wrap himself in a blanket, make a cocoon of it, then talk until he fell asleep, sometimes in the middle of a sentence. I would lie awake in silence, waiting for his words to find their empty place so I could focus on missing Olga, seeing her in my mind's eye and psyching myself into tears.

Once, walking to school, I thought I saw Olga ahead of me. My heart racing, I ran to catch her up only to discover that it was another girl. That it was a cruel trick of the eye. I spent the rest of the day in a daze, hardly aware of what was going on around me and the things people were saying to me. When the teacher asked me a question, I had no voice to answer her.

Seeing my despondency, my father asked me to come along with him to do some duck shooting. This invitation was the result of some serious discussions my parents had about my state of mind after Olga had left, and how I was showing early signs of withdrawing from the world when I became sad, and how hard it was to get me to respond. I overheard these hushed discussions, which would take place in their bedroom. I would catch their conversation in broken phrases and fragments, such as 'I can't get a word out of him. He's gone broody' and 'he needs bringing out of his shell' and 'a boy needs his father,' to which my father would murmur assent.

Duck shooting was a very adult thing to do, and I was supposed to feel privileged and adult to be going with him and his mates on their shooting expeditions. Frank was very jealous, and made a scene. He took no notice when our mother assured him that 'as soon he was old enough' he would be able to go duck shooting too; he knew he was being fobbed off.

We drove to a nearby lake before dawn one morning, and my father quickly built a bivouac of reeds and branches in which we could hide unseen from the sky. I learned this new word, bivouac, which had a nice, sharp feel in my mouth when I repeated it under my breath. It was a strange word and I didn't risk saying it out loud.

From his pack my father produced two cork ducks that he set floating on the lake. As he explained it, the ducks flying overhead would mistake the cork ducks for real ducks and assume that it was safe to land on the lake. Then, when they got within range of his double-barrelled shotgun, blam! blam! and they were dead ducks. Sometimes he waited until they landed and were easier to hit. That was not as much fun, of course, as blasting them out of the sky.

Ducks are not stupid, he assured me. They knew when the hunting season opened and liked to make themselves scarce, seeking ponds and little lakes where they could outwait the hunters. Flying high to keep out of range, they couldn't tell the difference between a real duck and a cork one. I watched him pull the trigger and saw the shotgun kick back against his shoulder. The dead ducks fell out of the sky and splashed into the lake.

They looked quite realistic, those cork ducks, bobbing about on the water, with grey-green wings and curved necks. They looked very happy and contented.

Every now and then some distracted hunter would shoot his own decoy, much to the derision of other hunters.

So I learned another word in its context: decoy. I was deeply impressed that something false could look so real as to lead a creature to its death. The idea frightened me. What if there were words like that, I wondered; words that looked okay from a distance, at first glance, yet up close proved to be false and empty. And dangerous. Decoy words.

The word bringer returns

It was after that first duck-shooting expedition that you came back into my life with your fine whisperings. I had almost forgotten you, forgotten our whispering place in the muehlenbeckia. Almost forgotten your secret transmissions, the creation of my mirror self, the way you could conjure words into flesh and set then to work in the world. Almost forgotten my gratitude.

I was on one of my expeditions up Conical Hill, and I was singing. The day was crisp and bright. The shadows across the winding path were sharp. As I sang I tried to jump from shadow to shadow, as if the light might hurt me. Then I would change over and jump from brightness to brightness, trying not to land on the shadows, as if the shadows might hurt me. Singing was a part of the game as each variation of light and shade had its own note, its own tonality.

I made up a melody, more like a chant, and used words from the invented language Olga and I had developed, modulating the sound to the world around me – deeper intoning for the large trees, high keening for patches of sky, a regular beat for the hard earth beneath my feet. My song developed during the weeks following Olga's departure; I was growing a skin over her memory. It was skin formed from song. On this occasion something different happened; I felt as if the trees and the earth, the shadows and the light, were listening to me, responding to me, that all the elements were picking up on my song and passing it along, spreading it far and wide. I was at the centre of spreading waves of melody, and that melody was gathering words as it spread. All the words of the world were there, infused into the song. I couldn't make them out individually, but I could hear them swell and break open as the music lifted them.

The feeling grew so strong I stopped, and the silence rushed in at me. You were there in that silence, all around me, waiting, expectant, holding within yourself the echo of my singing and all the words that ever were, words not yet hatched, words you were holding in trust. That echo drew me to you just as it does now. The first time it happened I felt that I was entering a sacred place, hushed with an eerie presence. The familiar winding path became unfamiliar. It led to places undreamt of and, when I turned to look back, gave me no clue as to where I'd come from.

Sensing your presence was scary and made me want to run back down the winding path for home. I didn't understand how a sentient being could be so close to me and remain unseen, yet realised that, in the moment, home did not exist, the town of Hanmer little more than a hope.

'Hello,' I said, my voice sounding small among the tall trees with their tall shadows. And an even taller sun standing behind them.

I felt a warmth in my body, the kind of flush you get when a friend is near. I didn't have a clear picture of you, what kind of creature you were, but I knew you were there and could hear me perfectly well. Any words I chose to speak would find a home in you. I felt you came from an empty place, like the Balashikha of the urban legend, and couldn't enter fully into my world because you couldn't get past the wall of mirrors. Like a creature from fairy-tales, you could only stay for a certain time, a few minutes, a few hours. Then the mirrors would pull you back and you would get lost among the reflections. The echo of my voice would go with you.

When alone with you, I had no problems talking, barely a stutter. Just as with Olga, I could babble away quite happily, and you understood me perfectly, even as you do now. You rejoiced in my words, took them and held them in trust. My words were a perfect fit for your ear. I didn't ask how you, a creature of silence, could be my word bringer, and I rejoiced with you.

I didn't get to the summit that day. I left the path and sat among the trees and talked to you by sub-vocalizing, a half internal whisper. I could feel your response in my body, and in the posture of things around me, a medley of sensations. I was happy because I was not alone; somehow I was met, and that's what mattered. I got up and started acting out my words, as if I could literally give them body. That was the beginning of the dance. My body didn't stutter.

When you withdrew my world returned to normality. There was no rush of sensations, no sense that I was connecting with an invisible being. I went home, feeling content for the first time since Olga had left. I had made a friend for life. An unusual kind of friend, but I knew I could trust you. I knew you would always bring me true words.

Over the coming weeks, I learned that I could best talk to you when close to running water, and that my singing formed a bridge between us. It was as if you found your voice in the sounds of the river. At the same time, the rush of water hid my singing, or swept it up, so there was little chance of somebody wandering along and hearing me. My first instinct was to keep you secret. Under the cover of the noise of the river, words and listening could thrive. I didn't just talk but sang and growled and made all kinds of noises. I danced about as if I could make words with my body – or maybe leave words behind. This played a part in bringing you to me, recalling you from the realm of mirrors; you would hear me and come to me. You would become the world and open yourself to me.

To my joy I discovered that if I sang I didn't stutter. Sometimes I would sing the most familiar of rhymes:

Row row row your boat gently down the stream
Merrily merrily merrily merrily life is but a dream.

The words would roll off my tongue just as smoothly as that stream took the boat, and I sensed that in some way the words were coming from you. My singing enabled me to sense your presence and your whispers.

I told my mother about you. I should have held my tongue. Her look warned me to say no more. She decided that you were an imaginary playmate, a decoy of the psyche, one I created to fill the gap left by Olga's departure. I heard my parents discussing the matter. I couldn't hear what they were saying, except at the end my mother said, 'The less said the better.'

Dead shot

There were further duck-shooting expeditions, but after a while I tactfully suggested that I didn't need to go. My dad thought I was overly sensitive to the killing of the ducks, but it was not that. I was a country kid, I knew that life came and went and we ate what we killed, but it was the deception of the ducks that affected me the most, their mistaken belief that they were joining other ducks on a peaceful lake. That the creatures died, deluded to the very last moment, preyed on my mind.

Instead, I took every opportunity to go up the river on my own where I could be alone with you and you could bring me some new words from far-off places and times. You couldn't utter them yourself, since you had no body, but float them into my mind on the uplift of your melodic form. Shadow sounds poured through my head and fused with my tongue of song.

Frank thought he was old enough to tag along. He would run after me, crying and bleating. 'I'll tell on you.' What exactly he would tell wasn't clear, but he had some dim intimation that I was up to something. I had to shake him off, or take him home. Sometimes I couldn't get away as I was expected to play his soft-toy games with him.

I didn't tell my parents that I saw ducks up the river sometimes too, and that it was nice not to have to hide from them and shoot them. I discovered that ducks were quite friendly and, if you weren't carrying a weapon, would come right up to you. My parents resigned themselves to this desire I had for solitude; my father shrugged his shoulders as if to say, 'I've done my best.' Frank looked disapproving. My mother gave me a shrewd look, as if she understood more than she was saying.

During my wanderings up the river with nobody but you to talk to, I began to love nature. It began with willow trees, the deep silent pool at the bend in the river. From there I could see the mountains, hard and sharp against the blue sky. I started examining things close-up too, the spongy bright-green moss that grew on stones and rotting wood, the ants, beetles and spiders scurrying about on insect street, the dragonflies hovering over their reflections in still water near the bank where the river eddied, watching the minute life beneath. All this to the happy patter of water rushing over stones. I discovered that if I looked at something long enough, without thinking too much about it, I could discern a hidden glimmering there.

I started to learn the names of things, especially plants, but the world of things seemed quite separate from the world of words. Even though things had names, they didn't need them. They didn't mind if you took their names away, for their names were not a part of them. They carried on quite happily without them, as could I. Names were not anchored to things, things were anchored to themselves.

I would take samples back home with me, and my mother would help me identify them. My mother was quite good with the common names of plants, and taught me to identify the gentle willowherb, the tough silver tussock and the spiny Wild Irishman. She showed me how to press leaves and flowers between the pages of heavy books. The only books we had heavy enough for the job was a set of hardback Charles Dickens' novels. Several of those in a pile worked fine.

Later, when the travelling librarian came to town with her magic bus, I discovered that these plants all had other names.

I also developed my love of mosses, lichens and fungi. The lichens dabbed bright colour on grey river stones. Mosses made shadowy, hidden places soft. Fungi grew in fantastic shapes, like creatures in a fairy-tale, and there were tiny flowerless liverworts with their peculiar spore-releasing stems. I began to keep a notebook in which I tried to draw each plant and would laboriously write out its name. Some names I loved to say. I learned that sometimes words do fit, the sound reflecting in some way the nature of the object. Fungi was my favourite; the word itself seemed to have a deep fungus-like aspect to it while the word lichen had a hard, scraping sound like the rough feel of it on smooth rock. When I learned how a word felt I had less trouble saying it. By looking through the notebook I could picture the plant in the wild, and remember trying to draw it, remember the pleasure I took in finding and collecting it. I would remember my amazement at finding the rare, rough woven basket-fungi looking like the ribs of a ball, looking as if it had been made by a human hand, and the bird's-nest fungi that looked as if it were full of tiny eggs.

I favoured the river because it was a living thing which harboured many other living things. It had a voice. It could be cheerful and bubbly or quiet and thoughtful. It could be fast and furious or sluggish. It could reflect my face like polished metal or hide it with turbulence. When I spoke, it carried my words away as if they were mere shadows on its surface. It had hidden depths, and it moved through time just like other living things. I also admired the hard, grey river stones for their egg like roundness and their inwardness. Later, I discovered that those stones were made of greywacke, a sedimentary rock, a hard form of sandstone. Sometimes you could find fossils in it which showed that this land was once under the sea. I didn't know that at the time, and would stare at the aquatic shapes in the stone wondering what they were. I liked the word, *greywacke* for its somewhat dissonant two halves. It felt like two words forced together.

I marvelled at the birds for their quicksilver cries, and the way they revelled in the freedom of the air; the black fantail for its flibbertigibbet manner, dashing about like bright chittering thoughts; and the hawk for its slow, distanced circling watchfulness. I was fascinated by the hawks because I was not fooled by their lackadaisical flight. I knew that at any moment they could swoop silently on some blissfully unaware rabbit or creeping rodent.

As far as the townsfolk were concerned, the only good hawk was a dead one. Farmers accused them of attacking new-born lambs. Once, when we were driving home from a Sunday outing, with Frank and me fighting in the back seat, my father pulled the car over to the side of the road and shushed us. Up ahead a hawk was sitting on a fencepost. It was as still as if it had, itself, been carved from tawny wood. My father slid his .22 rifle silently from its sheath under the driver's seat. Frank and I immediately stopped horsing around, our attention rivetted on the weapon. My father gave it to my mother who looked at it and back at him. He raised his eyebrows enquiringly. I could tell from the look on her face that she didn't want to do it. Her mouth was set in the way it did when she faced an unpleasant but necessary task, which was quite often; her life was beset with such tasks.

She nodded, quietly opened the car door and slipped out, rifle in hand. It was a hot, windless day and the sun made a streak of light along the barrel. Us kids were agog – was Mum really going to shoot the hawk? I'd never seen her shoot anything; Dad was the family shooter. She placed the rifle on top of the car door to steady it and took careful aim. She took her time. Dad, Frank and I watched avidly. Nobody breathed a word, not even Frank. The world seemed to hold its breath.

After what seemed like an age there was a thin crack in the air and the hawk toppled. It must have been a direct hit as the bird dropped off the fencepost without a twitch or cry.

'Dead shot!' my father cried exultantly. I reversed the words in my mind – shot dead, I whispered.

My mother showed no pleasure in the act. Or pride. She didn't even smile. There was a look on her face I hadn't seen before. I don't think she had the words to describe what she was feeling. Dad, however, was proud of her. All the way home Frank pointed an imaginary weapon everywhere and made shooting noises.

All the way home my mother stared out the window and said nothing.

Mythologies are weightless compared to mountains

During my lone trips up the river, I learned to move silently. If I was quiet enough, I might catch the shy, long-legged pied stilts wading daintily along the edge of the river, their heads darting back and forth. If I disturbed them, they would take to the air with their yapping cries, dragging their legs beneath them. The less noise I made, the more I became a part of everything I saw. That silence put me in a receptive state and best able to appreciate the quick life around me, the skip of light and shadow and the rush of birds.

The welcome swallows I admired most of all, small, slender birds with finely pointed wings and distinctive forked tails, a deep blue head, dark chestnut wings and breasts of orange-red. They could fly like a coloured stone from a slingshot so close to the river they might have been drawing their energy from it. My mother told me that they were called welcome swallows because they appeared to herald springtime.

The most common bird was the magpie. With so much colour everywhere, these birds were a study in black and white, as if cut from a pencil sketch and set free into our world. Their harsh cries were all black, as if they had something sinister to say. They were far from shy and far from friendly. Once, while climbing an old pine tree that grew near the river, two of them attacked me, screaming at the top of their voices. I guessed that I must be close to their nest, and climbed down as fast as I could. That didn't stop them. They kept at me, and I had to keep trying to put the tree trunk between me and their fury. Even when I reached the ground and ran away, they kept after me, diving at my head, shrieking. Only when I hid among some willows did they give up. They flew away, cawing triumphantly to one another.

Behind all this flashing movement and bird calls there lay the unmoving, silent mountains. I was in awe of these distant peaks, tipped white, for their remoteness, their stoical silence and their capacity for contemplation. They might be host to thunderstorms and furious winds but they held their peace. Shifting clouds might cover them, yet when the clouds had gone they remained, just as they had been, serenely indifferent. It seemed that nothing could touch them. The names we gave them seemed puny in comparison to their magnificence, even those names that carried mythological weight. Mythologies are weightless compared to mountains. The nearest, most visible peak was Mt Isobel, which didn't mean a lot to me. My mother could only tell me that Isobel was a Scottish name. Perhaps some explorer named it after his wife, she said.

Everywhere I looked I saw things that were unselfconscious in their corporeality, things that had no need of words, and would patiently suffer the names humans gave them. Later I was to learn that the buzzing of crickets, the chirping of birds, the sounds other animals make with their bodies and actions they perform, are a language more complex and diverse than humans give them credit for. I didn't see it that way at the time. Birds might celebrate and cows lament, but this great body of sound was profoundly different from the slipperiness of human speech, and nestled comfortably within a larger body of silence.

Despite a growing fascination with names, and my willingness to talk to you with all the words you had in store, I was happy to be away from the world of speech, adult words, words that might not mean what they say. I took refuge in the world of sights and sounds. I spent a lot of time walking, mostly on my own but sometimes with you. As I walked, all the words I had learned and were still learning would settle to the bottom of my mind like sediment, leaving my mind unencumbered. Words can swirl around things and obscure them. Only when words had faded could I see things in their nakedness.

One day I saw something that didn't belong, not to this world anyway. It was one of those luminescent, clear days. Colours seemed to glow from within, the sky was a baked powder blue and the wind had dropped away to nothing. Bird sounds were preternaturally loud, although there was little movement: the hard, almost mechanical cry of the kea, the long trilling of the grey warbler and the complex yodelling of the tūī . These sounds were familiar and I'd learned to distinguish them. I was clambering over some rocks, feeling the hard-worn stones with my feet, when I heard a harsh cry that was new to me. At first I took it for a kea, but it was too long and piercing for one of those croaky parrots. It was coming from high up, but was no skylark. Shielding my eyes against the sun, I was able at last to locate it, wheeling about like a hawk but too big for a hawk. It had a skinny, leathery-looking body, long narrow wings and long legs which trailed beneath it.

I didn't have a name for it at that point, but later I came across a picture of it in a book and recognised it as a pterodactyl. That was impossible, of course, even without knowing what it was, I knew it was impossible, but it was there and was uttering those hard, elongated cries. I felt how thin the bonds of time were, and how easy it might be to step into another sky just as simply as jumping from one stone to the next. I felt then the underlying unity of everything, all knitted together by light and movement. The one and the many; the many and the one.

I didn't have words to describe such experiences. Words fell short. After returning home from my walks it would take me a long time to find words again, a long time for the world of human words to return. When you disappeared, you took worlds of sound away with you. I would watch my parents talking, and only slowly did the import of what they were saying impinge on me. And only slowly could I respond to their comments or questions, and I never spoke of the pterodactyl. I didn't have words for it anyway.

They had their own understanding of this. They called me a dreamer and said that I was often 'lost in a dream.' That puzzled me. For a start, I was not lost. I knew exactly where I was and where the world was. Even when I closed my eyes, I knew what was near and what was far away. If I was lost, then where was everybody else? Besides, the way I was experiencing the world was the opposite of dreaming. I was experiencing the world in all its realness, a realness beyond words, not toying with phantoms or indulging in images the way a dreamer does. I learned that words do not always fit the world, are not always true to the world, and that is probably why I liked to get away from them.

Forbidden words

I discovered that there were forbidden words called swear words, words which have lots of power. These taboo words could only be used by adults, although of course children knew them all. I was fascinated by the idea that certain sounds were off limits, as dangerous as a cliff edge or swirling river pool. A world of submerged meanings, all to do with bodily functions. Things that would make kids snigger and sneer.

This came home to me when I was very young, under five years old.

I was in our backyard watching my father attempt to cut off a chicken's head. That poor chook was due for the pot. I could tell by the look on Dad's face as he approached the chopping block, axe in one hand, squawking chook in the other, that he didn't relish the task. His face was red, as if he was embarrassed. He looked like a big kid. Frank and I stood off to one side and watched. I held Frank's hand and he clung tight.

It was an awkward thing to do. Dad had to hold the struggling chook down with one hand and swing the axe with the other. He had to aim for its neck and make sure he didn't hit his own hand. He stood there holding it seemingly for ages waiting for it to fall still so he could get a clean swing at its neck. Finally the axe cut through the sky. The chicken's neck was partially severed, blood spewed everywhere, my father jumped backwards and the bird flopped off the chopping block and ran silently around the yard with its head hanging by a few tattered pieces of skin while my father shouted 'fuk fuk fuk fuk fuk fuk fuk' sounding like a chicken on her nest busily laying an egg. I pounced on the word with delight and so did Frank. My parents were not happy when we joined in, making the same noises as Dad. I stuttered on the 'k' saying 'far far far far far k k k k.'

Much to my father's disgust, my mother started laughing.

Charles Dickens

Words were like stones, strange and alien in my mouth, but my parents were much relieved. They smiled and laughed and felt good about me again. I kept talking, saying all sorts of words, it didn't matter what. In gratitude they bought me my favourite ice-cream, which was hokey-pokey. I liked that ice-cream as much for the name as for the taste.

After my brief speechlessness, my relationship with language started to change. The incident with the doctor had demonstrated to me that words were power, and that if I were not to be completely powerless in the world, I would need to master them. I could still go for walks up the river, I could still leave words behind, I just needed to use them again when I got home, put them on like a set of familiar clothes. That way I wouldn't draw attention to myself. You weren't much help with that. Your words were incantations that took me away from everyday speech.

I became a reader. While I still had trouble forming my letters, and shaping them into words, and still only spoke when I needed to, I found that reading was becoming easy for me. Words would flow off the page and through my brain in a steady stream. Since I didn't have to say them out loud, I had no problems with them. I started by reading children's books, those suitable for my age, but soon found I could read adult books too, almost anything I wanted to. Words on the page were no barrier to me. Without friction they slid off the page. I thank you for that.

The only books in the house were that dusty set of Charles Dickens' novels I was using to press flowers and leaves from my river expeditions. Now I put them to a new use. I opened *Great Expectations* and began reading. I loved the smooth, razor thin pages and the packed print, the faded, musty smell. It was so different from the *Secret Seven* books they had at school, with paper thick and rough, the printing large and chunky. The print of *Great Expectations* was small but thin and elegant. It lent a certain grandeur to the story. I discovered that reading was as easy as listening. It was a kind of listening. Once I could hear Dickens' voice in the lines, hear it with my inner ear, all I had to do was sit back and enjoy the ride.

I didn't have too much trouble with new words, either. I kept a notebook in which I entered new and strange words. I came to enjoy finding them, trying to shape them with my mouth as I wrote them down even though I mainly mispronounced them. I kept that notebook for years, even after I stopped using it. A new word was a discovery, like an unknown territory to be explored. That territory had its own topography, its own history, its own charm. Many of these were words that I'd never heard spoken aloud, so I would make up my own pronunciation. I did this when I was alone, so that people wouldn't laugh when I tried to say them.

I began to repeat words under my breath as I read them, and even began to do that after speaking. My spoken words would be followed by a whispery echo, and I would whisper away to myself as I read, quite unconscious of what I was doing. My parents were not exactly alarmed by this development, but they were amused and a little puzzled. My mother consulted somebody who was apparently an expert in bringing up children who assured her that my whispering was somewhat unusual but perfectly harmless. It even had a name: subvocalising. My parents were reassured to have a name to put to it. It was a little odd, but nothing to be afraid of, not like autism.

By my tenth birthday I had read four Dickens novels. My favourite was *The Tale of Two Cities* in which people are driven by grand emotions.

My parents didn't believe that I was reading them, they just thought I was looking at the illustrations. I couldn't tell them that I could hear the words, a voice in my head, and that I could *see* them, a long procession like an endless carnival doing their dance of meaning and significance, before passing on. My hours of sitting on the bank watching the river flow stood me in good stead. Just as my eyes would move back and forth, tracking the water as it flowed in and out of my vision, so I would track the words, flowing from left to right. Like a river they had a voice, a surface that could catch the sun, quiet depths where mysterious creatures moved and shapes formed and dissolved, different tempos according to the terrain and different moods they carried with them from the mountains.

My parents were happy that I was learning to read, at least to a certain point. Dad would suggest that I was spending too long with my 'nose in a book.' There was a tinge of pride in his voice when he made his complaints. He took to calling me the professor. When something needed doing around the house, he would suggest that the professor get his nose out of his book and do something useful. Often I would pretend not to hear him.

Mum was concerned that Dickens' books were too adult for me. Miss Haversham from *Great Expectations* was very creepy, my mother said, and the novel might have an unhealthy effect on my mind. Somebody lent her a copy of *Boys Own Adventures*, full of healthy, outdoor stories about hunting and canoeing, but I couldn't be bothered with them. They tried to be exciting but were really just boring. Nothing to match the adventures of heroes and heroines embroiled in the French Revolution.

We were what was called 'working-class' people. My mother had a series of jobs working in shops and my father did a variety of labouring work, eventually graduating to become a taxi-driver and used-car salesman. They had an ambivalent attitude to reading and education. They were driven by a desire for their children to have a better life than they had, and in their minds the key to that was education, the kind of education they never had. By means of education, their children would be lifted into the 'middle class' where we would have a more comfortable life. Yet they were suspicious of educated people who seemed to do no real work in the world, and got paid to do a lot of talking. There are those who talk and those who do, my mother would say.

'Take everything people say with a grain of salt,' she once counselled me, 'It's what they do that's important.' In her family, it was what you did that defined you. I understood that. I realised that there was often a gap between what people did and said. I understood that it was okay for me to become a talker, just as long as, like some educated people, it wasn't all talk and no action.

Reading Dickens had some unintended consequences. My vocabulary became coloured by archaic terms and usages. I still didn't talk much, but when I did I would say some very odd things, at least odd to the ears of the people around me, my peers and my classmates at school in particular. They couldn't understand much of what I was saying. Words that were normal to me were unknown to them. I couldn't find the right register for them, and so would prefer to read a book during playtime than play with the other children.

Cargill was the exception. He didn't care how I talked, or even if I talked at all; he had plenty to say, mostly about nothing. He ended up eating his lunch with me as the other kids got sick of him. So we hung out together even though we were pretty bored with each other. We tried to play some of the old games of getting into trouble but we were just going through the motions.

My parents had something new to worry about when my teacher told them that I was becoming 'socially isolated' and encouraged me to invite friends home after school. Mum took it very much to heart and contacted Cargill's mother to invite him to a sleepover. He had Frank's bed and Frank had the privilege of sleeping in the big bed with Mum and Dad. It took Frank a while to figure out if he was the loser or the winner in this bed swap. In the end he accepted it with good heart. From an early age he liked to look to the future instead of clinging to the past.

It all duly happened. Cargill took Frank's bed and talked to me while I read *David Copperfield*.

More than ever I would, after school, seek the solitude of walking, shedding the day's words, going further upstream than I had ever gone, ever closer to the mountains, content to roam for miles and, after dark, come home where Dickens awaited me.

Unfortunately, reading Dickens had little impact on my school work. We were graded on a simple scale of 1 to 5. 1 was excellent and 5 was abysmal. My report cards would show a 5 for everything except reading, which would be a 1. My teachers couldn't explain this paradox. It was as if my reading took place in a world quite different from the real world. I might know a lot of strange words, but that didn't seem to change anything. Once again my poor parents, who had been encouraged by my reading, became gloomy about my future. Dad took refuge in work, Mum in worry.

The magic bus

Our little town had no library of its own, being served by a 'library on wheels,' an old, pale blue Bedford bus with Country Library Service in red capital letters on the side. It opened like a pie cart, with a counter where you could stand and look at books as if you were eating pies. It was fitted out with popular works, many of them hopelessly archaic. There I discovered other nineteenth century novels to supplement my reading of Dickens, such as *The Count of Monte Cristo*, *Rob Roy* and *Tom Jones*, mainly books about adventurous young men. Upstarts, brave and prepared to step outside of their commonplace lives, take on all comers and woo the women. I also found *Frankenstein* and *Dracula*, works that haunted my dreams with the presence of the other, the frightening other that lurks below the surface of our minds, below our words, to step into the everyday world from the nether hells of strange forests and spooky old buildings. Reading Dickens was a good preparation for reading those two books.

The townsfolk didn't know what to make of Mrs Rockwell, librarian, bus driver, friend to all readers. It was as if they couldn't bring her quite into focus, like an image in a camera lens that wouldn't resolve. Mum's friend said she must be a spinster, a variety of the human female I hadn't yet knowingly encountered. That would be a neat box for Mrs Rockwell, as spinsters were allowed to do strange things like drive around remote, rural areas on their own with a bus full of books. The problem was, the box didn't quite fit her. Or she didn't fit the box. She didn't behave like a spinster, people observed. A hint, perhaps of the Merry Widow (another genus of the human female), or a style suited to the Independent Woman.

My mother had never encountered any Independent Women, and wasn't sure they existed. Men always ended up controlling the money, one way or another. Not that she begrudged Dad a little flutter on a Saturday horse race. I liked the word flutter. I saw money, mostly notes, sprouting wings and fluttering over the horizon. Never to be seen again. A flutter wasn't serious. It wasn't even gambling. It was just some money with butterfly thoughts.

The Independent Woman is most likely found at the racecourse, having a daring little flutter on the trifecta, or on a favourite to win in the last race, not scrabbling around with books in a bus.

No box entirely fitted the woman, and that couldn't be right. There had to be a box.

Dad brought back a full report. He'd gone to the library bus to see for himself, and to get an Ed McBain, 87th Precinct cop novel, books he called 'thud and blunders.' He found one, *Lady Killer*, and didn't have a lot to say about Mrs Rockwell other than she seemed to have an olive complexion which reminded him of a French woman he knew a long time ago when he was in the army. At the mention of this French woman, my mother got one of her 'the less said the better' expressions. Later, Dad was to come up with another theory. There was something about her voice, he said. And her name. He suspected that her name had been Röckel, a kraut name if ever there was one. That's what the Germans who came to New Zealand did, they changed their names to hide who they were. But they couldn't fool Dad.

Everybody was bemused by this periodic visitor in her book bus, while what her life might really be like, her dreams and secret enthusiasms, remained unknown.

On first impression, she was a somewhat austere woman who held herself stiffly, wore a short black jacket, a white blouse buttoned to her throat, and a dark skirt that reached all the way to her ankles. She also wore large round glasses that made her eyes look bigger than they really were. Her voice was clipped with a faint accent. The effect was curiously old fashioned, noticeable even to a little boy. In hindsight, I can see that she was attempting to dress conservatively, perhaps as her mother or grandmother might have, but compared to the practical, rough-and-ready dress of the Hanmer women, she looked different enough to be almost outlandish.

At first, she was rather stand-offish with me, keeping a sharp eye on how I was treating the books. Her manner suggested that her experience of little boys had not always been so happy, that they tended to bend the spines and leave smudges on the books with their grubby little fingers. She began to thaw when she saw me reading the opening pages of *The Hunchback of Notre Dame*, not just looking at them but reading them, not bending spines, and my fingers were not as grubby as she feared. That piqued her curiosity.

While her manner remained rather brusque, she took me under her wing and encouraged my wider reading. She was surprised to learn that I had already read *The Pickwick Papers* by Dickens, which she proudly offered to me as an alternative to the romance novels, westerns and murder mysteries she mostly stocked. She tried to hide her further surprise when I started chatting to her about Dickens' other books, and how scary Fagin in *Oliver Twist* was.

Mrs Rockwell wasn't fazed by my stuttering, and never tried to finish my sentences for me, which made her a superior adult in my estimation. Although she came by only every month or so, she became an important person in my development, a link with the great outside world, as well as the greater world of knowledge. She always tried to bring something to interest me, with the conscious pleasure of one who loves nothing better than to nurture young minds, a sacred task that my school, it seemed to her, was not performing very well. I gathered, from her chilly attitude towards them, that she didn't hold schools in very high regard.

In that musty bus I discovered some works of natural history that began to turn my interest in that direction. I found a book called *New Zealand Trees* written by JW Matthews. I noticed that the trees all had names in a strange language, which Mrs Rockwell informed me was Latin. I became fascinated by *A Weird Region* by T.W. Leys concerning the great eruption of Mt Tarawera in 1886 that wiped out whole landscapes including the famous 'pink and white terraces,' filling the air with smoke and ash, burning people's lungs. I was fascinated by the scale of the destruction and spent ages staring at the few photographs that existed of the now vanished landscape. Up until that point I had seen the world I had been born into, the mountains, the river, Conical Hill, as eternal. They had always been there and it had never occurred to me that it all might vanish in a few days.

I dreamed that Conical Hill turned into a volcano which burst apart and poured rivers of lava down into Hanmer, burying the town forever. The heat that preceded the lava exploded houses and trees even before it reached them. I saw the Molesworth boys trying to gallop away, their burning hats flying off their heads, their horses melting beneath them.

I woke up from that dream, sweaty and distressed. My mother had to come to me in the middle of the night and comfort me. I told her that the world could end any time, that nothing was fixed in place the way we thought it was, that disaster could strike as we lay in our beds just as it had in 1886, which happened at 2 a.m. as people were peacefully sleeping.

Mum's annoyance at being disturbed at her 2 a.m. translated into a suspicion of the book which had sparked my fears, in turn, translating into a suspicion of the Library Bus and Mrs Rockwell herself. What did that woman think she was doing, giving kids books like that? For a few days I had to hide the book from her sight, but the damage had already been done. I could never see the world in quite the same way again. Everything was contingent, the whole country poised over shifting tectonic plates, life itself flourishing briefly in a planetary envelope of delicately balanced gases. The Hanmer River might one day fall into an abyss, or vanish altogether. Conical Hill might vanish into some vast cavern beneath the ground. If it got hot enough the air itself could catch fire, all the houses buried under a desert of ash.

After all, I told Mum, the water for the thermal springs for which our little town was known was warmed far underground by heat from the earth's core, or so our teacher told us. What if one day the lava down there decided to come up through the same tunnels in the graywacke? It could destroy the town for sure. Mum told me not to be a Chicken Licken or a Foxy Loxy and scare people, particularly Frank, with what she called tall tales. 'You'll give your brother nightmares' she said.

Dad, who had been to war and watched cities reduced to rubble in the space of a few hours, did not agree with Mum that my fears were entirely fanciful. His grandfather Samuel Meer, he said, had been near

Mt Tarawera when it blew. He'd been only a child, not much older than me, but vividly remembered it all. He also told the story of 'a spirit canoe' seen several days before the eruption. He'd been with his parents and a group of tourists returning from the pink and white terraces when they witnessed a large canoe or waka approaching them. A row of warriors stood in that waka wrapped in flax robes, their heads bowed, their hair feather-plumed for death. A moment later the waka disappeared back into the mist and was never seen again. The local people said this waka sighting heralded the destruction of the region.

I had never heard Dad tell a story like that, or use the word waka before. He said it with some self-consciousness, but was determined to say it, I think because his grandfather had used it, the Māori word for canoe. That story made me think of the shooting I had heard on the logging road, the sounds of war, the boy on the logging road and the strange flying creature I had seen. I wondered if these were 'spirit dreams' that somehow heralded the destruction of Hanmer. The boy in raggedy shorts might be a spirit come to warn me. Perhaps fire would rain from the sky, perhaps a huge wave would come up from the ocean and drown even the mountains, perhaps war would come on the back of huge logging lorries.

I kept these fears to myself because I knew they would only worry my mother and puzzle my friends. I told Cargill all about Tarawera but he wasn't that interested. It was a long way away and a long time ago. When he woke up every morning, the mountains were still there. He wasn't going to get excited about something that happened way back then.

I was hooked on the magic bus, visited it every day after school while it was in town, and talked with Mrs Rockwell, who continued to unbend and show me all kinds of literary treasures.

The History of Four-footed Beasts and Serpents

I don't know by what fluke Topsell's *The History of Four-footed Beasts and Serpents* ended up in our bus, maybe a donation, but anyway there it was. Mrs Rockwell, told me that I was the first person to take it out. In confidential tones, she told me she kept the book on the bus only because she liked to look at it. 'I just open it at random and read a bit,' she said, as if confessing some infraction of the rules.

It was a rainy day when she sat me down on a little stool, the library bus's only amenity, usually used for reaching the higher shelves, and showed me Topsell's *History*. 'I don't know why I didn't think of it before,' she said. There was no one around that day. She and I were alone in the bus, our heads bent over Topsell's weird and wonderful illustrations, rain pattering softly on the roof of the bus. It felt as if the two of us were in a cocoon, sealed off from the world.

It wasn't the descriptions that interested me at first, but the pictures. Pictures of fantastic creatures both real and imaginary. What fascinated me was the way the imaginary and the real were mixed up, as if imaginary creatures did exist, and real creatures were at the same time imaginary.

Even the imaginary creatures were made up of bits taken from real creatures. I stared for hours at the drawing of the fearsome Hydra who had two eagle-like claws, a curled serpent's tail with scales and seven small mammalian heads with little round hats, like cloth crowns, and some with their tongues showing. And there was Lamia, a beast with the head and breasts of a woman, the forelegs of a bear, the hindlegs of a goat and the body of a serpent scaled like a dragon. She hissed like a snake or dragon. This delightful creature was a shapeshifter who preyed on handsome men and sucked the blood of children.

Then there was the manticore, described by Topsell as a deadly combination of man, lion and scorpion with a tail of venomous spines similar to porcupine quills, which could be shot like arrows into unsuspecting prey. This beast boasted a treble row of top and bottom teeth forming a grotesquely smiling mouth and, Topsell wrote, 'whose greatness, roughness, and feet are like a lyon's, his face and ears unto a man's, his eyes grey, and colour red, his voice like the voice of a small Trumpet or Pipe, being in course as swift as a Hart; his wildness such as can never be tamed, and his appetite is especially to the flesh of man.'

'Humankind can never stray too far from its nightmares,' Mrs Rockwell commented. She kept her voice low, not wanting to be overheard saying such things to me, I suspect.

After what seemed like an age poring over these pictures with the now enthusiastic Mrs Rockwell, whose glasses made her eyes large enough for her to look a little monstrous herself, I decided there could be no better life than travelling around the world seeking out strange and unknown creatures. 'There are still lots of species undiscovered' she told me. 'People think we know it all, but we don't. Especially insects. There are insects every bit as fantastic as Topsell's creatures.'

She didn't really want me to take the book home, because she kept stroking it, but finally let it go, admonishing me to look after it and not to take it to school where other kids could get their grubby little fingers onto it. She was very worried about those grubby little fingers. She'd be back in a month to collect it, she said. I solemnly promised.

I discovered that Topsell didn't write only about fantastic creatures, but told fantastic stories about known creatures. Apparently elephants were sun and moon worshippers who had evolved a complex set of rituals for their deities. He also believed that the blood of an elephant and the ashes of a weasel cure leprosy, and that touching an elephant's trunk cures a headache.

After reading this I told my mother, who often suffered from headaches, that she needed to touch the trunk of an elephant and for a moment, just for a moment, because her headache was so bad, she believed me. Then she chased me out of the house, telling me to take my 'silly book' somewhere else. It was worse than that Tarawera book, she declared.

I tried a few more ideas from Topsell on her, just to see how she would react. When I told her that apes were terrified of snails, she said 'Wow, I didn't know that' but when I told her that a sea-horse can eat a crocodile, she got angry again and once more I had to flee the house, *The History of Four-footed Beasts and Serpents* under my arm. Nor was she receptive to the idea that the horn of the unicorn was an antidote to 'poyson.'

Perhaps it's not so paradoxical that Topsell's fanciful book set me on the path that would lead me to the natural sciences, for his history also contained much accurate observation, such as 'It is the nature of a Dog, when he maketh water, to hold up his leg,' and 'Dogs have reason, and use logik in their hunting.' This mix of fact and fancy set the western mind on the path to empirical science just as it did with me. My desire to travel the world looking for strange creatures slowly matured into a more realistic ambition to go into the wild places of my own country and catalogue creatures humans barely knew existed.

Some of Topsell's observations, considered fanciful for hundreds of years, have proved to have some foundation, such as his claim that horses love music. Seen as ridiculous, experiments suggest that horses like certain kinds of music, classical and country music, but not jazz or rock. Some scientists pooh-pooh the idea that animals and fish experience pain, stress, and have dreams just as humans do. Once my mother solemnly assured me that fish felt no pain when taken out of the water and bashed over the head with a heavy stone, as the fishermen did. I found that hard to believe and I don't think she believed it herself, she was merely repeating something she'd been told.

Before returning the book, I took photos of some of the pages using Dad's Six-20 Flash Brownie camera. They were too blurry for me to read the text but caught some of the illustrations okay. Mum didn't like them and allowed me to keep them only if I solemnly promised not to show them to Frank.

Dreaming Topsell and a nameless dread

I dreamt of those Topsell creatures. In these dreams they were a part of the real world. Some were scary and some were not. They inhabited the streets as if they belonged there. I was the only one who could see them. Nobody would listen to me. I tried to show Mum and Dad, but they were too busy with other things.

The spiny bear ape arctopithecus was busy rooting around the boxes behind the Stevens sisters' café looking for discarded food. The sisters, both hefty women, were bashing it with sticks but it took no notice of them. A walking fish with the ears of a mouse and flattened, almost duck-beak mouth called the ichneumon, had taken up residence in the hospital pond. The groundsman was screaming abuse at it. Cargill brought an elongated dormouse with a bushy tail and built like a dachshund to school. He was telling kids not to pet it as it could bite off their fingers. In the school playground, a man-ape with a sunflower face was running in circles chasing the sun that seemed to be trying to escape him. A beast with several sets of teeth had become so hungry it had grown many heads in order to devour more people. Nobody seemed to notice it snatching people off the street. I tried to tell the adults, shouting myself hoarse, to little effect. Everybody just kept on going about their business.

My dream-self became aware of a brooding presence on Conical Hill. Although I couldn't see it directly, I knew that a creature with the body of a bull and a head of a giant hawk was watching me from the upper reaches of the hill where trees grew thickly.

Mum's voice, warning me not to stray too far, woke me up.

I lay awake for a while, listening to Frank breathing. I didn't feel relief that I was awake and Topsell's monsters were confined to my dreams and between the pages of a book. I could still sense the malignant presence on Conical Hill.

No matter where I was or where I hid, it could see me.

Dreaming of Topsell's creatures didn't bother me so much, it was like entering a huge book with 3D pages, more exciting than scary, but what did start to bother me was a corrosive feeling of dread as the evening, and bedtime, approached. It would settle over me like a mantle. If I could have held the sun back from sinking, I would have. I would have stopped time. I hated the way the closer the sun got to the mountains of the western horizon, the faster it seemed to go, that its final descent was precipitous and irrevocable. I felt scared and helpless. At that hour, you were never around to bring me the words I might have used to hold back the dark, a song I could sing in the face of that creeping feeling, which was a like a void seeping through the sky and the land, heralding a night much longer than the hours the clock marks off.

I felt that if Olga was still around, I would not be feeling this loneliness and dread that had apparently bred in the empty, wordless spaces she had left behind and was eating up all my meanings, the filaments of self that connected me to the world.

As the day began to settle and the shadows began to breathe, my heart would sink. I didn't want night to come on. I didn't want to have to go to bed. It was not that I was afraid of the dark, or that the dark might harbour Topsell's monsters, it was more amorphous than that. It made those kinds of fears look silly, for it was something deeper, a feeling of sickening anticipation. An anticipation of... the nameless, the void without form, the empty pits that open beneath the human heart, gravity's sinkhole. It was all the stronger for being nameless, unidentified; it remained simply a foreboding, a disquietude that grew more intense as bedtime got closer.

The only cure was to climb into bed with my parents, who became increasingly annoyed by it all. They didn't know how to reassure me. There were no monsters under the bed to banish, just this formless trepidation. Look at Frank, they said. He was just a toddler but he loved going to bed and sleeping all through the night, not drifting through fears as I was. The dreams that followed this dread were of fleeing and flying. At any moment the faceless might take on a face, the nameless find a name, and dread would turn to terror and self-possession to panic.

It took many years for this feeling to wear off. At some point my parents kicked me out of their bed and I staved off the dread by reading far into the night, mostly Dickens. 'He'd prop his eyelids open with matchsticks,' Mum commented. She didn't mind too much. As a child herself, she had read under the blanket with a torch and her own matchsticks, for her mother would disapprove.

Reading helped, but it wasn't until much later, as an adult, when I met the mighty Aria, that the feeling faded altogether. I was not alone, I discovered. Others felt it too. It's what lies behind the wine o'clock, cocktail hour. There's a feeling in the air. Somebody's eyes will have to meet the dawn. Aria was too psychologically robust to go with such mood swings, and being with her, something of her attitude rubbed off onto me. I could grow up. I could leave the frightened little boy in Hanmer. I didn't have to carry his fears.

That worked. But sometimes I wonder if the feeling might not reappear one day. In the future.

When I get old.

Language as a fantastic creature

In my child's mind words became all mixed up with Topsell's fantastic creatures, who were like a set of Dickens' characters, and I saw that language was the same. It too could take fantastic shapes, become discoloured, turn drab or grow brighter than lichen.

It was the names Topsell gave his creatures that alerted me to this, the infinite flexibility of words, the shuffle of syllables.

There wasn't just my English and Olga's Russian but a whole menagerie of languages, millions of weird and wonderful words I would never get to hear. Perhaps there were thoughts, kinds of thoughts, that can only be conceived in a particular language, concepts that have no equivalence in other languages. To get a true picture of the world, you would have to know all the languages there had ever been. Even then, your picture could never be totally true because there might be new languages in the future, or languages you never found out about. Like living creatures, these languages could thrive or die. When a language died, fewer people spoke it until just a handful of people, maybe just one person. When a language thrived, it transformed itself and put out roots, growing and spreading. Assimilating.

Languages are alive, I discovered. And suffered all kinds of varied fates.

This vision astonished me. I had always felt that the words I used, those you brought to me, were directly connected to the objects they denoted. Since any object might have a thousand names, does it have a name at all?

I tried to explain this idea to my mother, but she was sceptical. 'A tree is just a tree,' she said, pointing to the young Douglas Fir in our backyard. 'It doesn't matter how many names it has.'

That sounded very sensible, but I was not convinced. Does the tree have a name for itself, I wondered. Does Topsell's manticore know it's a manticore?

Later conversations with Mrs Rockwell would throw some light on this, but like the creeping dread that came on with the dark, I would never be able to tie a word to the world the way I had done. Language had become unstuck from the world; the relationship was purely provisional.

I didn't like this feeling. I think it helped create the evening dreads, the nameless terrors. Terrors that were formless because they were nameless. Because words wouldn't stick to them.

A time before this

Mrs Rockwell returned after a month, and pounced upon her Topsell which I dutifully returned, inspecting it for any sign of grubby little fingers. Finally, she pronounced herself satisfied, and produced a gift for me, two books on dinosaurs, *All About Dinosaurs* by Roy Chapman Andrews and *Dinosaurs* by Herbert S. Zim. I took these books home and eagerly read them. They passed the test of my mother's approval. She saw them as a great improvement on the freaky Topsell and didn't mind Frank looking at them. Dinosaurs were a healthy interest for a boy.

What I liked about the Andrews book was the account he gave of his many travels to exotic sounding places like the Gobi Desert of Mongolia, searching for dinosaur bones. I loved the idea of going to high places, the Gobi apparently reaching 5000 feet, whereas Hanmer was only 1300 feet. In my mind's eye I saw the Gobi floating way above Conical Hill, and was enchanted by the story that at night the sand dunes sang when the wind was up. I imagined being there and singing along with the sand, learning its language. I learned that dinosaur fossils had been found at the red Flaming Cliffs of Bayanzag (which I couldn't pronounce), and tried to imagine those cliffs and why they might be flaming. I saw them catching fire in the light of the sun. I imagined dinosaurs burning up in their fire. Sometimes I imagined that Olga was with me, and we went through many dangers together, even fighting living dinosaurs. Just when the danger was at its greatest, and we were about to be trampled by massive feet, the flaming cliffs would catch flame and the dinosaurs, now terrified, would run away. Olga and I would cling to each other in relief.

It was the Herbert Zim book, however, which sparked my interest in the names of these creatures. With Mrs Rockwell's help, I learned that their names were as fascinating as the creatures themselves. What else could the mighty brontosaurus be called? Here was a creature that lived up to its name. And the ponderous, hugely armoured stegosaurus fitted its name as well as my imagination. Stego and Bronto! Mrs Rockwell was as interested in dinosaurs as I was, and there was a gleam in her eye when she looked at the pictures in Zim's book of massive bone structures. I was learning that Mrs Rockwell's somewhat distant and frosty manner hid a warm and youthful heart. As we looked through Zim's book together, she became like a child, shyly at first but soon letting down her guard. She would laugh and pat my head and say, 'You're a solemn little chap,' and I would grin at her just to show that I wasn't all solemn.

I learned that the word dinosaur was made up of two words, a Greek word, *deinos*, meaning terrible or fearfully great and *sauros*, meaning a lizard or reptile. So a dinosaur was a fearfully great reptile. Mrs Rockwell wasn't quite sure why we used Greek names. And some used Latin words also, like the fearsome tyrannosaurus rex, which used the Greek word for tyrant and the Latin word for king – rex. That words could be made up of other words from different languages was a new idea to me, and made me wonder where all these sounds I was trying to make came from. From Mrs Rockwell I got the idea that words had histories just like living things.

When I saw my first picture of a pterodactyl I went hot and cold with astonishment. The proto bird I had seen had been extinct for thousands of years. I didn't tell Mrs Rockwell about how I had seen one in the skies over Hanmer and heard its harsh, elongated cries. She would certainly think I was making it up, and that would not have met with her approval. She would've become chilly and reserved with me. Little boys should not tell whoppers. I kept staring at the picture but could not make the memory go away, or substitute the picture for my memory. Only I knew what its cry sounded like, I thought. The books didn't mention that because the writers had never heard it. I could tell Mr Andrews and Mr Zim but what notice would they have taken?

Where are the dinosaurs now? I wanted to know. It was an urgent question.

'They all died,' Mrs Rockwell said, 'and nobody is sure why. Some scientists think volcanos were responsible, filling the air up with carbon dioxide which made Earth too hot and dangerous. Maybe Earth was hit by something from outer space. But nobody really knows. Not yet, anyway.'

A stream of sound

Cargill and I were at that age when trouble would come in search of us. It didn't have to look too far. We could easily be found hanging around the sawmill, too dangerous for kids, or lurking around the back of the town's only café, which people called a tea-room, where old buns and stale jam cakes were left in cardboard cartons for eventual disposal. Cargill and I agreed that it was a good idea to 'save' these from the rats. The café owners, two big lumbering women known as the Stevens sisters, Betty and Gladys, would chase us away if they saw us. For some peculiar reason it offended them that we could eat their home-baked sweets without paying, even though they'd discarded them, most of them dry with stale cream. Cargill and I would fight over the Sally Lunns because of the cream oozing out of the slit at the top. Cargill could stuff a whole lamington into his mouth and still talk.

I was keeping a watchful eye on the back door of the café in case the sisters came rushing out while Cargill rummaged through the cartons, when something strange happened. I was getting ready to say something, prepare my words because that way I wouldn't stutter quite as much, when a stream of sound issued from my mouth, or more precisely, my chest, rushing up through my throat and out into the world without any conscious volition on my part. These were not just random sounds, however, but words and patterns of words in some language totally unknown to me. It was as if I had magically learned how to speak another language. It felt as if someone inside me, some other being, was talking. Perhaps another me, like the articulate one in the mirror, only this time articulate in a foreign language. Maybe I'm speaking Greek or Latin, I thought.

It sounded strange in the ordinary air behind the café. And loud too, without any stuttering at all.

Cargill looked at me in amazement, mouth full of jam tart. I shook my head. Cargill tried to say something and bits of jam tart dribbled out of his mouth. I could do nothing but shake my head; the echo of those freakish, loud words filled my mind, pushing ordinary ones out. I was staggering around like Mr Washdike after a long night at the Rotherham Pub. I fell over backwards into a pile of cartons causing the top ones to come tumbling down on me.

The back door of the café flew open and Betty Stevens came rushing out. Seeing us, she looked both angry and relieved. 'I thought something terrible had happened,' she said, 'with all that yabba-dabba. Clear out, you two. Scram.'

We didn't wait to be told twice.

'What happened?' Cargill said when we'd reached the safety of the street. He'd managed to stuff some currant buns down his shirt and we ate them as we walked along.

'I don't know.'

'You said a whole lot of funny words,' Cargill said.

'Yeah,' I said.

'But why?'

'Beats me,' I said. I needed something to wash down the stale currant bun.

We arrived at the hospital gardens and slipped through the gate where I'd first seen Olga. Inside, in front of some shrubs, there was a park bench where we could sit and look across the grounds at the old alkies lizarding in the sun on their benches. They looked more like dried-up husks than people. They knew Cargill and me well, probably remembering the day we drained the hospital lily pond. They would jabber and point when they saw us. Cargill liked to poke his tongue out at them, which would make them jabber and point even more.

'I'm not telling my mum,' I said.

Cargill nodded. He had things he didn't tell his mum too.

'She'd just think there was something wrong with me,' I said. Besides, she always gave the impression that she had better things to attend to than my nonsense. 'She might take me to a doctor.' I thought of my stuttering and dismal performance at school.

Cargill agreed that that was not a good outcome.

'I'm not going to tell the teacher or the other kids at school.' Mrs Hurrell, my teacher, was a nice enough person, but a little too scratchy to confide in. Besides, she was in a position of power over me, and I was learning that it was best not to confide in figures of authority, even my parents, as any confidences might rebound in unexpected and unpleasant ways.

'I won't say anything,' Cargill said. I didn't believe him, not the way he liked to talk.

'You have to promise.'

'I promise,' he said.

'Anyway, it hasn't done me any harm.'

'You're not stuttering,' he said.

That silenced me. I was afraid to say anything more in case I started stuttering again.

The alkies had seen us and were pointing at us. They seemed to find us hilarious.

'See that one right on the end?' Cargill said.

'With a face like a horse?'

'Well, that's you,' he said.

'No, it's you,'

'You lie,' he said.

'Not me,'

'What about all those words? Were they real words?'

'Beats me,' I said.

Through that whole conversation I didn't stutter once.

The tongues of men and angels

Not telling anybody did not apply to Mrs Rockwell, who was fascinated by my account, although she was quiet about it at first. I could tell she was considering something very deeply, as if she had some important decision to make. Seeing the solemn look on her face, it occurred to me that Mrs Rockwell had been a little girl at one time, a kid of our age. It was hard to imagine. I couldn't see her without her large round glasses and stern expression.

Finally, she began to talk. She told me that what I had experienced was known as 'talking in tongues,' or glossolalia, and that I was not the first person to experience it. Although, she said, she'd never heard of children experiencing it.

'Some religious people believe it to be a divine language. The Bible tells the story of the apostles of Jesus who, after his death, all began uttering strange words when *cloven tongues like as of fire* descended upon them.' When she said, 'cloven tongues like as of fire,' her voice dropped a register as if she were suddenly somebody else.

She got up abruptly and paced up and down the aisle of the bus. Her face was set in a way I had previously seen with my mother, and I knew she was hiding an intense inner process. She looked grave and somewhat foreboding, which was the way she often appeared to people at first. Then something like grief passed across her face, and she gave me a tormented look.

At that moment a customer arrived at the open side of the bus. It was Mrs Rogers whose husband was the local mechanic. She placed three books on the sideboard. She didn't see me as I was sitting on the movable step off to one side.

'Have you got any more like these?' she asked, affecting a certain indifference.

'Travel books, isn't it? Mrs Rockwell said, sweeping up the returned books and placing them on a board that ran beneath the counter. 'We've got a new one by Freya Stark called *Iona, A Quest*, about her travels in Greece and the Levant.' She dithered about trying to find the book. That puzzled me as she knew where every book was, and never had problems finding them.

'I enjoyed her last one,' Mrs Rogers said, 'you know, the one about visiting Arabia.'

'*A Winter in Arabia*,' Mrs Rockwell said absently. Finally, she found the book she wanted and placed it on the counter. I wondered why she didn't invite Mrs Rogers into the bus to have a browse.

Mrs Rogers gave a guilty smile as she seized the book. The cover showed some stone ruins that reminded me of dinosaur bones. The book quickly disappeared into her bag, and with a quick goodbye she was on her way.

'She's hardly ever left Hanmer,' Mrs Rockwell said, half to herself. 'And all she reads are travel books.'

Recovering her presence of mind, she pulled a book down from the topmost shelf. It was a brightly coloured book called *Bible Stories for Children* which she gave to me without saying anything and was silent while I flicked through the book. There was Adam in the Garden of Eden giving names to all the animals, there was Moses parting the Red Sea, there was Daniel in the lion's den, Jesus preaching, and a group of men with cloven tongues like as of fire coming down on their heads. The cloven tongues looked like fiery birds dancing above them.

'Mum and Dad are not religious,' I said. 'I've seen some of these stories in a colouring-in book I had when I was Frank's age.'

Mrs Rockwell was uncharacteristically quiet.

'Is there really such a thing as a divine language?' I wanted there to be one, even if it was only spoken by angels. Mrs Rockwell didn't answer at first, and occupied herself by returning *A Winter in Arabia* to its shelf. When she finally spoke, she sounded faint and distant.

'Maybe, but glossolalia is just a string of meaningless syllables. It might sound meaningful but actually be meaningless.'

I tried to relate that to my experience behind the tea-room. I had no way of knowing if the sounds that came out of my mouth were meaningful or not.

She took the book out of my hands and closed it with a snap.

'My parents were Pentecostals,' she said, scratching at the back of her hand. 'They wanted me to believe it all, speaking in tongues and everything. But I saw them a bit like Father Christmas stories, or the Tooth Fairy. When I was a teenager, I realised that my parents were misguided, and that glossolalia has nothing to do with God.'

She looked around the bus almost fearfully. She'd made a red mark on the back of her hand where she'd been scratching.

'My parents died in a car crash a few years ago, but sometimes I think I can hear them singing hymns. My mother said Jesus's face appeared to her in the water.'

'I've seen lots of faces in the river. They come and go all the time.'

'Of course they do!' She seemed relieved to hear it. 'I'm glad you're my friend,' she said suddenly, out of nowhere.

'Don't you have many friends?'

'Not that many. Because... well... I'm a bookworm.'

I'd never heard the expression before, and I liked it. I imagined myself as a worm wriggling through millions of words.

'You're never lonely if you're a bookworm.'

I came away from that discussion with the word glossolalia on my tongue. It was a wonderful word to say, if I could say it without stuttering. It got my tongue jumping up and down in my mouth. If I stumbled over the second 'l' I almost tripped into speaking in tongues 'lal-lal-lal-lia-lia-lia,' a lovely string of syllables taking me off into la-la land. I sensed that if I wanted to, I could use the word itself, by chanting it, to bring on talking in tongues as if the word itself, if stuttered correctly, was a code that would trigger it. I tried it out a couple of times and it seemed to work. I could get all kinds of sounds coming out of my mouth, but only sounds that belonged to my own experience of language.

The dandy lion and other creatures

Cargill and I never talked about my experience again, although from that point on our friendship began to wane. It was nothing that you could put your finger on, and we still had adventures, but we were together less often, Cargill was spending more time with other kids and I was spending more time with books from Mrs Rockwell's magic library bus. I was happily becoming a bookworm.

Also, Cargill didn't want to talk about the things I wanted to talk about. Like God. He liked to make pronouncements on such things but not discuss them.

'God made the world,' he said one day in a tone suggesting that that was the end of the matter.

'Is god inside the world or outside of it?' I asked, keeping god in the lower case.

God with a capital is the one and only big I AM; god without the capital is demoted to being one god among many. I'd heard about the big I AM and didn't like the sound of Him. Mrs Rockwell didn't seem to like him either. My parents avoided any such talk, although dad would sometimes make comments about 'Bible bangers.'

Cargill was annoyed. 'God made the world,' he insisted, as if that answered the question.

Cargill, who had always been such a gabber-mouth, was becoming morose. He didn't talk as much now except to complain; he could complain endlessly, especially about school. Like me, he didn't do well at school. Sometimes he would fall into a brooding silence.

One day, coming out of one of those silences, he said, 'You know, I would really like to burn the school down. Right to the ground.'

Over the coming months, with Mrs Rockwell's guidance, I continued my exploration of different kinds of language. I told her about my father, the poor mangled hen and his 'fuk fuk fuk.' She was delighted by the story, and just as delighted with my theory that swearing was like the opposite of divine language. The evil and the good.

'That's an interesting idea,' she said.

She reached out to pat me on the head, but withdrew her hand at the last minute.

We would always sit on a couple of low stools used for library patrons. We couldn't readily be seen from the open street, a passer-by would have to stand on their tip-toes to see the top of our heads. But Mrs Rockwell kept one eye out, as she called it, and would promptly rise when a patron came along. There were steps up into the bus at the back, and sometimes we would be interrupted by browsers. Mostly we would create a little bubble for ourselves where we could explore things, like a couple of kids telling ghost stories at night.

I saw that this was analogous to my expeditions up the river exploring the physical world. With Mrs Rockwell, I discovered the joys of undertaking expeditions through the world of ideas where there were many weird and wonderful species to behold. Ideas had their own topography, history and evolution. Every idea seemed to have grown out of a previous idea, or ideas. It was both bewildering and exhilarating to discover that ideas rested on other ideas like a house of cards. The truth, however, was there to be discovered. Was ours the only universe? Would the universe really end with the death of heat? Was the universe itself alive? There were answers to these questions, real answers, and people had dedicated their lives to finding them.

Mrs Rockwell called that the language of science, which was the language of verifiable things, from distant stars to the gases that made up our atmosphere. A lot of this had to do with naming and cataloguing, and, it seemed to me, Adam's task of giving names to all the animals was never finished. I was particularly interested in newly discovered plants like the mysterious-sounding ghost orchid that was leafless and flowered only at night, the fungus with teeth, the voodoo lily and the fireworks flower, exotic sounding creatures that would have happily found a home in Topsell's *History*.

This growing interest in the natural world was fed by my lone walks along our river, which I began to call by its name – the Hanmer River, making two words out of it to get the 'n' before the 'm.' I began to register things that had always been there, in the background, unappreciated. Like the soft broom with its heady yellow scent, the way its small, pea-like flowers glowed like golden syrup in the late-afternoon sun. I enjoyed picking the dark pink flowers of the red clover and sucking them for their sweet juice. I admired the yellow flower of the sow thistle with its serrated leaves, another plant that I could eat. I learned to recognise the cloudy seed heads of the dandelion, a plant I loved as much for its name as its qualities. A dandy lion, my tongue hitting the two 'ds' like stepping stones, with the 'lion' fading on the breath. I recognised the delicate yarrow with its floating flower heads and gentle demeanour. I came to appreciate the stubborn dock with its long yellowish root, and when it came to smells, I couldn't miss the loud fennel with its sweet-sharp scent. I learned how to outwit the thorny blackberries so I could, in the autumn, eat their berries.

Mrs Rockwell told me that everything that grew had two names: its popular name and its Latin name. Naming, and seeking names, became my major preoccupation, and while I didn't leave nineteenth century literature behind entirely, my reading became more oriented towards natural history.

What fascinated me were the sonorous Latin names all the plants had, which became their official names, since the common names might change over time or be different from place to place. It was their Latin names which anchored them in a common language, for they were known by those names all over the world and by scientists who spoke different languages. They could be sure that they were talking about the same thing.

These Latin names caught me up, as they sounded so splendid and imposing, like the sound of distant thunder. The ghost orchid was called *Didymoplexis stella-silvae* which is a wonderful name to try to pronounce. Mrs Rockwell and I broke it up into syllables and learned to say it by chanting, as if it were a children's rhyme. We did the same with the fungus with teeth, known as *Hydnellum nemorosum*, the voodoo lily became *Pseudohydrosme ebo*, which we both stumbled over, and the fireworks flower the *Ardisia pyrotechnica*, which proved quite easy to say once you got the hang of it.

These official names had a solemn air of authority about them. I felt solemn saying them out loud as if I were taking part in some ancient ritual. Common names were evanescent; Latin names were firmly grounded in ancient history. By chanting the Latin names of these plants we were turning them into a liturgy of the natural world.

Enter the taniwha

One day Mrs Rockwell brought me a new word.

Taniwha. With the 'wh' pronounced as an 'f.'

It was the first Māori word I'd heard, or could remember hearing except for Dad's 'waka.'

Mrs Rockwell said it in a hushed, reverent tone.

She tried to explain to me that while the taniwha, often represented as reptilian, with spines running down its back like geckos or tuatara, sometimes with wings that made it look like a dragon, and sometimes looking more like a fish with a long, powerful tail, might seem like one of Topsell's monsters, the creature could not be dismissed as a mythological being. For some it was like a living presence, sometimes seen as a guardian spirit of a river or mountain. I immediately thought of the creature I had seen in my dream, with the body of a bull and the head of a giant hawk, residing on Conical Hill. That creature had been a living presence, one which I continued to feel after I had woken up. Maybe that creature was a taniwha which had changed its shape when it came onto the land.

'In some traditions, taniwha are terrifying creatures that capture people and eat them,' Mrs Rockwell said. 'They might even kidnap women to live with them as wives. Then they would be killed by a hero and the women returned to their families.'

This fired my imagination. I had seen pictures of St George slaying a dragon in which the dragon looked like a taniwha, so I saw the taniwha like that.

'But taniwha are not always monsters. They can be seen as protectors of tribes and sub-tribes. They are revered and people who pass by their dens must say a special charm or spell and leave an offering.'

I loved the idea that there were special words that could soothe and placate the taniwha. I was sure those words would have to be sung.

She showed me a picture of one found in a cave along the Ōpihi River, south of Christchurch near Timaru. It was a rock drawing, at least twelve feet long and three to four feet wide, showing three taniwha with interlocking tails. I took from this that the artist must have seen the taniwha as a huge creature, maybe as big as a dinosaur. It looked like it had the body of a serpent and the tail of a stegosaurus.

We talked about this with eager enthusiasm, saying the word taniwha as often as we could because we both liked the sound it made in our mouths.

Mrs Rockwell would say the word in special, hushed tones, as if it were a secret word. I had the feeling that she didn't want passers-by to hear us. Said in a conspiratorial half-whisper, it sounded mysterious, and saying it over and over made it sound defiant. It had the air of the forbidden about it that I liked.

After leaving the bus that day I kept whispering it to myself. Driven by an impulse I didn't fully understand, I made sure no one else heard me say it. I didn't want any questions as to where I'd heard it. It belonged to Mrs Rockwell and me.

It was our little secret.

True and original languages

'My father believed there was a divine language,' Mrs Rockwell said to me one day. We were looking through JW Matthews' book on *New Zealand Trees* and were having fun with the Latin names.

'He thought this divine language wasn't spoken by people.'

She always held herself upright as if on a boat in high seas when talking about her childhood and her parents, and she would scratch the back of her hand. Her voice would change too, become less adult and more sing-song.

'He thought it was what Adam and Eve spoke in the Garden of Eden. It was a language that came before common human speech.'

'Do you believe that?'

'I don't believe in the Garden of Eden. It's one of those myths that gets hold of people's minds. Once it's got a hold, it's hard to shake.'

'Let's just imagine that it's true. What language did God use to speak to Adam?'

'It would have to be Hebrew,' she said reluctantly. 'So, Hebrew became the true and original language of the Jewish people.'

'But what if it wasn't Hebrew? What if it was a special language only God spoke?'

'Angelica,' she said. 'That's what my father thought. Not just the name of a plant but the special language you're talking about. Angelica, the tongue of angels, a language not of this earth.'

That sounded very exciting to me, and I wanted to hear it immediately. I wanted to hear angels talking to each other in Angelica. I bet they didn't stutter. I bet it just flowed off their tongues like music. I felt curiously doomed when I realised that I would never hear it, only maybe after I was dead, and that was a big maybe.

'If it's not of this Earth, then I don't see the point in thinking about it.' She spoke like an insistent child, on the cusp of anger. 'We're never going to hear it. And it probably doesn't even exist. I mean, there's no way we can prove that it exists.' She looked around almost fearfully, as if her father was about to appear and tell her off for saying such things.

'Oh, I can hear it. Listen.' I began to chant some random syllables. It wasn't glossolalia but just made-up sounds. I tried to imagine how it would feel to be an angel and to want to sing.

Mrs Rockwell laughed. She seemed relieved. She joined in and chanted made up sounds as well. For a moment it was our very own unearthly language. An unsuspecting passer-by, perhaps heading into the local council offices outside which the library bus was parked, would have heard some strange and eerie sounds, as if ghosts had suddenly inhabited the world of books.

'Let me tell you about the strange case of Hildegard of Bingen,' she said.

'Who's that?'

'A very remarkable woman who lived a long time ago. Sometimes she wrote in a language nobody knew. It was called the *lingua ignota*, which is Latin for unknown language.'

'*Lingua ignota*,' I repeated, quite thrilled that it should have such an imposing name, just like a plant.

'She was the only one who could understand it. Some people think that she believed it was the universal language spoken by humankind before the Tower of Babel, and maybe even spoken by supernatural beings.'

'But how would Hildegard know it?'

'Divine inspiration. Like her music. She thought her music was directly inspired by God, so why not her *lingua ignota*? Or...' she leaned forward on the stool with great intensity, bringing her face close to mine, 'or she might have created it to be her own secret language. It was safe to write things in that language because only she understood it. Perhaps she could write things that she dared not speak.'

At that thrilling moment, a fantail landed on the counter and peered in at us chittering brightly. We both stared in amazement as the bird did a quick flutter around the library, hovering here and there as if checking out certain books.

'The bird has its own *lingua ignota*,' she said. She smiled with pleasure at the idea. The idea that a bird's utterances might be divinely inspired was not something her father would have approved of, however much he might like the idea of a divine language.

In my mind's eye Hildegard looked a bit like Olga, only grown up, sitting at her bare wooden desk in a trance writing her secrets out, letting them into the world but only in her special code. A fantail was hovering at her window, chittering away in its own tongue.

'I wonder what her secrets were?' I said.

The fantail, who might have known the answer to my question, swooped out of the bus and into the open spaces, diving to and fro.

'It's all just speculation,' Mrs Rockwell said suddenly, rising from her stool as if she had something better to do. 'It could be a made-up language. Like Esperanto.'

'Olga and I made up our own language,' I said. 'We had bits of Russian, and English, and made-up words.'

'You still miss her terribly, don't you?'

'I still do,' I felt myself go red in the face and felt like an idiot.

'Well, I think it's quite wonderful. I don't have anybody I really miss. My bus is my friend. Would you say a few words in your made-up language?'

'Okay,' I said. I hadn't forgotten. The words came out of my mouth just as they used to, fluid and without stuttering.

Mrs Rockwell attempted to make the same kind of sounds. I didn't like that. That language was for no one but me and Olga. I shouldn't have told Mrs Rockwell in the first place, now it felt as if something had been spoiled.

One day, when Mrs Rockwell and I had our heads together, deep in our explorations, my mother walked up the back steps into the bus with no warning. She regarded us both with deep suspicion, and I felt Mrs Rockwell stiffen and draw away from me a little. Mum had a way of ferreting out secrets that was quite uncanny.

'So this is where you are,' she said, as if she'd been hunting all over town for me.

She looked at me, but her focus was on Mrs Rockwell. Something transpired between the two women which was as hidden from me as Hildegard's secret language. I had the feeling I'd done something terribly wrong. My mother was an expert at making people feel guilty for some unstated infraction of rules that were never made clear; even Mrs Rockwell in her chilly mode was affected by it, and became quiet and dignified, as if she were a child trying to be an adult.

Later, my mother questioned me closely, asking what we were talking about and why we were sitting 'so close together.' Looking back now, I can see that she suspected some kind of impropriety, but at the time I knew nothing of that, and the incident left me unsettled. I continued to visit Mrs Rockwell when she came to town, but detected in her a certain reserve unlike her previous enthusiasm.

One day the library bus failed to come, and I never saw Mrs Rockwell again.

Part Two

Aria and the feedback effect

The big smoke

Do you remember our move from Hanmer? I remember Midnight, our black cat, staring wide-eyed at us from inside her travelling box. I remember the fear and hope on my mother's face, Frank crying and dad fussing with the car, which, I think, was a Buick Sedan he had bought to use as Hanmer's first taxi. I remember the mountains falling away behind us as if into an ocean. I remember a shooting star that seemed to fall on the road before us.

My father called the city of Christchurch 'the big smoke' and he couldn't wait to get there. He was tired of driving drunks to the Rotherham pub and back again in his Buick. He would never make any money or get ahead that way. And in the big smoke Mum might be able to find work. They talked a lot about the move, how they wanted to improve their own lives and give me and Frank a shot at higher education. I overheard Dad say that Hanmer was a 'dead end.' Opportunity beckoned from the Big Smoke.

Time gathered itself into a whirlwind. We moved from the open spaces of Hanmer into a pokey little flat in New Brighton, on the main street called Seaview Road, above a café opposite a movie theatre which played 'Sail Along Silvery Moon' every night when the movie finished. Frank and I learned to hate that bland song. We would cover our ears whenever it come on. Midnight took one look out the window at the main street below, with cars and trucks and people moving along the sidewalk and in and out of shops, and bolted out the door, never to be seen again.

There were no wild spaces, like the Hanmer River, no Conical Hill where I could talk to you, and work on my inner voice, the one that never stuttered. No mountains or cowboys riding in from mustering. No fragrance of Olga. Midnight took all of those things when she bolted.

Soon I found Brighton Beach with its miles of sandhills and found I could outrun the city, go north up the beach far enough to where there was nothing but sandhills, silky lupin and wild blackberries. And the restless, moody ocean. I could run half-way to the Waimakariri River.

You were there but your presence was fainter, less clear than at the top of Conical Hill or up the Hanmer River. It was as if the sound of the ocean had washed your voice away, and it was the ocean that was my word bringer. I thought maybe you'd fade out altogether just like the imaginary friend my parents thought you were. It seemed that your work was done. You had given body to the ghost realm of words. Perhaps I didn't need you anymore. Mum always thought I'd grow out of you.

At least the beach was a big, empty place. Mostly. Once I came across two people lying in the sand, one on top of the other, and they had hardly any clothes on. I scrammed out of that vicinity as fast as I could. At least the first time I did. Later, I would creep up and spy on such couples, for the beach north of Brighton was a popular place for lovers.

Funny, although she left before me, I felt I'd left Olga behind once we moved to the city. Olga and Cargill and Conical Hill and the Hanmer River with its chatter and its willow groves. I thought of Midnight padding through the miles to get there. Christchurch also had a river, the Avon River, but it was so tame it was hardly like a river at all. The Avon didn't talk to me, just slid on by, silent and secretive.

On the main street where we lived, I found a small, privately owned lending library, with the same Westerns (for the men) and Romance novels (for the women) and 'thud and blunders' that Mrs Rockwell stocked in her library bus. There was no Topsell, or dinosaur books. The library was run by a pleasant woman, Mrs Little, who didn't know much about books but had an uncanny memory for which books her regulars had taken out. 'This looks like a good one,' a customer would say, holding up a book enquiringly. 'You've read that one,' Mrs Little would say, 'but I don't think you've read *Midnight Rendezvous.*'

Talking to Mrs Little made me miss Mrs Rockwell. All Mrs Little wanted to do was give me Famous Five and Bobbsey Twins books. She did have an old copy of *The Count of Monte Cristo* but I'd already read it. What I did discover, however, in Mrs Little's paperback library, was a small selection of science fiction: Isaac Asimov, Arthur C. Clarke, Robert Heinlein, Robert Silverberg and Philip K. Dick. Mrs Rockwell had never mentioned science fiction, although I found in some descriptions of alien species an echo of Topsell's *History.*

Also reminding me of Topsell were the garish covers of the magazines like *Amazing Stories, Weird Tales* and *Astounding Stories of Super Science.*

The Creature from the Black Lagoon crawled out of the slime at the back of my mind to terrify me. Between the covers, however, I encountered the work of such classic writers as Jules Verne and HG Wells, who felt comfortably nineteenth century for me, as well as the unsettling stories of the younger Philip K. Dick who was interrogating the nature of reality itself, and which brought me out of the nineteenth century and seemed to catapult me into a future full of fake worlds.

Mrs Little didn't particularly approve – she still thought the Bobbsey Twins were the best – and would look rather scandalised by the covers of those magazines, which sometimes featured scantily clad damsels in distress about to be assaulted by tentacled beings, but would get them for me nonetheless and would take my couple of coins with a righteous air. Money was money, tentacled beings notwithstanding. I didn't exactly hide these magazines from my mother, but I didn't flaunt them either. Nobody said anything and one day I found my father reading one, a bemused look on his face. This was not Ed McBain.

Most memorable was a novel called *A Canticle for Leibowitz* by Walter M. Miller Jr, my first encounter with post-apocalyptic literature. Here was a story that spanned centuries and delved deep into the nature of faith. As I read it, I had the feeling that I was only picking up the surface of the story and that the book was charged with a half-concealed meaning just beyond my grasp. I was fascinated by the idea that a story could contain another even more powerful story hidden inside it, just as truth can hide inside a lie.

A few years later, I read a commentary by Percy Walker who claimed that the book was a cipher, a coded message, 'a book in a strange language.' It was that secret, strange language that held me in thrall as I read. I got the same feeling from Philip K. Dick's stories, simple on the surface yet with hidden meanings beneath, meanings that kept erupting into the text; stories of salvation and damnation.

If the dinosaur books introduced me to the notion of deep time in terms of the history of the earth, *A Canticle for Leibowitz* made me realise that humans too were subject to the depredations of the centuries. Languages themselves could grow old, die and be forgotten. In Miller's novel, a group of monks has a sacred text written in a language they can no longer decipher. It is only a single piece of paper, but the monks revere it as it was a relic from before the 'Simplification,' a fiery atomic holocaust that had plunged the earth into darkness and ignorance.

It turns out, however, that this piece of paper is no profound message from the divine realm but a shopping list: *Pound of pastrami, can of kraut, six bagels – bring home for Emma.*

All those centuries they had been worshiping a shopping list.

Behind this story of the delusions of faith there loomed the 'half-concealed' story, which was the story of our own time, a time overshadowed by the possibility of the 'fiery atomic holocaust' destroying our own world. Everybody did their best to ignore this horrifying possibility, but it was there, sneaking into our dreams and our stories.

I discovered that Miller had been partly inspired to write his one and only novel by witnessing the destruction by bombing of the abbey at Monte Cassino in Italy, built in the sixth century and used at the time of the war as a monastery. My father had been there, had taken part in the Battle of Monte Cassino, and had witnessed the bombing of the abbey. He would talk about it sometimes to his friends, but only when he was drinking. Maybe he had met Miller and never known. This helped make the book personal to me, and gave me a chill when I perceived, as a half-concealed truth, the way real events fed into the dystopian dreams of Miller and other science fiction writers.

I would take the book to the beach and lie facing the sea with the sandhills at my back, the book in my hand, time slipping through my fingers like a silken thread, imagining the bomb like a strange sun blossoming on the horizon, signalling the end of all that was familiar to me. I would distract myself from this vision by learning the Latin name for things around me, like the coarse marram grass that clung to the sand hills, also called bent grass or just beach grass, but was really *Ammophila arenaria*, a grand name for such a humble plant. Or the grey-brown sand hoppers with their black eyes that jumped around all over the place, and were really called *Talitrus saltator*. I wondered if, when they jumped, they had any notion of where they would come down. I also wondered if they got any pleasure from the sudden flexing of their abdomens that enabled them to jump.

In a few weeks I'd read all of the science fiction in Mrs Little's lending library. She kept careful tabs on what I was reading and began acquiring books to suit my taste. Mostly they were second-hand books she got dirt cheap, but I didn't care. My mother didn't begrudge me the few coins each book cost me to borrow.

My parents' gamble paid off. My grip on language grew more certain and my stuttering continued to fade. Despite a stubborn inability to spell correctly, my school grades began to improve, albeit sluggishly, and Frank made friends. He told Dad that he was going to make 'lots and lots and lots' of money. Dad laughed and said he wouldn't be surprised since Frank was a little go-getter, unlike me. Except he didn't add that, not out loud anyway.

My parents became more cheerful about my prospects. My father thought I might become a lawyer because I liked to argue about things, but my mother knew. 'He's going to study plants,' she said.

My interest in plants was piqued by my science fiction reading, as those authors were free to imagine all kinds of flora and fauna, and humankind's relation to them. Topsell had never imagined plants in his *History*, only strange animals, but surely he would not have been surprised by John Wyndham's triffids, and might have delighted in drawing them with their nasty, whiplashing tentacles.

As with Wyndham, the hidden 'half concealed' story behind many of these books was about a conflict between humankind and nature; the alien forces arrayed against the heroic humans were invariably hostile. The book that brought this underlying story to the surface most vividly for me was Harry Harrison's *Deathworld*. Harrison imagined a highly toxic, alien world in which the human colonists had divided into two camps, the settlers and the grubbers. The settlers, known as the junkmen, were engaged in a bitter, never-ending battle against the plants and animals of Deathworld, a battle they were losing, while the grubbers lived beyond the confines of the junkmen's city defences and had learned to talk to the planet's creatures, who turned out to be telepathic, and had come to some accommodation with them.

It was in the activity of Harrison's junkmen, who thought only of killing, and killed everything they could simply because they could, that I first learned of the feedback effect. As their weapons grew more destructive and sophisticated, so did the responses of the creatures of Deathworld, who mutated to better kill humans. This locked them into a death spiral as the weapons of each grew more deadly. It was an arms race the junkmen were losing. The grubbers escaped this death spiral by making friends with the alien species, and by killing only to eat.

In the games I played in my lone hours on Brighton Beach, I imagined that I was a grubber and could communicate telepathically with the creatures of the beach, particularly with the poisonous katipō spider (*Latrodectus katipo*) with its sinister-looking black body and jagged red stripe on top. My parents warned me about this spider, and told me to keep clear of it and to come home immediately if I was bitten, but I sought the hard-to-find spiders out, entered into a conversation with them, trying to induce the shy creatures to walk over my hand, telling them that I was a grubber not a junkman, friend to spiders and sand-hoppers, and that it had nothing to fear from me.

Maybe that worked because I never got bitten. I believed that the spiders could pick up my peaceful intentions, and even felt that they could speak back to me in their telepathic way, telling me of their hopes and fears. They told me they were getting hard to find because there were too many junkmen disrupting their homes, and invaders from abroad, like the 'false' katipō (*Steatoda capensis*), which was about the same size and also black, but with no red stripe. They were happy to meet a grubber like me who didn't want to kill them.

I didn't tell my parents about these conversations with the katipō because I knew mum would only worry, and she had enough on her hands as it was. I did tell Frank, however, and he was suitably horrified. He would never let a katipō, or any other spider, crawl over his hand. 'I would just squash it,' he said.

And then, one day, a book arrived in my hands which would change everything and put an end to my childhood.

Sex and survival

I had reached the last year of my primary schooling and the grand age of twelve. I don't have a lot to say about my years at New Brighton Primary school except that it was nothing like my little Hanmer school. The children were unruly to the point of riotousness and our poor teacher, a man of good will and generous heart, I believe, could hardly be heard above the out-of-control hubbub of the class room. Chaos ruled.

The situation became so dire that during the intervals and lunchtimes the teachers would patrol the playground breaking up any group of children larger than three or four members in case we ran riot, and keeping an eye on the little lunch shed in the playground to make sure the girls were not getting molested. On rainy days, when we had to stay in the classroom during breaks with no teacher in attendance, some of the girls would cluster along the back wall and allow the boys to put their hands up their dresses. The racket everybody made was deafening.

On such days the teachers would retreat to their staffroom and let it all rip.

There was a resource room in one of the buildings where we would sometimes be sent to get class sets of books and other material, and there a more silent and intense nefarious activity might take place. Sometimes a girl would ask to go to the toilet and go instead to the resource room where she would wait for boys to come and encourage them to put their hands down her panties. On one occasion I was sent to the resource room and found a plump, dark-haired girl from another class, and two boys who were 'feeling her up.' She didn't look that them but up at the ceiling. She didn't say anything but made encouraging noises.

I stood in line and took my turn to put my hands down her panties while she wriggled about, but I didn't know what it was I was feeling. I quickly withdrew my hand without discovering very much, although she sighed with disappointment.

I learned more the next time she was there and began to get the hang of it. I met that same girl in the resource room about two or three times in these guiltily intense, wordless encounters, so much at variance with the raucous activities in the lunch shed and the class-room on a rainy day. I never learned her name, but if we happened to see each other in the playground, which was not often as she was from a year-before-me class who had a separate playground, we would ignore each other and look the other way.

Finally, one of the girls, who was only twelve, got pregnant because of meeting boys after school, and the beleaguered headmistress interviewed all the girls from our class, which was the worst class, and the headmaster emerged from his office, his stubby strap in hand, and gave every boy 'six of the best' whether we were guilty or not. I took my punishment, nursed my hand and that evening you returned to me with a poem about a leopard, or maybe Bagheera, the panther from Rudyard Kipling's *Jungle Book*, leaping from rock to rock feeling his muscles rippling all through his body. I wrote it down as fast as I could in case you took it away again.

During that year, I learned how to shoplift and bully those weaker than me. It was bully or be bullied, and I was too much of a wild kid from the mountains to be bullied. We would buy fish and chips or sausages and chips wrapped in newspaper, open the top of the package, and raid the shops down Seaview Road, pretending to be innocently eating chips while slipping pens, pencils, erasers etc down past our wrists and into the package. Fountain pens were our top steal. When we got back to school we would open the packages, survey our loot and swap stuff with the other kids. The kids would cluster around us bold thieves admiringly, coveting our goodies.

That ended badly with the police getting involved and coming to the school to interview some of the boys, who had graduated from shoplifting to breaking and entering and hiding their loot on a little island in the Heathcote River, suitably named Naughty Boys Island. The sight of these two, tall, sombre looking men in blue stalking across the playground and in and out of classrooms had a sobering effect. Suddenly all the boys were good little boys and the girls pictures of innocence.

The two sombre men interviewed me in the headmaster's office, with the headmaster looking on. Glowering is the word. They seemed to know all about my shoplifting, which I then confessed, but were satisfied that I had nothing to do with breaking and entering, or taking girls of Naughty Boy's Island, or any other nefarious activities on that island.

'That class has a few bad eggs,' the headmaster said, looking hard at me.

Despite confessing, I lied about all sorts of things, about who was with me and what I might have seen in the lunch shed. I hid behind my confession the way a good liar will hide behind the truth.

That was one thing Frank and I could share. He'd learned the value of lying too, not just to stay out of trouble but to get ahead in the world and make lots of money.

'Dad lies,' he told me. 'He lies when he's selling cars to suckers. He calls them suckers.'

At that time my father had a partnership in a used car lot. A struggling used car lot. There just weren't that many suckers around.

Dad was not impressed when he heard about the shoplifting, and less impressed when he found out I'd lied to my mother, who first asked me about it having heard something from another mother. Police at the school is news that spreads fast.

'He's a sly, lying little hound,' Mum said to Dad in a voice that made his duty clear. This was the last occasion he took off his belt to administer justice. The welts from his belt remained on my buttocks for some days.

'I'm not doing this because of the shoplifting,' he said, 'but because you lied to your mother about it.'

I was too busy suffering from the belt to reflect on the strangeness of this.

There were two Māori boys at that school, brothers, whose names were Hemi and Mikaere, but the other kids tended to call them Jimmy and Michael instead. I was fascinated with the word Mikaere, which joined Olga's father's name Mikhail, as known variations of my own name. There had been no Māori in Hanmer, and I approached Mikaere to talk to him because I was curious and wondered why my parents had never spoken of the Māori people in our house. Mikaere was shy and hardly spoke at all. He met my eye a couple of times and that was it. The two brothers stuck together and didn't make friends.

One day, however, I had to approach them because I heard them speaking a strange language to each other in low voices in the playground.

'What language is that?' I asked them directly, thinking of the special language Olga and I had spoken and Mrs Rockwell's sacred language.

'It's our language, Hemi said fiercely. 'We call it te reo. The language.' I didn't at that point understand his sudden defiance, and thought that he didn't like me. Later I was to discover that Māori were discouraged from speaking te reo, and children had been punished for speaking it at school. Girls and boys alike would be strapped.

In order to get me involved in some wholesome activity, and take my mind off any criminal ventures that might be brewing in my brain, my parents got me to join the local branch of the Boy Scout movement. I learned to tie a knot or two, although that same criminally inclined brain was not suited to the military virtues of Boy Scout lore. Most of the fun occurred after scouts, when we would return home in the dark, throwing stones on people's roofs and running away. Eventually, the adults decided to close down the New Brighton chapter of the scouts because of our behaviour, and that was the end of that.

My year at New Brighton Primary School ended with a new word: *tsunami*. A word I couldn't spell no matter how hard I tried. One morning the whole school had to assemble in the playground after we were told that there had been an earthquake in South America and a fast-moving wave was heading towards New Zealand. The fear was, with Christchurch being so low-lying, that the wave would sweep over the sandhills and inundate the city, Brighton being first in line.

For once the children were quiet and subdued as we were led out of the school and across the road to where some properties were several metres higher than the streets. We gathered on that higher ground and waited, our eyes fixed anxiously on the sandhills in the distance, at any moment expecting a great wave to come surging up and drown the school. Maybe drown the whole world. Many of the kids were scared but I was excited. I couldn't wait for that wave to come bundling over the sandhills and race up through the streets carrying all before it.

It never came.

The coming of Silent Spring

The day I grew up I was in my grandparents' place talking to my grandfather.

They had moved from Scargill to Christchurch to be near us, I believe, and bought a little house in North New Brighton, in Grantley Street, just across the Rawhiti domain, in easy cycling distance of my school.

After school, I wouldn't want to go home and would cycle across the domain to stay at Grantley Street until the dark began to creep out from under the fences and the eaves of the houses.

My grandmother, a wonderfully kind woman who came from 'the old country' always contrived to have some scones just coming out of the oven when I arrived. Little boys were always hungry after school, ready for a scone with a little butter and raspberry jam. I loved her accent, which made her sound other-worldly. I liked to hear her wistful stories of the 'old country' and about her father, who was a violinist, a very straight-laced man who once farted loudly in church with such self-control he didn't turn a hair, which made my grandmother, a little girl at the time, laugh out loud and thus be identified as the cause of a disgraceful incident.

'Wherever you be, let your wind go free,' was my grandmother's favourite saying, and she would always say it to make me laugh.

My grandfather, although perfectly lucid, had lost himself in his past. He would sit with a large tray on his lap covered in photographs, a mosaic of memories he constantly moved around as if realigning his relationships. Beside him he had a shoebox full of photos from which he would draw new ones, often at random, and return some he'd grown tired of. Sometimes he would use both hands to shuffle the photos in the box, mixing them up as much as he could so as to surprise himself with what his hand might find.

I realised it was not just the images he was shuffling about and choosing, but the words that went with them, the names and the stories. That was the important thing. Each photo was associated with a different set of stories, a different chain of words.

He would talk to me about the photos and tell me about the people in them. 'Don't know who that joker is with your mother,' he might say, pointing to a photo. 'And that's your great uncle Samuel. He had a chicken farm, you know. Made a lot of money. But they were wowsers. They all were. That whole side of the family. I never had any time for him. He was as mean as they come. As mean as the devil himself. You know, I lent him the money to get that chicken farm started, and once he started making money he wiped me like a dirty rag. He'd look down his nose at me and your grandma. We were the poor relations! And look, that's me there, with your mother as a baby. She was very colicky, you know. Your grandma would be up for hours burping her.'

I tried to take an interest in all of this, and sort out my great aunties and great uncles, but the photographs were turning a cacky, yellow colour and, I realised, most of the people in them were dead. 'Dead as a doornail,' my grandfather would say with some satisfaction, pointing at one photo or another, or 'he gave up smoking before the war,' or 'he bit the dust during the Depression,' or, 'he was a soldier and bought the farm in Korea.' He always said these things with a certain relish. Being still alive made him one up on those dead friends and relatives of his.

'Photography turns the whole world into a cemetery,' he'd murmur while shuffling his past, maybe thinking of a re-deal.

The dead and the living were all mixed up together, sometimes in the same photograph, smiling at the camera or looking away. It gave me a creepy feeling, to have the dead so present, with my grandfather walking among them as his younger self. His world of memory had become a graveyard.

It was to my grandfather that I first spoke about the book that was changing my life: *Silent Spring* by Rachel Carson.

It's somewhat mysterious how this book came into my possession. It certainly didn't come from Mrs Little's lending library, she stocked only popular fiction, and my parents wouldn't have bought a book like that. They didn't buy books anyway, but did get books from time to time from the Christchurch Central Library. Mum had a questing mind her circumstances never allowed her to develop. She was a child of the Depression, and had to go to work at the age of twelve, as did my father. But, in Christchurch, her interests began to range far and wide, and it must be that she came across the newly published *Silent Spring*, maybe in Whitcombe & Tombs, the main bookshop in town. I'd heard her talking about the shop, and at first thought she was talking about a cemetery. It's hard to imagine her approving such a purchase, however, when every penny they had was spent putting food on the table for us kids.

And just maybe she left it on the kitchen table where I would find it after coming home from my grandparents' place, where, she would observe, I'd been 'scoffing Grandma's scones.' When I asked her about it, she didn't admit it.

The very existence of that book in our house was an anomaly. In the same category as the strange boy on the logging road, who I'd never forgotten, or the Pterodactyl in the sky over Hanmer. Sometimes things happen that just don't fit. More intriguing for me was the idea that Mum had deliberately put it where I could find it. Perhaps she wanted me to read it and understand something about the world into which I'd been born. Something she couldn't talk to me about, personally, but left it to Rachel Carson to say. How do you tell your children their world is going to Hell in a handbasket, and that the world they thought they would inherit was being ripped out from under them? The story of Harry Harrison's *Deathworld* was no longer a tall story about something happening on a faraway planet to imaginary people for the entertainment of readers. It was the story of our own world.

'The junkmen are in power,' I said with great earnestness. 'They're for real.'

Grandfather hadn't read *Deathworld*, but he gleaned something of my meaning. 'They call it planned obsolescence,' he said, setting out his photos as if he were playing patience with them. 'It was General Motors in the 1930s that started all that nonsense. They want everybody to keep buying new cars, so they say the old cars aren't good enough. They call it progress, but it's just a bloody con. Look at your dad's Buick Sedan. A perfectly good car. A classy car even. I don't know why he wants to trade it in.' He shook his head. Wonders would never cease. He was shifting some cards from one line to another. I could see there was some approximation of suits developing. One line had photos of my mother from birth, at the top, to near present day, her hair freshly permed, at the bottom. Another line featured my grandmother: Grandma at the top as a beautiful young woman standing on a railway station in 'the old country' clutching a purse, to a recent one of grandma sitting in an easy chair with her cat, both staring patiently at the camera.

'It's more than that.' I handed him a piece of paper on which was written a single word I had carefully written out, double checking everything as I went to make sure I got it right: *Dichlorodiphenyltrichloroethane*

'What kind of word is that? Is that a real word or did you just make it up? I wouldn't even try to say it.'

'It's a chemical. It's called DDT for short.'

'Oh that. Why didn't you say so. Bloody good for getting rid of pests in the garden. Grass grubs and porina. They'd eat everything in sight if you didn't stop them. Caterpillars by the thousands.'

He was creating a line of photos with me in them. Me as a baby on a rug. Me riding a tricycle down the main street of Hanmer, me in various family groupings, me heading off for my first day at New Brighton Primary, a brave smile on my face. There it was, the childhood of me, all laid out in a nice line. I suddenly wished he had one of Olga.

'Rachel Carson says that we're breeding resistance into the bugs, who grow stronger by mutating,' I said with great earnestness. She uses a new word: ecosystem. She says DDT weakens the ecosystems which fall prey to stronger, invasive species.'

'Does she indeed?' He made it sound as if he considered this Rachel Carson, whoever she was when she was at home, a pretty uppity woman. Mutating indeed!

I pulled the book from my school satchel where it had been lying in wait for this conversation. I had a passage already marked and read it out loud. I very much wanted my grandfather to understand it.

'No responsible person contends that insect-borne disease should be ignored. The question that has now urgently presented itself is whether it is either wise or responsible to attack the problem by methods that are rapidly making it worse. The world has heard much of the triumphant war against disease through the control of insect vectors of infection, but it has heard little of the other side of the story—the defeats, the short-lived triumphs that now strongly support the alarming view that the insect enemy has been made actually stronger by our efforts. Even worse, we may have destroyed our very means of fighting it.'

'I think Miss Carson has forgotten one thing,' he said, sweeping up the lines of photos into another jumble before setting them out again, this time more like a detective placing crime-scene photos and suspects onto a whiteboard. There was the miserly uncle Samuel, and beside him his wife with a thin mouth. Prime suspects.

'She's not just Miss Carson. She's Dr Carson. She has a degree in Zoology, and she's a marine biologist.'

'If you say so.' He considered me with deep scepticism.

'It's a fact. She's a scientist.'

'Yes, yes,' he said placatingly. 'I can imagine. But you know, women are all very well, and you wouldn't find a finer woman than your grandmother this side of the black stump, but they're not really cut out for this kind of thing,' he pointed to the book, 'because their brains are wired up differently, and sometimes, you'll find out in due course, they can't see the wood for the trees. Take this Dr Carson of yours, I can show you right now where she went wrong. It's very simple.'

'But you haven't read the book.'

'I don't have to. Look, she says we're breeding resistance into the bugs, which are growing stronger, right?'

'And weeds too.'

'What she forgets is that the bugs can't win. The weeds can't win.'

'Why not?'

'Because we're smarter than they are, silly boy!' He gave a great laugh 'A lot smarter. Have you ever seen a smart bug? If the bugs develop resistance, which I think's a bit far-fetched, we can just bomb them with something stronger. Those chemists know a trick or two. Now your Miss Carson didn't think of that, did she?'

I saw then that my grandfather was a junkman through and through. A divide opened up between us.

'I'd rather be a grubber than a junkman,' I said, but my childish grip on the novel was slipping. It wasn't so much a novel as a cypher, a coded message like *A Canticle for Liebowitz*. Maybe all these science fiction novels were coded messages carrying half-hidden meanings, especially the dystopian stories of Philip K. Dick. *Silent Spring* ought to have been a fantasy, but the fantasy had become the world. The junkmen had arrived here, in our world, and built a City of the Damned. Words had turned from sounds into things.

I suddenly saw my grandfather as a silly, bigoted man, and in that moment, I grew up.

'How old is this Miss Carson?'

I glanced at the back of the book, 'Um, I think maybe fifty or so. It says she was born in 1907.'

My grandfather nodded in satisfaction, confirming something he had suspected all along. 'And she'd not married? No? Well, she's probably a communist, or…' he tailed off. There were some things he'd rather not think or say. There were worse things than even being a communist. He'd heard that there were women who liked to sleep together, although he was not a hundred percent sure about that. If it were true, the cunning creatures kept it well hidden from his eyes.

'Your mother's headed in that direction, you know. She's a communist, although she won't come out and say it. She thinks Mao Tse Tung is trying to help all those poor peasants over there in China. Poof!' He laughed, perhaps at the silliness of the idea, or at the weakness of women's brains. Probably both at once. The next photo he put up was of an old bach at a beach, seeming to lean towards the water. The scene of the crime. There's my mother again and the joker he couldn't remember.

After that conversation, when I left, wheeling my bike from that little house in Grantley Street, I was a changed person. I looked at my grandfather's garden, carrots and lettuces and potatoes in neat rows, all carefully weeded, and saw it with new eyes. It was poisoned, and out of that poison monstrous forms would flower.

Adam the taxonomist

We weren't called baby-boomers in those days, but the effect of the tsunami of children born after World War Two was felt all through the education system. They had teachers they threw into the front line after a bare three months' training, calling them 'pressure-cooked' teachers, many of whom floundered in the classroom.

There were nine first-year classes, the third form, at Linwood High School, and they were streamed on the basis of our performance in an 'intelligence test' called the Otis test. It was filled with stupid questions:

'A foot is to a man, and a paw is to a cat, the same as a hoof
is to a what? (1) a dog; (2) a horse; (3) a shoe; (4) a blacksmith;
(5) a saddle.'

Or

> 'If the first two statements following are true the third is (?)
> Some of our citizens are Methodists. Some of our citizens
> are doctors. Some of our citizens are Methodist doctors.'

Or

> 'If George can ride a bicycle 60 feet while Frank runs 40 feet,
> how many feet can George ride while Frank runs 30 feet?

Or it asked me to identify the next number in a series, or the next shape in a sequence.

I neither knew nor cared and spent most of the test time flicking ink from my favourite stolen fountain pen onto the legs of my nearest classmates. I couldn't take any of the questions seriously, and was accordingly placed in the second-to-bottom of the nine classes. The classes were highly stratified. The first three classes were professional with French language learning, from which would come our doctors and lawyers and scholars. The second three were professional without French, from which would come our clerical workers, secretaries and other functionaries. The bottom three classes were called 'General' and from them would come our wood and metal workers, labourers, shop assistants and general no-hopers. I began to appreciate that the word 'class' referred to more than a group of children in a room.

My timetable was filled with double periods of woodwork and metalwork, for which I had no aptitude. I found myself among the other no-hopers and acted accordingly. I was caned regularly, as that was the preferred method for maintaining order and stratification. On-duty teachers patrolled the corridors and playgrounds, canes twitching, brooking no dissent. Other than idiots like me, who dared to drop water-bombs on them from third-floor windows as they strolled beneath, children steered clear of them.

I rebelled. Dropping water bombs on teachers wasn't enough. I was getting too much of the cane. Look at the welts on my backside. I told my mother that I would no longer go to school. That I'd run away if I had to. I said school was a prison and made people crazy.

My mother came to the party. It took a brave woman to front up to the headmaster, a chilly, remote man, who liked to wander the corridors in his black academic gown, casting stern glances to the right and left, and ask for her son to be put up into the professional classes. I would have to jump a class, the top General class, to get on the lowest rung of the Professionals. The headmaster did not like the idea. After all, what kind of chaos would ensue if parents started dictating what classes their children should be in? It would set a very bad precedent.

My mother prevailed. I shifted classes, and albeit slowly, my grades began to improve, particularly in biology. I had a feel for the natural world that was rooted in my childhood experiences in Hanmer, and my growing unease with what seemed like the random, chaotic nature of things was balanced by the order of living things. I found the seven major groupings particularly satisfying: kingdom, phylum, class, order, family, genus, and species. These categories created a comforting hierarchy, starting with the most general and over-arching to the most particular and specific. Seeing the secret patterns of the world gave me some hope. It wasn't all just a big, random mess with everything flying in all directions, but rather everything fitted with everything else. These categories and their names gave things solidity in the world.

The common Douglas fir was called *Pseudotsuga menziesii*, a wonderful name impossible to pronounce. It is embedded in the hierarchy of the class *Pinopsida* family *Pinaceae*, the genus *Pseudotsuga* and the species *Menziesii*. Very satisfying to know that everything was in its allotted place in creation, even the humble Douglas fir. David Douglas gave it its popular name, the species name came from Archibald Menzies, both Scottish naturalists, and its genus name meant 'not hemlock.'

I saw Adam as the original taxonomist, giving names to all the animals – "And Adam called names for all cattle, and all birds of Heaven, and all animals of the Earth... whatever the man called every living creature, that was its name." From this I concluded that words gave order to the world, and without words the world would be a blur of colour and shapes. At least to humankind.

I would do what Adam had done, for his work was not finished.

I would be a taxonomist.

Which entails the naming, description and classification of living things – finding words for things so that they might fit into their category, differentiated, visible to us human beings. Naming brings things into being. That gave me goosebumps.

There could be no higher calling than the discovery and naming of things.

My mother was not surprised by my success in biology, and was triumphant. The faith she had put into me had been vindicated.

'Michael's just a slow developer,' she said, having heard the term somewhere, 'but he gets there in the end.' She looked at me with fierce, all-consuming pride. And lit a cigarette.

A dark song against a blue sky

What I best remember about the Cuba crisis was the silence that descended on the classroom as the Russian ships with the cargo of missiles headed towards Cuba, towards an invisible line in the ocean which, if crossed, would trigger a nuclear war. It was as if words had lost their agency and faltered before the prospect of doom. At a certain point there was nothing left to say. Conversations petered out; the usual hubbub of the classroom faded. A fearful speechlessness reigned.

It would be no use crawling under our desks. We knew that much.

The teacher had his ear glued to the radio and would cast us anxious glances from time to time. We could hear the radio squawking like some alien life form. Death was on the wing. I could hear its dark song against the blue sky. The kids fell quiet under the arch of that dark song. The school playground looked totally normal. A kid wandered across it carrying a ball. Beyond the playground there was a woman pushing a pram. There was the distant, muted sound of traffic from Ferry Road. The Edmonds baking powder factory stood still and calm.

That speechlessness had fallen over everything in the face of the enormity overshadowing us, the way birds will fall speechless before a natural disaster like an earthquake or eruption.

My mind fell silent. All I could hear was the background hum of my consciousness. It was a maths class and I was staring at the algebra equation the teacher had written on the board, then forgotten as the drama of the crisis unfolded. The equation had become enigmatic, a cryptic message from the universe to the reasoning mind, while on a faraway ocean Russian ships crept towards Armageddon. This is where *A Canticle for Leibowitz* had started. It wasn't so much that reality was imitating fiction, rather fiction was becoming reality, the division between the two dissolving. The book was open, words had taken to the sky and turned into missiles.

Reality was making some strange genre choices. Every moment was a cliff hanger.

When the teacher stood up and announced that the Russian ships had turned back, the silence lifted and children began to murmur to one another again from behind their hands. The world resumed. A truck rumbled past the school, seeming to make it shake a little. The equation on the blackboard gave up its secret. Somewhere in the school, a cane would be whistling through the air. *A Canticle for Leibowitz* retreated into fiction once more. For the moment.

You're all I've got

My mother was hyper-aware that I was growing up, and it did not please her, especially when I began to notice a girl with curly, strawberry-blonde hair who lived down the road. She went to a different school, with a different school uniform, which added to her mystery. I would watch her as she walked, with determined self-confidence, past our place on her way home from school and back again.

My father had bought a corner store off Linwood Avenue, and was trying, as he put it, to 'make a go of it.' Sometimes the girl would come into the store and if I was about I would loiter close by, keeping a covert eye on her. I liked the way she carried herself, head held high, back straight, eyes clear and blue.

Her appearance put my mother on high alert, or rather my interest in her did, and Mum did not take to it too kindly. On one hand she was pleased that I was growing up and finding my feet at school, but at the same time was tormented by jealousy of any girl who might come within my compass. The strawberry blonde girl made her wrathful. She had outbursts my grandmother gently referred to as 'ing-bings.' When my mother was having an ing-bing it was best to keep clear. She would scream and shout and her eyes would turn into little hard stones. Dad said it was her 'nerves.' What these nerves were and where in the body they might be remained vague.

Afterwards she'd have a cigarette and catch up with herself.

I had to distance myself from my mother, who, to me, was becoming unpredictable and dangerous. One afternoon I had followed the girl home to see where she lived, and actually had a few words with her and discovered that her name was Emily. I liked the name. It rode lightly on my breath. Somehow my mother found out about this little development and came at me, snarling, 'What did you want to follow that bitch for?' Her eyes had gone all stony and she lifted her bony arm as if to strike me. Her dressing table, the same one from Hanmer with the three mirrors, was behind her and I saw her both from the front and back as she raised her arm. She looked like another person.

Using the word bitch was a big deal for Mum. She didn't swear much, and to call somebody a bitch was serious stuff. She didn't know anything about Emily. There was a load of implication in that word that hit me in the gut, but I didn't fully understand it.

I went hot and cold and stepped back in case she did strike me. She was a lot scarier than Dad. I was grateful that she'd never found out about my explorations with the girl in the resource room at Brighton Primary.

The interest in Emily didn't get very far, but my mother was triggered and went into one of her 'moods.' These moods were a different kind of ing-bing. She would chain smoke, become surly and cold and say as little as possible, mostly in a dismissive tone. They could go on for days. These moods upset my normally equanimous father more than the ing-bings, as everybody suffered as a result of them; the cold went everywhere. Mum's moods ruled everybody. The threat of them became a permanent feature of the atmosphere in the house.

A kind of darkness grew in the shadows of those moods of hers. The world became a half-submerged place full of hidden reefs and monstrous shapes.

Shortly after the 'bitch' incident I was in the shop after it had closed, doing some work there, when my mother came in, her eyes already stony. Dad had been training Frank and me to 'fill the fixtures,' which was to replace stock that had sold, while he went off and did something else. I waited in dread as Mum approached. I had a weird feeling, as if she'd been possessed by an evil spirit, and the chill of it was in my bones.

She came right up to me and pushed her face close to mine. I could smell the nicotine. Her pupils floated in the middle of the whites of her eyes, which had a faint yellowish tinge. Her voice was low and trembling with intensity. 'Don't you boys ever grow away from me now, will you.' Her eyes slid across to Frank who was happily putting some cans of Watties baked beans in tomato sauce on the shelf, labels carefully turned so they faced outward, just as Dad had shown him. Her voice grew threatening. 'Don't grow away from me. You're all I've got. All I've got.'

A familiar numbness swept over me. I couldn't think or feel anything, and I certainly couldn't speak. I had to remove myself from myself.

She swung away and walked off, the shadows of the half-lit shop swirling after her. I thought she was going to turn around and say something more, but she didn't. I think she wanted to. I think there was a lot she could have said.

Mechanically, I turned back to my task. Next to the baked beans would come the spaghetti. There was a box of it at my feet. I bent over to get some more cans, something I'd seen my father do many times, when it struck me – what about Dad? Didn't Mum have Dad? Not just Frank and me. How come we were all she had. I didn't understand it. She had her life. I had a spooked-out feeling I sometimes got from reading Charles Dickens. I thought of Miss Haversham of *Great Expectations*. A woman who no longer had a life. My insides felt raw and quivering.

'What did Mum want?' Frank said.

I had no answer for him.

The varieties of Aria

I fell in love with Aria's name before falling in love with her.

I had seen her among all the other students at our first-year physics class at Canterbury University, a tall girl rapidly shedding adolescent awkwardness, confident, bright-eyed, imperious. It was hard not to notice her.

'That's Aria Byron,' an acquaintance whispered to me one day as we were taking our seats, and the tall girl had come in late. 'I've heard she's top of the class.'

'Wow.' I was not top of the class. Physics didn't suit me that well, but was part of a General Science foundation course, and I was only just hanging on, my grades floundering around the C mark. I considered this A+ girl with some awe. I tried to imagine flying through the equations of renormalisation without turning a hair. Not for normal humans.

Her name became her. She seemed to spring into the air with each step. I would say her name under my breath as she came into the lecture room and took her seat. I started falling in love with her name, which is as light on the tongue as air itself and tends to lift on the wings of its own harmony. I didn't once stutter over it. Ar-ri-a. Aria means song or melody in Italian, more precisely a vocal solo, but its literal translation is *air*; its Teutonic origins relate the name Aria to a bird. In Greek, however, it meant lioness, and that was my Aria, a sleek hunter. In Persian the name means noble, and you finally have a full picture of her; a noble lioness who can move like a sinuous melody and whose element is the air.

When Aria later told me that her name was a shorter form of Ariana, the name her parents gave her, I was further enchanted, for in Greek, Ariana means pure or sacred, whereas in Welsh, it means silver, and in Hebrew, it means a beautiful melody.

All these meanings wove together to give me a picture of the woman; I could know her by understanding the meaning and origin of her name. That was more significant to me than Aria looking a little like Olga, with a rich abundance of dark curls, or how Olga might have looked when she got older.

Once I asked her why she shortened her name, and she said Ariana sounded too pretentious to her, too over the top, and she didn't want others to think that she thought she was above them all with her fancy name. To Aria, what other people thought was very important. She tried to shape herself around what others thought of her and did a good job of it. She wanted to be successful and shine in their eyes.

My interest in Aria's name sparked an interest in my own, which I'd long taken for granted. I had three names which all seemed to yield up important information on my larger identity. My first name, Michael, is a question: 'who could possibly be as great as God?' That makes me feel humble. It suggests that God (with a capital) is the word of words, that there is no other word that can be greater. I liked the idea that my name was a question, even though I didn't believe in God. Not the big I Am. If I was anything, it was a Pantheist, believing the divine to be immanent in all things, the hidden word, the hidden presence, the half-concealed meaning of the text that was the world.

Taxonomy leads naturally to Pantheism, the discovery of the many names of God.

My second name is Paewai, meaning driftwood, or perhaps 'water horizon' where the ocean meets the sky, in Māori. It was a mystery. Why did I have a Māori middle name? My parents were not forthcoming, and simply said that the name was 'in the family' and probably picked up because one of my ancestors 'liked the sound of it.' That was possible. I liked the sounds of words too, especially names, Latin names of plants, Aria's name. They said they liked the sound of it when they gave it to me.

I was almost satisfied, but asked my grandfather just to make sure.

'Paewai,' he said, rolling it around on his tongue as if it were a sweet with a tart centre. 'There are family stories that go back to the 1830s. Your great-great grandfather, on your father's side, is said to have taken a Māori wife. His name was Peter. I mean, I don't know if they were married, there's no paper work at all, no indication of who she was or where she came from. All that is known is that her name was Paewai. Story goes that she died young, giving birth to a child. Peter went on to have other children, and kept the name Paewai because of his love for the woman.'

'What happened to Paewai's child?'

'I don't know,' he said.

I didn't believe him. I believed that I was a descendant of that child. Paewai was a shadowy figure who bequeathed me only one thing, perhaps the only thing that was truly hers – her name. There are times I feel the presence which comes through a name. Driftwood often travels long distances before finding a beach. The sky has a long distance to travel before it meets the sea. Paewai had drifted, but there was strength in this, strength to travel whatever the distance, whatever the horizon.

My surname, Meer, is rich in resonances. Meere, in German, is a body of water, but as a surname, it probably derived from either the Old English word *mere*, meaning pond, or from *maere*, meaning boundary. That would fit, as great-great grandfather Peter Meer, who had a child with Paewai, probably came from the border area between Sligo and Mayo to the west of Ireland where the name is found. It is also close to the ocean.

Beyond not wanting to be Ariana, Aria had little interest in names or their associations, or the ritual nature of names. For her names were just names, and had no mythical or magical powers or qualities. We were both scientists, moving together through the years of study. Her area was engineering and her love was applied mathematics. She could eat equations for breakfast. For me, science begins in the imagination and ends with wonder; for her it begins with numbers and ends with engineering. As a taxonomist, I was steeped in the names of things; *in the beginning was the word.*

One of my great joys came later with the discovery of a new species of fungus high in our alpine regions, and having the privilege of naming it. The discovery of a new species is a big moment for any taxonomist.

Some will name the species after themselves, as if seeking immortality for their names, as if they can imprint themselves on the things around them. I had no such desires, and was happy to coin a Latin name from the colour of the fungus: *Aurantiacus mykēs*. Mykēs being both the Latin word for mushroom and like a short form of my first name, Michael.

The Big Bang

Aria and I met under thrilling circumstances, at least from a scientific point of view. I found myself sitting near her listening to a talk given by a visiting cosmologist on the ground-breaking discovery of what he called the 'blackbody background temperature' of the universe, or the 'microwave background radiation' that permeates the universe.

It was an exciting story. Two scientists, Arno Penzias and Robert Woodrow Wilson, working at the Bell Telephone laboratories in New Jersey, discovered a mysterious noise in their receivers that was not any interference pattern. It was spread evenly over the sky both day and night, and was a hundred times more intense than anything they expected.

The visiting cosmologist, whose name I've forgotten but who looked more like a rugby player than a scientist, was exhilarated. This discovery, he said, was solid evidence for the Big Bang theory of the creation of the universe, against the Steady State theory according to which stars are dying and being born all the time. This microwave background radiation was the echo of the Big Bang itself, a reverberation, a sound fossil left over from that cataclysmic event. When did this happen? That was still being worked out, but it was certainly many billions of years ago.

There were lots of questions and excited chatter. Some 'steady state' advocates claimed that this discovery was not definitive, but the mood of the evening was against them. One enthusiast described the Big Bang as the great cosmic orgasm that brought the universe into being. This was greeted with good natured, tolerant laughter.

The cosmologist was something of a showman. He drew several crosses on a deflated balloon and then, when he blew the balloon up, the crosses moved further away from each other as the rubber stretched. This, he said, was how the universe inflated, especially in its early phases, and it was probably still going on. The universe creating space for its own expansion.

After the lecture I joined a group of mostly physics students, who didn't want to stop talking about it, outside under a dome of winking stars as the lights went out in the lecture hall and everybody else went home. There was all sorts of excited speculation. Did the Big Bang create time? What was before the Big Bang? How did suns and galaxies of suns form? What would happen? Would everything contract again into a Big Crunch? How did gravity fit into all this?

Aria spoke forcefully about the areas of physics this opened up. 'It is a wonderful time to be a mathematician or physicist,' she said, her face glowing with intelligence and animated thought. I was drawn to her, to her dark, excited eyes and volubility. She spoke with passion about a 'linear accelerator' that was being built underground at Stanford, a three-kilometre-long tunnel or 'waveguide' to produce a beam of charged particles, electrons accelerated to almost the speed of light using hundreds of klystrons, which were special kinds of vacuum tube used to amplify microwaves. It would be operational in a couple of years.

It was heady stuff, gravity defying words floating up from the street to the stars, concepts exploding, a big bang of mind flooding our bodies with energy.

Soon there was the only the two of us standing there, outside that dark lecture hall, with me matching her loquacity, telling her all about the intimate and supportive relationship between fungi and lichen, and how a little splotch of colour on a rock could be as exciting as a splotch of stars in the far sky – at least for me. I told her how fungi was capable of running sophisticated chemical tests on the elements it encountered, how, in one case, a fungi learned over several weeks to break down the deadly poison nicotine into something it could feed on.

She believed me. I believed her. We believed each other even when we disagreed with each other. It was a joyous discovery. We retreated to a bar that was open late and went on talking way into the night, until the management kicked us out.

I learned that she was not only intelligent and impressive but beautiful, and could flash with fire or soften with empathy. She was as fascinated with me as I was with her. She'd never met anyone who still read nineteenth century literature and could talk with enthusiasm about Dostoevsky and George Eliot. She even tried to read *The Brothers Karamazov*, but didn't get very far. Those two brothers, she said, Ivan and Alyosha, meet in a café and have a conversation that lasts for *eighty* pages. 'That's crazy,' she said. 'How could anyone read that?'

I read some books she gave me on cosmology and quantum physics, cautioning me that they were out of date now. I fared better with them than she did with *The Brothers Karamazov*, well enough to form some opinions. I learned enough to assert that I didn't agree with Everett and Wheeler's many-worlds theory because it led to too many infinities, but I was mainly faking it. The maths was beyond me.

In the face of all this exalted stuff, I became aware of what a humble task taxonomy is, no mind-shattering discoveries, no Big Bang moments, just a meticulous cataloguing and naming. I took pride in the humble nature of my calling. With Aria I became attractively self-effacing. I was not leading with my ego. This impressed her, so I cultivated it. I became a very good listener. That charmed her, so I cultivated it even more. I began to shape myself around her.

Eventually, we ran up against the boundaries of our ability to comprehend one another, but that didn't seem to affect our capacity to have fun in bed, which is where these intense night conversations led us. In fact, those differences in the shapes of our minds seemed to fuel our physical interest in one another, and we had some marathon love-making sessions that lasted longer than the conversation between Ivan and Alyosha in *The Brothers Karamazov*, and were as cataclysmic as the creation of galaxies out of sub-atomic particle excitation and gravity.

I came to learn that, while she could get excited by big ideas, her interest in maths was essentially practical. Maths enables us to build things, and to her that was the highest value. The better the maths, the better the things we could build. She didn't question her underlying faith in progress. Discovering the microwave background radiation, and confirming the Big Bang theory of creation was progress. It was humanity itself making these stupendous discoveries.

While Aria did not always understand me, it was with her that I learned to speak freely. The embarrassments of my childhood seemed to fall away, although I never did learn how to spell our contrary language, and avoided handwriting wherever I could. With Aria, I learned to find words to express my disagreements with her on matters of science and religion. To keep up with her I had to be articulate. She was a materialist and a reductionist, while I favoured mystical experience and the elaborations of theory. I had to find a language, a bridge to arc across the gulfs between us.

Our relationship worked because we challenged each other, each of us wondering how we could love somebody who was so profoundly mistaken about the world. We spent a lot of time searching for the right words, the most telling words. 'QED,' we would cry after finalising the development of some line of thought. I preferred the full Latin quote, *quod erat demonstrandum*, which basically means game over. It rolls off the tongue like some booming, final judgement from the great God of Reason.

I fell in love with words as I did with Aria, I became intoxicated by the sound of them, their music and their charm. Especially their ability to move a person to love. There was a melancholy song around on that very theme:

'It's only words, and words are all I have
To take your heart away.'

I would read poetry aloud just to hear the sound of them chiming in the air. I preferred the Romantics, particularly Shelley, and the twentieth century inheritors of that tradition, Pablo Neruda and Octavio Paz, and enjoyed the rhetoric of Martin Luther King, a master wordsmith.

Aria and I made love with the same vigour that we argued. Our love-making was like a conversation made up of sensations. She would pursue her sensations with a single-minded dedication that inspired me. It seems a little cruel now to say that our love making was focused on the rising curve of her sensations, my responses measured by how they fed into hers, but that's how it seems to me. I would be satisfied, all right – emptied might be a better word. I would lie beside her unable to speak while she chatted away. She could talk immediately afterwards, while I lay speechless. It could take me an hour to recover the power of words, and then they came slowly.

This impressed Aria, who put it down to her erotic mastery. It made her proud to be able to fuck me into silence. It was better than winning an argument.

During that time, you were not about very much. You discreetly withdrew from my life as my intimacy with Aria grew. Perhaps I no longer needed you to be my word bringer since Aria and I gave flesh to words together. They were like creatures bent on exploring one another, eager to meld concepts and thoughts into new forms.

There was not much room for you in a life noisy with the hubble-bubble of words; it's my silence you need. Like the silence which now, much later, rules my life – a huge and empty interiority in which you can thrive, at least for the moment. I didn't miss you. I even thought of you as the imaginary playmate my parents thought you to be, left behind when I grew up and learned how to use words. I almost forgot that you had brought me to the brink of words when I was young.

But you were still there, in the background, invisible, hidden, but ready should I ever need to turn to you.

Occasionally, even at the height of my love affair with words and Aria, Aria and words, my language would falter, and in the middle of trying to say something to Aria I would get struck dumb. All the struggles I'd had with language as a child returned. I felt as if I had to learn how to talk all over again, and I couldn't, the language was beyond me. The slipperiness of ordinary words, their power to wound as Olga had been wounded, their inherent impossibility, came rushing back. I was a child again, silent before the immensity of the world and the awkward fragility of speech.

They're rolling out the drums again

My grandfather had been right about one thing. My mother was up to something, going out at nights to meetings and talking for ages on the phone to people she referred to as 'fellow travellers.'

She'd joined the campaign for nuclear disarmament, CND, because she said she had to 'do something for the world.' Not just talk. Talk's easy. Talk's just hot air. There were two kinds of people, the talkers and the doers. The only question was, which kind was I going to be. Finally, I had grown up. I had learned to talk, mostly without stuttering. That was good. And I had a girlfriend. Well, there was plenty of time for that sort of thing. What was needed now was action, a public outcry against nuclear weapons. We came close with Cuba. Too damn close. We need demonstrations, maybe sitdowns as Gandhi had used. New terms came into the house. Passive resistance. Civil disobedience. These were more than just words, they were words of power, rallying cries. Placard words. Other terms came into the house too: brinkmanship, cold war, nuclear stand-off, arms race, radiation sickness, nuclear winter and the grandaddy of them all – Mutually Assured Destruction. There was the twentieth century in a nutshell. MAD.

'It's all madness,' she said, 'and the madness has to stop. Only a public outcry can do it.'

My mother had come into her power. There was a lot of triumphant smoking. The truth is an unstoppable force, she said. And the truth will out. Truth will bubble up through a cauldron of lies until it reaches the top, at which point it is released into the human mind as revelation. And it is out of that truth that action springs. Action was what brought about social change.

I went with her on one of her marches. Twenty or thirty people walked along the road carrying 'Ban the Bomb' placards. It was a quiet, almost sad affair, with many of the participants being old. Old lefties, mum indulgently called them. There were hardly any young people.

'That'll soon change,' Mum said. 'Things in Vietnam are heating up. There's a nasty little war brewing there, you mark my words.'

Another cigarette face down in the ashtray.

At such moments my mother evinced something of the power of an Old Testament prophet, a jeremiad energy which gave wings to her words. She was becoming, in her circle, a prominent personality. An unstoppable force in her own right.

Dad was not swept up in enthusiasm for the cause, but he was sympathetic. Not exactly a fellow traveller but a benign presence. If Mum was enjoying it, Dad approved of it. After all, it got Mum 'out of the house' – that was the important thing. She was not like one of those wives you saw in adverts swooning over a new washing machine or fridge. A hitherto hidden zealotry had surfaced in Mum's character, and Dad had no intention of standing in its way. 'She needs an outlet,' he said. He treated the whole thing with a good-natured tolerance. It was true, he had to admit, nuclear war would be crazy, and if Mum could stop it, all on her own, she would. If anyone could, she could. It was also true that he was happy to sit at the kitchen table on a Saturday with his radio, listening to 'the trots' or rugby, keeping company with a flagon of beer, while his wife went out to save the world, which God alone knew needed saving, and somebody had to do it, while other somebodies could just take an hour or two off.

The tribunal

A bombshell arrived in my letterbox one day, exploding my world. Opening that fateful envelope threw me into an abyss. War and peace, these were no longer abstractions to me. The war had arrived in my letterbox. The child of war I'd seen on the logging road in Hanmer came running through the house, the sounds of distant artillery suddenly not so distant.

The bomb of bombs loomed over all of us.

Nuclear nightmares were in the air, and some were making art out of it. There was Kubrick's *Dr. Strangelove or: How I Learned to Stop Worrying and Love the Bomb*. The final image of good o'l boy Slim Pickens riding the big bomb as it fell through the sky towards Moscow, whooping and waving his hat like a cowboy rodeo rider, was an enduring image of the age.

Aria was not as excited by the movie as I was. 'I thought Peter Sellers was supposed to be funny,' she said.

'He was funny though,' I said.

Aria couldn't see it.

Then there was Philip K. Dick's *Dr. Bloodmoney, or How We Got Along After the Bomb*. There was a sense in which this book was more unsettling than Kubrick's movie. Dick's fiction was possessed by a brain-scrambled madness that enacted an explosion of scenes barely held together in a plot line. That brain scramble was the coded message of that book. War tears your mind apart.

Aria didn't think much of it. 'It's a pretty poor effort to throw a story together. It's ramshackle.'

My mother had been right about one thing. A nasty little war did brew in Vietnam, and our country was directly involved. We were going to send troops to stand by our American and Australian allies to hold back the tide of communism, which was about to engulf Asia and the Pacific, or so the story went. There was a lot of emotional talk about what we owed the Americans for the Battle of Coral Sea during World War Two, which turned the Japanese back and stopped them from invading our shores.

Mum was triumphant in her rightness. The anti-war movement had arrived. I was part of a generation that refused to be cannon fodder. Now thousands were marching, not just a few old lefties and fellow travellers waving Ban the Bomb placards. The young people were on the move. Lies were being unmasked. The young found the words to speak truth to power. Never had belief in the efficacy of words to bring about material change been so high.

The bombshell arrived in our letterbox shortly after I turned eighteen. It was an official notification and my first military order. I was to turn up at such-and-such a place at such-and-such a time for a medical examination. I'd been drafted. America had just concluded a deal to import our lamb. It was a meat for meat deal. We'd send a contingent of soldiers to Vietnam to kill Vietnamese while Americans enjoyed our lamb.

I did not comply with the military order. We were one of the very few countries in the world that had a process for dealing with 'conscientious objectors' other than just throwing them in prison. The conscientious objector had to appear before a tribunal and explain why they were refusing military training. I believe the tribunal had been set up to accommodate Seventh Day Adventists and other pacifist groups within Christianity. Their defence was simple. It says in the Bible 'thou shalt not kill' which couldn't be much plainer.

That wasn't going to work for me, so I set about devising my own defence based on morality and logic. I would argue that the development of the nuclear bomb made war redundant, or at least crazy, as nobody could win a nuclear war, and any war could escalate into a nuclear war at a moment's notice. War didn't make sense any more. It was war itself that was the threat to humankind.

I wrote out that document on an old Olympia manual typewriter, painstakingly banging every key and whitening over mistakes with sticky stuff called Twink. Never had so much depended on my command of words. Life itself, maybe. Or prison. I chose every word with trepidation. I had read about the war, and the Allied program to spray vast areas with a 'defoliant' called 245T. More precisely, 2,4,5-Trichlorophenoxyacetic acid. The military said it was safe, but I didn't believe them. *Silent Spring* came back to haunt me, and a growing realisation that all wars were wars against the planet, against life itself. And wars thrive on lies. They always say their chemicals are safe. Of course they do.

I wrote myself into my convictions, and by doing so, discovered myself. Was I prepared to go to prison for this? Yes, I was. I had to lean on my words like a blind man leaning on a stick. Could I put my weight here? Was the ground firm? Would this hold up? Hold me up? Each carefully chosen word carried a heavy burden. They would sit on the page for a while until I crossed them out, fed a new sheet of paper into the Olympic, and re-wrote the page, reaching for new and better modes of expression.

My arguments did not impress the tribunal, which consisted of five men who viewed me with great suspicion, and who grilled me for five hours. It was clear that they had not read *Dr Bloodmoney*. They came up with various hypothetical situations such as what would I do if someone attacked my girlfriend while we were, say, walking in the park. I said that there was a difference between defending your girlfriend and training to go off and kill other people in their own country while poisoning their land at the same time.

This argument did not go over well. Several members of the tribunal became agitated and red in the face. There was one man, however, who showed no reaction at all, but simply regarded me with a mask-like calm. I figured him for the secretive Security Service. He spooked me more than the others. There was a clergyman who regarded me tolerantly. The angry ones were clearly military, because I'd just told them that their lives had become meaningless, that war itself was the enemy. They kept staring at my statement and back at me as if I were a creature from another planet. I was. I was from *Deathworld* and I had a message for them.

As the questions wore on, I became more frightened but also more determined. These men I'd never met had power over me. They could crush me. They could determine the shape of my life. They were junkmen and didn't like grubbers. I was just a kid who had gotten too big for his boots. A spell in the army would do me a lot of good, they suggested.

In the end, they brought out their big word, their big gun. Cowardice. It was more than a word, it was a weapon they would use to destroy me. Wasn't I in fact just being a coward? I could see this word was pregnant with significance for them. Cowards were the lowest of the low, and a coward was someone who didn't want to die or be poisoned for life. In World War 1 they shot cowards, shot their own terrified men fleeing the slaughter of the trenches.

I would have been happy to have admitted to such a definition of cowardice, but that would have landed me in prison for sure. Instead, I had to find my courage and tell them outright. For me, opposing war, all war, was a moral imperative brought about by the nuclear age, and I would be prepared to go to prison for that imperative. I would not obey any military commands and I would not go into the army to join the 'medics.' I was surprised by my own determination. The longer they harangued me, the more determined I became.

I had no one in my corner except for my father, who said nothing. Dad had come to the party. He had even returned his medals and his Royal New Zealand Returned and Services' Association badge. 'They should know bloody better,' was the only comment he made before the tribunal. I don't think my mother's activism had finally got through to him; he had quietly come to his own conclusions.

While they sat behind their desks, in spirit the members of the panel were encircling me, a pack of Topsell's creatures, looking for a weakness, sniffing the air for blood, howling their rage at each other. The thought of Mrs Rockwell feeding my mind from her magic bus, bolstered the courage I needed to see through those hours of interrogation. Life was possible without killing. Of course it was. How could we think otherwise?

Eventually they let me go, but the atmosphere in the room was seething. They were happier dealing with Seventh Day Adventists who they could look down on. I represented something new and threatening to them. A rationality that directly opposed their own. I was consigning them to the dustbin of history.

For the next few days, I waited for the army to arrive and haul me off to prison. I had a prison bag packed. My parents were supportive, Dad in a quiet, respectful way, Mum churning with excitement. This was her son, making his stand. Let nobody forget that. *Her* son! She'd light a cigarette before she told them, just so they knew how important it was. He might be a slow developer but he gets there in the end. She was thrilled to the core and wanted to live it all, vicariously, through me. I couldn't let her do that. I had to shut her out, and that made her sullen, at least for a time, until the excitement returned. My son!

A couple of weeks later I got a printed card in the mail. The card said that I was registered with the government as a 'conscientious objector' and would not be called upon for military duty.

Already I had other things to think about.

The sounds of te reo and funny smelling cigarettes

In the early days of our relationship, Aria and I liked to go to parties. I think it was to show each other off to the world, to feel how nice it was to hold hands in front of others. And to leave together, knowing we would be going home together, sleeping together and waking up the next morning together, perfecting the art of sitting up in bed drinking coffee together and talking about the previous night's party.

Mostly, there were familiar faces at these parties, friends who loved to get together on Friday night determined to see Saturday morning in with a headache and a mouth that tasted like an uncleaned bird cage. Some would boast of these hangovers as if they were an achievement of sorts; the bigger the hangover the better the party – right? Others might be suitably ashamed. Others might swear off alcohol forever. But by the next Friday they would be back again for another round. The same old faces, the same old hangovers.

As the decade wore on, however, some new faces began to appear at these parties, American servicemen escaping the Vietnam debacle by going to McMurdo, the American settlement in Antarctica just a short walk from New Zealand's Scott Base. These guys were radically different from your average homegrown Christchurch student. Christchurch had little experience with black people, and we were fascinated with their shiny, ebony skins, their loose-limbed grace and easy-going bonhomie. They talked as if they were singing jazz, and their arms danced around in time to their voices. They walked as if they were dancing. They spoke in loud confident voices, cut a swathe through the local girls, and were emissaries for a new cultural movement, bringing with them The *Fabulous Furry Freak Brothers* comics, Grateful Dead albums and funny smelling cigarettes containing a herb they called giggle weed.

Plenty of giggling went on.

Aria didn't approve of giggle weed. She liked to be serious even when a little drunk (she never got too smashed) while I took to it like an old friend. It suited me down to the ground, more than the demon booze which was already getting the better of some of our friends. I didn't mind a giggle or two here and there, in the right company. We did a lot of talking. I found receptive ears to my anti-war views among these visitors who were grateful to have escaped Vietnam and related stories from their buddies who had not been so lucky, about how nasty the war was and how some of their friends were getting sick from the defoliant 245T.

It was at one of those parties, in a miasma of giggle weed smoke, that I met a shy boy who had been in my class during that last raucous year at Brighton Primary. I had forgotten all about Mikaere, whose name was a Māori version of my own. A few puffs of the magic dragon loosened our tongues and soon we were sharing less than fond memories of Brighton Primary. I learned that the girl who got pregnant that year at the age of twelve, whose name was Katrina, now had three children and a miserable life married to a petty crim, one of those 'breaking and entering' boys from that time, who spent more time 'inside' than outside, leaving Katrina to bring the kids up on her own. Mikaere's brother, Hemi, had volunteered for the army and was now in Vietnam shooting other brown skinned people for the white man. Mikaere was sad about it. He hated being separated from his brother, who might never make it back home again.

I told him about Mrs Rockwell and her taniwha, and how we loved repeating the word which seemed to have a music to it, and how she'd said it in a special tone of voice, low and almost conspiratorial.

'She might have been part Māori,' he said. 'Some Māori pretend to be Spanish, or Greek, even in their own country. She knew what she was doing when she said taniwha in a low voice. Kids got beaten.'

I could hardly believe it.

It wasn't long before we got onto my favourite subject, names and sounds of words. I told Mikaere about discovering the Latin names for things, and how they could make the humblest of plants sound grand. He understood, and told me how he loved the Māori names for creatures, especially birds, because they were beautifully onomatopoeic.

'Take *whio*,' he said. Called in English the blue duck, which has no poetry to it at all. Not like this,' and he gave a whistling call 'whio-whio-whio.'

'That's very cool,' I said.

'Then try this one, *kākā*. The brown parrot. That's exactly the sound it makes.' Loudly, he croaked 'Kaa kaa – kaa kaa,' and everybody stopped talking for a moment to look in our direction.

'Kaa kaa!' I squawked at them, and they shrugged and went back to what they were doing. Aria, who was sitting with a group of big-brained particle physicists, laughed and gave me a 'are you going crazy?' look. They were talking about some German cat that didn't seem to know if it was alive or dead. She looked flushed and vivacious. She was on her favourite subject, the glorious age of technology which humankind was entering

Mikaere was getting excited. He loved the sounds of these words and was ecstatic that I was enjoying them too.

'And that other parrot, the *kea*. That's exactly how it sounds, and he called in a loud, sharp voice. 'Kee-aaa, kee-aaa.'

I joined in and we filled the smoky air with our cries, 'Kee-aaa!'

This time only a few people paused to look our way. We were old hat by now. Aria gave me a 'yes, you have gone crazy' look. Oh well, it was just a matter of time. But she loved me anyway.

One of the black American servicemen joined us. He was so lanky that when he sat on the floor beside us his knees were nearly knocking on his eyeballs. He listened with great interest. Mikaere was explaining the name of our night owl. 'The white settlers, the pākehā, called it the morepork because that's what they heard,' and he gave the eerie cry, 'more-pork!' and the serviceman joined in, 'more-pork.' Then I joined in and the three of us started up, 'more-pork!'

'Get a life!' somebody called.

'The whities heard that because they were hungry for meat,' Mikaere said.

'Right on!' the serviceman said.

'But Māori, they heard something different. They heard it like this – ruu-ruu, ruu-ruu,' and the serviceman and I joined in, 'ruu-ruu, ruu-ruu.'

'So the bird is called the ruru,' Mikaere concluded triumphantly.

'This is a gas,' the serviceman said, and proceeded to roll up what he called a 'stick,' which was a giant twelve-paper, funnel-shaped joint. It had to be twelve papers, no more no less.

'Tell us some more,' he commanded as he got the stick alight. At first it looked like a red eye lazily opening and closing. Then it looked like an old steam-engine train leaving the station, it was blasting out so much smoke.

So Mikaere told us about the prosaically named (in English) yellow-eyed penguin, which in te reo was *hoiho*. And that was its cry, hoi-ho.'

The three of us lifted our voices:

'*hoi-ho, hoi-ho!*'

A fine old time was had by all. Wine and 'the 'stick' passed around from hand to hand. Aria's laughter pealed brightly through the haze. She was talking about the technological wonders that awaited us to a resolute-faced scientist, possibly the soberest person in the room. It took us an hour to do the fifteen-minute walk to her place as we kept stopping to kiss and moon at each other. Making calf eyes is the expression.

Much to my regret, I didn't see Mikaere again. We might have become friends. I heard that he'd gone up north to be with his family after his brother was killed in Vietnam.

Hesitations of form within the grey

Bringing Aria home to meet the folks was not a good idea. Once was enough. Dad was nice enough, if a little bemused. Mum tried to put a good face on it, but was roiling inside. I caught her glancing at Aria with what I recognised as hatred. She wasn't aware that it showed on her face. She was wrestling for control over her feelings. Some other bitch was after her son.

We ate the classic roast lamb with potatoes, gravy, peas and spinach from our garden. Aria was blissfully indifferent to Mum's evil eye. At least at first, but as the dinner wore on she became unsettled. She knew something was wrong but didn't know what it was. It made her talk too much and she spoke at length about the joys of mathematics, which wasn't a big conversational winner.

'Everything's mathematical, she said. 'Even a snowflake, even a piece of music.'

Mum was deeply suspicious of this. 'Even the bomb,' she said.

'Yes. Even the bomb. It wouldn't be possible without maths.'

Mum had heard enough. 'There's such a thing as moral responsibility,' she said tartly. Moral responsibilities loomed large in Mum's mind.

Aria had to agree. Mum had a way of doing that, saying things that brooked no argument. She sucked a lot of smoke into her face and stared at the table top.

While we were still in the shop off Linwood Ave, Aria lived on the other side of town, in a little apartment on Dean's Avenue, which meant crossing Hagley Park to get there from town, but we always chose to meet there. As far as we were concerned, my place was a hostile zone.

I'd get the bus into the square and walk up past the university and across the park, a walk I always enjoyed, not just in anticipation of seeing Aria, but for the trees and open spaces of the park. Sometimes I'd sing to myself and cast around to see if you were about. I could be my own secret self for a while, just as I had been in Hanmer.

In the early evenings, Hagley Park often hosted a mist that rose up wraith-like from the Avon River, hovered over the grass fields, and provided the tall trees with gauzy skirts. The sounds of the city became muffled.

One evening the mist instead of thinning out continued to thicken. I had to feel the path with my feet. Trees loomed up at me suddenly, silent and implacable. There was another world here, the one the trees knew. I couldn't see it. I could only see the grey, and hesitations of form within the grey, like a world coming into being.

The mist that hid my world hid my words as well. I lost not only the things around me, but their names. As the mist grew thicker, and the world was buried away from my sight by a grey veil, the words that described that world disappeared with them. I was walking through the wordlessness of that obscurity. I was shorn of all but a few words, emptied of the world. Since there were no things, there were no names. I was giddy with emptiness. With wordlessness.

I was speechless.

As I slowed my usual brisk walk to a careful stroll, a strange cry came out of the mist, and the flapping of leathery wings. Somewhere out there, floating in the formlessness, was the pterodactyl I'd seen as a child. Not just one but several, a discordance of them, sounding grim and exultant. I fancied they were closing in on something, ready to rip it apart with their long, saw-toothed beaks. In flight, they sounded like canvas snapping in the wind. I put my hands over my head as I had done when magpies attacked me, and sought shelter under an elm tree. Its broad trunk was solid at my back. The genus *Ulmus* in the family *Ulmaceae*. The Latin words held the world in place. At the same time there was a shadow in them, in their etymology. Elm trees were associated with the Underworld. They had a special affinity with elves who guarded burial mounds, their dead and the associated passage into the Underworld. It felt as if the solidity of the world was being eaten away at from within. All the epochs and geological eras of deep time were there, just beyond my grasp, the boundaries between them dissolved by the mist. Just there, a few steps ahead, beyond the elm, linearity disappeared and times and distances became entangled.

I kept walking, yet felt as if I were not getting anywhere, as if I were walking on an endlessly moving path. That sensation faded as the mist thinned and the world of names returned; as things reappeared, language returned, the world reassembled itself. Movement resumed. My identity resumed. I was once more a person with a place, a place that fitted the person. I saw that my identity was a provisional thing, easily threatened; the dissolution of time was always only a step away. And while all the words in the world might be there one day, the next day they could all disappear. Everything would return to a mixing pot in which time lost its arrow, turned back on itself, became a complicated dimensional object that existed outside of, and prior to, language.

Later, I attempted to describe this experience to Aria, but she was not impressed and said that I was too mature to get spooked by a bit of mist. I said I wasn't spooked, just emptied of words, but to her that meant spooky. No matter how good you are with words, you cannot convey to another an experience which they have not had, for they will only translate your words into their own experience. Spooky was as near as Aria could come to relating to my experience; for her, mist did not erase the world of names, just hid them. They were still there, even if she couldn't see the objects to which they belonged. For her it was sensible and simple.

That realisation brought an element of sadness into my relationship with Aria. Ultimately, we are alone in our world of words. Our words might coincide from time to time, but we can never be totally sure that we are talking about the same thing.

B-cell lymphoma

My relationship with Aria took a big step forward after my mother died. That came out of the blue. Within weeks of being diagnosed with large B-cell lymphoma, she became very ill, and her mind buckled under the strain. No use throwing an ing-bing with death, which was unresponsive to her moods. Towards the end she would ring me up at Aria's, where I was spending most of my time, and say, in a deep, unrecognisable voice. 'Come now, come over now.'

'It's like she's possessed,' I said to Aria.

'The cancer's probably reached her brain,' Aria said.

On one occasion I rushed over to Mum, thinking the end was near, and she came at me with a carving knife upraised. She was wearing long, scraggly pajamas and a loose dressing grown open at the front. Her arms were apocryphally thin, her skin mottled, her face as grey as putty. She had seized the knife from the kitchen table, and her mouth was pulled up in a rictus of hate. It was me. I was the one who betrayed her. Not Frank, not Dad. Me. She was going to fix my wagon once and for all.

Another time I found her on the toilet with a bottle of whisky, a burning Benson and Hedges cigarette and a bunch of pills. A quick death wasn't quick enough for her. She wanted out. She gave me a sickly smile, like a child caught out doing something naughty.

Other times she lay exhausted on her couch, her tartan blanket over her knees, smoking cigarettes and in too much pain to talk, staring stricken at the world around her as if she didn't recognise it. She would reach out for a word, a word that signified salvation, like 'chemo' or 'remission,' or her little friend 'willie white cell' who was busy rushing about in her body snapping up the cancer cells.

The way she stumbled over 'willie white cell,' getting lost with the double 'w', reminded me of her efforts to teach me how to talk without stuttering. She would utter some phrase and get me to repeat it over and over until I could push through the sticky parts. She preferred common sayings like 'a stitch in time saves nine' which I couldn't say without getting stuck on the 'stitch,' or 'a fool and his money are soon parted', which I could say quite smoothly until I got to 'parted.' As she lay dying, I tried to remind her of this, tossing off 'a stitch in time saves nine' with consummate ease, hoping perhaps to distract her with some pleasant memories, something which might make her laugh since she had often found my efforts to talk funny. Instead, she just stared at me with her eyes like two clouded marbles and said nothing. The doctors suggested that she couldn't talk because she was in a state of shock and in too much pain. I'm sure they were right, but I thought I detected, in her hard stare, a stubborn refusal to partake in any way in the life from which she was being so cruelly torn.

Meanwhile, my father sank into vagueness, lethargy and sherry.

Ultimately, he was a practical man. Dealing with a disintegrating personality was way beyond him. Beyond me too. Frank moved in with some friends and never came home.

There was no going gentle into that good night for Mum. She raged against the world and her life, and fell into suspicion and bitterness. She wasn't a Christian but that didn't prevent her from believing in Hell. As far she she could see, everybody was hellbound, especially those who had never loved her. Especially me. Of course, I had betrayed her. Of all her betrayals, that was the hardest she had to bear. Towards the end she came to grips with the understanding that I didn't love her, couldn't love her and, even as she went down kicking and screaming and remonstrating, wouldn't love her.

One winter evening the cold moved into her bones and stayed. I found her, cold as clay, lying on her favourite couch with the tartan blanket on top. A cigarette had burned down to the filter in the ash tray. I woke up Dad who did his best to pull himself together.

'Poor old Mum,' he said.

It turns out that Mum, unbeknownst to anybody, had taken out shares in a company called Brierleys, which had prospered, and there was what she described in her will a 'little nest egg' for me and Frank.

'I can't believe Mum put her money with that arch capitalist Ron Brierley, Frank said. 'Wonders will never cease. She was not so crazy after all.'

'That's not all,' Dad said. It turned out that, not trusting the banks, or the tax department, Mum had also buried wads of cash under the house in glass jars and golden syrup tins.

Enough to cover her funeral expenses and then some.

She wasn't going to be a burden to anybody. Even in death.

Right at the end she had satisfaction is knowing that she had paid for her own ticket to Hell.

The panic merchants

It so happened that Aria's apartment in Dean's Avenue came up for sale shortly after Mum's death, and while Mum's 'Brierley money' was not enough for a deposit, Aria's parents, who lived in London, stumped up the balance and we were suddenly landowners, set up like a proper married couple with a modest mortgage, except we weren't married.

We were a couple, looking forward to doing postgraduate work in our respective fields.

'The world's your oyster,' grandfather said to me on the day of my graduation. 'And there's Frank, heading off to Aussie. That's where the money is, of course. Britain is moving closer to Europe. It costs money to ship stuff, like butter, to the other side of the world. We're going to be the tail end of nothing down here. Too far down under for anybody to care.'

As my grandfather grew older, he grew more malign. I could see my mother in him, just at certain moments as he readied himself to pass judgement on something or somebody. We never spoke about *Silent Spring*, although I did mention 245T and its use in Vietnam.

'Commies have got their own way over there,' he said. I knew he didn't approve of my conscientious-objector stand, although he didn't say much about it. I think my grandmother had warned him against it. A peaceful house was all she asked for.

He did, however, profess to an interest in the earth sciences, and if he'd had the opportunities I had, he'd have studied geology. 'It's all in the rocks,' he said. 'The Christians have their Bible, we have our rocks.' Visits from Mormons and other 'holy rollers' as he called them, had incensed him against religion. 'They think they can come poking into your life,' he said. 'Busybodies is what they are.'

On the strength of this, I shared an article I'd read called 'No More Ice Ages?' from a book called *Fact and Fancy* by the writer I knew for his science fiction, Isaac Asimov. In discussing the carbon cycle, he made a rather simple but compelling argument. Nature wisely 'sequestered" carbon under the ground, where it became stored energy. During a big volcanic eruption, that stored energy could be released, flooding the air with carbon dioxide, a heat-trapping gas, so upsetting the energy balance of the planet. Enough volcanos and the planet would heat up. However, humans could take the place of volcanos and flood the air with carbon dioxide and methane from our industrial processes. We were sucking up the stored energy and, by burning it, amping up the climate.

If I thought my grandfather would dismiss the idea out of hand, I was wrong. He gave it a lot of thought. 'They call it progress,' he muttered. While he was a core defender of capitalism, and the right of ordinary blokes to make an 'honest profit,' he was made uneasy by some of the unforeseen consequences of the world we were building, and was beginning to wonder if there was any such thing as an honest profit, which was a commie thing to think.

'It'll be in the rocks,' he said, 'if it's happened before, with the volcanos. Or the ice. All they need to do is take some ice-core samples and analyse the atmosphere of past times.'

'That's a very good idea,' I said.

'I think you'll find that there's no cause for panic. We'd have to put a hell of a lot of that stuff into the air to make any significant difference.'

He didn't like the idea that humans could affect us in such a big way. We were after all, small, insignificant creatures, and the earth was vast. We were a piddle in the ocean.

'The panic merchants always have another end of the world coming up,' he said.

He considered his own deceased daughter as one of those 'panic merchants' but he wouldn't say so. All that hoo-ha about the bomb and look, we already had The Limited Test Ban Treaty. The world was heading in the right direction there.

'They've got it in hand,' he said, 'and it will be the same with this CO2 thing. They'll be on top of it long before it causes any trouble.'

I was not so sure. Over the subsequent weeks, and further studying atmospheric chemistry, I became convinced that Asimov was right, that the heating of the planet was already well under way. Grandfather thought that this was because I was young and hot-headed, and had been infected with my mother's commie ideas.

I tried talking about it with my university colleagues, most of whom were bemused or only vaguely interested. Maybe so, but it's hundreds of years away, was the common response. A good theory but it lacks hard evidence, was another. Aria listened politely but had other fish to fry.

I did however find one willing ear, an older woman and senior in our department, Dr Janet Holden, a tough, no-nonsense woman, who, after hearing me out, had more to say on the subject.

We were sitting in the staff common room where, as a post-grad student I was tolerated, especially when accompanied by a tenured staff member. The room was nearly empty, and the afternoon sun coming through the window seemed to be making the dust motes dance. I had the feeling that this room had slumbered for years as time had passed it by. It was as worn as the leather of its couches.

Janet had been in the botany department forever. Tall and imposing with a mass of grey hair, she was the elder of the department, although she had never risen above an associate professorship.

'It's because I'm a woman,' she said when I asked her why she had never been granted full professorship. 'I speak my mind, enough for some of these wussies. They get heart palpitations every time a woman speaks up.'

Janet liked to smoke but fought against it, calling it a 'filthy habit.' I sat and watched her tearing a cigarette to pieces and scattering the tobacco into the ashtray while she told me that the Asimov article, which she'd read, was based on the earlier work of a scientist called Guy Callendar who, back in 1934, wrote a paper suggesting that human activities had raised the carbon dioxide content of the atmosphere by about 10 percent since the beginning of the century.

'This was disputed because it was thought that the ocean would suck up our CO2. Then along comes Charles David Keeling. Have you heard of him?'

I hadn't.

Janet settled into her lecturing mode, the mode in which she felt the most comfortable.

'He set up a monitoring station on Mauna Loa, Hawaii, in the late fifties to measure CO2 in the air. His measurements showed a clear upward trend in the amount of CO2 in a short 18-month period. They call it the Keeling Curve and there's no escaping what it means.'

Governments and the fossil fuel industry were keeping quiet about it, and Janet and I both knew why.

'Money doesn't talk, it swears,' she said.

I'd heard that line somewhere before.

Some staff members wandered through and she fell silent. She stared at the tobacco in her ash tray. 'I think you're right. The heating has already started. The Franz Joseph glacier has been thinning and retreating since god knows when.'

'Jesus! How long do you think this's been going on?'

'Since we started burning coal. When the first smoke stacks went up. I'd say late seventeen hundreds at a guess.'

At that moment it all became real to me. It was like entering another dimension and finding another earth there, an earth that humans were slowly cooking. It was like a Harry Harrison Deathworld sequel. The junkmen, not knowing any better, had gleefuly adopted the energy sources most dangerous to them, and every other creature. With their vast might, everything was at their mercy, the grubbers included. But even the junkmen could be brought to see reason, surely.

'Once governments find out, they'll put a brake on this before it gets out of control.'

I knew enough organic chemistry to know that if you add energy in the form of heat to any given system, turbulence sets in, which turns into cascading feedback effects, which turns into chaos and disorder.

'Will they, though?' Her voice dropped to a conspiratorial whisper. 'I've heard that back in the 40s the big-oil people commissioned a study by their own, hand-picked scientists on the long-term effect of CO_2 emissions. And what I heard was, their scientists told them straight out. Long-term emissions will heat the planet, atmosphere and oceans, as well as acidify the oceans.'

'But nobody's said anything.'

'That's right. They're sitting on those reports. And they'll keep on sitting on them until their fat arses catch fire.' She laughed, loudly, and it sounded shocking in the afternoon somnambulance of the staff common room.

She pulled out another cigarette and examined it as if she'd never seen one before. 'Filthy bloody things,' she said.

'They killed my mother,' I said.

'Is that right?'

'Or helped her along her way.'

'I feel funny about all of this,' she said. 'I know it's real but it seems unreal. And it's not hundreds of years away if it's already happening. It's funny to be talking about it.'

'My grandfather would call us panic merchants.'

'Good on him. I imagine we could be called a lot worse.'

Over the next couple of weeks, I abandoned my study of fungi, lichen and liverworts, and began researching planetary systems. The issue had taken over my life. I could hardly believe that it was sitting there in front of everybody, with nothing being done. No investigation, no royal commission, no government committee.

Combing through old newspapers in the library, I discovered a reference to a 1965 memo to President Lyndon Baines Johnson disclosing the link between CO2 emissions and climate change, showing federal climate action could have started decades sooner. That memo was the smoking gun. But what could LBJ do? He had a war machine to maintain, warmongers to keep happy, commies everywhere, anti-war protesters filling the streets chanting 'Hey, hey, LBJ, how many kids have you killed today?'

The Miami Herald reported that the memo was written by a visionary called Donald Hornig, who outlined preparations for an ambitious environmental program and a plan to address 'pollution.'

> 'Pollution is now one of the most pervasive problems of our society,' Johnson declared, announcing his intention 'to give high priority to increasing the numbers and quality of the scientists and engineers working on problems related to the control and management of pollution.'

The article said that increasing CO2 could raise average air temperatures, with the result that 'polar ice could melt and the oceans rise to swallow up our cities.'

The *Herald* emphasised that this wasn't 'idle speculation or science fiction' but was based on warnings sounded by 'reasonable scientists in and out of government.'

When I read this, hope flared. The cat was out of the bag. The memo was on Johnson's desk. Newspapers were picking up on it. I eagerly related these discoveries to Janet Holden, who was as excited as me but pretended not to be. Several times in our discussions her cynical mask dropped and I glimpsed, behind the grey hair and wrinkles, a youthful enthusiasm and hope against hope.

'Maybe reason will actually prevail,' she said, 'Wonders will never cease.'

As the months wore on, that hope faded. Johnson got side-tracked pursuing a futile war. His hold on power was beginning to slip. Meanwhile, the fossil fuel industry and its allies, the National Association of Manufacturers, the Manufacturing Chemists Association, the U.S Chamber of Commerce, and the Automobile Manufacturers Association, set about suppressing the CO2 story. Mention of the memo and Johnson's plans disappeared. Misdirection began with a claim that the world was actually headed for a new ice age.

It wasn't only the facts that were being buried, but the very language available to properly describe our world. A language of description was slipping away. If you don't have the words you can't think about it.

'It'll come back to bite them on the arse one day,' Janet said, 'but by then it will be too late.'

Her old cynicism returned with a vengeance. It made her older. I wanted to see her youthful smile.

'Don't let this take over your life,' she said. 'It can become obsessive. Suddenly you find you've lost your balance.'

'Is that what happened to you?'

'Years ago. I had to watch a forest, filled with trees, some of them five-hundred years old, get destroyed in a matter of weeks. That gave me a lot to think about.'

'But how do you keep your balance in a world that has gone out of balance?'

Janet was still peeling cigarettes, adding to the pile of unsmoked tobacco already in the ashtray, a little golden pile. 'You just have to keep going.'

'Going nowhere fast.'

'Doing whatever you can. What else can you do?'

Doing whatever you can usually means doing nothing at all, I thought. I felt raw, as if I didn't have the padding others had; my mind could flay me alive. It shredded everything the way a grater shreds a piece of fruit. I needed to get out. I suddenly had the desire to go to Hanmer. It would be just like it always was. I would walk to the lookout at the top of Conical Hill. I would feel myself back in among the mountains. I would hear the whoop of the Molesworth cowboys riding into town after the mustering. See Mum clapping her hands to the sound of a dance tune, Dad swaying his large body to Louis Armstrong, singing along with 'What A Wonderful World.'

Techno-optimism

I began to feel that the people around me were living in a fantasy world not of their own devising, a carefully crafted fantasy world with all the knobbly bits edited out or smoothed over. In that world, technology would solve all our problems from nuclear power that would provide us with endless electricity 'too cheap to meter', new generations of wonder chemicals to grow more food and control nature, computers to do all our mental heavy lifting and robots to do the physical heavy lifting. Utopia was just around the corner. That was our evolutionary advantage. Dealing with pollution was another technical problem, and talking about it irritated these optimists.

I went to upbeat talks with Aria on how technology would develop over the next hundred years or so, with no mention that the world would be facing unprecedented temperatures and violently volatile weather. Theirs was a cultivated ignorance. The growing shadow beneath was suppressed. Like a stream that's concreted over and is forced underground, the shadow was banished to our subconscious and manifested only in dreams and fantasy novels like *Lord of the Rings*.

So the techo dream steadily grew further away from reality. People who thought of themselves as hard-headed realists moved deeper into fantasy.

I had reached the point where I had all the words you could bring me. Your gift was complete. There were no more words, only the ones we had. We were at the limits of language. I wanted words that were the opposite of a spell, words which would break the spell. People would then come out of their dream and say, 'Look what's happening, look what's happening, let's do something about it.'

It was my peak words moment, but also peak frustration. It's one thing to speak, quite another to get what you want across to others.

Even Aria didn't get it. Well, she got it but just didn't think it was important, certainly not important enough to brood over. I used your best words in the best order and little came of it except for more love-making. Even that had become frustrating. The sex was as immersive as ever, but our minds were not meshing. In our circle of friends, most of them science students, Aria was the high priestess of techo-optimism. Her words were all shiny and impervious, a bright, depthless edifice. Artiface. A priestess in a suit of bright armour, dystopian misgivings bounced right off her, shadows withered. Faces were lit in the sodium-vapour-lamp glare of her certainty. Nothing would stand in the way of the triumph of humankind. One day, she said, we'll have telescopes floating in space strong enough for us to be able to see right back to the beginning of time. Imagine that.

She had plenty of admirers. She was seen as an exemplar of a new kind of woman: professional, awesomely smart, ambitious, self-directed and destined for great things. And good looking into the bargain. What was there not to admire? She could have had any man she chose, the story went, and some wondered, if not aloud, how come she'd ended up with me. The oddball.

Aria was too good a scientist to deny the chemistry behind global heating, but her interests were primarily personal and practical, getting ahead, keeping on top of things, keeping the money flowing. These things loomed much larger in her mind than a possibly overheating planet. After all, we did have a mortgage to pay. I seemed to forget that sometimes, she said.

She became frustrated with my anxieties. 'Life's in front of us,' she said. 'Let's get on with it.'

The Orwellian language feedback loop

I began to make sense of the phrase, 'the decline of language.' I don't know where I first heard the phrase, someone talking about political discourse during the McCarthy era in the U.S. I think. It's all about repression. By repressing a few key concepts, you can hammer a whole lot of other words out of existence; reality disappears from view. You can degrade words by misusing them, putting them in the wrong context, appropriating them for your own devious purposes.

Language is in decline when it no longer fits the reality we're trying to describe.

I was drawn to the idea that the problem lay with language when I saw how Aria's words were like a bronze shield, deflecting my words with ease. I also resisted the idea because I couldn't see how language, per se, could decline; the words we need are all there if we choose to use them. Then I encountered an essay by George Orwell called 'Politics and the English Language' and I began to appreciate the complexities of the relationship between words and their meanings. He wrote:

> 'Now, it is clear that the decline of a language must ultimately
> have political and economic causes. But an effect can become
> a cause, reinforcing the original cause and producing the
> same effect in an intensified form, and so on indefinitely.
> A man may take to drink because he feels himself to be a

failure, and then fail all the more completely because he drinks. It is rather the same thing that is happening to the English language. It becomes ugly and inaccurate because our thoughts are foolish, but the slovenliness of our language makes it easier for us to have foolish thoughts.'

I saw this process reflected in the feedback loops kicking into play on a planetary level. Ice reflects sunlight back into space, so helping to keep the planet nice and cool. As the Arctic ice melts, areas of dark water that open up can absorb more heat, so melting the ice even faster, and so on. Until eventually there will be no ice left and nothing but foolish thoughts with which to consider it.

Feedback loops playing out in the world and in the world of words. The suppression of the language of scientific description, in the case of global heating due to CO2 levels, had political and economic causes all right, and made it harder to talk about those things, which in turn helped suppress that language even further. And so on. Until the words catch fire.

Orwell concludes that:

> One ought to recognise that the present political chaos is connected with the decay of language, and that one can probably bring about some improvement by starting at the verbal end. If you simplify your English, you are freed from the worst follies of orthodoxy.

This galvanised me. Good rhetoric, shorn of bureaucratic decoy words and slippery propaganda, would connect directly to the truth of things. That truth would be like an arrow, a magic arrow that would fly right through the shiniest of lies, the darkest obfuscations, the buckle and twist of mind.

I sharpened my rhetorical skills on Aria, and later on my friends and colleagues. I was driven by the belief that words mattered, that words could change the world, that there was a potency in words that would bring about a new order of things. 'The truth will out,' as Mum used to say, and I felt the force of that. Truth has a way of bubbling to the surface, no matter how fervently it is repressed. Words that unlock our understanding cannot be kept at bay; lies are constantly being undermined by the reality of things, that's why there always has to be new lies or rigid enforcement of the old ones.

I didn't have close friends among my colleagues at work, and my newfound passions didn't win me any. My colleagues began to regard me warily, or try to placate me. Like Aria, they had other fish to fry. They had children to feed and a mortgage to pay.

'We'll muddle through somehow,' they said.

I dreaded the time when reality would be debased into a worthless product of junk language, and the language of lies became the language of thought. The language of lies is the language of insincerity, a way of hiding one's true intent from others and even from oneself. As Orwell said, 'The great enemy of clear language is insincerity. When there is a gap between one's real and one's declared aims, one turns as it were instinctively to long words and exhausted idioms, like a cuttlefish spurting out ink.'

Long words and exhausted idioms, I couldn't get that phrase out of my head. I kept running into them everywhere, in every weaselly obfuscation. We'll muddle through somehow, but maybe not. Maybe that spurting ink will turn everything into a murky blur and we will lose the world to shadows.

The multitudinous names of god

Perhaps it was because my words could find no purchase in Aria's mind that I began to take field trips away from the city, to remote areas, mountain or river, to do the important job of cataloguing, not just recording what is known but discovering patterns and variations, and sometimes new species.

The meticulous cataloguing and naming became a sacred task. The simple ritual and repetition of each day: my pen, my notebook, my magnifying glass. A pilgrimage along some mountain track to find, perhaps, a scarlet mistletoe on a silver beech tree. The scratching of names on paper. The careful indexing. These things reinforced a growing sense of mystical connection to the world, a connection that had its roots in my earliest experiences as a child, and which needed no language.

By now I knew the Māori name for much of the flora and fauna, and enjoyed chanting them as I walked along. The ordinary cabbage tree was called tī kōuka, a sound which came from deep at the back of the throat.

Then there was the whimsical whauwhaupaku, the five finger, sounding like a whisper. There was tawhai for the beech and pāpāuma for the broadleafs. And my favourite, the huruhuru whenua – for the common fern the shining spleenwort – which when spoken had to be sung.

Getting my tongue around these words threatened to take me back to my old stuttering ways, but in chanting them I shed my petty self. I could feel the words vibrating up through my body from the earth beneath my feet. To anyone passing by I must have sounded like a mumbling monk toiling towards some distant temple. I didn't have to struggle with language. Once I had found the sounds, and opened a passage for them in my body, all I had to do was sing.

The best thing about the field trips was that I hardly had to talk to anybody, and what talk there was remained on the everyday, practical level – places to go, good camping spots, good tracks, old forests. Even when you love it, talking is exhausting, especially with a brilliant person like Aria; digging for the right words, testing meanings, weighing sounds. Especially when an Aria type of person can easily deflect words, diffract meanings, mute sounds. Out in the field I needed no more than the articulation of the wind in the trees or the rough gossip of a river as it rushed over stones and through fallen branches. Everything nameless until I named it, everything held in miraculous balance.

The world of humankind, and its creeping doom, lay many worlds away.

I read a story about a group of monks whose earthly task it was to chant all the names of god, and since the names of god are multitudinous, this task lasted many millennia, stretching over many generations, and as long as they kept chanting the universe maintained its existence. But names of god are finite, and when the last name was chanted, the universe winked out of existence.

Who would know any of these multitudinous names of god if not for the humble labours of the taxonomist? I didn't believe in 'god' as a supreme being lying outside of space and time. Rather, for me, god was all possible forms of existence; god was the creation. I didn't have to 'find' god because everywhere I looked was god. Discovering a new species was like finding a hitherto hidden name of the divine. Nature was like an ancient scroll, continually revealing its mysteries.

I determinedly kept god down in the lower case. It was either that or return to the nineteenth century practice of giving all nouns capitals, an idea that appealed to me. A tree would become a Tree, a river would become a River, love would become Love; everything would become Divine by virtue of the capital letter. The modern trend, however, is to get rid of capitals wherever possible. I can see a time coming when they will disappear altogether and even our own names, the last bastion of the capital letter, will succumb to the lower case. Then god will have to put up with being just another noun, and not the Noun of nouns, and we will have to accept that the divine is not standing alone in splendid isolation, separate from everything, but is the expression of the lower-case nature of Everything.

Sometimes I would make up stories, just as Topsell did with his *History of Four-Footed Beasts and Serpents*, about the places I was in and the plants I was cataloguing. I made up stories about the love affairs of fungi, the secret world of the bush wren and the lofty passions of mountains. In doing so I created a private menagerie of myths and legends, often built around names or the meaning of names. I made up a legend of how one of our volcanic mountains was banished from a community of volcanoes and exiled to a distant coast for its uncontrolled passions, and the strong words it used to declare them, only to find that my story echoed the Māori legend of how Mount Taranaki and Tongariro fought a titanic battle for the favours of the beautiful, bush-clad Pīhanga, with the defeated Taranaki forced to flee to the west coast of the North Island. That apparent coincidence gave me the idea that the memory of the land lives in the land and not just the human mind. The natural world, the universe itself, is imbued with memory.

I could feel the way everything fitted together: kingdom, phylum, class, order, family, genus, and species each inside the other, each of the other. Each within its memory.

In a dream I saw the mosses and lichens in the alpine regions as a deck of cards, each with their Latin and Māori names inscribed in italics. With them, I was building a house of cards that reached ever higher. It required more care with each additional level to keep the pyramid of names intact; words standing on top of words. Then a soft wind blew off the sorrowful Mt Taranaki and it all collapsed, folded in upon itself, from the outside to the centre, swift and silent – the disintegration of names.

After these sojourns in the wilderness, I would return to the city steeped in its silences, barely able to talk at first, having to rediscover the language of social interaction, having to fit back into the world of humankind and rediscover my relationship with Aria.

A man of ambition

On returning from one field trip spent in the rarefied atmosphere of the Alps, I found a change had taken place in Aria. She was acting oddly. She didn't ask me about my trip, or try to engage me in vigorous discussions on the virtues of materialism, and every so often I caught her studying me out of the corner of her eye. One day she asked me if I had any ambition. I wasn't sure what to say. 'Maybe write articles for *National Geographic* magazine,' I said. 'I can take my own pictures of photogenic mushrooms and mosses.'

We were in our city apartment, in our kitchen at the small formica table where we ate. It was a humble little table, but Aria was proud of it. It was, she said, an original from the 1950s. We were drinking Earl Grey tea out of Royal Dalton cups which had been a gift from her mother, and an inheritance from her grandmother. I was just as happy to drink tea from an enamel mug, as I did on my field trips, but knew better than to say so. Such attitudes might be indicative of a lack of ambition.

'I mean,' she said, 'do you want to live in this poky little apartment forever? Don't you dream of having a house of our own, you know, in the right area, with a bit of a garden and roses? You could have your own office. I could have mine.'

It was a seductive vision. It has been called the three-quarter acre pavlova paradise, and it was increasingly out of reach for people like us. I didn't like to think about it. I agreed with her and thought about something else. I thought of one of the Department of Conservation huts with four bunk-beds, a rough wooden table, and a fireplace. I could be happy there, with no ambition to bother me, the day's specimens laid out on the table for closer examination, my notebook open, the right words on hand, a mountain wind rattling outside.

'You'll never make any money working on contract to the uni,' she said, wiping the tabletop with the side of her hand as if sweeping up crumbs. 'The rate you're going you'll never finish your PhD.'

She was right of course. I was happy enough living from hand to mouth, but she wasn't making much money either, even though she had tenure. Tenure was the magic word that guaranteed her job, sort of, but not enough money to think of buying a house 'in the right area' which meant Merivale or Fendalton, without a crushing mortgage. Unless she had a partner with ambition.

Was I that person, she was starting to wonder. She was starting to stare into the middle distance. Maybe she was wondering why we hadn't made plans to marry. Maybe she was starting to wonder a lot of things, like how her life was slipping away day after day, like how she was running but not getting anywhere, like how there had to be more to life than what she was getting.

'I'm a cynic and a pragmatist, Michael. I live in the real world. I need a life more structured than this. I want a proper plot, you know, a real storyline with a payoff at the end. I want to be what people comfortably call 'comfortable.' I'm past apologising for being ambitious. I want to live in a story that gets somewhere, has an aim, fulfils its terms, doesn't just meander gloomily from one thing to the next. Is this all you want?' Her fingers scratched the smooth table top as if seeking purchase. 'I just don't know if I am the right person for you.'

Once you have a thought like that, it's very difficult to get rid of it. I could see where this was heading, but felt helpless to change it. What use would my reassurances be? Placating phrases died in my throat. There was no use uttering them. I had a sinking feeling in the pit of my stomach. I did not want to make its acquaintance.

'We can't have a baby here,' she said. 'We need more space.'

I thought she was getting ahead of herself. The only person I'd ever thought of having a baby with was Olga, and I'd been five years old then.

She sipped her tea without enjoyment and rubbed the formica tabletop as if it were Aladdin's lamp and a genie would appear to grant her three wishes. Big wishes. Everywhere she looked she saw my lack of ambition. Our apartment was too cramped. I was never going to get ahead cataloguing plants and learning the names of things, however useful that might be. You can recite the innumerable names of the deity day and night and not be a buck richer.

As we talked about our future that day, and in the days following, something peculiar began to happen. I was not at a loss for words. I had plenty of words, more than enough, and so did she, but none of them brought us any closer. Quite the opposite, the more we talked the further apart we became. Communication was supposed to be the key to a good relationship, but not in our case. It was paradoxical and frustrating. Trying to build a bridge with words was a futile task. We searched for the right words, the words that would fix everything up, but there weren't any. That experience brought home to me the difficult truth that words in themselves won't bring people together; more likely in fact create divisions, suspicion and hostility. Our words kept slipping away from their meanings like beaten dogs. What we wanted to say was never quite what we said.

I sought the phrases that would restore the heedless times we'd once known, when life was long and desire was strong. Now dissatisfaction had moved into our little apartment with every intention of staying, and it was a tyrannical guest. That glowering presence seemed to hover in the corners of the room the whole time. We walked on eggshells around it.

Everything depended on finding the right words. And the right words were never quite found. Our love-making lost its edge. The stars lost their shine. Words lost their heart.

I began to feel that Aria was deliberately using words to push me away, to create distance. Far from being a mode of communication, words were destroying what communication we had. As in a Dostoevsky novel, patterns of words served as smoke-screens behind which intentions lay like coiled snakes and the truth was hidden. The dotterel pretends to have a broken wing in order to lead predators away from the nest. We found lots of broken-winged words. We needed them to lead each other away from our vulnerabilities.

Then we started shouting. Words were not loud enough in themselves; by upping the volume we tried to compensate for their lack of efficacy. Hard words and loud voices. Too big and loud for that small apartment. Hard words left me washed up on a shore of broken syllables. Things said couldn't be unsaid, as they say. All those hard words had us bleeding from the mouth.

I called it the wounding.

The particulars we argued about don't seem to matter much now, talking to you. You can make them up for yourself; they are always the same. They are always about the clash of dreams and realities, hopes and hurts, projections and disillusionment, money and powerlessness, the impoverishment of our realities compared to the richness of our psyches. The particulars vary from case to case, but the underlying conflict is always the same. Words can only take us so far, I realised, and that's not very far at all. Beyond them lies the seething ocean of resentments and hurt, love and desire, hope and fear.

Little wonder these arguments became increasingly punctuated by long, wounded silences. In those silences, our bruised words crept back into their boxes.

One evening the silence grew so thick and heavy, I said, 'Is something wrong?'

'Nothing,' she said.

In this context, nothing means everything. Nothing was a decoy word. Nothing was a trapdoor to hell. Nothing was a mirrored wall encircling pain. Nothing was not a word so much as an anti-word.

'Nothing?'

'Nothing.'

And there it was. No thing.

Then no thing became a thing.

Another man.

A colleague who worked in the physics department. A brilliant man, every inch Aria's equal. A man of ambition. A man who had wrangled a prestigious job at the Stanford Linear Accelerator, which had finally become operational. A new era of experimental physics was about to open up. The wonders of the subatomic world would be revealed through the collision of charged particles. Quantum theory would be put to the test. And he would be there, this brilliant man, on the cutting edge, and the equally brilliant Aria would be by his side. A luminous pair orbiting around each other, powered by their ambition. That's what she saw in her mind's eye. That's what she wanted. What she really, really wanted. She'd get a job there, maybe on the engineering side. It wouldn't take her long, I had no doubt.

And, let's face it, I was but a humble cataloguer of fungi and lichens. A chanter of the names of god. I couldn't see Aria being happy in a bunk bed in a Department of Conservation hut, making tea on a billy over a fire and fussing with some specimens. I didn't have anything to match a particle accelerator, three miles of high-tech tunnel, where a person could feel they were playing god, bringing particles into existence, albeit briefly, probing the heart of creation.

Our doom was sealed.

'You're a nice guy, Michael,' she said, 'but these days nice is not enough.'

These were the hard truths I hadn't faced. You need the killer instinct to make it in the world, and I didn't have that. It was missing from my genetic make-up. I was a grubber. I just wanted to sing the names of things back to them. So my life had no structure. I was an amorphous, structureless being. A random particle.

All night it weeps little wax tears

In the last stages of our relationship Aria began to lie to me, and so I started lying too. Lies are like that – they're catching. They create their own feedback loop. Lies breed in the dark corners of the deceiving mind, and from there they spread to every aspect of our lives. Cuttlefish ink. In the resulting confusion, lies thrive and continue their insidious work. Lies terraform our lives to create an environment in which they can prosper. They are parasitic life forms.

Aria would tell me she was going into university to work. 'People who want to get ahead have to keep at it,' she said. No slacking off. Nose to the grindstone, ha ha. So the specific lie hid behind some general truth, a lie in camouflage. In fact, she was going to meet her new man, the particle physicist who was making something of himself, a cool dude whose name was Dave, a man who was going places. A man who apparently never slacked off.

When she returned, smelling of sex, I would tell her that I too had been working, making something of myself, a lie more obvious even than hers. The more she berated me for not having enough ambition, the less ambition I had and the more I pretended I did.

Feedback loops everywhere.

Lying seemed easier than facing the truth. Lies were cowardly words; truth delayed was truth betrayed.

At first she was keen for me to believe her lies, and did her best to make them believable, but after a while she didn't care and her lies became careless. I pretended to believe her, and tried to make that pretence believable, but it was an empty gesture. I stopped believing in her even when she was telling the truth. Our lies became weary, and in this manner the truth might reveal itself. Lies become tired but the truth never does. Nor does the lover's desire to be constantly talking about the object of their desire. I got to hear a lot about Dave. Once she started talking about him, she talked about little else.

Dave, apparently, was not only a genius at physics, but a fountain of wisdom, a man who had all the answers to life's ills. A man who had discovered a truly scientific approach to having a positive attitude and getting ahead.

'Dave says that the world is what you make of it,' she said. She got a special, reverential tone when she began a sentence with 'Dave says.' Anyone would think Dave was the only one who had ever uttered a bromide or indulged in platitudes. 'Dave says that our personality creates our reality.'

'Do tell.'

'No, really. Your moods harden into a personality. The energy you send out into the world helps create your reality and hardens into a belief system. Neurons that fire together wire together.'

'And so, by magic, CO_2 loses its heat-trapping properties. Pollution goes away all by itself because my neurons are firing together.'

'Of course not, but you need the right attitude to deal with any problem. How can you sort out the world if you can't sort out yourself. You're putting all this energy into creating these negative neural pathways. Dave says...' She pushed at her hair and her eyes grew misty. She was falling into a reverie. I wondered if they did it in the lab, briefly, among the whirring machines, or if they went back to his place for the full course. The more I wondered, the more I bled.

Fuck Dave, is what I said, except I didn't say it out loud. I internalised it so it could harden into hatred for this pretentious prick. As for Aria, she was too besotted to see these ideas for what they were: bullshit.

'Dave says it's how we think and train our brains to process information that really differentiates us.'

And Dave, let's not forget, had done a lot of information processing, having written his doctoral thesis on Cygnus X-1, a strange astronomical creature that was acting like an anti-sun whose gravity was so extreme that nothing could escape it, not even light. It was the ultimate gravity sink, sucking everything into it. Dave's thesis was on what the physics of such an object might look like, how common, everyday particles might react to such extreme gravity.

How exciting!

We had a final dinner together at an Italian restaurant the day before she moved out. It was our last supper, conducted over ribollita and red wine. We struggled to find anything to say. Even the wine could not unlock our tongues. Around us couples were murmuring to each other, carried along by candlelight and currents of feeling. Those same currents had already beached us. Our love had run out of breath. I remembered our first meeting, outside the lecture hall and how we'd talked deep into the night. Neurons that fire together wire together.

We ordered, hardly looking at the menu, and ate mechanically.

As we sat there, I was reminded of a poem by the medieval Chinese poet Du Mu that Janet Holden had shown me when I told her what was happening to me. She'd surprised me with the breadth of her reading, and I had the feeling, from the melancholy way she recited it, that something similar had once happened to her.

Too much love
Somehow became
No love at all

Over this farewell bottle
We can't manage a friendly smile

Only the candle
seems to be able
to feel for us

All night it weeps little wax tears

Part Three

Cliffs of Fall

The mission

A heavy-lidded tuatara stared down at me indifferently from two hundred and fifty million years of evolution. There was a primeval certainty in that gaze. Sometimes described as a living fossil, through natural selection, this creature has achieved an enviable stabilization of form. It had been around for some two hundred million years. When I looked into its three eyes, the ancient cosmos looked back.

'She keeps me humble,' Janet Holden said.

I wondered how she knew the tuatara was female.

Beside it, on the wall behind her desk, was another photo, this one of the female mayfly in the order *Ephemeroptera* with its curved, slender, segmented body, long thread-like double tail and ribbed, translucent wings. It had a fragile beauty.

'The tuatara can live to be over a hundred, but the poor female *Ephemeroptera* might only live a hectic five minutes. Just long enough to mate and lay eggs. They have no mouth since they have no time to eat. And yet, they predate our tuatara friend by fifty million years.' Her voice had taken on the rather severe tone she used for students. She often spoke with emphasis, as if she were expecting disagreement or talking to somebody slow on the uptake. 'She keeps me humble too.'

'All this humility of yours is a bit too much for me.'

'Ha ha. I got you there, didn't I? You didn't see me as the humble type. Well, I have these two characters on my wall to remind me that very few creatures escape extinction. Almost every creature that has ever existed has disappeared. These friends of mine,' she gestured to the wall, 'are the exceptions.'

She snapped her fingers, sending millions of species into oblivion.

'We *Homo sapiens* have had... what? about three hundred and fifty thousand years. That's how long it took us to fuck up the planet. Maybe it's time for us to bow out. Hand the world over to our inheritors. *Rattus rattus*, maybe. She gave a twisted grin. 'We're too big for our boots.' She gestured to the photos. 'These friends of mine were here before us and will be around after we've gone.'

'You sound positively gung-ho about it.'

'Oh, I am. There's nothing special about us, except perhaps our belief that we are better than everything else.'

I thought about my grandfather and his declaration that humans were so much smarter than bugs. 'You do know how to cheer a person up.'

'Ha ha. I'm a ray of sunshine, I know. This business with Aria has soured your outlook, Michael. Thrown you into a tailspin. But just think. You've been saved the folly of having a child. That's worth a sigh of relief.'

She got out a cigarette packet. I could see she was about to shred one. I wanted to leave. I didn't know if I could live through the deconstruction of another cancer stick.

'You're mocking me.'

'Not at all.'

'Baiting me, then.'

'No, no. I just want you to see the upside of all this doomy stuff. Extinction is as natural, and inevitable, as death. Look at the broader picture. There's life after *Homo sapiens*. We'll be nothing more than a strata of plastic in the geological record, an embarrassment soon forgotten.'

'The broader picture.'

'That's right. The broader the picture, the less important we become. That's why I've never had the patience to read novels. I tried a couple once, but they seemed obsessively concerned with the mating rituals of the human species.'

'Maybe because that's what most interests humans. They say birds sing about their eggs.'

'But we're not birds. We can see the broader picture. Why all this focus on the evanescent emotions of individuals? People's loves and hates, so important to them, really just come and go on a passing breeze. After all, the individual experience is embedded in the larger, collective experience. Separating the two is something of an illusion.'

She was in full lecturing mode now. Her voice had risen as if she had to throw it to the back of the lecture hall where students might be dozing off. 'With all this focus on the individual, we're in danger of forgetting that we are a gregarious species. We draw our meaning from the greater whole. Individuals can't find meaning on their own, I mean purely within themselves. They find no meaning and so become melancholy, like you are. But you like reading novels, don't you?'

'Mostly nineteenth century novels.'

'How quaint. Why?'

'I find them soothing. They take their time. No fast cars. No aircraft, no phones, no movies or tv. People rode horses or horse-pulled carriages. Those writers had the space to complete their thoughts.'

She shook her head. 'Each to their own, I suppose. It takes all kinds to make a world and so on. I draw comfort from the great passing parade of evolution, but that's probably due to my training. For me, evolution is like a great poem, but never finished, always changing. Some people find the very idea of deep time giddying. They want to reach out and hold onto something that isn't moving. But everything's moving, species coming and going faster than you can say god bless them.'

She fell silent and stared moodily at the cigarette she had still not started to dismantle. Her expression was a mixture of stubbornness and grief. I remembered the Du Mu poem and wondered if she had ever loved anybody. She never spoke about such matters. Perhaps she held such 'evanescent' things in little regard. Perhaps she'd once had her heart broken and had never recovered.

She remained that way, deep in thought, for some time, as if she'd forgotten I was there.

'If all things are evanescent, then all things are equal,' I murmured, mostly to myself. Within the giddy spaces of deep time, the lives of both the tuatara and the *Ephemeroptera* were but brief flashes.

Now there were two people sitting together each lost in their thoughts. I was remembering how recently, by accident, I saw Aria with her new love, Dave, the wonder of modern manhood. With his impressive height and resolute jaw he looked every inch a man of ambition. Here was a man who had his neural pathways sorted! Here was a man with a vision! A man cut out for a larger role in life. A man who could hunt down those evanescent bosons, make sparks fly in his particle accelerator. Nail them to the wall. A man with Aria on his arm. A man of destiny. They didn't see me. I slunk into the shadows, but not before I had witnessed her hand lightly on his arm, her face upturned in laughter, her dark auburn curls shining in the sun. A face full of hope. And love. The knowledge of her happiness wounded me. The fatal thrust. Cauterise the wound, I told myself. Use true words. Only true words can kiss it better.

Janet fiddled with the cigarette. There was a slight tremble in her fingers. 'I don't know. I just don't bloody know.'

I didn't know what she was talking about, and didn't ask. It would come out, whatever it was, or not.

'Is there anybody else on the horizon? That's what happens in those novels, isn't it? Always somebody else comes along. A new ritual begins.'

'All in the past as far as I'm concerned.'

'Aw, come on now, don't give me that.' Thinking about my dismal love life seemed to cheer her up.

'No, it's true. I've lost the art of chatting up girls, if I ever had it.'

'Isn't it like riding a bike?'

'Not for me. I can't find the words. My social skills have dropped to zero. I'm like a fish out of water. Aria did me in, well and truly. Anyone fucked by Aria stays fucked.'

Janet was delighted. 'Don't be so turgid. Aria's quite a woman, I'll give you that. I wouldn't want to tangle with her. But you'll find that there's life after Aria, there always is. You're still young enough, your bell still rings, I assume.'

'She took a whole lot of me with her. Words, precious words. The word bringer only brought me so many. Aria took most of the best ones.' A lot of those words had been like our children, shared concepts, shared constructions of thought and image.

'What the hell are you talking about?'

'The word bringer. He came to me when I was a child and brought me words, taught me to speak. Gave words body. But I realise now, you only get a certain number of words in a lifetime. It's a bit like Scrabble, you only have so many letters, you have to make your words with what you've got. In the end the bag empties. No more letters. Aria had her hand in my bag and has stolen away a whole lot of words and phrases. Don't ask me what they are because they're gone. I feel around for them and come up empty.'

'What nonsense. And besides, you're being silly. You have all the words you need to talk to anybody you want, and that includes chatting up girls. It's not that hard. Most girls like being chatted up. It bolsters them. Makes them feel they're attractive.'

'You're missing the point.'

'No, I'm not. I'm just saying what someone always has to say in this situation. You have to get back in the saddle, literally as well as metaphorically.'

I looked up at the tuatara and wondered about its love life. Did these spiny-backed ones even have a love life? It was doubtful. Males have no reproductive organ, so reproduction occurs by the pair rubbing their cloacas together. That's not as sexy as it sounds, since a cloaca is nothing more than the chamber into which the intestinal, urinary, and reproductive canals empty.

Topsell would have been entertained by these creatures, especially their 'third eye' on the top of their heads, which has a retina, lens, and nerve endings, yet is not used for seeing.

'Okay, you don't want to talk about it,' she said. With one swift movement, she split the cigarette down the middle and the dark yellow tobacco spilled out into the ashtray. She poked at the little pile with her finger. 'They put chemicals in it to keep it moist,' she said. 'You know, work is the answer to these problems of the heart. You're a scientist. You're after the truth.'

'With a capital T.'

'Absolutely! I'm very old fashioned that way.'

'That's very quaint, Janet.'

'Don't be silly. You do too. Remember – the truth will out.'

'I'm not so confident anymore. The truth may be as ephemeral as your *Ephemeroptera*,' I gestured to the mayfly. 'It can be degraded, co-opted and destroyed.' I thought of George Orwell.

'More nonsense. Come on! You are a scientist, aren't you? You know that the moon is not made of green cheese. Or any coloured cheese for that matter. No matter how many people claim it is. Or believe it is. It's not a question of belief.'

'Okay, you're right. You usually are. You're like Aria in that respect. She's always so totally right. Even when she's wrong. I don't know how she does that. It's an amazing trick.'

'If you're not careful you're going to get all bitter and twisted. As I said, there is life after Aria. Just as there was life before her. Were you ever in love, I mean before Aria?'

'Yes.'

'With who?'

'Olga?'

'Who's Olga?

'It doesn't matter.'

'Okay, so you loved before Aria, you can love again, after Aria.'

'She took a chunk of me with her. I can't explain it. As I said, I don't have the words. I feel locked in, blocked out, frozen in wordless time and space. The world is made with mirrors. It's like when you're asleep and can't breathe. You have to make yourself wake up and make the image in the mirrors move. In my case, I can't do that. I'm paralyzed. The next breath is beyond me.'

'Okay then, drama queen. I've got the answer. Some serious fieldwork. And right up your alley. This is what I wanted to talk to you about.'

She opened a book and showed me a photograph. I recognised the tiny bird, with its greenish wings and chalky breast, as the boulder-hopping, bobbing, rock wren. 'What do you know about it?'

'Not much. I'm more into mosses, lichens and liverworts.'

'It's odd, no one really knows how they survive the winters. Maybe they hibernate. Their nests can be as warm as thirty degrees, when outside it is below freezing. You're going to have to get up to speed on them. Do some research.'

'Why?'

'The pīwauwau only live above the tree line, between nine-hundred and two-thousand-five-hundred metres above sea level. We have some evidence from DOC that predators are spreading into higher alpine zones because of creeping temperature rises. At least that's our hypothesis. Our little friends *Rattus rattus* love nothing better than a little delicacy like the rock wren, whose nests are in crevices or on the ground, making it easy for *Rattus rattus*, and stoats, who happily thrive above the tree line.' She was slipping into her lecturing voice again.

'So?'

'I'm sending you to Mount Cook National Park to get up above nine-hundred metres and record any sightings. Also check out their food source. Beetles, spiders, flies, caterpillars and caddisflies. They also eat berries and grass seeds.'

'Why me? There are others, like Moana and Terry. I mean, proper ornithologists. It's their department. I could bring you a report on rock moss, or the tough little *Oreobolus strictus*.'

'You have the patience, Michael. But there's something else. A sort of secret between the two of us.' She tapped the side of her nose.

'Now I'm intrigued.'

I'm not including the planet heating hypothesis in the aims of the study, which the threshold guardians,' she pointed the ceiling 'have to sign off. At the moment any suggestion that we're heating the planet might be seen as dangerously fringe. Even gathering evidence might seem suspect. Can you imagine Professor Crock-of-Shit approving it.'

I pretended not to be a little shocked at this description of our Head of Department, a scholar of some renown.

'So we are co-conspirators?' I liked the idea. I felt a trickle of life through my system. Maybe there was life after Aria. Life as a secret agent for science.

'Sooner or later, as the evidence rolls in, this is going to go mainstream. We don't have to draw outrageous conclusions. The evidence will speak for itself. If predators are moving upward in alpine regions, that can only mean one thing.'

'The environment's changing. Getting warmer.'

'To get the funding, I'm framing this as a routine census operation. It's been five years since the last rock wren count. Sightings have been few and far between. We can suggest they're becoming an endangered species, for unknown reasons of course. Leave the conclusion for others to make, but write me a separate report on any evidence you might find on alpine warming. When this thing breaks, we want to be ready.'

'I think I'm feeling something.'

'Good Lord! Don't be too hasty, cowboy.'

'I like this secret mission. The guerrilla scientist. I can get into that. It gives my life some meaning.'

'I thought it might.' She looked at the cigarette she had not yet pulled apart. 'I'm trying to quit shredding them. I'm not free of them yet, obviously. I carry them around everywhere.'

'Have you got a clear idea where I might go?'

'There's a track called the Ball Pass Crossing to the West of Mount Cook. Well... sometimes the track is nothing more than markers. It'll get you up over two thousand meters, rock wren country. You'll have to leave the trail at some point to get a wider sample area. You have the gear?'

'The very best. But I'm still not sure I'm the best person for the job. That's your call.'

I stood up, thinking the interview was over.

Janet was rolling the cigarette back and forth across her desk. 'There's something else,' she said.

I waited. It was not like her to hesitate, or look embarrassed.

'A dream. A kind of cringe-worthy dream. I was a temple priestess. I had robes and a tiara and everything. Don't laugh. I know it's corny. And here's me the hard-headed scientist.'

'Nobody said you were hard-headed. And I'm not laughing.'

'I've dreamed about her before. She's beautiful and imperious. She's like the mother of mothers. And serves a demanding goddess, which is some big granite creature I can't quite see. I am a powerful priestess. I have lots of servants and underlings to carry out my instructions.'

'I wish I had dreams like that. My dreams are all about getting lost, or losing my underpants in public.'

'You were in my dream, some kind of palace hanger-on. A lowly individual. I ordered you to go and find a certain mythological bird, maybe a fenghuang, a Chinese firebird, a bird who reigns over all other birds.

From fiery embers, a phoenix ascends,

With wings of dawn, its radiant form blends.

The Fenghuang dances, a cosmic ballet.'

I thought of Topsell and tried to remember if he had included a phoenix in his *History*.

'So I was a lowly individual was I?'

Well, not too lowly. It was a dangerous mission. You were to bring her back to the palace where I could put her in a cage. I was jealous of her, you see.'

'Are you jealous of somebody in real life?'

'Not that I know of. I gave up jealousy when I was sixteen.'

'What happened then? What did I do?'

'You set off, as you were told. You were an obedient underling. You said something strange to me, just before I woke up. You said you were being hunted.'

'Hunted?'

'That's what you said. When I woke up, I researched fenghuang and found an ancient source which said that she is made of... she began to read from a text in front of her, in full lecture mode now "...the beak of a rooster, the face of a swallow, the forehead of a fowl, the neck of a snake, the breast of a goose, the back of a tortoise, the hindquarters of a stag, and the tail of a fish. "'

'I don't think I'm going to be able to find one of those. Maybe with bit more funding…'

'Ha ha.'

'An obedient underling. You're applying this dream to real life?'

'As near as I can get. If you think of the temple in the dream as representing this august Temple of Knowledge in which we nest like little cooing spotted doves…'

At that moment, under the timeless gaze of the tuatara, I had an intimation that if I accepted this job life would never be the same again. The fenghuang would awaken and something of the magnitude of an earthquake would open up the ground to swallow me. Swallow everything up. Then I would appear, transformed, in some other place. A shiver went through me.

'Are you all right? You look like you've seen a ghost.'

'I'm all right. Someone walked over my lowly, obedient underling grave.'

Dostoevsky's mirror

I made my preparations as if I were going away for a very long time. I told myself this was just another field trip and I'd be back in a few weeks but it didn't feel that way. It felt like an occasion, a grand departure, a big farewell. It was as if I were leaving the world. This grew out of the feeling I had at the end of my conversation with Janet Holden, that mysterious, anticipatory shiver.

It was as if I were going to die.

I put that feeling down to the break-up with Aria: the breaking down of the world, the word. The world as flesh. The world would peel away, taking me with it. Our homes would be ripped away from us by the forces we had unleashed. Not even the mountains could protect me, but I would run to them anyway, a bit like the 'sinner man' of that song. The rock couldn't hide me, but in its shadow I could hide my eyes. Aria would go away and take the world with her. Soon the crumbs from the table would be stale. Then no more crumbs. Just rock and sky.

I hastened to finish reading Dostoevsky's *Demons*, as it was too thick and heavy to take with me. Too many words. Besides, I had to leave the nineteenth century behind. The mountain winds would blow away the centuries. The novel disturbed me. It portrayed a world where hideous deeds and political violence lay behind smooth words and youthful certainties, the supercilious and the cunning were on the ascendant. All their talk served to hide things away. It was just like the modern world. The trick in the novel is that there are no demons, just people, for it is the people who are the demons. The novel was a mirror, and in it I saw our own faces staring back at us.

I decided I should visit a few people to say farewell. The list was surprisingly short. A couple of friends and colleagues. I discovered, when Aria left to fly to a fascinating new future in California with her fascinating new man, that most of 'our' friends had been her friends. They couldn't be bothered with me. I say this without rancour as Aria was indeed a bright star in the firmament, outward-going and engaging, not to mention beautiful, so it was natural for her to be the glue in our social web which, when she left, fell apart.

I did have one friend, Jimmy James, who stuck with me, at least for a while. He saw me as his drinking buddy, although he did most of the drinking. He was a geologist who assured me, with great earnestness, that since earth's climate was changing all the time anyway, I shouldn't worry my pretty little head about a bit of CO_2. I realised, listening to him expound on the beauty of rocks, that he was very much like my childhood friend Cargill, who'd also liked the sound of his own voice, and our friendship mainly consisted of me listening while he sounded off about things that interested him.

When I took leave of him, however, he clapped me on the shoulder in a comradely way. 'Go tell it on the mountain,' he said.

'What do you mean?'

'I'm not sure. It's a song. You should hear Paul Robeson singing it. Send shivers down your spine. It came to me when I thought of you up there on Mt Cook, scratching in your notebook. When you tell it on a mountain, the whole world can hear.'

He must have been a little drunk when he said that. I didn't know what he was talking about.

I also visited my grandfather, now in his nineties. He was still in the same house in Grantley Street. Grandma had died but he stubbornly lived on, only reluctantly accepting help with shopping and domestic chores. He sat in his old, familiar chair, but now his box of photographs was pushed to one side and his tray, which he kept on his knees, was empty.

'Your father's got the dementia,' he said reprovingly, as if this was due to some inherent weakness in my father. He'd never been totally convinced by his daughter's choice of husband. 'Early onset, they call it.' There was a touch of satisfaction in his voice, a little snort of contempt. He was proud to have escaped dementia. 'I've buried a daughter to cancer, I don't want to bury my son-in-law. There may be such a thing as living too long. I've had my fill of people.' He pointed to the box of photographs, 'the past is full of people, wham-bam, they all went their own way. They're all dead now. Dead as doornails. I used to like to remember them, arrange my memories, but now I can't be bothered. I don't care what happens, I just don't want the dementia. It terrifies me. They see things, you know, that aren't there. I had a friend who got the dementia. Bill. Bill thought he was living with a cat. He even bought cat food and put it in a bowl. He'd see the cat all around the place. But there was no cat. There never had been. He added the cat himself. I don't want to start doing that. I don't even like cats that much. Your grandmother did though. Bev loved her cats. I know she's gone, but sometimes I pretend she's still here, maybe in the kitchen making some tea, or maybe she's just popped around the corner to buy butter or bread. I don't want to start thinking like that or I'll end up like Bill with his imaginary cat.'

'I don't think you're in any danger of losing your mind, Grandad. You don't miss much.'

'That's right. I know my right hand from my left. But some things I've never quite made up my mind about. Your mother was a commie. I was disappointed with that. Then you stood against the war. I had to admire you for that, although, you know, we had to hold back the commies. I always thought your mother was responsible for you being a conchie. Bit of military training never hurt a young man. But you had guts, I'll give you that. I always thought you read too many books. It does your head in, reading all the time. Bev used to read those women's magazines. They did her head in. I always preferred gardening. The more you can grow, the less you have to buy. I'm past it now. I've got a guy who comes and mows the lawn. I've had to let the garden go. Did you say you were going to see your father?'

'Yes. I'm leaving town for a while. Doing some field work up near Mt Cook.'

'It'll be as cold as a witch's tit up there. Don't get frostbite. I heard of a bloke who got frostbite and lost his toes.'

As I left I noticed that indeed the weeds had won against the chemicals, at least for the moment, and the garden was flourishing with golden rod, dock, clover and buttercup. I suspected at some point Grandad would just get it all sprayed. Those weeds were worse than commies.

That was the last time I saw my grandfather.

Do you remember that Russian girl?

Meeting with my father was another kind of mirror. The slippage between words and their meanings was reflected in my father's state of mind. Pieces of language floated around in his mind, attached to memories, while the memories themselves were not attached to any coherent narrative. Time had turned into bubbles.

'You always did like to get away from it all,' he said, sounding very composed, almost scholarly. 'You used to wander up the river on your own when you were hardly five. You were a strong little bugger. Sometimes Mum and I wondered if you'd ever come back. You'd bring back frogs and put them in a jar.'

I didn't know where the frogs came from. They were a bit like Bill's cat. I'm not sure that there were frogs in Hanmer. My father might have been remembering something he did as a child.

We were sitting in his neatly maintained living room in his modest retirement village apartment. Morning sun, coming through the sliding doors, made a neat, light square on his beige carpet. He loved order, having everything in its right place. That way he knew where he was. His body did at least. He could put out his hand and find the teapot. He was still able to live alone, but that wouldn't last. One day he would wake up and fail to recognise his own room.

Neither of us talked about when he would need to go into care.

'Do you remember that Russian girl?' he said. 'The girl you were friends with back in the day? What was her name?'

'Olga.'

'That's right. You brought her home to dinner one time.'

'I don't think so,' I said. 'I went to her place for dinner.'

He gave me a querulous look, as if maybe there was something wrong with my memory. 'You brought her home. We ate meatballs, because that's what they eat in Russia. Mum had a terrible time trying to make them.'

I didn't argue. And besides, maybe he was remembering something I'd forgotten.

'I saw her the other day,' he said.

'What...?'

'Oh yes.' He spoke with absolute assurance.

'She'd be all grown up now. Probably married with kids.' I laughed a little at the idea. Would I know her if I saw her in the street, I wondered.

'Of course,' he said, but sounded dubious. Memories don't grow up. 'You said you were going to marry her. Mum and I had a good laugh about that.'

'I'm sure you did. That was a long time ago, Dad.'

'Not that long as the eagle flies.' He laughed at the sight of time turning into space.

'Where did you see her?'

'I was with Grace,' he said, referring to a friend who often took him for drives. 'Olga was just walking along the street. Carrying a skipping rope.'

'Oh.' Like a carry-over from somewhere else, I thought. Another time, another place, another story. Still a child, skipping into eternity.

'They didn't really fit in, you know. They could hardly speak English. Her dad opened a shop. He was built like a beer barrel. I went in once to ask for soup. He thought I was asking for soap. But I wanted soup. He couldn't say soup.'

He laughed.

'Soap! He could have done with some, I reckon. Those Russians don't take baths, you know. Her mum was like a little fat hen.'

'I uh, don't remember much. Except Olga.'

'You need words to remember things. As soon as you said her name, Olga, I could see her plain as day, coming down the street after school looking for you. Mikee, she called you. If you don't have the right word, you can forget things.' He pointed to bowl of fruit and vegetables on the table. 'That purple thing, what is it?'

'It's an aubergine.

'Aubergine,' he repeated. 'That's a strange word. I'd forgotten it. You see, because I couldn't remember its name, I didn't know what it was. It looked very strange sitting there with the apples and potatoes.'

I thought it looked strange too. 'It's sometimes called an eggplant, or a mad apple.'

'Mad apple,' he said. He was losing his way among these words, struggling to find his feet in the conversation. 'I saw Mum the other day. She didn't even look at me or say hello.' He laughed briefly. 'I think she's leaving me. She's in love with the doctor, you know.'

'Do you mean Mum, I mean my mother, your w-wife, or your m-mother?' I stumbled through that one, feeling ham-fisted with words. I was on the edge of stuttering again, just like I used to do with Dad when I was young.

'Who? They all have mothers, you know. I thought you'd know that. It's like the girls. All the girls have legs, have you not noticed? I see them everywhere. It's a crying shame. Next thing they fall in love with their doctors. Next thing they're reaching for their coat hangers. It's the same old story. Every time you turn around someone'll take a piece of you. A bit like a roast turning on a spit...'

His voice trailed into a mumble. Somewhere he was turning a roast on a spit, watching the fat splatter into the fire. Maybe a long summer evening, friends around for a beer and a barbeque. The echo of light chatter and laughter. Kids playing with someone's dog. Was that a real memory or something that was supposed to have happened?

He stared out the window. Another day was happening out there. Not much else. A lot of coming and going to little effect.

'There's another thing. You had a friend no one else could see.' He laughed. 'I don't know if they ever came home for dinner, because you never introduced us' He laughed again. 'This friend didn't have a name and I thought that was peculiar, since you were so big on names. Everything had to have a name. I don't know why I remember that now. My memory's got all churned up. That Russkie girl believed you, poor wee thing. She said she could talk to your friend too.'

He laughed, longer this time, and when he came out of the laugh he was in a different place. He looked at me accusingly, 'These women who come in the morning. I can't really look after them, you know. I've got enough on my hands. What with one thing and the other. This business with Mum....' He trailed off into a mumble again. The square of light on the floor had shifted.

'They're your helpers, Dad.'

He regarded me intently, and with some suspicion. 'Listen, I must have had an accident. I can't remember things properly. I've been waiting for hours for the doctor to come. Mum and I...' He stopped half way through his sentence and looked around. It was a long way to the end of the sentence. Meanwhile the beginning of the sentence was lost to time and distance. He stared at me, stricken.

As I was leaving, he clapped me stiffly on the shoulder. Up close I could see how old he was starting to look. It came as a shock. We get used to seeing people the way we remember them. In some way his face was older than Grandfather's.

He grinned at me, and I could see a young person's face hiding inside the old.

'Next time you come, bring your sister,' he said. 'She's a sweet kid.'

Capturing the ineffable in the net of mind

I paid a final visit to my meditation group. In the dark days after Aria's departure, I came across them by accident. In the public library, I got talking to an earnest young man who was searching for books on Buddhism. He and his friends would get together and meditate or chant. The idea of people getting together and not talking intrigued me.

Most of the group, except for a serious young woman who worked at the bank, were of the stoned hippy variety who sat around ostentatiously with their legs crossed, their eyes closed and beatific smiles on their faces, humming or chanting AUM, which is the primordial sound of the universe, something like the Buddhist version of microwave background radiation that got the cosmologists so excited.

I enjoyed the silence, the freedom from words. I could rest easy, away from the babble of language. The chanting didn't bother me too much.

After the meditation they would talk about their experiences, erecting gaudy edifices of sound, their breath rushing in their throats. They were dogged by the hopelessness of trying to describe the indescribable, to capture the ineffable in the net of the mind. Words can wear their meanings like colourful cloaks, but beneath the cloaks you find a great flapping nothingness.

It was the nothingness that interested me, for it was real while their ideas were like fireflies in the deepest night.

I found the ongoing discussion about who and what the divine force was tedious. Developing a set of fixed ideas about it seemed like a fool's game to me. The quest for certainty in a provisional creation is doomed to failure. It wasn't words I wanted to take away from those sessions. I wanted to be touched by an energy beyond thought.

In the silence I could feel myself expanding, spreading through space and time, growing lighter, airier (not Aria), free from the time-bound bonds of words and their associations. Words were a burden I could leave at the doorway to silence. I'd be free of them one way or another. Either I'd leave them behind or they'd leave me behind. Or both. One day you would come. You would be as tall as the sky. Like some god, you would stoop down and withdraw words from the world.

There was a truth in that wordless state that words could not approach.

Sometimes the group chanted together, but I didn't join in. I may not have known the meaning of the sounds, since they were in a foreign language, Sanskrit probably, but they created pre-determined patterns in the silence, ripples in the mind, stones thrown into a still pool. I noticed that the woman from the bank didn't chant either.

It took a long time for all that shouting between Aria and me to fade away. My first meditations were full of the raucous noise we used to make. All I could see was that candle from Du Mu's poem, slowly burning down into a shapeless mass while our voices did the same.

I found I could engender my own meditative silence at home, the same little apartment I'd shared with Aria. Somehow that apartment had grown bigger since Aria left. My meditative silences made it even bigger. A few short steps from the fridge to the sink to the toilet to the bedroom – who needed more? I wanted to strip my life of all superfluous things.

Sometimes I returned to the wilds of North Brighton where I'd tried to outrun my adolescence. I liked it out there in the tussocky largeness. The blackberry memories of spying on lovers or searching for katipō spiders or leaping from sandhill to sandhill as if I were weightless. I could meditate in those wilds. In fact, it didn't feel like meditation at all, just a natural state of receptivity, a state I knew well from my childhood. I didn't have to do anything special. I didn't have to do anything at all.

Some who lose a relationship become desperate to hook up again. To find a replacement. Somebody to fill the void. I was perverse; I liked the void. The void took me beyond words. Beyond the needs of words, because words are needy things. They get hungry. I could lie on my back in the tough marram grass and look up into the great throbbing heart of things as empty as a bell jar. I felt like an ant gaping at infinity.

I wasn't trying to find god or anything fancy like that. I knew that I didn't have to 'find' god because god was everywhere I looked, even in the darkness of the human heart. I just wanted to enjoy a moment's peacefulness in which I could observe what arose and what passed away without fear or favour. That didn't seem like too much to ask. These moments provided me with a brief holiday from myself and my preoccupations; there was nothing particularly spiritual about them.

My interest in the meditation group faded, but I paid them a final visit. I felt warm towards everybody. They all smiled and welcomed me. They put their hands together in greetings. We were just human beings, mortal, perishable, and we could never be greater than ourselves.

Charlie's place

Charlie's Café was the last outpost of the city, a jumping off point into the great unknown and an intermediary zone to land in upon returning. A decompression chamber of sorts. Situated in a decaying corner shopping centre that boasted a dairy which never seemed to close, a pre-loved clothes shop which never seemed to open and a family-owned pharmacy which also sold film rolls, Charlie's had the unloved feel of a business on the skids. The 1940s red-bricked buildings looked ripe for demolition. The shop verandas looked saggy and the windows above them filled with dust. At one time this might have been a busy corner, with local people coming to shop, now there wasn't much but an occasional kid shooting through on a crate-scooter.

In Charlie's I was nothing, a nobody, just another transient sitting at a table drinking mediocre Kona coffee. Charlie's represented neutral ground for me; I didn't have to pretend to do anything, or to have any ambitions, or be working on anything, I could just sit in that very ordinary café and watch ordinary life going on around me. I didn't have to appear as if I had a life to go back to, a partner waiting for me at home. I didn't have a fancy new pager to check, a diary to consult or papers to peruse.

In Charlie's I was between worlds.

I was first drawn to the place because it had almost nothing to recommend it. No polish, no style, no atmosphere, no pretentions. Just an ordinary tea-room. A dozen tables with red-and-white chequered plastic tablecloths. You could get a milk-shake, a cup of tea or coffee, a choice of cheese and tomato sandwiches (toasted if you preferred), or asparagus rolls – and for sweets, lamingtons, custard squares or raspberry slices with pink icing on top.

I stumbled on the place by accident when leaving town one time, on the run from shouting matches with Aria, and found there a soothing anonymity. The scruffy-looking red-haired girl waiting tables was perfectly indifferent to me. I could drink my coffee, read my newspaper, and let the world go its own merry way. Sitting at one of Charlie's unremarkable tables, I could take a step away from my life. I had momentary glimpses of my life as if it were lived by something else. Above all, except for a mumbled thanks to the scruffy red-head, I didn't have to talk to anybody.

I hadn't realised how debilitating those rows with Aria had become, how they emptied me, how they smashed the delicate veins of language I had been cultivating to better understand the world. It was in the wounded silences between the shouting matches that I began to understand the carbon cycle, the finely tuned energy balances that marked the Holocene and the shit storm that was on its way. It was as if the breakdown of my relationship was nested within a larger breakdown I could barely conceive.

Just around the corner from Charlie's was a motel with the ridiculously bland name Belle-view Motel. Perhaps it was so named because it had no view. In its lack of pretentions, it was a perfect match for Charlie's, right down to the chequered plastic tablecloths. Its rooms were exactly what you might expect from a cheap motel, a perfect place to spend twenty-four hours of extended anonymity.

The large woman who ran the Belle-view Motel, and who spent most of her time sitting in her tiny office in front of her TV screen, didn't show the slightest interest in me, which suited me fine. There was no breezy chatter about where I had come from or where I was going. With a face composed into a graven mask, she would sit in a perpetual half-dark with the prattle of the TV washing over her in a constant white noise.

It suited my purposes. I could lie around and listen to the city unfolding in the morning, or read a nineteenth century novel, or perhaps some early naturalist like John Lewis, Richard Maybey or Thoreau, and listen to the bash of traffic from the streets. These were hours I owed to nobody. If I didn't want to say hello to the man who walked his dog as I passed him on my way to Charlie's, I'd walk straight on as if deep in thought.

Sometimes I listened to the concert programme on the radio. I liked Bach's clinical approach to improvisation, but also enjoyed the Romantics for their bombast. I was drawn to the female composers like Fanny Mendelssohn and Clara Schumann as well as Edvard Grieg and Gabriel Fauré. In these composers I sensed a preoccupation with and surrender to nature. For them, human suffering took place on a grand, cosmic scale, not a tawdry Belle-view Motel's level. Lying on a cheap mattress and staring at the grimy ceiling, I could re-live scenes from my life with Aria as if they belonged to some grand passion play while the music boomed on.

Grief can make the world feel unreal. Everyone becomes an impostor. Music can reconnect us with ourselves, bring our tears to the surface, bring us trembling back into the world. In that state, I came to understand that the true me, the real me, was still a child, moving with the wind and shadows and in no need of a name.

It was while lingering over an after-breakfast coffee at Charlie's, on my way to the Alps on my secret mission, that I met Chad. In retrospect, I find it odd that while I knew Chad only fleetingly, he had a profound effect on my feelings about the world. I had reached a pivot in my life, a turning point, a point of no return. My visit to the Alps would change everything.

A nineteenth century novelist might have described Chad as portly, but he was a thick-set man without much surplus weight. He had thinning hair, a blunt, no-nonsense face and bulging eyes. Like me, he was flicking through the morning paper. He slurped his coffee loudly and made a choking sound as he read an article.

'Christ almighty!' he said, loud enough for everybody to hear. 'These people should be shot. Put up against a wall and shot.'

Charlie's was nearly empty. There was an old guy with long, thin grey hair and an olive-green quilted jacket, and a woman in shorts and t-shirt who looked like she'd dropped in for coffee while out for a jog. I suddenly imagined that her name was Shona. They glanced at Chad without any great interest.

'Shoot who?' The waitress with the curly red hair and skinny, bloodless fingers was called Glenda, according to the little badge on her blouse. She was at the counter, doing some calculations on a piece of paper and didn't sound that interested in the answer, rather distracting herself from a boring morning.

The loud man took the bait, 'The politicians. Every bloody one of them.' He looked around as if expecting murmurs of sympathy. None came. He tapped a thick finger on the newspaper as if summoning judgement. 'You know what they're on about now? Setting up a tribunal to hear Māori grievances under the Treaty. Grievances! Grievances for Christ's sake! I've got grievances, plenty of them. They should set up a tribunal to hear my grievances.'

'That would be a bloody joke,' Glenda said. She seemed to be considering the sad custard squares sitting in their perspex cabinet.

The loud man stared loudly at her. He turned and looked at me aggressively, as if I were responsible for everything that was upsetting him. He glared at the old man in the quilted jacket, who regarded him steadily, and the woman in shorts who was departing rather quickly.

'Bloody liars, that's what they are.'

I looked as neutral as I could. He did not seem like the sort of person to engage with.

'What's this crap about Māori grievances? Christ! They should be glad to be alive. We conquered them, didn't we? They almost died out. Pity we didn't finish the job.'

'That's not funny,' Glenda said. She'd paused her calculations and was giving the loud man hostile looks from the counter. 'Shoot you more like it,' she said. She looked at the custard squares but they had nothing to offer.

Chad pretended to look taken aback. 'Well... fuck me,' he said. 'Well... you're just a fucking ginga, what would you know?'

Glenda shrugged and went back to her calculations. Her fingers were hooked around her pen like claws. 'Enough to know a moron when I see one.' Her voice crackled at the back of her throat.

He gave me a raised-eyebrow look, inviting me to join his mock astonishment. He seemed pleased at the response he'd provoked.

I grinned at him and he grinned back.

'Never trust a ginga,' he said.

It was time for me to hit the road, but the loud man stood up, gathered his coffee, came to my table and plonked himself down in front of me.

My fault for breaking the golden rule: never smile at a crocodile.

'I'm Chad,' he said, 'and I'm a farmer.' Such a bald pronouncement reminded me of AA meetings where someone stands up and says, 'Hi, I'm Chad and I'm an alcoholic' and everybody says in chorus 'Hello Chad.' He stared at me as if waiting for me to take issue with him over his declaration. He stared at my face, checking out my skin colour.

'You've got a very Anglo-Saxon name,' I said.

'I do? I didn't know that.'

'Chad. It comes from the old Ceadda. It means protector and defender.'

'Well fuck my brown dog! How did you know that?'

'I'm fascinated by names. In Welsh it means battle warrior.'

When he grinned, he looked like a kid barely out of primary school. 'Now you're talking!' He thumped the table and the coffee cups jumped. 'If they think we're just going to stand by and let this shit happen, they've got another think coming. They'll suddenly find they're dead meat. I've had a gutsful.'

'What of?'

'These fucking tree huggers for a start.'

Chad was one of those rabid individuals who see sinister implications in any measures a government might take for the public good. For them, there was no such thing as the public good, just their own, individual interest. And they turned nasty when crossed. Such people somehow managed to be both complacent and angry at the same time, and had a tendency to use violent imagery, like putting people against a wall and shooting them.

'I hate to break it to you, Chad, but I am one of those tree-huggers. Maybe not physically, but in my mind. Without trees we'd be dead.' I wanted to tell him that tree-huggers were not new, that back in 1730, in Rajasthan, India, a group of women sacrificed their lives protecting sacred trees from the emperor who wanted to fell them to build a palace. Over three-hundred-and-sixty people were beheaded by the emperor's soldiers, but I didn't want to give Chad any ideas.

Chad considered me with a mixture of revulsion and rage. He looked as if he were about to tear my head off. 'And you'd come onto my land and tell me how to run my farm.'

'Maybe. I mean, what if you, or any other farmer, were mistreating your animals, starving them maybe. Don't you think somebody should intervene in such a case?'

'Why would I mistreat my animals? Why would any farmer? After all, they're our livelihood, you dipshit. We don't need any government,' he spat out the word, 'coming onto our land and inspecting our animals. My animals are probably better fed than you. Especially if you eat the crap in this place.' He looked over at Glenda to make sure she was taking it in, and at the old guy in the quilted jacket who seemed entertained by the proceedings.

I knew it was hopeless. I knew before I started. He was a junkman through and through. He believed that his power over his land, his rights as a landowner, were absolute. Subject to no higher power. I was wasting my words. I might as well have said nothing. This whole conversation was futile.

Glenda, dispensed with her calculations, came over and slapped Chad's bill on the table. 'Eggs on toast, two coffees' she said in a scratchy voice. Her skin was so pale her freckles stood out as flecks of gold.

'Isn't the second one free?' Chad said, looking aggrieved.

'That was yesterday.'

Chad was nonplussed. He was at a loss for words, but I suspected not for long. He looked at me, inviting me to share his astonishment and outrage, and I grinned at him. I was enjoying his little performance. For a second he returned my grin, then resumed his outrage.

'I take that personally,' he said in a wounded voice.

'You can take it any way you like', she said, 'you still gotta pay.'

Chad looked at me, 'She's fucking lippy,' he said.

For the first time Glenda smiled, but it was not a complicit grin, rather a saccharine sneer. 'Gingas have sharp *claws*,' she said, hooking her bloodless fingers into eagle's talons.

'What happened to customer service?' Chad asked me as he dug into his pocket for the money.

The old guy winked at me as I walked out of Charlie's.

I checked out of the Belle-view Motel and headed for the hills.

Go tell it on the mountain

In the mountains I feel shorn. Like a sheep that's lost its wool too early in the season. The addictive city person who leaps into the furious business of manufacturing a self, or at least the illusion of a self, fades fast in these vast, chilly spaces. The unimpeded wind and deep silence between peaks soon strip me back to my essentials. I have no need for the paraphernalia of an everyday personality.

I can walk upright under a tall sky without any props. I can think about Aria without falling into a gravity sink. I can gaze out over the world of humankind with something approaching serenity, and in full cognisance of my mortality. I don't have to live up to anybody's expectations. I don't have to pretend to be ambitious or aspire to the grandiose. I don't have to maintain a public version of myself. I can ground myself in observing nature; observation seems to be my natural condition. I don't have to think, just watch and listen, feel and smell. And take my cue from creatures who have nothing to prove.

I was frightened at the thought of being without you. With you just a whisper away, I am never alone, at least not that awful existential aloneness that so besets humankind. You had been absent before, but mostly when I had no need of you. When I was certain of my words. When Aria filled my life I hardly ever sought you out. Now, however, with the world clawing at me, I needed you as confidant and companion. I feared a growing darkness of mind.

I argued with you long into that first night in the mountains while setting up a base camp to the west of the Ball Pass Crossing. You were as hard and sharp-edged as the adamantine found in Marvel Comics. I had never seen you like that. Always, you had been about warmth and receptivity and the comfort of true speech. You were there when the emptiness grew too endless. Now, you were withdrawing. It was up to me.

This was my chance. My freedom.

In my tiny mountain tent, at base camp, I began a journal consisting mostly of lists, lists of plants, animals and insects, cross referenced to times, places and altitudes. I jotted down a few observations on what I saw, and took photos. I knew the real value of my work would lie in the data I collected. I kept another list, this one of species I would expect to find but didn't. That was just as important as the first list.

Sitting there on that first night, with my journal on my lap, I felt something approaching contentment. For the first time since Aria had decamped, life seemed possible again. Life, if not love. In the meantime, I'd settle for life. It was a perfect evening. The stars were bright and sharp and there was no wind. The air is rarely still on the mountains, so when the wind drops the stillness can seem like magic. The sudden stillness of the air. The eternal stillness of the mountains. The chill purity of snow. The silence of a star-filled sky. The rush of mind continued unabated, of course. Mind was driven by its own winds. I could hear it, like a cacophony of whispering voices. In the city I was hardly aware of it. Up here I could catch phrases and tones, snatches of conversation and a voice that drones on like a never-ending radio broadcast.

The mountains come from deep down and reach high. Their voices still boom across the sky. Their thunder reverberates through our feet. Their massive presence is an antidote to quantum infirmity; their bleak insistence is no conman's tale. You can die fast up here or live a million years.

I began to think of myself in the third person. A necessary displacement. Standing aside from myself, I could see that this individual known as Michael Paewai Meer was a pastiche largely determined by the self-reinforcing patterns of his life. He was a zombie person driven by his hungers. All that silly business with Aria. The Icarus flights into pleasure. The crashing with burning wings. The foolish agonising. This Michael Paewai Meer was not somebody I wanted to identify myself with at that moment. He was like the blindfolded slave pushing a grinding wheel. More precisely, perhaps, he was a social construct, a simulacrum, programmed to do what his creators wanted him to do before discarding him. Well, I could discard him first. Get it over with. If I had to die to the world, so be it; without death there is no renewal, I told myself.

When the winds did come, they blew more than just the city cobwebs away. Everything not nailed down gets blown away. Michael Paewai Meer was nothing more than a cluster of cells clinging to a rock and seeking out the crevices, but it felt that what was left of him was as real as it got, windblown but integral, shorn but whole. Red blood and white bones.

I liked the mountains because there was nothing I could do but concentrate on the task at hand. The grinding wheel eventually grinds up the slave and his hapless cries. The mountains don't care about humanity. Theirs is a monumental indifference. Caring can be a problem if you care about something which is already doomed. I was not reminded of humanity every time I left my tent, not reminded of Aria's beautiful face, of heartbroken streets and sad custard squares. The falcon flies straight and true.

The mountains offered no comfort. Doom was nothing new to them. They saw a vast continent ripped apart, and reborn, thrust up out of the ocean. Earthquakes and cataclysms ruled.

Maybe that's why I felt so at home there, nestled in my particularities like a bird with its nest in the crevices.

First there is a mountain

During my first year at university, a song by the singer Donovan became popular that contained what I thought was a nonsense lyric:

First there is a mountain
Then there is no mountain
Then there is

On singing these lyrics to myself I would run the words together, *firstthereisamountainthenthereisnomountainthenthereis* which must have been the longest word I ever tried to say. The words seemed like a lot of silly nonsense until I was old enough to go up into the mountains and see for myself, watch them disappearing as the mist rolled in, reappearing briefly before buried in the grey sky again.

There was mystery in the way something so huge could appear, disappear and appear again.

From my vantage point to the east of Mt Aoraki I could witness this wonder several times a day. A cloud would come and bear the mountain away, then the light would come and restore it Donovan's lyric reenacted many times.

Mountains are always masters of mystery, I decided. Like that other mystery, love. First it's there, then it isn't, then it is. You see it, then you don't see it, then you see it. Perception's own three act drama.

There was almost nothing of man's works up near the clouds, just an occasional stick with a yellow top to mark remnants of an old track, or an artful arrangement of stones. The rest is jumbled rock and sky.

And memory.

Memory is like a second, ghostly landscape superimposed on the physical one, I realized as I gazed at the imposing mountain. We walk through both worlds at once. There are crevices and cliffs in both, and what appears to be an easy path may not turn to be so easy. A shale strewn slope may turn into a room where a little boy lies on a bed reading a book about strange and unlikely creatures. A valley may become a street on which cowboys ride after mustering. That isn't fantastical realism, it's just the way the mind works. For all I knew this dual world might run through all of nature, wherever there is any memory or cognition. A bird might remember the nest in which it hatched even as it enjoyed the open-winged skyway.

In the end the physical landscape and the mental one became hopelessly entangled. Quantum entanglement of dimensions. Most of the time this was not evident, but up on high it became a stark truth, a rock face scribbled over with thought.

The mountain was like a metronome. It rocked back and forth between night and day. There was a music in it I couldn't quite hear, but I could sense its time signature. Walking on the mountain, there's a lyric in the air.

A spark of life wrapped in a few feathers

In the morning, after a quick breakfast of coffee and trail-mix, I scouted around base camp. I didn't see anyone else, not even on the Ball Pass Crossing. The weather had held and there was only the occasional ruffle of wind to disturb the stillness. I didn't see any rock wren, but I was not surprised. The *Passeriformes acanthisittidae*, also known as the pīwauwau, or mātuitui, was a tiny bird for such big names. No bigger than a sparrow, shy and secretive, and weighing no more than a handful of rice, its green back and yellow front made it easy to miss in the jumble of rocks and moss.

Despite Janet Holden's wise words about how de-rigueur extinction was in the life of the planet, I felt this pretty bird deserved a better fate than to become rat food and disappear, unmourned, from the face of the earth. I couldn't bear the thought that they'd already gone extinct. It's one thing to sit with Janet in her comfortable office, or the gloomy privacy of the staff club, and talk calmly about extinction events, quite another to sit on a mountain side and listen vainly for the chatter of a tiny wren.

My feet took me upward. I had a primordial urge to reach the highest point my feet could reach. I left the Hooker Valley track, and the Hooker glacier to the west of Aoraki Mount Cook, and made my way up the eastern slopes towards some of the lesser peaks, keeping a sharp eye out for the little birds.

I kept my eye out for other things too. Rat and stoat droppings, anything that might indicate the presence of predators.

The first plant that caught my eye was the dome-like, ivory-coloured flower cluster of the penwiper, *Notothlaspi rosulatum*, a plant that flowers in its second year and then dies, stubborn yet fragile. Mate and die. I took photographs, carefully noting the location of each one, trying to get a picture of the diversity of the field. I scratched around and looked under rocks to see what sort of insect life I could find. Everything I saw was carefully recorded. I got pleasure from that exhaustive cataloguing, fitting everything together as if it were a puzzle. The apparent disorder of nature gave way to underlying patterns and hidden connections.

I did miss talking to you, even though I was prepared for your absence. A couple of times I started talking as if you were there only to realise there was a big empty space you had vacated. I had that big empty space inside to mirror the big empty spaces outside, the wedges of sky between the mountains, the silence of the long scree slopes.

My companions were my old friends, fungi, mosses, lichens, liverworts. I took lots of photos of *Umbilicaria hyperborea*, a fungus commonly known as blistered rock tripe, which can live on the most barren of substrates, bare rock, acidic wood, bricks, tiles, and even asphalt. I admired fungi and lichens that could do that, cling to sterile even toxic surfaces where nothing else could live. No competition.

There was also *Stereocaulon corticatulum*, a fructose lichen, found up to 3,000 metres. From a distance it looked like delicate white crystals rising two or three centimetres, or frosted flowers, but it was as hardy as life got.

I also noted widespread *Sphaerophorus melanocarpus*, which can be found almost as high as the *Stereococaulon*, and which appears to grow white bonsai trees. There is a whole world inside their frozen forests.

I took lots of photos, and realised I was happy. I still liked those impossible Latin names, and rolled them around on my tongue as I climbed. Once more I was like a mumbling priest scaling the heights of heaven, treading out his pilgrimage in sacred syllables.

I was making my way towards a point I called Mt Nobbly, a crest of rock five hundred metres or so above me. I planned to camp in the lee of it while I scouted around for signs of rock wren. That I hadn't seen any yet was starting to bother me. I thought it was just a matter of attuning my eyes to the rock and the hard light.

Previous studies suggested a decline in population, but to see none at all implied they were gone. At least from this area. I didn't want to think that, didn't want to have to peer too hard into cracks and crevices or between boulders for a spark of life wrapped in a few feathers.

When it's ready it will show itself, I thought. Or maybe when I'm ready it will show itself. I discarded both ideas, seeing in them the beginnings of superstition. If they're around I'd see them, eventually; if they weren't around, it didn't matter how ready I was.

When I reached my Mt Nobbly the top half of the mountains were beginning to float in the light, separated from their dark foothills fallen into shadows. It was little more than a vantage point. Behind it was a boulder-strewn slope, ideal rock wren country. Come to me, babies! Let's get some shots in this flinty light. But none showed their tricky little faces.

The top of Mt Nobbly was a flat surface where I could sit like a child with my legs dangling over the edge. I could sit there and bang my heels against the world and look down at the distant tree line, little more than a dark blur, where the mountain beech ended. Ball Park Crossing looked like a thin scratch. The landscape was unmoving, while colours from the sky passed over it. The eternal stillness of the mountains. The chill purity of snow. The silence of an empty sky.

A song my mother used to sing came to mind. She sang it because her mother had sung it. I used to sing along with her, and could do it without stuttering.

On top of old Smokey,
All covered with snow,
I lost my true lover
From courtin' too slow.

I told her that old Smokey must be a volcano.

On top of old Smokey,
I went for to weep,
For a false-hearted lover
Is worse than a thief.

Beside me, on the rock on which I was resting, was a perfect example of a *Placodioid* lichen, with dark yellow, crusty circles. *Rusavskia elegans.* The name slipped into my mind, comfortable and familiar. Was that Olga, hiding inside the name? It seemed primeval to me, a scraping of life on a rock, a patch of colour as antediluvian as life itself. Except in spectacular circumstances, mountains are the most solid ground you can walk on, and the flora that grow here are ancient. Mists roll in and out and winds do their worst, but mostly the rocks remain unmoved and the *Rusavskia elegans* holds tight to them.

Before the light faded, I put down my pack and checked out the boulder-strewn slope. The boulders were like huge versions of the stones of my childhood river. The slope was like a river-bed made for giants. I moved slowly and carefully. I watched out for movement. Rock wrens are rock-hoppers, always on the move. I might walk right past one sitting still, but movement will give them away.

I was disappointed that I didn't see any; their absence saddened me. The world was a much emptier place than it should have been.

A brief pause between eruptions

I had the best gear on the market. Previously, as an investment in future field work, I'd spent up large. My backpack was made of tough canvass and leather strips, light-framed and designed to fit snugly on the human back; the sleeping bag, with hood, was like a fluffy dream, and the self-inflating mattress popped up out of a coil of plastic no bigger than my hand like a genie out of a bottle. I had a weatherproof torch with a powerful beam, a mini gas-cooker, a billy, and several pairs of thermal underclothes. My quilted vest was padded with duck down. I had tea and food bars. I was ready for nights in the wild away from my base camp and my tent.

Darkness gathered in the sky like an invading army, then came down fast. I found a level spot between two giant rocks, somewhat out of the wind, and made myself comfortable. I boiled water for tea and crunched on a protein bar. Before inflating my space-age, ultra-thin, ultra-tough, mattress, I went a good distance from my camp and had a crap under the stars, using a little trowel to bury it as best I could. My torch made a thin, cold beam in the vast dark. I aimed it at the sky as if I could illuminate the stars. There must have been some fast-moving high cloud because the stars came and went as if uncertain of their existence.

It was too dangerous to wander about in the dark. I sat on my flat rock and sensed the great range of mountains around me. The sense of the solidity of the mountain beneath my feet was a comforting illusion. Given a big enough time scale, even mountains are ephemeral.

What is this, our little country, but a brief pause between eruptions?

And I'd be a goner

Before settling in for the night, I used the torch to have a look around for wētā, who have the grand name Anostostomatidae which, if you can learn to say it, rolls rather magnificently off the tongue. Looking a bit like an overgrown cricket, these creatures could be found in alpine regions, and tended to come out at night to forage. I read that new alpine species of wētā had been recently discovered and wondered if I would spot one.

I had no more success finding a wētā than I did a rock wren.

Soon I was snug inside my sleeping bag. My physical tiredness was delicious. The sense of the landscape around me was overwhelming yet comforting. There was nothing moving but the wind. Nothing to chip at my rest but the stars, big and bright and sharp now the cloud had cleared. Sleep came without needing any enticement.

So did dreams. Tearful with homesickness, I was approaching earth from deep space. It began as a tiny speck and grew steadily larger. As it grew, my hopes surged. When it filled my vision, however, I saw that all the oceans had boiled away, the atmosphere had burned up, the mountains were sullen and denuded, no flakes of *Rusavskia elegans* in the crevices, and the planet was nothing more than a barren stone in space.

Suddenly I was back in Hanmer, in the middle of a wide river bed. Around me were large greywacke stones talking to each other in some gritty tongue. Olga was there and she was singing in Russian. Her voice floated above the hard language of the stones, loud and clear and sweet.

My father was there too. He looked like a large, shambling mountain man. He'd come looking for me and got lost. Now that he'd found me he asked me if I'd like a beer.

In the morning, I set out to explore a couple of ridge lines to the north of me, following the slope of boulders, keeping a sharp eye out for that quixotic bird. I moved as quietly and unobtrusively as a clumsy biped can. I even tried to dampen my thoughts as I suspected that birds could hear them, especially if they were loud. Birds always know when you are looking at them. I sat as still as I could, giving the rock wren the opportunity to show itself.

I had plenty of opportunities to check out the mosses, lichens and liverworts. Besides the *Rusavskia elegans,* which made me think of Olga, I identified some foliose lichens, *Parmelia signifera,* which sounded like the name of a woman of some significance, and *Umbilicaria* with their wrinkled lobes, which made me think first of my mother, then of you, mother of my words. What looked from a distance like an ice-white crystalline structure turned out to be the fungi *Stereocaulon corticatulum,* which can grow up to three thousand metres.

I found microscopic flowers, a tiny snow *hebe* in some rock crevices. Since they aren't usually seen this high, I noted them down as possible further evidence for the upward movement of flora.

A roll call of survivors, they are, the hardiest of the hardy. There should be photos of them on Janet's wall.

I took lots of photographs, which I would later use to build my report.

You need to be conscious to apprehend time, I thought, staring at these little blobs of life clinging to the rock. They can keep themselves going for many thousands of years and not know a single passing moment. That's the wonder of it. I envied their indifference to time and death. Death has no meaning to a fungus. Its spores carry the memory of life back to its very beginnings in the primordial swamps.

With that suddenness typical of the mountains, the clouds came down out of the sky, and a wet wind blew the drizzle back and forth. I didn't care too much. I'd lost the view but not the lichen, gleaming under droplets of water. I decided to backtrack to a spot on the ridge where I'd seen a flattish area to camp.

The wind dropped and the drizzle gave way to mist. I was blundering around in a raincloud.

It was slower going on the return journey. I had to make sure of every step. One slip up here and I'd be a goner. Even a twisted ankle could prove fatal. My base camp seemed worlds away; the great grinding city was in another universe altogether.

I didn't try to go too far. Aside from the danger of slipping, I could also get lost. I imagined the mist lifting to reveal a landscape I didn't recognize, with no way of knowing how to return to my base camp.

I quickly chose a spot where the slope was gentle and I couldn't roll. It was the best I could do. I sat for a while and waited for the wind that would send the mist on its way. Imperceptibly at first, colour began to leach from the world; the white mist turned grey. I inflated my mattress, climbed into my cocoon and waited for the dark to arrive. I zipped everything up as tight as I could, since mist like this will eventually soak through everything. I left a tiny gap through which I could see a little and breathe. I hoped I didn't have to pee until morning. I didn't bother turning on the torch. There was nothing to see. Best conserve power wherever possible.

Being so far away from humankind made it easy for me to imagine the world without humans. Little would change as far as these mountains were concerned.

During the Permian Extinction Event 250 million years ago, the ocean lost almost all its life. Global heating left sea-creatures unable to breathe. As temperatures rose and the metabolism of marine animals sped up, the warmer waters could not hold enough oxygen for them to survive. They drowned. That round of heating was caused by the massive emission of carbon dioxide by volcanic upheavals in Siberia.

Now we were entering another great extinction event, with humans playing the role of volcanos, and no matter how high I climbed, I could never escape it. My very purpose in being here was to calmly and methodically search for evidence of it.

I took some gulps of air and waited for sleep.

Hypsithocus hudsonae

Huddled in my cocoon for that second night, I had to face the stark reality of my situation. I had come up here of my own free will, and yet felt abandoned, like a child from a folk tale taken into the wilderness, deserted and left to die. I had a world full of words, but they had no purpose.

You made yourself scarce just so that I might feel this total abandonment.

One day you would leave me and take all of your spells with you, leaving me finally, and irrevocably, speechless. Then I would be well and truly helpless before eternity. There would be nothing to hold me upright. That day was coming at me full tilt. An abyss was opening up between me and language.

The world outside my cocoon was a vast, unknown ocean made up of night and mist. My consciousness was no more than a brief whirling shape on that ocean, brought into being by heat and light and just as easily dissolved by those same forces. Little wonder that extinction was the general rule of life. Alter those forces even slightly and those whirling shapes vanished.

Turning on my side, I had a view of a lump of rock I'd avoided when choosing my spot. From this perspective, it looked like a little mountain all of its own, with its ridges and sheer walls. I even saw what I thought were tiny spots of *Lecanora farinacea*, a crustose lichen, looking like miniature forests, but since there was no real light, just a sourceless glimmering, I couldn't be sure. Then I saw something I could be sure of, a little alpine shield beetle, looking monstrous this close up. A member of the chunky *Hypsithocus hudsonae* species.

'Hello little lady,' I said, glad to have something to talk to. 'You're pretty high up in the world.' As far as I knew, *Hypsithocus hudsonae* couldn't survive much higher than eighteen-hundred metres, and I was already higher than that. This was a female, capable of carrying between twenty and forty eggs. I had to produce my torch and use some precious power in order to see them, but there they were, arranged along her abdomen as if neatly planted by a careful gardener. I wondered what she was doing on her little mountain after dark. Looking for a dry spot to lay her eggs probably, maybe even attracted by my warmth. To her I would be like a big warm rock, a haven in the cold darkness.

I turned off my torch and kept an eye on her. It wouldn't pay for her to get too snugly. I wouldn't want to roll over and squash her. She seemed quite content to sit where she was, facing me, perhaps, like me, listening to the drips of moisture falling off the flap of my cocoon. This flap protected her little mountain to some extent.

As I lay there, inviting sleep, I seemed to enter into communication with the beetle who, I fancied, was here to guard over my slumber, and to ensure that my dreams did not overwhelm me. The soils up here were too thin and bitter for the micro leaves on which she relied, she told me. She could lay her eggs, but what would her offspring live on? Where were the succulent roots upon which they could feed? Where would they go on these bare, windswept rocks?

She would die soon, maybe before she got her eggs laid, maybe before I woke up in the morning. For her, every moment was a life-and-death struggle. I began to cry. Not muffled sobs but what my mother would call 'bawling your eyes out.' Tears hot as lava running down my cheeks, scalding my flesh. I couldn't say what I was crying for exactly: the beetle who could find nowhere to lay her eggs, Aria who was slipping over the horizon of my emotional life, my father losing his way among his thoughts, a world full of dying things. It didn't matter. These were tears that had been bitten back by falsely comforting words.

The beetle didn't cry. She continued to be stoic and meticulous; she had a job to do. Her only requirement was the necessity of the moment, and the moment after that. All she had to do was live.

Time lost its footing. Caught between one moment and the next, the mountains glided into a motionless world.

Up here, beyond the thick veil of noisy words, the universe began to show through from behind, membrane after membrane, delicate as the beetle's wing, the one and the many, dimensions interwoven with dimensions. Stars enfolded into space.

I saw myself in my cocoon, a larvae of grief, writhing about, pulsating with the energy of tears. I had no idea what would emerge from that cocoon. Above, in the night sky, the galaxy spun on its vast axis, a great nothingness at its centre. A beetle was crawling from star to star, from one starry arm to the next, in the opposite direction to the galaxy's spin, giving birth to worlds.

A tiny sphere of feathers

I woke up with cold dew on my face, staring at the galaxy. At some point I had unzipped the top part of my sleeping bag so that my head was open to the elements. The mist had gone. The little beetle had gone.

As soon as I stood up, the mountain on which she'd mounted her vigil was nothing but an anonymous stone at my feet. Above, the stars were arranged, fat and newly laid, in a dark without end. The ridge on which I'd been lying dropped away to sheer nothingness.

Bit by bit, the shadows drained away; bit by bit the world came into play. Mt Aoraki caught the first light. The first, faint brush of orange. I might be the only human being to have viewed this scene from exactly this vantage point and watched the sun pull the mountains up out of the face of the deep. Whatever else happened between now and eternity, the slow crumble of time, this moment would exist because I was there to witness it.

As I packed things away, taking care to put everything in its right place, I kept glancing northward, towards distant peaks but was looking at two days tramp at least – creeping along ridgelines was slow work. Two days there, two days back. I would run short of supplies.

The weather didn't feel good. Wind and sleety showers threatened. I thought of the rock wren who, some thought, could freeze themselves over the winter and unfreeze in the spring. I decided to return to my base camp. I'd replenish my stores and head off in a different direction, maybe west this time, towards Aoraki.

I scraped some lichens into sample bags. Their chemical composition would be analysed; another fragment of human knowledge would be added to the store.

The clouds were beginning to stack up in the west against a blue background. A front was coming in from the south-west; it would be in my teeth as I descended the ridge. I took plenty of care, especially when the rain arrived. In my mountain gear, I felt more like a spaceman walking on the moon than a man out in the elements. I clambered rather than walked, taking every precaution.

I didn't pause anywhere for long. The rain was nothing like the previous night's hanging sheets of mist, but nasty, windblown and full of little icy fragments, reminders of what a storm up here could be like.

I didn't remember the river. Maybe it was dry when I made my way up here. Now it was a swollen stream, turbid and freezing. There was no obvious way to cross over. I sat on the hard stones and stared at the opposite bank, so near but so far. I could almost jump it, but that was a big almost. I'd have to go upriver or down to find a crossing.

I was about to get up when I heard three short, high-pitched notes coming from the other bank, clear above the white noise of the stream. Rock wren! I held my breath, waiting to hear it again, searching the rocks across the stream, ready with my camera for a quick shot. The call wasn't repeated.

There was a movement among the rocks. I thought I saw the bird, but my eye might have snagged on the movement of water around the rocks. Such a tiny sphere of feathers, so easy to miss, or be mistaken.

There was a large, flat rock I could use as a stepping stone right in front of me. I could be across in a moment, maybe find some droppings, even glimpse the bird itself. It would take two short jumps, to the rock, and then to the other bank. It looked easy enough, but I wasn't sure how slippery the flat rock was. I couldn't see any signs of rock moss. It looked dry enough. It was time to take my chances. The other side was close. A wren was close, I was certain. I threw my pack across with a good heave. The stream was swift but narrow, bubbling against the stepping stone, threatening to wash over it.

I did all the calculations I could, then took the first jump. I teetered, but my boots held to the rough surface of the stone.

Now for the other bank.

Just one jump away.

Part Four

Balashikha

Inside the mirror wall

The suburban streets of Balashikha are long and empty, as if they have all the room in the world in which to stretch. Streaks of light and shadow are anchored to the facades of buildings.

Silence reigns.

Between the vacant houses and apartment buildings, their windows opaque with ochre dust, grass grows lank and untamed. Along the verges, wild flowers decorate the grasses with spots of colour: the purple *viola incisa* looking like an orchid, the mustard-tipped goldenrod and a magenta splash of peony.

Walking down the middle of the street, I am alone with my footsteps. Shuffling leaves accompany my shoes like a whispering audience. There is only the machinery of night and day, the passing hours gliding by on slippered feet and the mingled scent of flowers.

I have the city to myself, except for you of course. I feel you everywhere. For all I know you created the city, brick by brick, out of myth and memory. The apotheosis of your art, perhaps your final canvas. I wouldn't put it past you, and I have never known the full extent or the limitations of your powers. Or even who you really are. I was all too ready to relegate you to a secondary existence, a fantasy, a bit like the imaginary playmate my parents conjectured, little more than a metaphor for the arrival of language. It was you who put buttercups in my mouth.

I saw you as a word bringer, but you are more than that. You are a world-bringer. You need capitals: World Bringer. That looks better. I don't know how many World Bringers there are in all the realms, or if everybody has one, but I have come to see you as a demiurge, a fashioner of worlds. You are a cosmic entity, a confluence of unimaginable energies. I've had plenty of time to wonder which demiurge you might be, one capable of approaching a young boy as he walked upriver singing out his grief at the loss of his dearest friend, pulling him into the world of words, assemblages of sound as befits his species. I hope it wasn't

Yaldabaoth, an archon with the face of a lion and the body of a serpent, half flame and half darkness, who now rules over tormented souls as Lord of Chaos. Rather I see you as Ariel, spirit of air, of elemental entities and beasts. Wielder of fire. Mother of Aria. I could imagine Balashikha as a creation of Ariel, formed in the vortex of your dance, from the syllables of light and dark you broke open.

Humans are rowdy creatures. We fill the world with noise. Without people around, the silence becomes like a shimmering pool. Everything is caught in its image. The sounds of restless leaves or wind exploring the grass become a part of it. I am held as a shiver in the pool.

A blue jay flies across the sky, making blue ripples.

I was born from that shimmering pool. It was my mother. It nourished me in my bed of stars. It ushered me into the empty city when I was barely conscious. It gave me limbs and a mouth. It gave me the city to roam in, like a big empty house. It gave me songs from some remote time, ancient melodies I could sing to keep myself enchanted. It gave me all the time Ariel could create to find my feet, to roll back the boundaries of self, to lose my old past and grow a new one.

Once I had a life different from this one, a life in which I had a real mother and father, and a brother too. And grandparents. And Aria. Friends and colleagues. Projected from memory, that life was like a film pasted thinly against the Balashikha sky.

Despite patchy layers of dust and rank growth, the city is caught in the timeless zone of fable. Like the dark forest in which Hansel and Gretel found themselves, the city is both imaginary and real. If there is a place I can lose the world, it is here, in the unhurried quiet of the backrooms and backstreets and abandoned fountains of the empty city.

There are no people, or dogs and cats for that matter, but there are beetles and birds everywhere. There is the great tit and the yellow tit with their high-speed chirping; the great spotted woodpecker, always knocking like a visitor denied entry; a common tern crying out for an ocean. I've heard antique melodies from these birds. And the susurration of tiny creatures running their errands down on Insect Street. Beneath them the silence is unruffled.

Once I realised there were no people around, my muscles lost their tension. I remember people, streets full of them in cities that smoked like thuribles swinging on their chains. Snatches of popular songs hiding in pockets of air. I remember the whining sound of traffic, exploding voices and dreary monologues, the booming of war and suffering, the cries of oppression, the gathering of the last wave, the bleaching of humankind. A furious mutation. Blood and guts, fire and fury. A world gone wrong.

That was only a moment or two ago, it seems, but my years in Balashikha are stretched. Time here is like a bent guitar note. My memories fade among the vacant streets, silent parks with their tall pine trees, and where the Pekhorka River passes quietly into history.

If I walk far enough in one direction, I come to the mirrored wall which smoothly encircles the city. I go there to meet myself just as I did as a child in front of my mother's dresser with its triptych of my face. Although the wall bends imperceptibly, my image seems compressed. Compressed in time too, from subtle changes in the glass, for I appear to grow older and younger as I walk beside myself. I can follow the wall around to my starting point although it takes three days to do it. The wall is seamless, not a break anywhere. A miracle of rare device.

I remember a story about a ship called the *Mary Celeste*, found abandoned floating in the Atlantic, but with the crew's personal effects, food and a cargo of alcohol undisturbed. Balashikha is like that. While perishable goods not in a freezer have long since returned to fragments and fungal spores, the shops are full of tinned food and regular goods, the houses are full of clothes and personal belongings. Electricity hums. Street lights turn themselves on at night. Even the dust tidies itself away. It is as if everyone just walked out.

Perhaps some great disaster threatened the city, and everybody simply downed tools and made a run for it. What kind of disaster, was an unanswered question, as was why people didn't return when that disaster failed to strike. It must have failed, I reasoned, as the city seemed unharmed. No flood or fire or slurping mud had been through here; no meteor had struck. No invasion of wild, Topsell-like creatures. Perhaps the disaster had been a great wave of silence that that swept the land, people fleeing before it, fearful of losing their voices. The animals running with them. People and animals falling over each other trying to escape. Only the birds and the insects wouldn't care. Bird cries were impervious to the silence, in fact they thrived on it. It was their natural medium.

All this is speculation, but in the absence of any credible explanation, such conjecture is better than walking around in the complete absence of explanation. I would rather fabricate some narrative, however implausible, than accept the inexplicable.

Balashikha is quietly rewilding itself. Electricity still hums through its wires, but its foundations are returning to earth as the city settles into its past. It decays, only sluggishly, as if caught in slow-motion, and unevenly, time apparently embedding itself in some areas while passing over others. Currents of time wind through the city like a braided river. Things caught up in it surrender to their mortality. Other areas remain as if untouched, islands with the pristine feel of something newly created. Some of the buildings have gone wrinkly, mossy and bedraggled, with broken window panes and musty smells. Others still shine freshly in the morning light, shopping malls where muzak still plays on an endless loop, cans of food that look as they have just been placed on the shelf, supermarket doors that slide open and shut. Leftover pieces of conversation haunt the air.

All over the city machines are turning themselves off and on as if operated by ghosts. Dustless windows gleam and traffic lights still blink. I feel I might encounter other shoppers going about their business, pushing trolleys or carrying shopping bags, the air suddenly lighting up with chatter. At any moment everybody could reappear and life resume its normal course.

That doesn't happen. Everything from the freshest to the most decayed, is caught like a fly in amber, in one suspended moment.

In some places the funereal smell of time is overpowering, in other places the air is as fresh as the first morning of the world. The demiurge who created this city, be it Ariel or some like being, did not attempt to banish death from its dreaming streets, or prevent slow pockets of degradation from spreading. I found a dead seagull on Lover's Bridge. Crows had pecked out its eyes. Its eye sockets were teaming with ants. Ants are a sure harbinger of time.

In some places the stench of decay has been subdued by the smell of wild flowers in bloom. In other places wild flowers hang their heads.

Time creeps up from behind. It eats things from the inside out.

The world is only a step away

Although I know I'm alone, I keep thinking there are other people. I expect to run into someone but it doesn't happen. It's easy to imagine people slipping in and out of the shadows when my back is turned, or that people have gathered somewhere else, in a park or stadium. That at any moment somebody might come walking around the corner. A marching band in full regalia perhaps. That within seconds I might be engulfed in a clamorous carnival. That carnival moment is there, just a step away. At any moment the world might come swirling in.

Sometimes I hear the sound of parties, people eating, drinking, laughing and dancing, but those sounds fade to nothing when I search them out. Like will-o-wisps of a swamp, the sounds of reverie vanish down the empty streets, or turn into the billboard-rattle of the wind.

Once I woke in the morning to the roar of traffic, but as soon as I looked out the window of the apartment I had moved into on Gorky Street, the grinding sound shut off and the street was empty. The shops, which include a bakery, a hairdresser, a dairy advertising Jin Ling cigarettes and a fruit and veggie shop with a large sign showing a smiling orange with white teeth, all looked open for business. At any moment customers might appear: an old woman wearing a headscarf carrying a small loaf of bread emerging from the bakery, a municipal workman in blue overalls slipping into the dairy for smokes, a child on their way to school loitering around the fruit and veggie shop, a dark-haired young mother pushing a pram. I could almost see these people, and others like them, going about their daily business.

There is a big roaring world there, just a step away, but I'm separated from it, caught here in this amber time, which I can always hear in the background, a distant white noise, the hiss of passing life.

In some parallel dimension, the life of this city goes on as usual. I can sense it but can't enter it. I am one displacement away.

I walk in the middle of the street in case someone dashes out from a shop and startles me. Sometimes I hear footsteps coming behind me, but when I turn, the street is empty. That big roaring world cannot be caught by surprise and cannot be stalked.

Often I sing when I walk, as I did as a child. I began singing to you, because you prefer song to speech. You like your words to make musical sounds in the air. I'm happy to oblige and end up singing to everything, the buildings, the trees, the passing skies, threading my voice through the songs of the birds. Singing is my major recreation. I don't sing any particular melodies, or lyrics, rather I let my voice carry me wherever it wants to go, finding the notes that harmonise with the world around me and the tempo of my footsteps.

One morning I woke up to the sound of strident military music. I couldn't find my own voice in that stentorian roar. I thought that if I listened for too long I would turn into a statue of some conqueror holding a sword aloft. Or an army marching off to war. I would start to see blood flowing in the streets from martyrs of lost causes. The fear I felt, lodging in my gut like a piece of shrapnel, was that war would come and the city would be deluged in flame. I have no special protection here.

I followed the sound and found it coming from an empty band rotunda in Balashikha Park. It faded quickly after I arrived, the ghostly musicians having packed their instruments away and moved on, leaving their last notes hanging in the air with the murmur of seats just vacated. It occurred to me that I had died and was a ghost, separated forever from the world of humankind by the thinnest of membranes. I resisted that idea since I had all the bodily functions of a living, breathing soul; I've never heard of a ghost eating and excreting.

Once I heard a voice making solemn pronouncements in Russian, echoing through the city as if the god of Patriarchy himself were speaking. It had the gravity of an official declaration, like the imposition of martial law. I traced it down many halls to a government department that controlled huge loudspeakers which had somehow turned themselves on. I found a control panel and flipped switches until it stopped.

Sometimes I have the uncanny sense that columns of soldiers are passing by. I'm not sure if they are arriving or departing, but there is a weariness in their tread and the trace of a homesick song in the air.

Sometimes I hear thunder in a clear sky like thoughts breaking the sound barrier, the trace rippling through the streets and shaking up the air. I do a sad, slow dance through the streets to evoke the end of wars. I can't make a difference from here, but I can weep for the needless death of children and collect those tears, harbour them for the reckoning to come.

In Balashikha I am protected from the madness of the human world

– but for how long? Time might be skewered here, and move in swirling eddies, but there's no escaping it. I live as a child, but there is smoke on the water. We cannot be children forever.

Once I heard the sound of falling masonry and found that a bronze dome on top of the Transfiguration Church had tumbled to the ground, bringing its cross with it. The church now looked like someone caught in the rain without their hat. The fallen cross looked like a person lying uncomfortably on their side propped up on an elbow.

Fire in the hole

One day the air turned a rusty red colour and there was the smell of smoke in the air, of burnt forests, chemicals, plastic, hair and flesh all mixed up. I feared that a wave of flame would engulf the city, and me along with it. I kept glancing at the sky, as if expecting huge flames to rear like Godzilla over the city, or flow through the streets like lava. There was an ashy taste in my mouth. I feared that the mirrors would shatter and melt, that the air itself would catch fire.

The birds fell silent. There was just the occasional croak of a crow. I walked the streets from memory through the swirling smoke. The heat was suffocating. It was an avalanche of heat. My clothes stuck to my body like smouldering sacks, so I removed them. With no one around, my nakedness didn't matter. Here I was, the sedulous ape, seeking cool stores and bags of ice. I put on a mask to keep the ash from my lungs. I blinked into the world, trying to clear my vision. I had to concentrate on my breathing, for the heat sat heavily on my chest. I lay on the cool marble floor of the East Gate Hotel lobby and tried not to move. Even the slightest movement would create heat. When I closed my eyes, fiery worlds passed by, blobs of red and orange.

I tried to remember my early life in Hanmer, the snow swirling out of the iron-dark sky, the frost that turned grass into crystal slivers and etched itself into windows, breath that froze in the air as it left the body, hands that went numb inside their mittens, nights spent shivering under prickly blankets, puddles turned to ice after rain, but these images wouldn't hold. They buckled and melted, dissolving in the furnace of heat.

I lost track of the hours and the days in a hectic fever. At any moment

I could die. Between breaths. Between thoughts. Like some medieval sinner, I could tumble into the fiery depths. If I couldn't sweat it out, I would take it with me.

And then one day it stopped. A dragon's breath had passed over us and moved on. A cool wind blew from the north. The world welcomed it with a song.

I got up from the marble floor and went looking for something to eat.

The very image of you

Yesterday, I found a picture of you in the Art Gallery of the City District, done in the classical style: Ariel looking like a medieval archangel with a candle in one hand and a sprig of leaves in the other, a sublime smile on its genderless face, bringing light to the world, dispensing wisdom. I read that the artist was unknown, and that the painting dated to around 1650, from Columbia, part of a series known as *Arcángeles de Sopó* and, in this artist's vision, you were the archangel of divine war. I liked that, the divine warrior. The idea clothed my thoughts in medieval splendour. In some way, however small, I was worthy of your smile.

The artwork is reminiscent of Raphael, the same sense of tender beauty. Of course, Christians would see you as an archangel, for they think in hierarchies. I prefer to think of you as nature's demiurge, the catalyst that brings life forth from the raw materials of creation, a living entity that can speak, as you did with me, and able to take a body, like the divine androgyny of the image of you hanging in the gallery, and yet be spread through the lines of time and space in nature's own particle accelerator.

I carry this image of you everywhere I go. I no longer have to imagine what you look like. Here, at least, you have settled into corporeal form. I find it comforting to think that you were here before me and will be here when I'm gone, that you whisper into the ear of other children struggling to speak. It gives me a different conception of who you are. I have read that William Blake saw angels, and said an angel dictated his verses to him. I'm certain that was you. You gave him his mythology, just as you led me to the garden of names.

It felt a little like desecration when I took down your picture from the walls of the Art Gallery of the City District and walked out with it. I felt like a brazen thief, but I decided to hang it in a luxurious room in an oligarch's mansion in which I've taken residence.

While this image cannot contain the totality of you, it leads me to you on long afternoons when there is little to do but make peace with time.

A man, a woman, a child and a river

I see smoke rising from a distant chimney and I discover I am not alone after all. It takes a human being to light a fire in a fireplace. I am full of trepidation. I am fine on my own, living in the present tense, scavenging for food, walking empty streets, visiting some of my favourite spots like the blue temple of Archangel Michael, and the Monument to the Street Cleaner.

And you are here, hanging on the wall in front of my bed. I see you every morning when I wake up. Your dark wings and red cloak are the first things I see. The candle you are holding lights the world. You have hatched into a powerful presence, keeping this realm in balance. You can see past and future. You may take away the words you gave me, but the gift will remain, wrapped in your voice. The singing will continue after my mouth has been stilled.

I leave my mansion in Gorky Street with the same trepidation. I have to go many miles, across the Bridge of Lovers and south, to Malakovka, where the Pekhorka River flows under highway P105, to get to the house with the smoking chimney. It is a two-storey, semi-detached dwelling in the suburbs. The house is yellow on one side and grey on the other, but in structure the two halves mirror each other.

Each half has a double casement window, and from the window of the yellow house, a face is staring down at me. Recognition is instant. She is still a child, looking no older than when I'd seen her last, disappearing out of Hanmer in the back of her father's DeSoto Firedome Sedan, waving through the back window. She gives me a little wave and for a moment the two scenes coalesce; the two windows become one window as the past collapses into the present.

I wave and she vanishes from the window. A few moments later the yellow door opens and Olga comes running out. It really is Olga, that same roundy face framed by shining dark curls. Those same deep, troubling eyes. I struggle for breath.

As we hug, I understand that I too am still a child, even though years have passed in Balashikha. All along I'd been a child. I lived in another world once as an adult, but those images are taking on a curiously faded quality, like a fabric that has spent too long in the sun and holds only the memory of once-bright colours.

I remember striding across Hagley Park towards Rolleston Ave and Riccarton where Aria and I lived, thinking about fungi and mosses, losing the world in the mist, awakening on a mountainside where I had a conversation with a little chafer beetle and fruitlessly search for a rock wren. I see that life from the outside, viewing it from a periscope, as if that life were somebody else's, a fiction I'd assembled to provide me with a past. Those memories are as jumbled as a Canterbury river bed and fade among the crags and streams and flowing sunlight.

Strangely, the images of that other life grow sharper and more real the further back I go. I see a man, a woman, a child and a river, a wilderness full of strange and unlikely creatures from the musty pages of an old book. I remember a bus full of books and a librarian with glasses that made her eyes look big, conducting me through a circus of words that would eventually lead me into the real world. I remember a pterodactyl hovering in the sky just beyond arm's reach. I remember a path that wound back and forth up a hillside, and a sycamore tree with seeds that spun in the air like tiny machines. I remember having a tongue that kept tripping over tricky words, or words that might turn tricky at any moment on the tongue. I remember crying at night because the sounds I made with my mouth didn't make any sense in the human world.

And Olga. I remember her. A shy girl in a long, pleated skirt. A girl crying at the nasty names kids called her; shining with smiles at the dinner table while her father served me pelmeni; walking with me up to the deep pool at the bend in the river where we watched for trout and laughed in our own made-up language while the shadows of the willow trees played on the surface of the water.

My parents thought I made you up as compensation for losing her, but you would have come to me one way or another. I was born with you already in my mouth. I needed you to find words for me. When Olga left you simply came out from behind her shadow. Now she's back, and we don't have to let our memories burden us. Memories don't settle here in the mirror city. They slip between the covers of the day and are soon gone. They climb into old cars and are carried off into history. And like a memory, you too can make yourself scarce. You can disappear behind the bright facades of childhood and back into time's womb, leaving me with the words you once gifted me.

Olga and I are shy and don't know what to say. We just want to look at each other. We keep circling each other to make sure we are there, front and back and from the side. I see her like hundreds of snapshots run together, her face a collage of stills. When we do start talking it isn't in English but the language we invented many years ago. We are both delighted to re-discover it, and since much of it consists of gestures and facial grimaces, it is comical and makes us laugh.

We walk through the streets oblivious to the empty city around us. She wants to know everything that has happened to me since that day she waved goodbye, and I want to know the same about her. We have a lot of talking to do. Memories return as we begin to talk about them.

We end up back at the mansion I'd adopted in Gorky Street, and then walk back to her semi-detached, which is more comfy for the two of us. There are a thousand houses where we might live, but we need just one room to make our own.

We go everywhere together, often holding hands. We go to our favourite spot, the Rock Fountain, where we sit and watch the upflung drops of water sparkle in the sun. Or we go to the Stone of Memory to Victims of Political Repressions and put some flowers on the black marble plinth like true pilgrims. We go to the grand Homestead Gorenki and wander through the august halls and high-ceilinged rooms as if we were rich and powerful people with important things to do: treaties to sign, wars to declare or undeclare, debtors to be freed, criminals to execute. Our favourite haunt is the Mystical Castle, an ornate gothic building that harbours all kinds of histories in its corners and cubbyholes. We decide it is haunted, but also blessed. To sleep there overnight, in one of its ornate beds, is to tempt unforgettable dreams. The one night we do spend there I dream that the moon fell to earth and rolled like a huge marble clock-face down the street, smashing everything in front of it.

We are happy to be children. Time seems so far away. There is plenty of food, and firewood for the winter. We have the choice of homes to live in, we can have a winter and summer residence if we want to. A different residence for every day of the week, a different suburb for every month. There are no adults to tell us what to do. You don't qualify as an adult, and Olga and I agreed that it was okay you coming along and being with us. Olga can talk to you as I can, and you listen to her just as you listen to me. You have become a part of Olga. Ariel's spirit is everywhere.

We don't intrude on each other's silences. Sometimes I go out alone and wander about but always know where Olga is. My feet never get lost when it comes to finding their way back to her.

We construct our own art installation on an intersection. It is made of bits and pieces we find all over the place. Not just paintings and prints but everyday objects from garden rakes and shovels to kitchen accoutrements, crockpots and toasters. Lots of television sets and screens. Our junkpile stretches as high as we can get it. We join everything up with wire and call it Memory. It grows as we add more things to it. At the pinnacle we put a door lying flat and place a bicycle, upright, on top of it. It looks as if someone has just peddled in from the sky.

We became each other's pleasure

Despite evidence of decay, it's easy for me to slip into the belief that Balashikha will go on as it always has, that the streets will never be shaken out of their fantasy, that I will never wake up in the morning and smell smoke in the air, or see the sun burn holes in the earth, or watch the wind knock down buildings, or hear the drone of approaching bombers.

These streets are laid out as if for dreaming. We cross the Bridge of Lovers from one side of ourselves to the other.

One day we children awoke to find ourselves grown up. It seemed to happen overnight. Somehow, we'd missed noticing getting taller, older, bodies filling out. We'd stayed children until we weren't. We stared at each other in shock, both feeling it was silly of us not to have seen it coming. The years must have passed us by, sneaked by on slippered feet.

When we became self-conscious about holding hands, I knew the end of this Arcadian era was near. I finally got to see Olga as a grown woman. Her hair was long and dark and lustrous, her figure brimming and full, her face alight with humour. This must have happened slowly, yet suddenly it was a *fait accompli*.

'The days are long but the years are short,' Olga said.

What miracle is this? I wondered. That we had to come to this deserted city to grow into the adult love we couldn't have in the world we were born into. We had to cross worlds to get here, break boundaries of time, space and probability to make it to these streets where we might, finally, find each other. I saw that the city was like the made-up language we had as children, built from the imaginations of both of us yet manifested in the real world, in this case as streets and buildings, parks and rivers – and a sky to go with it. Love finds a way. The mirror reflects it back to us.

We found ourselves wandering the streets, loitering on the Bridge of Lovers, staring down into the lazy waters of the Pekhorka River, lost to time, marvelling at the consummate ease with which the water slid into our world and out of it again with barely a ripple, spending hours in a daze, only half aware of what we were doing, lazily capturing a few words here and there and letting them go like undersized fish returned to the ocean.

At first, we could barely look at each other in our adult form; soon we could barely look anywhere else. Soon we didn't want to look anywhere else. We fell into each other. We became each other's mirror. As we grew, our bodies reached for each other like two trees in a fairy-tale. We became each other's pleasure.

We slipped into making love with the same ease with which the hours passed and the river passed on under the mirror and out into the other world, or so I imagined. It hardly felt strange or new, rather as if we had always been making love, right from the very beginning, whenever that was. We would lie soaked in a common sensation, hardly able to distinguish who was feeling what. Our love-making was long and languid and seemed to have no beginning or end. We had nowhere else to be, and nobody to interrupt us or intrude on our thoughts.

I remembered the words of an old pop song my mother used to sing.

If I was the only girl in the world
And you were the only boy
Nothing else would matter in the world today
We would go on loving in the same old way

We became unsure of our origins as we remembered other lifetimes. We returned to those other lifetimes in our waking memory as well as in our dreams. There was a time when everything was green and verdant and quivering with life. Before then an age of ice and bright light. We had been many people, a fluid consciousness that wove in and out of time and physical bodies with the ease of the wind moving in the trees.

'I can't stop thinking about Hanmer,' I said. 'I dream about it and wake up crying. Why should it haunt me?'

'We were free then,' Olgo said. 'We didn't have to think of the next day, or the day after that.'

A time before the past and future came into view with its logjam of memories, I thought.

Now that we were adults, the streets grew heavy with the passing days. My reflection in the mirror wall was of somebody older than my years. Does sand in the hourglass run faster as it sinks?

You were there but didn't have much to offer. You just hung on the wall, a painting no more no less. Only the candle in your hand still burned. I wondered if you were fading out, no longer needed. You had no more substance than a patch of errant mist.

You wake up back in your old skin

After that first love-making, which seemed to go on for many days, we meandered into the luxurious East Gate Hotel on Lenina Prospekt, sat on deep, comfortable couches in the main lounge, stared at the black marble facings and drank the most expensive wine we could find, offering each other toasts in honour of our new status.

'I wonder if we will ever live a normal life,' Olga said. 'You know, have children of our own, find a community, live a happy life... or die here in our mirrored city, never finding any other life but his one, this in-between place.'

'We're safe here,' I said.

'I don't think so.'

Neither of us knew why she said that for there were no obvious dangers, but it sent shivers through us. Somehow, she spoke the truth.

Memories of our life in Hanmer, Olga's departure, my subsequent life and meeting Aria, grew stronger with every passing day. It had a pull like the tug of gravity. We grew certain that the world was still out there somewhere beyond the mirrored wall. We began to carry our other lives around with us. At first, they had a faded quality, as if we were remembering a dream, then becoming more real as our love grew. I discovered that love is not blind at all, but rather sees all; it is hate that is blind. Since we hid nothing from each other, we hid nothing from ourselves and our pasts were right in front of us.

I didn't want to remember those dismal events leading up to my separation from Aria, but there they were, those mortifying scenes of shouting and miscomprehension, fresh as just-plucked fruit.

Olga had her own scenes to deal with, memories that made her grim.

'I married a Russian named Torv because he was handsome, had a good job, and my parents wanted me to marry a Russian. They wanted to keep the old country alive in a strange land.'

'Is Torv a real Russian name?'

'Short for Torven.'

'Sounds like old Norse to me.'

'Danish,' she said. 'It just sounds like a Russian name.'

'What happened to him?'

'He did his best for me and our two children until vodka unravelled him. Bottle by bottle, he drowned our love.'

'I'm sorry to hear it.' I was also suddenly jealous of Torv for having two children with her.

'It's a very Russian story,' she said, and laughed. A snorting laugh. 'A solid and dependable man fallen from a fatal weakness for the bottle. It's the same old sad tale Russian wives have had to suffer for generations. I couldn't talk to him. He drowned my words. Alcohol has a way of dissolving speech.'

'What happened?'

'I got out. Took the kids and ran. He would have tormented me to death otherwise. With his tears and his fists.'

'It's a good thing you got out.'

'The awful thing is, I still love him,' she said. 'If he came around the corner with that loopy smile on his face, all that old love would be right there again. My foolish heart.'

'That doesn't apply to me and Aria,' I said. 'If Aria came walking around the corner, I'd have to cross the street.'

She laughed, but a shadow had crept into her laughter.

'Aria and I were left with bafflement and emptiness. When the passion wore off we were left high and dry.' I remembered the restaurant and the candle that dripped little wax tears. 'A whole lot of words lost their body. It was love that had given our words substance.'

As I said these things, I remembered them. Especially the bafflement and emptiness. I wish I could find a place where I could forget them.

'Even you and I can't last forever,' she said. 'According to the fairy-tales, we have to return to the world, the world of people. We'll have to pick up our lives where we left off. That's the rule with these tales. You wake up back in your old skin.'

'No, we won't. I'm not picking up anything. I refuse.'

'You can't refuse. You must return to the real world. We can't stay in the fairy-tale world.'

'You think this is a fairy-tale?'

'Yes.'

'But we have lived a lifetime here.'

'We are indeed blessed,' she said.

The past couldn't catch up with the present

After that conversation things began to change. The tips of the tall birch and spruce trees of Saltykovsky Forest began to grow rusty. The pine trees in the Dancing Forest, twisted into rings, hearts, and convoluted spirals bending to the ground, lost their momentum. They no longer looked as if they were dancing, but rather locked in contorted postures. There was a sour smell to the earth. A thrush began to sing in the middle of the night. The streets and the buildings had a stretched look, as if they had been holding themselves in place for too long. The colours of dawn no longer rang quite true.

The present turned into the past while the past couldn't catch up with the present. Memory unfolded backwards. I arrived at the day I first saw Olga. She was standing in the shadow of the sycamore tree, out of sight, watching Cargill and I pull the plug on the hospital pond. Maybe we could return to that moment and live our lives all over again.

We were relaxing on the Bridge of Lovers in a mellow summer morning, enjoying the feeling of water sliding beneath us and watching the sun coming up over the city skyline, when we saw a second sun rising in the south-east. Shadows multiplied and went pale. Some withdrew altogether. We were surrounded by light. The river sparkled.

'That can't be happening,' I said. 'There can be only one sun.' I was afraid that everything was unravelling and the rules governing our fairy-tale world were coming unstuck. Glitches were developing in our alternate reality, if that's what Balashikha was. Our world was forming cracks, like an old sidewalk.

Olga said, 'Have you ever heard of Hou Yi? No? He was an ancient Chinese superhero, Lord Archer, blessed with extraordinary skill with the bow.'

'Wasn't his wife Goddess of the Moon?'

'Yes, that's another part of the story. What I'm thinking about though is how Hou Yi was forced to shoot nine suns out of the sky, because instead of following each other in an orderly way as they usually do, all ten suns appeared at once. They were like naughty children. The temperature on earth became unbearably hot. Mass chaos ensued. Crops shrivelled up and people fainted in the streets as the earth began to burn. Seeing their opportunity, wild monsters emerged from the shadows and began to prey on humanity.'

'This is starting to sound familiar,' I said.

I thought I saw the rim of a third sun in the north-east. We might be caught there, on the Bridge of Lovers, holding hands, as the conflagration engulfed us. 'It takes a fairy-tale to catch the real world.'

'That's true. Anyway, Hou Yi took his mighty bow and shot nine of the suns which fell from the sky and turned into three-legged ravens, leaving only one, the one we see today.'

'Where are our superheroes when we need them? And why three-legged ravens?'

'Wait a minute,' she said, 'I see what's happening.'

'Tell me.'

'There's only one sun, the first one.' She pointed to the east where the first sun had cleared the horizon. 'The other two are reflections in the mirror wall.'

'Why haven't we seen them before?'

'Because the mirror has grown, look!'

She was right. Overnight the wall that encircled our world had grown upwards, taking in more of the sky, looming larger on our horizon, creating multiple dawns.

We gripped each other's hands tightly.

As the days went by we watched the mirror wall not only grow taller, but arch inward, reflecting the city from above as if there were a sister city on another planet, floating upside-down in the sky. We could lie on our backs and look up at that other world that was, at the same time, our world. We examined it with binoculars to see if we could spot ourselves looking back at us.

'I think the sky is turning into a bowl,' Olga said. 'Pretty soon we'll be living in a glass cocoon.'

'What will happen to us then, I wonder.'

Would it lock out the sun? Would we be blundering around in the dark? Already there seemed to be more shadows than there should have been.

We became fearful of what would happen. We lost the carefree moment. Lost it in the streets, which were starting to look spangly and strange. We kept glancing at the sky, looking over our shoulders to make sure everything was still in place. We started to listen for thunder. I had dreams that the mirror shattered and the city was turned into an inferno of falling pieces of sun and sky.

People in the mirror

One morning I set out alone to walk a section of the mirror, driven by a growing impulse to find a way out. Perhaps there was some way to slip between the mirror images and leave the city. We existed here only by virtue of the poetry of streets and sky. If we could break that spell, the mirror wall might shatter and Olga and I could walk free, for, over time, our contentment had given way to claustrophobia. We loved our aloneness yet suffered from it, loved the city but were trapped by it. It was a cage surrounded by seemingly infinite reflections of ourselves, shadow beings who followed us when we followed the mirror's circular path.

While the wall seemed to be smooth, offering a continuous reflection of ourselves as we walked, it was in fact composed of tiny slender panels that multiplied our images endlessly. Because of those panels, which I surmised enabled the glass to curve, our images were discontinuous. As we walked, we flickered in and out of being, too fast for the eye to catch, just momentary presences. I noticed it when going up to the glass and examining its construction minutely, as I would have, in my other life, examined moss or fungi.

This time I received a shock. The mirror wall reflected the streets I was walking, but they were no longer empty; people thronged the sidewalks and passed in and out of buildings. Some were dressed in the everyday clothes of working life, while others were dressed brightly, as if in a parade. It was a mirror world. The streets where I stood were as empty as ever, while my reflection stared back at me from a busy world. People passed behind or through my reflection, laughing and talking, or silent and preoccupied, taking no notice of me.

After a while, however, they did notice me. At first there were just a few nervous glances in my direction, as if I appeared to them out of the corners of their eyes, like a ghost or spectre. Something they'd rather not see. They would hurry on, their eyes averted. Then a little boy, no more than five or six years old, came right up to the glass and peered at me, his hands shading his eyes, which were wide with wonder. I stared back at him but that did not put him off. I pulled a funny face but he took no notice.

A woman came up behind him, his mother I imagined, joined the boy and peered in at me, cupping her eyes as he was doing as if looking through a window. I waved at them, and mouthed a hello. They didn't respond.

'Hello!' I shouted but they didn't reply.

More joined them. Casual passers-by or people on a mission, they paused to cluster around the glass, peering in as if at an exhibit. I made some hand gestures, an invitation to communicate, but no one responded in kind. The woman I thought of as the boy's mother took out a camera and started taking pictures. Others did the same. Camera bulbs flashed. They hardly seemed to react to each other much, although one man took another's arm and pointed off to my left. I didn't know what he was pointing at, unless it was the distant church of St Nicholas the Wonderworker on Ulitza Karbysheba, the tip of which showed above the houses behind me.

I approached the glass, moving slowly, dropped to my knees and peered at the little boy, whose face was now only a hand-span away from mine. He had a solemn look and didn't respond to my smile. I made a silly face at him and he didn't respond to that either. The adults clustered closely around, never taking their eyes off me. They were fascinated and perhaps a little repelled. I didn't know how I appeared to them. Perhaps the image they saw was not the one I saw in the mirror, superimposed on them like a ghost in their midst.

I did a pantomime for them to indicate that there were no people on my side of the glass. I don't know if they understood me as all they did was stare, but I was suddenly overcome by a yearning to be among people again, people who were not just images. I wanted to step through the glass and merge with the crowd, say hello to the little boy and something polite to his mother. My pantomime turned into a dumb show of grief. I was lost to the world, or the world was lost to me.

Up to this point, I'd heard nothing from the other side of the glass; theirs was a silent world. But even as I became aware of that wall of silence, distantly, there came the sounds of a busy street, cars tooting their horns, trucks changing gear, human voices coming and going. The sounds came in waves. I looked beyond the people to what I could see of the streets. I had trouble recognizing them. I couldn't place them in Balashikha. The park in the background looked like Christchurch's Hagley Park.

The little boy lost interest first. His eyes slid back to his side of the glass. He turned away. The woman followed him. She was carrying a shopping bag from which stuck a long loaf of French bread. The others became distracted and started talking among themselves. I could her the faint buzz and hiss of their voices.

I pulled myself out of the mirror world and ran back to tell Olga what I had seen.

Slipping into non-existence

When I took Olga to the same spot in the mirror wall, it showed nothing but the empty street. There was no little boy, no passers-by, nobody on a mission, no bustling traffic. They were there, I felt, those people. Maybe just a street or two away, between the images, between the clock hands. At any moment they might appear, coming around the corner of October Street in a ragged procession. Faintly, on the wind, I would hear the sound of a brass band.

None of that happened. Olga and I just stood there looking at ourselves, watching ourselves grow a little older. I didn't know what to say to her.

Our conversation became more constricted as words disappeared from our vocabularies, swallowed by the past and hidden there, as if hidden in the mirror world. Our made-up language shrank. Words that had come easily could no longer be found though we searched under our tongues and in our hearts. Our reflections in the mirror wall were curiously foreshortened, making us seem more compact, as if our images had to be squeezed to fit into the glass.

We dropped any made-up language and spoke English. That helped for a while, yet soon English words too began to slip away from our tongues. I was reminded of when I stuttered and had to jump-start every word. I was regressing, losing my precious command of the language and returning to my dyslexic state.

We went to the highest point we could find, the roof of an ambitious apartment block overlooking Gorensky Station, to look out beyond the mirror wall, if we could, to mountains or even distant cloud. All we could see was a blurred horizon line, curiously colourless.

'I'm sure we used to be able to see the....' I searched for the word, '....mountains. You know, in the far... distance.'

'I'm sure too.'

'But what if nothing exists beyond...' I wanted to say Balashikha but couldn't find the word '... here?'

'I don't believe that,' she said.

'Neither do I.'

After all, the rain that fell and the sun that shone all came from beyond the mirrored wall. The inside could never be free from the outside. No dream is ever secure, ever insulated from the world. No prison is ever foolproof. The rest of the world must lie beyond the wall, even if we could no longer see it; we both felt that to be true and more than mere speculation. As the wall grew, we only had the sky to reassure us that the other world existed. Even that sky, however, slowly became abstract as if it were more the idea of a sky than the sky itself.

Bits of our world were slipping into non-existence.

'I don't like the way things are ch-changing,' I said.

'It's time we got out of here,' Olga said. 'We've run our course. Memory is becoming grainy.'

She was right. This blurred outside world now had a mental analogue. Our ability to see beyond the event horizon of the city to our previous lives was, after coming up sharp and clear, being degraded by some force we couldn't discern. It was all becoming curiously colourless.

A grainy copy of itself

It seemed as if a light mist fell over the city. Everything became a little blurred, even things nearby, but there was no moisture in the air. It was as if the world had become an imperfect memory, a little grainy, a copy of itself which lost a little more substance with every passing day.

Distances shrank, while objects close up seemed further away. We went to Balashikha Park and gazed up at the tall, shrouded pines that seemed more like illustrations from a child's book than real life.

'Maybe this is a fairy-tale,' I said, stumbling on a cluster of words, 'except there are no wicked wizards or witches or stepmothers. No R-R-Rumpelstiltskin to weave gold from s-s-straw for the price of our first child.'

'I think they're here,' Olga said. 'They're just hiding. The fairy-tale has to end for them too. In the end their spells and plots come to nothing. As with Rumpelstiltskin.'

'I don't like that idea.' I wanted there to be magic in the world right up until the last possible moment, even if it meant a Rumpelstiltskin or two. Without magic there was no world; we lived within its compass. Aria could never see that, Olga knew it in her bones. Balashikha gave shape to it.

A great sadness came upon us both. Soon we would have to say goodbye, and it felt as if we had just found each other. Our tears mixed with our kisses. Love's shadow had found us. We began to dream of the children we would never have. We heard the sound of their laughter in the Pavlinsky Park playground, and cheers and whoops from behind the curtains of the Malenky puppet theatre. I found a copy of Topsell's *History of Four-footed Beasts and Serpents* in the Balashikha library and longed to have a child to share it with.

Food didn't quite taste the same. It was running out of taste, becoming as ash-like and bland as the air we breathed. At night there was a faint, pearly gleam to everything. I thought the mirrored wall, which was turning into our sky, was reflecting an after-image of the day, or maybe bouncing the moon around. We lost the ability to sleep soundly, and would wake up feeling tired and un-refreshed.

We found ourselves walking the perimeter of the city near the wall. We didn't have to articulate what we were doing. We were looking for a way out. A hole in the wall. A tunnel under it. Anything. There was nothing. We were thoroughly trapped inside our dream.

'Let's try to smash a hole in it,' Olga said.

I found a heavy steel mallet and swung it with full force against the wall. The mallet leapt back at me like an angry animal.

We seldom left each other's side now. I no longer walked alone as I grew more insecure the further away I was from her. The city was no longer a friendly place that would always lead me back to her. Streets I thought I knew took me places I'd never seen before, avenues with rows of silent apartment buildings. I might turn a familiar corner and find myself in some unexpected place. The geography of the city was beginning to come apart.

Once Olga and I tried to make the short walk south from Pekhorka Park to the Children's Library on the Volga Highway and encountered a stand of pines that shouldn't have been there. Where the trees began, the street ended abruptly. Olga stopped and didn't want to go any further.

'If we keep going south we have to hit the Volga Highway,' I said.

'What if...' Words escaped her. Maybe she thought we'd never emerge from the forest. A Hansel and Gretel lost forever. Maybe she thought it would take us... somewhere else. Holes were opening up in her thoughts.

A deer appeared at the edge of the forest, a doe. It might have been a hind. I couldn't think of the difference. Perhaps hind was only for female red deer. I couldn't remember and that bothered me. There were holes in my thoughts too.

She was a soft grey colour, with white patches on her throat and beneath her wide, dark eyes. She stood unmoving, watching us.

'She's beautiful,' Olga whispered.

She was so well camouflaged she appeared to merge in and with the forest behind. A little wind stirred the shadows on her coat. In that moment I could well believe that she was a princess or goddess in magical disguise, well believe that she was a supernatural being able to move between worlds.

To ground my thoughts, I tried to remember her Latin name, identifying a female grey deer but the Latin escaped me. At one time I would have known it; I prided myself on my memory for Latin names. Suddenly she was nameless, mysterious, floating between sunlight and shadow.

'If she runs back into the forest, we'll follow her,' Olga said.

'Perhaps she can lead us out of here.'

The doe turned her head away from and us and looked into the forest. Her ears twitched.

'She can hear something,' I said.

Slowly she merged with the trees and disappeared.

Holding hands, we entered the forest, feeling like we were children again, trapped in a fairy-tale, following a magical deer to some enchanted place. Maybe the hut of Baba Yaga, the bony-legged, iron-toothed one who ate children and whose hut ran around on chicken legs. And, like a little Hansel and Gretel with our breadcrumb memories, we would stumble into her clutches. Then she would fatten us up for the feast.

As we walked on, the shadows around us deepened, as if late afternoon were coming on in the middle of the morning. We appeared to be following a faint trail. We turned no corners, however, and I felt we were still moving south. We looked for the deer but didn't see her.

'Maybe we should turn around and go back,' I said. I was starting to lose my nerve.

'I don't think so,' Olga said slowly.

I looked back and saw no trail. The trees had closed in behind us. A little further on and we both stopped.

'Can you hear that?' Olga said.

The sound of running water. And not far off.

'I has to be the P-P-Pekhorka River. But it runs from north to south.'

'But it turns west before it passes under the wall,' she said.

Just as we caught a glint of the river, we saw the deer again. She was on the other side of the river, still as stone, gazing at us. She seemed to appear and disappear as the light shifted.

To the west of us, the trees were bent out of shape, twisted and truncated. Some reached skinny branches for the sky, others bunched heavily at ground level. It was like looking into a drunken forest.

'We're at the wall,' Olga said.

It took me a moment to see it; it was the glass distorting the trees.

'We can't be.'

We'd walked the perimeter of the city but never come across this spot.

'But it is,' she said.

The Pekhorka River passed smoothly under the wall. We both watched it.

'I think that's why we were led here,' Olga said. She pointed to the doe, 'She's showing us something.'

'Can you swim?'

'I can try,' she said.

Under the watchful eye of the deer we waded, fully clothed, into the middle of the river. The glass did not extend into the water.

'It should only take a few moments to s-s-swim under it,' I said. 'But let's hold our b-b-breath for ten seconds, shall we?'

'Get good and clear of it.'

'That's the idea.' I laughed, wondering why we hadn't thought of this before. Perhaps because, deep down, we didn't want to leave.

'Together,' Olga said.

'Together,' I said.

The doe watched impassively as we took some deep breaths and clasped each other's hands. Silently, I sent her my thanks.

'I hope we're together on the other side,' Olga said.

We dived and swam with the flow, keeping hold of each other's hands. I felt nothing but the soft embrace of the chilly, murky water. There was no sensation of crossing a threshold. I counted to ten and pushed for the surface. We stood up together, the water coming up to our midriffs. We were still in the forest. The mirror wall was still in front of us. Two astonished bedraggled faces looked back at us.

'That's impossible,' Olga said. 'We should be at least ten metres downstream. Let's try again.'

I hesitated. I had a bad feeling about it. I wanted to get out of that river and back onto solid land. I felt that the river could carry my mind away downstream while my body drowned and washed up on the bank still on the wrong side of the mirror.

'Let's count to twenty this time,' I said.

'Okay.'

Once more we dived under and swam. As I started counting her hand slipped out of mine. I looked around, but the water was too murky to see anything. There were just vague shapes, the kind the wind will make behind a curtain. I counted to twenty, trying not to rush it, and made for the surface.

The mirror was still there, just a couple of metres away. I stared at my solitary reflection.

Olga was gone.

A pointillist canvas

For two days I walked the streets of Balashikha alone, not caring where they led. I didn't try to make it back to the East Gate Hotel. At first, I told you that I would find Olga, the greyness would lift and bright sunlight would once more fall on Balashikha, food would recover its taste and the wine its tang, but I soon fell as silent as you were, as the empty streets were. You didn't have any words for me.

I often found myself at the Bridge of Lovers, staring down at the treacherous water.

'Olga is down there somewhere,' I said.

You didn't say anything.

That peculiar dry mist that was turning Balashikha into a pointillist canvas now crept up behind me as silent as a cat. Streets stretched off into nothingness, the past closed off behind me. I had to feel my way with my feet and hands to find food. Sight was becoming useless, time conjectural, words inconsequential. I felt as if we were in a cocoon that was slowly tightening. Like the alpine tiger moth whose Latin name escaped me, I would split the cocoon and emerge as some new creature into the world.

At the end of the second day I found myself at the Temple of St Catherine, climbed to its highest window and looked at the greyness, and the granular buildings. There was nothing here but the beating of my heart.

You appeared before me. You were dressed in splendour as a Russian Patriarch, with a silver gown laced with gold and a domed hat. You wanted to reassure me using ancient philosophies of eternal life, but they did not move me. I accused you of deceiving me but you were not moved. You wanted to be a steadfast presence for me, yet I seemed to see right through you as if you were the world on a spring morning.

You didn't have to tell me what I already knew.

My time here was up.

Part Five

The Fool

My last conversation ever and some sad custard squares

I lay on my cheap mattress in my cheap room in the Belle-view Motel and stared at the grimy ceiling, Edgar Allen Poe's short stories on my chest. I had arrived at the Belle-view Motel weary after the long journey down Highway 73 to Christchurch from Balashikha, pushing my trusty post-war Citröen Traction Avant as fast as it would comfortably go. I'd nodded briefly to the owner who was still sitting in front of her TV screen as if she'd never left, words emerging from the screen in a monotonal blur, and went directly to my room. I'd been here before, and here I was again.

I felt like a swimmer with the bends.

Had I seen a rock wren or not? I couldn't decide. Had I lived a lifetime in an empty Russian city with my childhood girlfriend? It didn't seem likely, but there it was, laid out in my memory like a carefully tended garden, complete with bridges and spires. It took pride of place alongside my life with Aria and my early life in Hanmer. It was not up to me to dispute my experience. It is not as if I were living a realist novel where everything has to make sense and bend to cause and effect. Life was not really like that. At least my life wasn't.

For the first time I noticed tiny cracks on the ceiling that looked like a map with roads going nowhere. I could follow any one of those roads to the edges of my life. Hanmer, Christchurch, Aria, were layered in my memory. My years in Balashikha hung before me like an aurora in shifting curtains of colour. Blues and greens festooned with streets and buildings hung from the ceiling. Almost iridescent. I had to face the fact that I'd lived a whole lifetime in the mirrored city, that I'd lived and loved and had my day there. I didn't try to make sense of my experience, interrogate myself as if I were a suspect. I didn't have any answers.

A nineteenth century novelist would either edit it out or spend many pages trying to account for it and explain it all away, perhaps relegate it to the status of a dream, a chimera of mind, a compensatory fantasy. I was under no such compulsion. Let the mind scratch away all it liked. I didn't question my experience any more than I questioned the moon in the sky. All I had to do was learn to walk in its light. Feel what its like to be a Rip Van Winkle in my own world even if I hadn't aged. I could walk along the road and take coffee at Charlie's as if nothing had happened, as if I were just the same as everybody else. I could lie on the smelly mattress, stare at the ceiling, and wonder, without prejudice, what to do with the rest of my life, which road to take.

I had no idea what was about to hit me.

Staring at the lines in the ceiling made me think of constellations and the mysteries of creation. Because of Aria, I hadn't lost my interest in cosmology, and the weird physics behind some of the universe's phenomena, like neutron stars and black holes. Science was becoming more exciting than science fiction. Both neutron stars and black holes were described as gravity sinks, places of such intense gravity that almost nothing could escape them.

Words are subject to their own gravity sink, I thought. They swirl about and disappear while the black hole, the gravity sink itself, swells a little.

Still mapping the ceiling, and clutching Poe's stories, I must have slipped into sleep because I found my bed had turned into a stone slab, and I was bound to it, like Poe's hapless hero in 'The Pit and the Pendulum,' staring up at a huge curved blade which was swinging back and forth with a whistling sound, slipping closer with each pass. This blade, however, was not made of steel but of silence. Soon that silence, honed to an edge on the mountainside and in Balashikha, would slice into me, split me wide open.

I woke up uneasy, heavy with the sense of portent.

No more lying around. I'd resurfaced into this world, I was over the bends now; I had a life to go back to, threads to pick up. That was simple enough, but why did it suddenly seem so impossible? Or perhaps more accurately, why did it feel as if it wasn't going to happen, as if my fate had other plans. I didn't like to think of it that way, because I didn't believe in fate, except perhaps as the consequences of our own actions, and didn't like the feeling that something was lying in wait for me, and had been doing so since I was a child taking those first fumbling steps into language.

That feeling was a hangover from the dream, I thought as I put the book aside and got up. Too much Poe.

I walked to Charlie's under a perfectly ordinary sun on a very ordinary day. Bits of suburban life passed before my eyes: a paling fence, a dog following a scent along the fence line; a man spraying his lawn; a child running home swinging a school bag, its buckle catching the light; traffic shuffling by, a wary cat, the brief ideogram of a sparrow in flight, a gull heading east. Scribbles on a blue sky. The paraphernalia of everyday life.

Compared to Balashikha, the whole world was in hectic motion. Everything whizzing and fizzing, me along with it. The one thing I needed in the world was a cup of coffee. The rest could wait.

Glenda didn't look so good. Her copper-coloured hair fell lank about her bony shoulders, her face looked pale and pinched and her freckles didn't glow. She looked as if she had just stumbled in from a world of perpetual twilight and lamentation. She was placing a plate of custard squares in the display cabinet as I came up to the counter. Even the custard squares looked fresher than she did.

'Haven't seen much of *you*,' she said.

I was taken aback until I realised that she was not accusing me, that it was just the way she emphasised her words. I was the only customer. Glenda came over and, hardly seeking my consent, took the chair opposite me.

'I'm sorry,' she said in a scratchy voice. I've heard it referred to as vocal fry or creaky voice. It's a timbreless crackling. 'My *boss*, like, wants me to do a *survey* on what people like the most about Charlie's. *Hello!*' She placed emphasis on some words, making it seem as if she were being sarcastic the whole time. 'So what do *you* like about the place?'

'That I don't have to talk to anybody,' I said. I didn't mean to sound unkind since she seemed like an okay person. She looked crestfallen. She rubbed the freckles scattered across her upper cheeks and nose as if she could erase them and, in a curious gesture, breathed into her hand.

'Ha ha, I get that.'

'I'm sorry, I didn't mean...'

'Na na na. *Dude*, it's all good. But, like, this place is pretty *crap*. Like, where's the *ambiance*?'

'That's why I like it, you can tell your boss. It's not pretending to be anything but a coffee joint with curling sandwiches. It's not trying, you know.'

She nodded, 'Yeah yeah yeah. I totally get that. I *hate* those *try-hard* places. But... well I'm *literally* bored out of my brain here. Like, talking to you is the *big moment* of my day, maybe even my *week*.'

We had a laugh at that. She pushed some lax ginger curls off her face.

'What about Chad?' I said.

'You mean...' she pointed to the table where he usually sat, and bulged her eyes at me.

'That's the guy!'

'He's literally a *fascist pig*. He hates *immigrants*. That's his big thing. Like, he thinks because I'm a ginga I must be a slut. He's always on about freedom, right? but he's a control *freak*. He'd like to control *my* body that's for sure.'

'You've got him.'

'I don't want him. I just want to, like, yeah, stay the fuck *away* from him. The way he looks at me.' She shuddered.

No sooner had we uttered his name than he came through the door as large as life and looked around with distaste. He recognised me but chose not to greet me. He was carrying his newspaper rolled up in his fist like a truncheon as if he were about to swat some flies.

In the world of fiction, coincidences are bad form. They violate the principle of causality, are seen as a cheap narrative trick, but in real life the universe has no such scruples, and co-called coincidences are inextricably woven into our everyday lives. Neither Glenda or I wanted to see Chad, so in he walks. In such moments, there seems to be a trickster at work, a joker in the rationalist deck. Maybe some demiurge like Ariel having a joke at our expense.

Chad took his usual place facing the street, his back to us, pushing the chair back with a loud scraping noise and spread out the morning's newspaper. I couldn't help but feel that he took a certain satisfaction in presenting us with his back, but it didn't last. After Glenda had returned to her sanctuary behind the food cabinet, Chad turned, gave me a sour look and said, 'You're the tree-hugger, aren't you?'

It's time for me to find another café, I thought. I'd lost my anonymity in Charlie's. Glenda felt free to come up and chat to me as if we were old friends, talking about Chad as if he were a familiar buddy of ours. Chad felt entitled to call me a tree-hugger.

'And mountain hugger too,' I said. I stared into the black depths of my coffee. I should have held my tongue. Something was approaching at full speed and I didn't know what it was. I felt like I was on flight TE 901 heading straight into Mt Erebus. Disaster might only be a few moments away.

My comment didn't seem to register with him. He was thinking about something else, glowering down at his newspaper and up at me.

'Earth Day,' he said with contempt. 'What a lot of bumfluff.'

Reluctant to talk to him, I gave him an enquiring look. Perhaps he thought that was an invitation. He came over to my table, sat himself where Glenda had been, and shoved his newspaper under my nose.

It was open at a two-page spread on the recent United Nations Conference on the Human Environment in Stockholm. I'd known nothing of this. My heart surged as I scanned the article, Chad watching me like an angry bull. The conference had adopted a series of principles for 'sound management of the environment' including what was grandly named the Stockholm Declaration and Action Plan for the Human Environment. There were details about this action plan, which included observation and assessment, management programmes and international coordination. Picking up on the conference, the UN was setting up its own Environment Programme.

I loved all those capital letters. It made it all sound so official and important. At last! I thought. There are some adults in the room after all. Some common sense is creeping in. Things are being done. Steps are being taken. Our living world might yet be saved. I wanted to jump up, throw my hands into the air and shout 'Hallelujah!' While my back was turned, something wonderful had been happening. The politicians would wake up and all would be well.

There was a small side-bar story on Rachel Carson whose book *Silent Spring*, the article said, 'inspired the Stockholm conference.' Yes! I was vindicated. Others had read that book and it had changed their lives, just as it had changed mine, bringing into play a new level of awareness. An awareness that could change the course of history.

Chad was regarding me with ever-deepening suspicion. 'Dangerous stuff,' he said. 'World government by bureaucrates. What a nightmare. Red tape everywhere. Busybodies running about telling us what to do. That we can't do this and we can't do that.'

'There are other nightmares,' I said, remembering my childhood dreams featuring Topsell's four-footed creatures and others like them. Suddenly, I saw Chad as one of Topsell's creatures. A four-footed ogre who had learned how to walk on two feet, which made him extra dangerous as he could use his front legs to rend and tear. A junkman who'd morphed into this true form, with several mouths, and eyes on the end of rubbery stalks that writhed about as he focused on things. There were many teeth in those mouths, big teeth like those of a bear. His voice was a deep, angry rumble, like a volcano.

'The *limits of growth*? What limits? These people just hate progress.'

He pointed to another side-bar story I hadn't noticed. It concerned what was called 'the Club of Rome,' which had brought together scientists, economists, national and international public servants and industry representatives from 53 countries. This report, the article said, 'called into question the benefits of growth, raising an alarm as to its impact on the environment and on the foreseeable shortage of energy resources.'

Chad watched me read avidly. His hairy, bearlike ears had turned into vents that allowed steam to escape in energetic little puffs. His teeth were all over his face.

'They hate to see people getting ahead and making something of themselves. Eeyores and doomsayers and pointy-headed freaks.'

'You should talk to my ex,' I said. I hardly recognised the sound of my own voice. It rang strangely in my ears, like somebody else's voice. My words sounded bodiless, weightless.

'Panic merchants,' he said, slowly shaking his head, which had become very shaggy. It was easy enough for me to dismiss what I saw as a hallucination, but what if it was more than that, that this Topsell Chad was the true and original form of the junkmen, whose actions make an enemy of nature and so become its most virulent expression.

'They hate oil, these idiots. And coal too.' He jabbed the paper with a hoof-like hand. 'They're on about that Torrey Canyon oil spill. Christ, that was years ago. Listen to this. It says, "It led to an oil slick spanning 270 square miles, contaminating 180 miles of coastal areas." What they don't tell you is that there are bacteria that gobble up petroleum. Some of them live off the stuff. It's gone soon enough. No more problem. I mean, fuck me, what are these people on about?'

I looked at the section of the article Chad was pointing to. 'Maybe they didn't like how it "killed over 15,000 birds and thousands of fish, including marine plants." Not a good look.'

'Boo hoo,' he waved his arms in the air, 'bloody birds bounce back quick enough. They lay eggs you know. Dozens of 'em. More little birdies come. 'Tweet tweet.'

He flapped his arms as if they were wings.

I'm sure he was trying to be sarcastic but looked more crazed than derisive. His eyes on the end of their stalks looked as if about to strangle each other.

'And fish too. They have babies as well, you know. More little fishies come along. Gloop gloop.' His wings turned into fins.

I could have finished the conversation at this point. Frozen him out. Gone back to my coffee and contemplations. After all, what were these provocations to me? Perhaps things would have turned out differently. Time would have taken a different track. You might have persevered, stayed with me a while, made sure that words maintained their integrity for a little longer, kept the gibberish at the door.

Instead, I opened my mouth and said, 'There's one little problem with these oil chewing microbes of yours, Chad.'

'Do tell.'

'They break oil down into methane.'

'No more problem,' he said, looking very pleased with himself.

'Big problem,' I said. 'Very big problem. Methane is a heat trapping gas. We're already changing the balance of gases in the atmosphere. We're pumping these heat trappers into the air as if there were no tomorrow.'

He considered me with repelled fascination, 'You're one of those greenhouse effect people, aren't you? I've heard about you guys. You're getting your knickers in a twist over a few atmospheric gases. Carbon dioxide is fucking plant food. At least it was when I went to school. You'd have us running around panicking over plant food!' He shook his head. It was a mad world, all right.

I became aware that Glenda was watching us avidly, no longer pretending to be doing any work. A little colour was coming back into her face. Her freckles were beginning to glow. Wow! Something interesting was happening at Charlie's. Wonders would never cease. She'd have a story to tell her friends at the pub after work. Chad was aware of her too, and I had the feeling that he was putting on a performance partly for her sake, to show her how easily a man like himself, firm and resolute, could crush a worm like me. She was his gallery and he was playing to it. Maybe he really did fancy her. Maybe he secretly liked 'gingas' which was why he heaped abuse upon them, calling her a slut and so on. He wanted her to be a slut so her could fuck her.

'Yes, Chad, carbon dioxide is a plant food. In the right proportion. If you overfeed goldfish, they die. But consider this, if you are going to pump heat-trappers into the atmosphere you will end up…' I gave a little laugh, '…trapping heat, right? How could you not? So the planet heats up. You're adding energy to a closed system. Eventually humans turn up their toes and die. We fry. Bake or broil. Or drown. The only question is, how long will it take? A hundred years? Fifty years? Twenty years? Just think, you might live to see it all. You might be lucky enough to live to see your farm wither and blow away.'

Chad's expression changed from repelled fascination to hatred. His face turned a strange puce colour. My Topsell Chad turned into a hissing serpent, the head of a snake on the body of a bear. I had crossed the line. He was ready for the kill.

There was a curious little pause in time when everything was suspended. Time will do that. Hesitate for a moment in its onward flow. At that very moment the door opened and the old guy with long, straggly hair and a quilted jacket came into Charlie's. I remembered him from last time. This was quite a reunion. The woman in shorts and running shoes would turn up next. We could sit around and reminisce about old times. The old guy went to the counter to order something. Glenda took a sandwich from the cabinet. She gave me an oddly triumphant look.

Chad appeared not to see the old guy. In his rage he only saw me. He was struggling to get himself under control. His mouth was moving but he wasn't eating. He was chewing on the words he would shortly spit at me. For him it was all about being angry; his anger was all the proof he needed that he was right. His incredulity was his only argument; because he didn't believe something, it wasn't happening.

'You're a fucking dipshit-arsemonkey-fuckhead-buttmunch-commie creep. You don't see it, do you? It's a fucking conspiracy to take away our freedom. We can't spray this and we can't burn that. Our cattle can't piss in the river. They can't even fart. On our own fucking property, what more.' He narrowed his eyes like a man of great cunning. 'It's property rights these commies are after, you know. They're coming for your property rights, they're coming for your prosperity. They're coming for your freedom.' He didn't try to keep his tone down to respect Charlie's ageing customer. His mind was galloping at full speed. *They* were coming for everything.

I had another chance to shut up and change the course of my history. I could have opted out right there. I didn't have to keep this charade going. Chad would always talk past me. Through me. Over me. Around me. His 'fucking conspiracy' was more comforting to him than the raw truth. He was dead serious but at the same time there was a manufactured feeling to his outrage. He was stoking it up. He loved stirring himself into a fury.

A deep weariness crept up on me, as if my very blood had grown tired. The uselessness of it all! It was that slippage again between words and their meanings. Words turning bodiless, weightless, and floating into space to be lost amidst the firefly stars.

And yet, I persisted.

'You've heard about the Woodstock festival of 1969, Chad?'

'I don't do drugs.' He smacked his lips together sanctimoniously then smirked at Glenda, or at least in the direction of Glenda, who had retreated once more behind the cabinet while the old guy took his coffee and sandwich to a table by the window.

'The first performer was a seventy-two year old black man called Richie Havens, and his song was a cry for freedom. There were generations of slavery behind that song. *Freedom*!'

'What's your point?'

'You're perverting the word.'

'Are you calling me a pervert?'

'Of a kind. Your 'freedom' means letting corporations run rampant; it means savagely repressing any efforts to deal with the underlying situation; it means replacing common sense with blind stupidity. The word 'freedom' has lost its mojo, Chad. It has become uncoupled from justice and the aspirations of the dispossessed and downtrodden. It's become a blanket justification for atrocities. Words are cheap, and can be cheapened even further by people like you.'

'You talk like a crazy man. A commie for sure. What kind of job do you have? I'll bet my last dollar that you're sucking on the tits of the Nanny State, gobbling up *my* tax money. You talk like you do. You've probably never worked a day in your life.'

'I suggest you read George Orwell. He understood how words could be turned inside out. Truth becomes lies. Freedom becomes slavery. Down the gravity sink they go.' What effort it took to talk, and to what little effect. The black hole only grew bigger and more voracious.

Chad began to look alarmed. He looked appealingly at Glenda and the old guy as if to say, look what I have to deal with. Glenda met his look with bold insouciance, the old guy stared into his coffee.

'You know, Chad, it doesn't make any difference what you believe or I believe, whether you rant and shout or die. Our beliefs are just straws in the wind. The planet doesn't care. It's not listening. Men argue, nature acts. Your war against nature is a losing one. Nature always wins. You junkmen don't seem to grasp that. Your war is self-defeating. Even if you win, you lose. Like nuclear war. You take everything down with you.'

There was a loud graunch as Chad pushed his chair back. His face had gone from puce to deadly pale. 'Cuckoo! cuckoo!' he cried, sounding like a demented bird, looking around him as if for sanity. 'Nutcase alert! Loony Tunes! Fruitcake fry baby! Yo ho ho and a bottle of rum.' He spoke directly to Glenda and the old man, 'They'll cook up stories about the end of the world to pull the wool over our eyes while they put their hands in our pockets. The big steal. You'd better believe it.' He spoke like a man with a firm grasp on the larger fatalities of life, a hard-headed realist who knew the score.

Glenda tried for a withering stare. The old man took no notice. He appeared to be deep in thought.

'Well fuck my blue duck.' He turned back to me, dragging his chair back to the table. 'Who are you anyway? Some kind of agent provocateur? Which nuthouse did you escape from? Don't panic now, take it easy, the boys in the white coats will be here soon.'

'I'm a scientist.'

'Whaaat?' What new madness was this? 'A scientist!' He made it sound like a swear word. I might as well have said I was a cockroach. His voice brought a boot down on the word.

'Absolutely. I'm a botanist. I catalogue and count. It's called taxonomy.'

'Is that right? *Tax*onomy. *Tax tax tax.* That's all I seem to hear.'

'It's nothing to do with tax. It's about counting.'

'Counting what?' he looked around for Glenda. He wanted to be sure she was listening. He'd given up on the old man.

'Bugs mostly, and mosses, lichens and liverworts.'

'What do you mean count them.'

'Well... for example, I'll take a certain area, say a square kilometre, and count all the *Teloschistes fasciculatus* in that area.'

'What the fuck?'

'It's a fruiticose lichen that grows in dark yellow clumps, mostly in alpine areas.'

'You're taking the piss.' He leaned forward, tipping the chair onto two legs as if about to spring. His arms and legs had grown bulging muscles good for springing.

'No, not at all.' Although, I didn't add, those dark yellow clumps look a lot like your face.

Chad shook his head in disbelief. 'You get paid to count lichen on rocks? *My* tax money going to a dribble head like you to do something as useless as that! Who pays you? DOC? The university? Like I said, sucking on Nanny State's tits. Game on! Get paid for being a busybody and fucking with people's freedom, with people's property. Let's ride the environmental gravy train. Toot-toot. Oh those tits! Those nanny tits!' (A side glance at Glenda.)

I opened my mouth to say something, to bite on some words and found there were none. Only their empty husks. There was a cavern inside my chest where words go to die. This most ordinary of cafes suddenly became a broken no-man's land where there were no words to be found and the most ordinary of objects defied description. I saw a ghastly parallel to my rows with Aria. The rising curve, the collapse and exhaustion. The confrontation with futility. The abdication of words. Words turning into helium balloons.

Meanwhile something extraordinary was happening in Charlie's. Chad had pushed his chair back with one of those terrible graunching sounds, had risen to his feet. The bottom of the shirt disappeared into a pair of mustard-coloured slacks that looked a little too big for him. He tore open his shirt and paced between the tables shouting, 'They want my money, they want my house, they want my farm, the shirt off my back, the shirt off my fucking back. And the fucking bank won't even give me a loan. They turned their nose up at me because I stink of cow shit, the snooty city bastards. That's the only reason I came to this shithouse city, and they wouldn't give me anything, not a measly dollar! All they want is to ruin me, take the shirt off my back. Well, I'll give it to them. I'll give you the shirt off my fucking back right now, you can have it and we'll cut out the middle-man.' He started pulling his shirt free from his pants. His pale chest and waist were exposed. He was a big, solid man. Glenda hid behind the food cabinet but I could see her shoulders shaking from laughter. The old man considered Chad disinterestedly, as if he were an errant piece of furniture.

In one movement, Chad pulled the shirt from his back, revealing the loose, sun-reddened flesh of his neck and his pale chest. Naked from the waist up, he looked vulnerable, like an innocent kid being razzed in the schoolyard. Like the victim he saw himself to be. His Topsell body shrank into human form. He stood staring down at his shirt in his hands. It was a very ordinary striped shirt. The kind of shirt a farmer wears when he travels to the city on business, maybe visiting a bank to get a loan. I expected to see tears running down his face. He looked up at me, contemplating the next stage of his drama, which was handing his shirt to me.

'Ah fuck it,' he said.

He stamped over to my table, seized his newspaper with one meaty arm and turned to go. He began to flush with embarrassment, his pale body turning mottled.

'Getting an eyeful?' he said to Glenda, whose hands covered her face but who was staring out from between her fingers.

When he got to the door, Glenda called out, her voice crackling like fireworks, 'Wait a minute sir, you haven't paid for your second coffee.'

'Get fucked,' he said grandly, and departed.

On the street, he quickly put his shirt back on. He didn't look back.

Glenda came out from behind the counter. She looked animated. Her freckles were glowing, her hair sparked with electricity. She had a big grin which showed her slightly crooked front teeth. 'What was that thing you said?'

I stared at her. I had to dig deep for the words in a graveyard of words. The last words I would utter.

'*Teloschistes fasciculatus.*'

'I mean, like, that's a real *thing*?' Her eyes opened so wide I could see she was wearing contact lenses that made her eyes look green. 'I've never seen anything like that. That's fucking *awesome*.'

I felt lighter, freer, like manacles had fallen off my wrists.

I nodded. I had no more words. Not ever. It was over.

She shook her head. Her curls swung vibrantly to and fro. 'I've never seen *anything* like that. That guy's *dangerous*. He's *violent*. He was making *fists*. He coulda gone for you.'

I shook my head.

'Speechless, huh? Getting of telling *pricks* where to get off? I know I do. I told my *mum*, I don't have to be polite to *arseholes*. It only encourages them. You gotta freeze 'em right *out*.'

I would've like to say something. To release the tension. Anything. Something we could've both laughed at. It wouldn't have taken much. All I could do was smile. I felt helpless and liberated at the same time. My head bobbed around in the air like a helium balloon, finally bobbing in her direction. I smiled, must have been a loopy smile because she didn't smile back. Not at first. Then I got a sly, complicit grin. *It takes one to know one. I spy with my little eye.* Followed by a wide-open grin.

'Hey!' She flashed me a glance from under her curls, 'Maybe we should, you know, like, go out together.'

Eat your heart out, Chad. I get the girl.

My brother's keeper

I went directly home, straight down Riccarton Road. I stopped for nothing but red lights. I didn't pick up any food to restock the apartment or top up the old Citroën with gas. Despite the noisy clatter of the engine, the car seemed pregnant with a silence that welled up within me and spilled out into the world, pushing the engine noise to the periphery. I had not yet read the Persian poet Hafez's pronouncement that a day of silence can be a pilgrimage in itself, but I was learning; silence was endless. It had no edges and therefore no centre. Infinity was opening up at the end of Riccarton Road.

Something had happened to me in Charlie's, in my confrontation with Chad, and I was coming to grips with what that was. Somehow, I'd reached the limit of the spoken word. There was no room in my chest and throat for them, just my breath flowing in and out, and yet words clawed at the inside of my head.

Surely I could talk to myself. To you. My word bringer, and now my word taker. I was never at a loss for words when it came to you, to us in our private space. I opened my mouth to talk but still there were no words. I hummed and sang without words as I had done as a child before you brought words to my door. I felt both terrified and exalted. Cursed and blessed. The silence billowed out, creating a space for itself. I flowed into that space with a feeling of joy and relief.

At the same time, panic hovered in the wings. Wouldn't I be suffocated in this silence?

Had you really gone for good? Had you taken all your words away with you? I didn't believe it. I was sure that if I pulled over and tried to write in my journal, I would be able to. I was speechless but not wordless.

Was this involuntary or an elected thing? Did you pull the plug on me or did I will this to be? Had I simply had enough of this weary world of woe, given up out of disillusionment? This either-or question didn't quite capture the experience. It felt more like a mutual abandonment, a divorce by consent. Perhaps it grew out of the ever-widening gap between words and their meanings. Perhaps it was because the world was drowning in words and nobody could breathe anymore.

More insidiously, it might be a symptom of the breakdown of chronology, of the narrative integrity that gives speech its context in the wider world of meaning. Coherent narratives were breaking down. I had my own breakdown of chronology to deal with. I had gone to the mountains, the Southern Alps to find rock wrens, wrapped myself in my cocoon, emerged as a child in the empty city of Balashikha, lived a lifetime there with Olga, deep in the mystery of love, watched that city slowly disappear into opacity, died, at least I think I died, and found myself on State Highway 73 on the way to Christchurch in my Citroën to pick up the threads of my old life, tears streaming down my face.

Looking at that sequence of events, I can feel the disapproval of the nineteenth century novelists I loved so much. The pieces of my life didn't hang together. Tolstoy would never have allowed such a lacuna to occur in his narrative. Or, if one did occur, he would spend the rest of the novel trying to knit it all back together, keep tight the chain of cause and effect. Perhaps they didn't have to deal with the kind of experience I had, or the extremes of dislocation of modern humans, the unmaking of reason. Maybe Dostoevsky would have understood.

I had been struck dumb, yet felt that I could talk if I really had to. If I had to call for help, for example. If I summoned the words, they would come. Surely, they would come! The world of language was there at the tip of my tongue. Was this not perhaps a throwback to my stuttering years, the ultimate stutter, lost between one sound and the next, never to recover? Or was I sulking because there was no way of restoring words to their innocence?

I tried to say something to the empty car. Maybe I could talk to the car. My Traction Avant liked a bit of encouragement and didn't answer back. Maybe that was the problem. I'd been bruised by my confrontation with Chad. Maybe I could talk if there was nobody around. I struggled. It was a physical battle. Eventually, I made some kind of sound. It wasn't a word. It didn't have the shape of a word. Even a made-up one. It wasn't a recognizable letter of the alphabet. I remembered how, as a child, I could induce glossolalia just by saying the word over and over. I fought panic. I am not trapped, I told myself. This is not a soundless room. This is now my home.

Struck dumb by the world or struck down by the will, it made no difference. I now lived in Silent Street. That is where you would find me. I had been cultured in the silence of Balashikha where I had lived for so many years. I could survive this.

My apartment had an unused, dusty feel. And it had grown smaller again. It was like a jacket that fits a little too tightly. Its silence was old and dusty too. At the same time the walls had absorbed all that shouting and yelling Aria and I had done. The walls held it in memory. The echo was still there.

My phoneMate answering machine was blinking. Aria had bought it so as not to miss a single message from Dave. I resented the machine because it reminded me of her. Of those final, ignominious days. And because it represented the unwelcome intrusion of her lover's voice into our space. What time was it in California? Night time? When I thought of them, they were spending their days doing exciting, important things, probing the heart of creation in their particle accelerator, and their nights doing other exciting things like fucking each other's brains out. Living the dream. There were no in-between states, not in my mind, anyway. I remembered how our bouts of furious fucking left me breathless and wordless, my brain turned to mush, and I wondered if it was the same for him, the particle physicist, or did he leap purposefully from between her long athlete's thighs ready for the next cosmic challenge. Before Balashikha I spent long hours thinking about things like that.

For a moment I thought the message might be from her. A conciliatory message, perhaps, conceived between bouts of fucking and cracking open the universe.

It was not. It was from brother Frank in Australia, where he had been busy making his fortune just as he planned. His hearty voice sounded strained, '...don't know where the hell you've been. Someone at the university told me you were doing field work in the Alps. I guess you're still into lichens... and things. Finally got through to Aria and she tells me that you two have broken up. And you never told me. Jesus in a jumpsuit! That's bad. Breaking up, I mean. I hope you're handling it okay. Always liked Aria. She knows what she wants. Mavis and I are sorry about that. We always liked Aria. She has her head screwed on straight, you know? We're coming soon... to see Dad. He's losing it. We need to see him, you know... and you too, of course. It's high time we had a good old ketchup at the barbie. Ha ha. We're flying out...'

I hit the off-button and the talking machine stopped. A truck rattled past giving the apartment a tiny shake. Always liked Aria. Of course you did. You were even jealous for a while, until you met Mavis. Even after you met Mavis. Aria knows what she wants. She has her head screwed on straight. Damned right. Aria knows how to have an impact. She's vivacious. She impresses people. She can work a room. She impressed Frank well enough. High time we had a good old ketchup around the barbie – Jesus in a jumpsuit! And I never told you. It should have been the first thing I did after Aria decamped. Grabbed the phone. After all, I am your brother. Yes, yes. *Brother my brother*. Hey Frank, Aria's shot through. Traded me in for a turbo-charged model. No, I'm fine. Great. Sure. Never been better. Got the rest of my life in front of me.

The phone started up again. I didn't answer it. Thoughts were roiling through my head but there were none for my mouth. No use answering the phone if I was strapped for words. Frank loved his monologues but would eventually ask me a question. Then the trouble would start.

I stared at the phone until it stopped ringing. A moment later the phoneMate crackled into action and Frank's voice emerged, 'Guess you're still not home. Well, Mavis and I are flying to Godzone tomorrow, Tuesday twelfth. There're a few things to straighten out. Will see you then. Byiee.'

Godzone. Always with a capital letter. Bye with three syllables.

He was curious about my break up with Aria, but more than that he didn't want Dad dying on him while he was in Aussie. That would make him feel guilty. Neglectful. I suddenly remembered him as my little brother, trying to follow Olga and me to our secluded place under the willow, at the bend in the Hanmer River, crying out 'Wait for me, wait for me.' Which we didn't. I loved Frank, but had never told him so. Love wasn't a big word around the house.

Now our roles seemed to be reversed. He was acting like the big brother. He was the one who would straighten things out. Get things back on track. Michael was a wonderful person with a soft heart, but he really didn't have a clue. Michael had this tendency to wander off track. Mum had made it clear to him in thousands of little ways that after she and Dad passed on, he would be the one to look after his older brother who, not to put too fine a word on it, had always been a bit funny in the head. He even had a sweetheart at the age of five. How silly is that? It's a good thing he counts bugs or whatever he counts. It keeps him focused. Keeps him from meandering off. Aria was good for him because she kept his feet on the ground.

I could see that Frank would be bringing Mum along with him, dead but still alive, her judgements ringing through the years, ringing through Frank's head. *You have to keep an eye on your brother, Frank. He's barely fit for this world.*

And then there was Dad. Something else to straighten out. Frank had always been a bit afraid of Dad. Seeing me get the belt put the fear into him. Unlike me, he managed to avoid the belt most of the time. He'd learned from my example. But he never trusted Dad, and trusted Mum instead. That was his mistake. Mum was a lot more cunning than Dad, who was straightforward by comparison. She was often the one who would fire him up to take off his belt. She was the one who could see around the corners of my mind to what she identified as devious intent. She knew me better than anybody did and that alone made her dangerous to me.

I realised I was standing, unmoving, in that inhospitable little room that was our 'living room', but felt more like an extension of the kitchen, staring at the phoneMate sitting on its self-important, compact-pine hall table as if it were some malicious living creature, with words filling my head. It was as if, now that I was no longer talking, there was more room in my head for words to go tumbling, a river of them, carrying their images off down to the great sea of language. The floodgates were open. All that stuff from childhood. I wonder if we ever get to leave it behind.

I realised, also, that I was afraid. Afraid to meet Frank and Mavis. More taniwha creatures. How would I deal with the world, in a practical sense, if I had no words? After all, people see with their words; I would be like a blind man. People negotiate the world with their words; I would lack agency. I had to be careful that Chad's 'men in white coats' didn't come and take me away.

Idly, I picked up a wooden frog Aria had bought from a flea market for a few dollars and left behind when she went to California. It came with a short stick which, when passed over its ribbed back, approximated a croaking sound. It usually sat on the window sill overlooking Dean's Avenue. I had turned it to face that direction so it wouldn't spy on me. It seemed like she'd left a little part of herself behind, a little froggy emissary, to keep an eye on things. Check out who I brought home, perhaps. Now it stared up at me as I rubbed its stick over its back to make it talk. Even this wooden novelty toy had a voice. I remembered my teddy bear, Cedric, which, when turned over, croaked 'Mama!' Even Cedric had had a voice.

They had no cause to be afraid.

That night I dreamt I was still in the Belle-view Motel. I had never left. I had decided to live in that half-way room forever, staring at the cracked ceiling. Lie low and get old. I wouldn't have to wait too long; getting old would come along soon enough.

What I liked about the room was that it contained nothing at all personal to me. It was not and could never be *my* room. It was a generic motel room. Even my suitcase, stuffed with the past, was shoved under the bed. The walls were bare except for a cheap print of an approximate daisy. The only object I recognised was the wooden frog, which was not mine but Aria's, to be thrown out at the first opportunity, leaving the room totally faceless.

When I looked out the window I saw the Alps. The snow on them was so pure in the moonlight it hurt my eyes. As I looked at them, they changed. They became bare and denuded like corpses made of rock. I couldn't look at them for long. If I tried to focus on them, they changed their shape. At first, they looked like a sea lion resting on the horizon, head raised, then like a human with an outsized jaw in profile.

There were creatures out there too, much closer to home, in the suburban streets of Upper Riccarton on the road to Sockburn, creatures with eyes as big as dinner plates oozing through the slime of shadows, or whose eyes bulged out of their heads like Chad's. Some had teeth and some had claws and some had arms hardened into clubs. Some had foreheads made out of iron for head-bashing. I saw my mother there as I had seen her in my very first dream, with loud music playing, when she turned into a pig and gathered me in her trotters for a dance, a four-footed creature who had learned to walk on two feet. In this latest dream however there was no music. The saints had already come marchin' in and had marched right on out again, and my mother was just one creature among many, hiding from their memories and the incessant whispers of their deaths.

My dream-self lay on the motel bed and stared at the cracks in the ceiling, which became like a roadmap through a drab, featureless territory. None of those roads led to Sockburn. A silence had fallen like the silence at the end of creation, when the last echo of the Big Bang has faded, when the last word has been erased. Columns of people were moving along the roads. They were weary and footsore and their eyes were cast down. They didn't have the strength to talk. A voice-over began, a smooth-voiced narrator saying, 'This is the last chapter of the human story. These are the last generations of humankind. Pity them. Pity them. Weep your scalding tears.'

With a heavy heart, I turned to Olga. We had often wondered where the inhabitants of Balashikha went, whether they just vanished off the face of the earth, but no! here they were, trudging down the long road that petered out into a web of narrow tracks.

I wanted to tell Olga that the mystery had been solved, that we no longer had to wonder about the fate of those people, that we could rest content, but she wasn't there. The words died in my throat.

Before I woke up, a demon-like creature appeared before me, looking as if it'd stepped out of a medieval painting, Hieronymus Bosch's *Garden Of Earthly Delights* perhaps, or a creature that didn't make it into Topsell's History. It had a serpent's head and a cat's body. And yet it looked sad, as if it had spent too many lonely years in Hell. I was overcome by the urge to confide in this creature, to tell it all my secrets before it consumed me. But no sooner had I opened my mouth to talk than the creature thrust its scaly head close to mine. 'Hold your tongue!' it said.

I woke up, alone, in my empty apartment, the first traffic cranking up along Dean's Avenue.

A touch of pantomime

'Why don't you say something, anything at all?' Frank said, brushing the sweat from his brow. 'You can't just say nothing.'

Apparently, I could. It's exactly what I did. I made them tea and poured it for them. I'd bought some gingernut biscuits, which I remembered were Frank's favourite. He liked to dunk them into his tea and suck on them. I tipped them onto a plate, a blue-rimmed one that had belonged to Mum. I fussed around. I was like a dancing bear. But I didn't talk. Not a word.

At first Frank thought I was just playing the fool. He quickly became exasperated. 'It's actually not bloody funny,' he said.

I agreed with him. I wasn't laughing.

I'd decided not to write notes to people. Once I started doing that, there'd be no end to it. I could nod and shake my head and do facial expressions. A shrug. A touch of pantomime. And that was it. That's as far as it went. I wasn't going to learn sign language.

'I know how you feel,' Mavis said with a red-lipped smile. 'Last year the wife of a friend of ours, Joe Coony, up and left him and he was so grumpy he didn't talk for two weeks. He just grunted. Whatever anybody said to him, he would just grunt. I reckon it was grief. Grief stopped up poor Joe's mouth. He had nothing to say.'

'That wouldn't happen to you, would it, sugar?' Frank said in a pandering voice, quite unlike the tone he used with me. 'If I left you, I'm sure you'd have a lot to say.'

'Fuck, yes. You'd get an earful. In fact, you'd never hear the end of it.'

Frank attempted one of his hearty laughs. 'Anyway,' he said to me, 'you can talk to us okay.'

'We're family,' Mavis said. To Frank she said, 'so you'd better not let those sheilas at the office get the better of you.'

Frank tried for another laugh with no more success than the first. Sheilas at the office? What sheilas? A piece of tea-softened gingernut dropped onto his trousers. He quickly picked it up and popped it into his mouth. He was giving me sideways glances, as if he was going to catch me out in some way, maybe catch me muttering to myself.

In most respects I was quite normal. I could smile and nod and cook a meal. I seemed perfectly composed and didn't appear to be a danger to myself and others. The psychiatrist Frank was to insist I see confirmed that. Frank wanted a proper diagnosis, and even though I knew it was a waste of time, I went along with it. The psychiatrist gave me a battery of tests, a physical check-up with MRI scans and all the rest, as well as some written tests. Those I was prepared to do. I didn't mind ticking boxes if it kept everybody happy. Frustrated, he declared me to be sound of mind and body. There were no physiological issues, as far as he could see, and my rational faculties were working as well as anybody's. His profound diagnosis was that I was simply refusing to talk, that this was a deliberate, conscious thing. He muttered for a while about 'selective mutism' but soon gave up on that; there was nothing selective about my mutism. I think he wanted to put a bolt of electricity through my brain just to see what might shake loose.

'It's a bugger that she ran off,' Mavis said to me. 'We liked her, didn't we Frank? How…' I thought she was about to say, how did you manage to lose a woman like that, or maybe how did you manage to hold onto her for as long as you did. 'I mean… the two of you… she wasn't really… compatible, was she Frank? For chrisakes Frankie-wanky, say something. I don't know what to fucking say.'

'Compatible,' Frank said. 'Ah… incompatible.' He grabbed hold of the word as hard as he could and wiped his face with his sleeve. He looked hopefully at his wife, as if she might bail him out of this desperately awkward situation. She took the wooden frog from its perch on the window sill and began to fiddle with it, rubbing its raised spine and making croaking sounds.

'You're an outdoorsy sort of person, Michael. You always have been. Frank told me that when you were kids you were always wandering off. Your parents never knew where you were. You enjoy… camping and that sort of thing.' Her tone made it quite evident that she, personally, did not enjoy camping and that sort of thing. Mavis was ten years older than Frank with a face worn by life's struggles and regular infusions of gin. Skinny enough to be described as scrawny, she wore a cream-coloured fluffy jumper and tight black slacks, just like Dinah Lee did a decade before. Her hair was done in Dinah Lee style too, a fringe with a styled curl on each cheek. She had all of Lee's records. She was dressed to look about twenty years younger than she was, and lived in a world where kids still did the blue beat and hung out in milkbars.

She wanted a drink and didn't know what to do with her hands, so turned the frog over and over. It looked as if it were trying to escape from her clutches, its haunches tense for the jump.

Frank was sitting opposite me at the mottled-green formica table Aria admired so much, in one of the matching kitchen chairs with tubular steel legs that creaked every time he shifted his weight, a corpulent man who wouldn't have been out of place in a Charles Dickens novel. Like someone from a previous era, he had braces to keep up his trousers, which he wore high above his waist and a large white shirt damp beneath the armpits. He would have looked a treat doing the blue beat. He wiped his forehead with the back of his sleeve again. 'You can't just say nothing, Michael. Sing me a song or something. You used to like to sing. You used to sing under your breath all the time. You used it to get around your stuttering.'

I wasn't sure that was quite true, but didn't try to correct him. That was probably going to happen to me a lot now. People would say things about me to my face and I wouldn't be able to argue with them. Frank seemed to get the same idea. It gave him a lead.

'Actually, if you want to know, you were horrible to me. Often. Once, you ran off with that Russian girl and left me stranded. You were supposed to be looking after me. I bawled my eyes out until some adult found me and took me home. Mum was ropable. If you'd been there, you'd have got whacked for sure. By the time you got home it was nearly dark and Mum was too worried about you to whack you.'

Tender family memories. I wondered how many more lingered in the wings. I'd be listening to a lot of monologues. I assumed what I hoped would be a sphinx-like look. It was a look I'd be working on over the coming months.

'Ah fuck it,' Mavis said, 'let's give him a couple of fingers of whisky. That'll loosen his tongue. I could use one myself. Haven't you got some of that duty free in your bag, Frank?'

'I sure have.'

'Well don't stand on ceremony. Let's get this party on the road. We'll get this sad sack oiled up.' She put the frog on the couch beside her, readying her hands for a drink.

But Frank didn't immediately move. The grin on his face was fixed. In my cramped apartment he seemed too big for the room even though he was sitting down. In his bulk he reminded me of Dad. He didn't look that comfortable either, nor relieved at the prospect of pulling out the whisky. He didn't want to be there, facing what he had to face. To me he said, 'If you can't talk, make a noise. Remember, when you used to stutter you would make a noise and that would help you talk. Like I said before. Or singing too would help.' His voice was oddly thin for a big man.

No Frank, I don't remember that. I think you're grasping at straws.

'Do you know the words to "Who Stole the Sugar"?' Mavis said. She was perched on the edge of the couch now, anticipating that first drink. 'We could have a little sing-along.' In a high quavering voice she sang:

'Who stole the sugar from your lips at night
I only know there's gonna be a fight
Over you... over youuu...'

She moved her hands, palms outward, back and forth as if she were dancing.

Frank didn't meet my eye. He busied himself with pulling the forty-ounce bottle of Black Label from his bag and lining up three glasses. His hand shook slightly as he poured. He gave one to Mavis, pushed one over to me and took a hefty slug himself. The drink seemed to stabilize him and he settled deeply into his chair which creaked ominously.

Mavis held her glass high. 'Here's to... happy times,' she finished lamely.

Our glasses met in the air. They drank. I put my glass to my lips and pretended to drink. A little of the oily, poisonous liquid wetted my lower lip and the fumes went up my nose.

'The fact is...' Frank tailed off, took a deep breath and started again, 'The fact is, old son, Aria wants to sell her share of this apartment. You have to find a buyer for it, sell it, pay her off and get on with your life.'

'Here's to getting on with your life,' Mavis said, holding up her glass.

'Get another relationship. The world's not short of women, you know. Make some money. Join the fucking gym. Snap out of it.'

Holding his half-filled glass, he got up out of the chair, which squeaked with relief, looked around, apparently unsure what to do, where he might have wanted to go, then returned and sat heavily in the same complaining chair. Looking defeated, he stared at the table top, and traced the flowing pattern with a sweaty finger. 'Christ it's hot,' he said. Heavy, low-lying cloud had brought a humidity we weren't used to in Christchurch. 'Have you heard a word I've said?'

I nodded.

He took another slug.

'Come on, bottoms up,' Mavis said in a jollying along voice, the voice you might use with a child to get them to do something they were reluctant to do. She led by example. Again, I pretended to drink.

'*Who stole the sugar from your lips at night,*' Mavis sang. 'It was probably those office sheilas,' she said, looking sideways at Frank and holding out her glass for a refill.

Sitting opposite Frank in my tubular steel chair, I shifted about, mirroring Frank's movements. Both our chairs creaked. For a moment, we were unmistakably brothers. At the same moment we both looked away. I looked at the walls Aria had insisted on painting white. Why did everything have to be so white, even an off-white?

'You'll have to list the property with an agent. Get things on the move.' He spoke, while filling Mavis' glass, with the distaste of someone delivering bad news. He knew that break-ups were messy things, and had always steered clear of them himself. I don't think he'd ever contemplated breaking up with Mavis, but how would I know what went on behind their closed doors, or what he really might have got up to with those office sheilas.

'So, we have to get it on the market straight away.' He said 'we' indicating perhaps his willingness to step in and take a role. I couldn't allow that to happen. Listing a property for sale couldn't be that hard. All I had to do was go into an agent and write all the details down. Nod and smile like an idiot.

Frank had lived his adult life in Australia, and had travelled across vast, stony distances to make money. And make money he did, pots of it. Now he had plenty, he was impatient and angry with people who didn't. Whingers should do what he had done and get up off their arses, make their own money instead of trying to get their grasping hands on his. Then they could eat and get fat like he did. Frank would have got on well with Chad, had they ever met. Frank was a Chad lite. A junkman by instinct. They sang from the same self-made-man songbook. Now he was concerned about me because, while I was not poor, at least not yet, I didn't have pots of money and, worse, I totally lacked the drive and now the capacity to make any. In a world full of money, it was a sin to be poor. For all their differences, he and Aria also sang from the same go-getter songbook. Aria would not have liked Chad, but he would have admired her ambition, as Frank did. Chad and Frank, and Aria too, would have concluded that it was my own fault that I lost Aria. I forfeited her because I didn't measure up.

Now I had become a worry to them. My share from selling the apartment would keep me going for a few years – and then what? Cheap, grubby hostels? The street? Homelessness? Fear not, brother. I am not as helpless as I seem.

The report I'd written on the absent rock wren had proved something of a hit. The Department of Conservation liked it and was keen to give me more field work. I'd turned the report into an article for *New Zealand Geographic*, which they'd paid me for, and welcomed further articles. I can write, mostly at night, allowing words to pass through my body and out through my pen or typwriter, bypassing my throat.

I had no guarantee that this tightly focused relationship with language would last, or when my hands might fall still at the keyboard.

In the meantime, I could look forward to a possible, if precarious financial future. In that I was not so different to everybody else. Nobody was safe. When it came to the future all bets were off. Money could burn. Banks fall over. Roads could get washed out. Crops fail. Supply lines fall apart. Supermarkets empty. Species vanish. Cities drown. This was the age we were entering.

Besides, homelessness was my condition. I was as homeless as a dandelion seed bouncing around in the air. Soon that seed would find base camp. Not talking had opened up a lot of spaces in my head. I was not afraid. Where my thoughts might land and take root, there was my home. At least that's what I told myself. I wasn't going to take on my brother's fear.

Frank geared himself up for the next round. 'Okay Michael, here's the deal. Aria's coming back here in a couple of weeks. She wants to see her mother and she has stuff to do. She's only got a few days. She wants you to find a buyer for this place so she can sign the papers when she comes and get it all over and done with.'

I nodded my head again. I was discovering that life became very simple when all you could do was nod, shrug and shake your head.

Maybe I should feel grateful to you, Aria, for breaking it off before its inevitable death rattle. I think of the years of misery you saved us. You can take the money and run. Make a clean getaway. Aria, my song of the air that blew away. All the way to California where all the fun things in the world happen.

Mavis was on her feet doing cute back and forward movements with her hands the way Dinah Lee might have done,

'Youooo don't know what you did to me
When you said you're gonna be leeeavin' me.'

'Jesus in a jumpsuit,' Frank muttered as he recharged his own glass. Funny how those glasses kept emptying.

'Don't you like my dancing?' Mavis said in a wounded voice.

I grinned at Frank. I couldn't help myself. He didn't grin back. He seemed to be having trouble seeing the brighter side of things, which was his forte. What if I never spoke again? What was he going to do? Was he his brother's keeper? As if things weren't bad enough, with the old man in hospice care. The sooner he could get back to Aussie the better. Across the ditch he could get on with the business of making money and not have to worry about shit like this.

Mavis collapsed back onto the couch and lunged for her drink. Once she had it secured she gave a deep sigh. 'What a fucking shit storm,' she said.

Frank nodded gloomily. 'Melbourne doesn't seem so bad,' he said.

'Good on a good day,' Mavis said, seemingly pleased with this vacuous comment.

Frank kept nodding.

I caught a glimpse of what had kept them together over the years. A mutual vacuity, supported by a nip or two, that had stood them in good stead through the vicissitudes of life.

Without warning, I was hit by images of the life Olga and I had led in Balashikha, how we'd loiter on the Bridge of Lovers and watch the soft, slow movement of the Pekhorka River; how, in some mafioso's mansion, we discovered a large four-poster bed with a maroon satin canopy and creamy white silk pillows where we could lie and watch the morning sun slip through the panels of leaded, red-and-green stained glass windows, and how we would wander through Elk Park holding hands in the rich yellow light of the afternoon, keeping a watch for the mythical elks who, we always felt, might put in an appearance at any time.

This was not a fantasy. My empty city was a real place. We had lived and loved there. It was there that silence had grown within me the way a pearl forms within an oyster, layer by layer. My conversation with Chad in Charlie's had cracked open that oyster to reveal the pearl of silence within. Now I carried it with me, sewn into my tongue. Its soft glow filled my head.

With the fastidiousness of the half-drunk, Mavis took the wooden frog from the couch and placed it carefully on the window sill behind her, in the exact same position it had been. It faced Dean's Avenue as if it was about to leap into the great world beyond. She got up again, not to dance but to whisper something into Frank's ear.

He nodded grimly. Now that I wasn't talking, there were certain things I was not allowed to hear, apparently. I suspected the time would come when she would say whatever she had to say boldly in front of me as if I were deaf as well as dumb.

While Frank was thinking and nodding, Mavis took the opportunity to refill her glass. She knocked it back and smiled at some rosy memory of her own. 'A chick-a-chick, a chick-a-chick-a-chang-chang,' she sang softly.

'Well, we'll get on our way,' Frank said. He made no effort to move, however. It was as if he was stuck to that uncomfortable chair. Stuck in my zone of silence. Without the social niceties, he couldn't find a way to break off.

'I wonder how Piddles is getting on,' Mavis said in the pitiful tones of a child. Piddles was their cat a friend was looking after while they were away. She made it sound as if Piddles might be pining away to nothing without them.

'Not talking is not going to solve any problems, you know,' Frank burst out loudly. 'It's just going to make them worse.'

I didn't think I was trying to solve any problems. It was just that words were no help to me.

'You can't hold out forever.'

He was probably right. Frank had always been the smart one. He could do maths while I could only stare at the numbers. He could cite much of the periodic table while I could only sing along because I liked the sounds of all those strange words, like the chanting of a magic spell: fermium, erbium, flerovium... I wondered if he could remember the periodic table now. I wondered just how flabby his mind had grown.

'I hate these nor-westers,' Frank said, mopping his brow again with his sleeve. 'I'd forgotten about them.'

Everything was better across the ditch, even the weather. He polished off his drink and stared out, beyond Mavis, through the window to Hagley Park, the calm playing fields and trees and the glint of the Avon River, as if trying to remember something. It looked tranquil, despite the muffled roar of traffic. I saw how little it would take to turn the place back into the swamp it had once been. Pterodactyl City. An underwater dreamscape. Then my nice little cramped, overpriced apartment with a view would be worth precisely nothing. Perhaps the nearby Waimakariri river would break through its stop banks, return to its braided ways, and rediscover its old outlet to the sea right through the middle of the city, right through the comfortable suburb of Merivale. Not such a merry vale. With enough sea level rise as Antarctica melted, not only was my vision likely but inevitable. I wondered if I'd live long enough to see it.

With a brisk, decisive movement Frank capped the bottle and stuck it away in his travelling bag before Mavis could pour herself another shot. Mavis pouted.

'We'd better get going,' Frank said. His chair shuddered as he got to his feet.

They looked at me as if expecting a response. *I'll sleep among the fishes.*

'Christ, I don't know,' Frank said. It was beyond him, his brother turning autistic. He'd never heard of anything like it. It wasn't like the flu. If I wanted to opt out of the human race there wasn't much he could do about it. Frank was a practical man. He knew when to cut his losses.

Like a good host, I saw them to the door.

Away with the fairies

Since my life in Balashikha, I had taken to walking the days away, following the sun and escorting my shadow from east to west, following the course of the Avon River through Hagley Park to its spring source in Avonhead. Walking kept my blood moving. I could dream or let dreams go. Think or let thoughts go. Since nothing would be spoken, all thoughts were equal.

I liked the park because, while the traffic noises never faded, its comparative silence mirrored the inner silence left by the absence of voiced words; there was nothing more than this skein of unvoiced thought. But this absence did not feel like a lack. I was reacting to the silence, processing it just as I would process noise. That silence was more than just an absence. It was more like something alive, something that made a shape for itself in the world. It had a quality and a dimension all its own. In short, it had substance. I could listen to silence, enter the dimension of it and learn from it. Engage with it as we might engage with words, react to it as though it were a song, a roar, a bang.

This was the silence I craved all along: not an absence of noise but a freedom from my tiny, petty self. Time now flowed freely from past into present and back again. I no longer had to narrate myself in words, and found myself moving through the trees, listening, eavesdropping on what I once thought of as silence, which was only the gentle noise of time going on without me.

There is a heady freedom to all this. While doing circuits of Hagley Park and the Botanic Gardens, I can let my mind float wordlessly along with me, like a child's balloon bobbing around tethered to a silken thread. I can carry the sky with me while keeping an eye open for flora and fauna. I may see a sacred kingfisher with its startling blue wings watching the river, or a black-necked Canada goose stalking picnickers. I have not lost the habit of cataloguing and will often take out my notebook and record the time and place of the sightings. 'Adolescent song thrush, *Turdus philomelos*, Garden kiosk, 11 a.m. Nov 15th.'

There are plenty of thoughts on hand and my mind would have me believe that thoughts were more important than observation. Since abandoning speech, I had come to believe that all this thinking was pathological. Birds and animals don't have this internal monologue, and are sensitive enough to pick up what we are thinking. I noticed that when I stilled my mind to a distant murmur, birds would come closer to me, dogs will seek me out, cats jump on my lap.

By not thinking, the world comes closer.

Walking made it easier for me to evoke Olga. Hand-in-hand, and in a daze of time, Olga and I had walked every street and byway of Balashikha. Hagley Park is not unlike Elk Park. It is flat and there are trees, a river and the sound of birds. I could easily imagine Olga walking by my side. Sometimes I had the uncanny feeling that she was there, right beside me, I only had to turn and look.

The Avon River, whose Māori name is Ōtākaro, is a domesticated river, especially where it flows through Hagley Park. As tranquil and unruffled as a swan's feathers, it goes about its business without fuss, overhung by willows and lofty, mostly exotic trees, and sprinkled with ducks. Arm in arm, lovers stroll along its banks. In springtime, the park is a festival of blossoms, while in autumn orange and russet colours rule. A river with all the pretty trappings.

There is a stylish walking bridge arching across the river to the Botanic Gardens, and I liked to linger on it, pleasantly merging it with memories of the Bridge of Lovers in Balashikha. Sometimes I played Pooh sticks with myself, finding two equal twigs, dropping them on one side of the bridge, then dashing to the other to watch them emerge, keen to see which one might have come out ahead.

On this occasion, however, I didn't linger. My thoughts pulled me back into narrative time. I was thinking about Frank and Mavis, how keen they were to get back to Aussie, and what a bother I was to them.

Oh brother my brother, elected silence sang to me, and beat upon my whorlèd ear. It was not about you, or Aria. Or even Olga. It was about a world that has forgotten how to listen, about beings who hear only their own crash, bang and clatter, the distant sound of rigs roaring up Rolleston Ave, heading west and south, ugly and strident.

The deeper the inner silence became, the less capable I was of talking. When I wrote, it was my fingers that did the talking. It wasn't just people. I had tried to talk to a dog and found I was like a stutterer caught between sounds and couldn't go forward or back. The dog soon lost patience.

As I walked, a light evening mist developed out of the humidity. I was reminded of the thick mist that swallowed all the names of things when I was a student, and how scared I'd been; I'd clung to the names of things in those days. I remembered the treacherous alpine mist that threatened to swallow me up, and the preternatural thickening of air that dissolved Balashikha. This mist was nothing so dramatic. It was light and gauzy, putting a soft, drowsy edge to things. It sat delicately on my skin and clothing, and gave the trees a sheen. There were people moving in the distance, like shadows come to life. Voices were distant and muted. As if, in sympathy with me, the world had fallen silent too.

I entered this wordless place as if it had always been my destination, arriving as a traveller might at a river seeking a way across. It had always been there, arrival only a matter of time.

I didn't mean to give offence. If I was a fool, I was everybody's fool. You might poke fun if you wish, write me off as an aberration or mental case, hardly worthy of consideration, if it gives you satisfaction. You might walk past me with your nose in the air, take pleasure in scrubbing me from your thoughts, expunging me from the record. That's all right, allowances need to be made all round. If you laugh, I will laugh with you; the joke is on all of us, after all.

Because I was not filling my mouth up with words, a hitherto submerged level of reality became discernable to me. Like those science-fiction stories that had informed my youth, half-hidden meanings lay buried in that mist. As with a palimpsest, there was a world hidden behind the appearance of things, behind the words that described the appearance of things. It was there in ghostly counterpoint to what we perceive to be the real world.

I walked through the mist in a daze of wordlessness. In many ways I was still a child. I had never grown up, just wandered into another world. Like Balashikha, a mirror world.

I can walk through the mirror to the other side, but I can't return.

Labyrinthine ruins

'We gotta go and see Dad,' Frank said. He'd booked their ticket home, and was not keen to discharge his final familial duties. He felt much better with that ticket in his back pocket.

I nodded.

He'd said it several times now. He was struggling with something. He didn't want to go, but had to.

'I'm not going,' Mavis had said. Seeing Dad scared her. She'd rather stay behind at their motel and flick through the *Australian Woman's Weekly* or watch some morning TV.

'I'm driving,' Frank said. His tone brooked no argument. Perhaps he thought that because I couldn't talk, I couldn't drive either. Perhaps he just wanted to be in control, to have something he could control.

On the drive to the hospice, Frank was uncharacteristically quiet. He hunched over the wheel and stared glumly at the street ahead, cursing every time he had to stop for traffic. The bluster had gone out of him. 'What a fucking shemozzle,' he muttered when the traffic grew thick.

Our father's dementia had reached the stage where our visits hardly registered with him, or if they did, he couldn't remember them. He was rapidly growing incapable of speech. He and I were a matched pair when it came to talking. I didn't mind sitting in silence with him but Frank did. He wanted to prod Dad into rational speech as if that would pull him back into reality.

Dad was restless, and kept looking around as if there were things happening we couldn't see. He had his own internal version of the mist that hid the world, and half-submerged meanings that were slowly being submerged. He murmured a little but few words emerged. He stared right through Frank and me as if we weren't there.

'That's Mum,' he said distinctly, his face lighting up like a child's. He pointed to a woman who was passing by the open doorway to his room.

'Is he talking about our mum or his mother?' Frank asked me, momentarily forgetting I wasn't talking.

Dad's voice fell into a mumble, telling some kind of story, I think, a long involved story that trailed off into nothing. His mental landscape was a world of labyrinthine ruins. Bits of it were crumbling the whole time. Soon it would be all gone.

His room opened to a little circular garden. I watched the sun play with the daisies in the garden and tried to ignore the rubber sheet that lay over his bed and the institutional smell, a mixture of urine and disinfectant. We sat in silence. Frank's eyes were fixed on me meaningfully and I began to discern his strategy. *You see,* his look was saying, *you want to end up like this?* Dad was losing his mind while I was throwing mine away. Dad was ill but I was a fool. There was still time for me to snap out of it, to come back to the world before the distance became too great. Frank was doing his very best in a trying situation to bring me around. He hoped that visiting Dad would knock some sense into me.

I smiled at Frank and took Dad's hand. His whole being was vibrating like dry straw rattling in the wind. His mind was like a window banging. He was losing solidity, clinging white-knuckled to the arms of his chair, hanging on for dear life. Monsters crawled out of the holes in his consciousness. They had insect bodies and human faces that screeched at him with scratched-glass voices. Drugs barely kept them at bay, and he could still hear them. He kept looking around to make sure they weren't creeping up on him.

He may not have known who I was but knew somebody was there. At the touch of my hand, his grip on the chair softened a little. 'Mum walked right past me,' he said with a little laugh. 'Never said a word.'

It's all right, Dad. You can let go. There is no anchor. The little you can remember will soon be gone. You won't remember death, even as it steals up on you. I wonder if you remember the little bivouac you constructed to hide us from flying ducks, or your glee at shooting them out of the air as they came in to land near your plausible decoys, your pride as you tied their legs together and threw them over your shoulder. Probably all that is gone. Your own mother and father have passed the doorway of memory. Their voices have fallen silent. You can let go. Let your hands fall. It's best to forget the dead.

The three of us were silent. I imagined Frank was remembering things too, but maybe not. Frank was always looking to the future; for him, the past had no appeal. More likely he was thinking of the drink he would have with Mavis when he got back to their motel. Unlike me, he was not one to get caught up in echoes.

We had nowhere to go until it was time to leave. Frank gave Dad an awkward hug. There was a bead of sweat on Frank's upper lip. He couldn't get out of the room fast enough. He didn't look back to see if I was following, turned in the wrong direction and set off determinedly down the corridor, heading deeper into the building with lumbering but determined steps. I followed slowly, waiting for him to realise his mistake. There were rooms on either side, many with their doors open. In one room there was a man lying motionless on his bed like a corpse. In another there was the woman Dad had mistaken for Mum. She was sitting on her bed staring at photographs on the wall.

Several doors ahead of me, Frank came to a grinding halt. He looked back, saw me, and looked ahead. There was nothing ahead but more corridor. 'Fuck it!' he said in a strangled voice, turned and walked back towards me. He walked straight past as if I wasn't there. I followed. We emerged into a large room where a dozen or so dementia sufferers sat around sunk in silence. There was no conversation. Frank made a headlong dash for the door to freedom. The door had been locked to prevent patients from wandering away. There was a key kept in a drawer at the desk by the door but Frank had forgotten that. There were no staff members around and Frank began to panic. He shook the door. In that moment his greatest fear was that he would never get out of the place, that he'd be locked in with the demented people.

'Fuck fuck fuck,' he said, each word a small explosion in his mouth.

I moved around him and calmly took the key from the desk drawer. I calmly unlocked the door. Frank gave me a deeply suspicious look as he pushed past me to get out.

'Let's get the fuck out of here,' he said as we left the hospice.

The elephant in the room

Aria did not look happy, just care-worn, aged, and jet-lagged. I wondered how she was faring with her new life, her new relationship. I figured I was better off not knowing and such details can be tormenting. Life wears us all down one way or the other; our prospects are seldom realised the way we imagine they will, our dreams are always one step ahead of us. Like will-o'-wisps leading the unwary traveller into the depths of a swamp, our visions dance and flicker seductively before abandoning us in the sucking dark.

At first, she refused to meet my eye. In a brisk, no-nonsense voice she talked about her flight, her mother, the unseasonal Christchurch heat as if everything was normal. When I didn't speak she got flustered, then angry, then frightened, then resigned. Then all of those things mixed up together.

'You see what I mean?' Frank said.

'Are you sick?' she said, standing in front of me, peering into my face.

I shook my head.

'What do the doctors say?' she demanded of Frank.

'That there's nothing wrong with him.'

'Nothing wrong with him', Mavis echoed.

'Then why aren't you talking, you bloody idiot?' She grabbed me by the shoulders and I thought she was about to shake me as if words could be shaken out of my body.

I shook my head again. The great negator, that was me.

'This is some kind of fucking drama,' she said, throwing her hands into the air. 'He's throwing a hissy fit.'

Frank and Mavis nodded furiously in agreement. They were sitting side by side on the couch, Mavis fiddling with the wooden frog, turning it over and over, while Frank did his best to look as if he wasn't there. He couldn't get comfortable, shifting his bum back and forth. I kept getting distracted by the sequined frock Mavis was wearing.

'You haven't answered the phone. I had to ring Frank to find out we had a buyer for the apartment.'

She and Frank looked at each other helplessly. Mavis looked at me as if I were a distant object.

'The apartment was snapped up,' Frank said, sounding as if this had been the result of his own efforts.

'I'm too tired to argue,' Aria said with a deep sigh. She plonked herself in the kitchen chair she'd always preferred and scratched distractedly at the formica tabletop, the table she'd once so happily found for the future she'd so happily anticipated.

That I was not arguing struck everybody, Aria most of all. She had no one left to argue with but herself. I didn't take any satisfaction in that. Frank shrugged his shoulders. He was doing a lot of that lately, mirroring me.

'Drama, drama fucking drama,' she said, addressing the table top. 'I always thought you never grew up,' she said.

Frank nodded in agreement, happy to be one of the adults in the room.

I smiled. It wasn't an appropriate smile, but I was happy, happy to be free of her, to be free of everything. The apartment was sold and Frank and Mavis and Aria would soon be scooting back to their lives, grateful to get away. All they had to do was make it through this scene. All they had to do was survive the drama.

'I always thought you were on the edge,' Aria said. 'Lack of affect, I think they call it. Something like that.'

My serenity took a dive and my mouth tasted as if I'd just crunched up a pickled onion. A snarky voice in my head was telling me what I might say if I was talking. *Yes, Aria, I'm sure you did. The important thing for you is that you were right all along. You have been vindicated. I was never going to make it. Never getting it quite right, always slow on the uptake. You saw that writing on the wall. It's a good thing you got out when you did, don't you think? But there's no satisfaction in being right, is there? Somehow I've escaped as if to another country, and that rankles.*

I made myself stop smiling; I didn't want to infuriate her any further. My silence spoke for itself as far as she was concerned. Yet she wasn't quite ready to give up.

'For Christ's sake, Michael, you've always had something to say for yourself.' She turned to Frank and Mavis. 'When push came to shove, he was never short of words.'

Frank nodded, 'But he did stutter.' He looked at Mavis for support, but she was intent on the frog.

'He soon got over that,' Aria said dismissively. 'He was always full of himself.'

Frank looked uneasy. People had said the same thing about him. More than once he'd been called a blowhard. *You're not blowing hard now though, are you Frank?* the same pickled onion voice said in my head.

'Maybe he's in love,' Aria said meditatively, fiddling with her coffee cup. 'They say love can strike a person dumb. In extreme cases.'

Frank didn't know what to say. Such a thought was way above his pay grade. Mavis looked up knowledgeably, as if she might know about such things, or that it behoved her to appear knowledgeable about such things. Perhaps there was a Dinah Lee song on the subject.

Aria turned on me, 'What's her name?' she said in voice full of splinters. She turned back to Frank and Mavis, 'Apparently when he was a kid he fell in love with a Russian girl. He was only five years old, for Chrisakes. They probably played doctors and nursies.' Her laugh was as brittle as breaking glass.

'I remember that girl,' Frank said. He was like a drowning man who'd been thrown a lifeline. He turned to Mavis, 'Now... what was her name?'

'How would I know?' Mavis said.

I didn't want Frank to remember Olga's name. I didn't want to hear it coming from his mouth.

'Cat's got his tongue,' Aria said to the room. She banged her coffee cup down, got up, and tried to pace around the room. It was too small for pacing. She took several deep breaths. She would count up to ten in order to get a grip on herself. It was an old trick she had learned to curb her impatience. Some things don't change. 'Cat's got his tongue,' she repeated.

I wondered if she knew the French version, I throw my tongue to the cat, which is a lot more colourful.

'I don't know what to say, Michael,' she said. She sat back down like someone about to get up again soon. To Frank and Mavis she said, 'I guess it wouldn't matter what I said. I could tell him the moon was made of Swiss cheese for all he'd care.'

Frank tried to laugh as if she'd made a joke. His bum was rubbing a large dent in the couch. Mavis wasn't sure whether to join him or not; after all, the moon did look a little like a round of Swiss cheese.

The silence became mossy. Something heavy and unspoken hung in the air. Aria lifted the coffee cup to her lips, but it was empty.

'Oh, and by the way, I finally got to read *Middlemarch*. Remember, you said it was the finest novel written in English in the nineteenth century, maybe ever. It was a bit tedious at times, but I see what you mean. It's all about the position of women in society, isn't it? A woman locked in a loveless relationship. Maybe you thought I could relate to that.'

Despite her sarcasm, she was reaching for our halcyon days when our talk ranged far and wide over literature and science. I don't know what she thought that would achieve, or what difference it would make if I did start blabbing away about George Eliot, or about the pathos and tragedy of the novel? Would it take us any further? Would it illuminate our own pathos and tragedy?

At the same time, it was curious that she'd finally read the novel, and I wondered why she had bothered. Was it to feel closer to me over there in California? Did she maybe miss me and my tedious lichens, mosses and liverworts? Maybe she'd just got bored hanging around the mighty particle accelerator doing maintenance work, watching her man get ahead instead of her.

'Oh Michael, Michael, Michael, Michael!' she chanted, as if the repetition of my name alone might change something in the world. She rocked back and forth on her chair and looked at me as if to say, 'How did we come to this?' but she didn't say anything more; for the moment she too was speechless. Then she began to cry in little self-pitying sobs. My pickled onion voice had no pity – or guilt. *No Aria, these are crocodile tears and they really don't suit you. You make your bed, you lie in it, Mum used to say.*

'Maybe we should all have a little sing-song,' Mavis said, and she began singing in a high quavering voice, '*When the red-red robin comes bob-bob-bobbin' along, sweet song...*'

Frank had the sale papers all ready and produced them like a magician pulling a rabbit from a hat, producing a pen with the same flourish. 'Let's get this show on the road,' he said.

Aria nodded fervently.

Mavis sang,

'Wake up, wake up you sleepy head
Get up, get out of bed
Cheer up, cheer up the sun is red
Live, love, laugh and be happy,'

Aria signed. Aria and Frank gave a big sigh of relief when I signed. I was no longer a property owner. They all watched me as if some miracle were taking place. Frank smiled with relief. 'Done and dusted,' he said, brushing his hands together.

'Gonna pack my cares in a whistle
Gonna blow them all away'

As if that signing released the floodgates, he and Aria and Mavis all began talking at once. It was as if they could make up for my not talking by flooding the room with their brisk voices. In this way they cobbled over my silence. All the talk was of flying. How long it took, how much it cost and how much leg room there was in economy seats. Aria made quite a long speech about the food, which she found quite disgusting although she ate it anyway. 'You've got to eat something,' she said. Frank talked about the hazards of the weather. Turbulence made him sick. 'After all, you're just bumping around in a tin can thousands of feet in the air,' he said. Mavis added that a couple of drinks was the answer.

Their talk surrounded me like a lot of birds fluttering in a cage.

It didn't last. After all, they didn't have that much in common. It started to come apart when Aria began talking about her work with the particle accelerator, and the exciting field of matter-energy research, in particular the search for super symmetrical particles, a kind of mirror image for all the known fundamental particles. 'We can create these particles,' she said, 'but they only exist for an instant.'

Frank's eyes began to glaze over. Mavis stared at Aria and nodded furiously as if she understood everything Aria was saying. I looked out the window at a perfectly ordinary seeming world. A man taking his dog for a walk. A puff of white cloud in a blue sky. Seagulls flying inland. The sound of a fire siren in the distance.

Pretty soon they were all talking about how they had things to do, places to go. Frank and Mavis to their motel to start packing, they had a flight to catch, and Aria had to go back to her mother who was on her own and a source of worry to her. Her problems were similar to Frank's – she didn't include me – in that she had to find care for an ailing parent. Costs were daunting. She'd be returning to California in a few days. Work called.

I was nothing more than the elephant in the room.

They couldn't get away fast enough.

As I watched them leave, another verse of the song Mavis had been singing ran through my head, not in her quavering tones but in the robust, somewhat drunken cadences of my parents, the way they used to sing at parties in Hanmer:

'What if I've been blue, now I'm walkin' through fields of flowers
Rain may glisten but still I listen for hours and hours
I'm just a kid again doin' what I did again singin' a song
When the red, red, robin comes bob, bob, bobbin' along.'

The big cop out

I met Janet Holden by accident in the corridors of the university. I'd left some papers in a locker and wanted to retrieve them. The university had not attempted to employ me after my contract with the conservation authorities ended. Perhaps they'd come back to me when there was more field work.

'Hello stranger,' she said brightly.

I nodded and smiled. I liked Janet. She was a smart cookie. I would miss our gloomy conversations, her cigarette shredding. Talking to her always made me feel that I was not alone in the way I saw the world. Her pessimism was like a breath of fresh air. There was a hard-bitten practicality to her that I responded to. No easy outs for Janet. She liked to face the world in all its madness fair and square.

When I didn't speak, she looked harder at me. 'So it's true, is it, what I've heard? You're not talking. You don't do anything but nod, smile and shake your head.'

I nodded and smiled.

'Fascinating,' she said. 'Have you seen a shrink?'

I nodded but left out the smile.

'And what was the upshot of that?'

I shrugged. You can say a lot with a shrug.

'Of course. Come on, oh silent one, have a cup of coffee with me. Maybe I can loosen your tongue, you know, if it's just got stuck to the roof of your mouth.'

Because she bore me only good-will, I went with her. We found a quiet table in the student cafe and lined up our coffees. We stared down at them as if we could read our fortunes there in the whirly cream on top.

'Is this some grand, heroic gesture?'

I shook my head. Students passed our table, to and fro, taking no notice of us. We might have been invisible. A group sat at a table near us, talking animatedly, hands flying, eyebrows flying, teeth glinting.

'The only thing it's going to do, you know, is make you complicit. And that's a shame. Silence is no act of rebellion. It's caving into the lies of the world, an abject surrender. Silence is an unblown whistle, a disappeared activist, a dismembered journalist. Silence slides down one generation to the next, keeping pain a secret.'

I nodded. She was right, of course.

'People tell me human nature is the problem. I don't think so. We've just surrendered our power to the bullies and the greedy gutses, the liars and despoilers. All we have to do is toss the tossers out of power. Your silence doesn't challenge the established order, far from it, it supports it. Even a dog will scream when run over. One final yelp of protest. But you, you're happy to die in silence. A martyr to nothing.'

I didn't feel the least bit like dying. I felt more alive than I'd been for a long time, as if, in my silence, something had awoken inside me, some slumbering force once hidden by the wild whirl of words, a leviathan of unknown dimensions rising up from the deep in a spray of light. I dreamed of a big cat, a panther, who could move sure-footed through its silence, invisible in the dark. I would wake up at night with my head singing. If I was sleeping in the park, which I did when the weather was warm, the night sky would show me the constellations of the heart. The soft air would brush my skin with a lover's touch. There were no words to screen me from the world.

She stirred her coffee as if she had sugar in it. She was struggling to stay calm, stung by what she saw as my betrayal. She was getting angry because I was no longer her mirror. I had become opaque. She could no longer read herself in me.

She brought herself under control and sipped her coffee without pleasure. I saw that her grey hair must at one time have been a light blonde, and I started to wonder why she had never married, if there weren't perhaps some tragedy in her past she hadn't shared with me, a tragedy that left her alone in the world.

'So you're going to run away to the mountains again, or some other remote place. Take refuge in your mosses, lichens and liver-whatevers, I suppose.' She tossed her head. 'You're going to hide away from people. Run if you see them coming. Cross to the other side of the street. What do you think you are? A Zen monk? Those Zen monks are full of crap. They only live in caves to get away from temptation. Then they boast that they have overcome their desires.'

I didn't think Zen monks did much boasting, but I took her point. I was not, however, running away. There was nothing to run away from. There was just a whole lot of people going places, from here to there; some happily, some sadly, some full of energy, some tired as hell, some full of aggression, some full of greed, some full of hope, some full of emptiness, some certain of themselves, others lost. And maybe some like me with nothing more to say.

'But how are you going to live?' She looked around helplessly, 'Order a cup of coffee, whatever? We have to talk our way through the world, that's how it is. That's how we are.'

She probably couldn't imagine how easy it was to get around a city without talking. You can go into a supermarket, do your shopping and leave without uttering a single word. And I tended not to frequent cafes. Cafes are for chatterers. I went to Charlie's once, just for old times' sake. Glenda was no longer working there. There was an older woman with grey hair and a tired face behind the same sad custard squares, and she could barely muster a 'thank you.' Chad didn't turn up. The old guy in a quilted jacket walked past but didn't come in. He didn't so much as glance at me. I sat there in the perfect anonymity that had first drawn me there.

'It's all very symbolic and everything, but you're not going to be able to sustain it. We're social animals, gregarious by nature. We talk, we talk all the time, like birds in the trees. The whole world is cocooned in a net of words. You can't escape them. People are constantly cross-referencing their experiences. Gossip makes the world go round.' She pointed to the students at the nearby table. They were laughing and talking ninety to the dozen.

The pickled onion voice in my head had lost its tartness and was coming through in overlapping fragments. There was a gentle resignation in it, like a dying exhalation. I saw word bubbles appearing above my head as if I were a cartoon character. They appeared then popped out of existence.

> *I'm not trying to escape*
> *from words words words*
> *I just can't speak speak*
> *speak or hold your peace*
> *hold my peace*
> *my piece*
> *I have spoken my piece*
> *and my words have gone*
> *their own sweet way*
> *away, far away*
> *way away*

'You're cutting yourself off from people. That's the net effect. I mean, we're here now, but it's a one-sided conversation. I'm not going to come here and sit with you just to hear the sound of my own voice. This grand gesture of yours is futile. It's totally self-defeating. People will wipe you off as a clown or a fool. Or a bit mental. You won't like it. I bet it won't last.'

I was reminded of a novel by Italo Calvino about a man who, as an adolescent, took to the trees and never came down. He lived his entire life in a network of branches, ignoring all pleas to return to earth, even ignoring the prospect of love. I admired that man. Perhaps his original gesture had been an act of petulance, but he lived it, followed it through to the very end. Like him I would live among my branches of silence and hear the sound of human voices from afar.

'And you're not consistent. I mean, you're writing your articles, which are very good by the way, Yes? Well, you're happy to use words then. So don't be a hypocrite and talk to me now. Just fucking say something.'

There was a difference, of course, and she could see it even as she spoke. I could write words and tick boxes; it was talking that had gone, those fly-by-night words. Nor would I carry a pad around and write things down for people. Frank had tried that one. Words were only available to my body when I was writing. My fingers could take words for a walk, that's all. Maybe Janet was right. Maybe I couldn't earn enough from my writing and would have to talk myself into a job at some point. Maybe I'd fall in love and find words waiting for me on a pillow. Maybe an enchantment would take a hold of me and my voice would soar into meaning. Or maybe, as I already suspected, even that tenuous connection to words would fade.

'I don't know,' she said, sipping her coffee without satisfaction. 'It's bloody frustrating is what it is. You'll nod and shake your head and won't write any notes. I mean, we could sit here and write to each other and you wouldn't have to say a bloody word. Have you thought about that?

I shook my head.

'We're not going to meet again, are we? Not unless you come to my office on the off-chance of finding me. We're only here now because we ran into each other by accident, right? Right. So that's not going to happen again because you won't be working here. You'll have no reason to be here. Come to think of it, why would you bother trying to see me, or anybody for that matter, when you've got nothing to say? You don't make a date with someone just to sit there in your holier-than-thou silence. It's not just frustrating, it's bloody depressing. Who else am I going to talk to around here? Everybody's so busy getting on with it. You were a bit of a Jeremiah, but you were the nearest I had to a drinking buddy. We only drank coffee, but, you know, the principle's the same. Now you've pooped out on me, and that's a loss. You've copped out, dropped out, resigned from the human race. I'm going to miss you, you silly bastard. What happened to you? You were passionate in the face of the world's ills and humanity's madness. Now you're turning into a corpse right in front of my eyes. Do you realise that? You might as well be a zombie, you know, just aimlessly shuffling around. Yeah, I know, words are cheap, but you'll pay for your silence. What's going to keep you on the go? What's going to get you up and out of bed in the morning? Where's the fun in it? Where's the joy in it? Have you thought that you might be suffering from depression? What do the shrinks say? Maybe there's a pill you could take. A word pill. Just chuck it back and, lo and behold! words will flow. The dam will break and you will joyously discover the beauty of talking. You'll get through this. I know you will. I have faith in you; you have faced the worst and pulled through. You're having an episode, right? Right. The episode will end. You will rejoin the human race. We'll rejoice and get drunk and say whatever stupid thing comes into our mouths. That will be fun. When did you last get bad and drunk? I bet that would loosen your tongue. You can't bottle it up forever, you know. Throwing a tantrum's not the answer. It's wilful nonsense. So you go to the garden and eat worms. Then what? After you've had your fill of worms?'

I laughed. She just looked so funny getting all steamed up. She didn't laugh. For a moment she looked crushed. I took her hand and squeezed it. I didn't want her to think I was mocking her. She pulled her hand free and banged the table. This was happening to me quite often. Our coffee cups jumped up and down. The students at the nearby table paused and looked across at us. Janet didn't care. She raised her arm as if she was going to slap me across the face.

'Ask yourself, oh silent one, where is all this leading? I mean what's the moral of the story? What are you leaving us with?' Her hand hung in the air. 'All good stories have a moral, you know that. A little nugget of wisdom or insight that we can take away with us. Your journey leaves us with a big fat nothing. A sulky silence.'

She stopped talking and there it was, my sulky silence.

'The only conclusion I can come to is that you think you're better than everybody else, the chattering apes around you. Do we disgust you? Are you nauseated by humanity, like that French writer? Do we want to make you puke? Have you puked all your words? Would you rather be on a mountain top looking down at humanity from a great height? That great height is the measure of your egotism. Do you feel superior to everyone you meet? All the silly sods that expect you to talk, to answer a civil question. Your silence is a fucking portcullis, did you know that? It's a big steel grid between you and the rest of us. You'll never have another relationship, that's for sure. A relationship is built on closeness and closeness is built on communication, but why the fuck am I telling you this? You know this as well as I do. I shouldn't have to be saying these things. You're not stupid, although I'm starting to wonder. You're just going to give the big fat middle finger to everybody, friends and strangers alike, and wank in your room, if you still have a room. If you still have any balls. It's no good giving me those Mona Lisa smiles, or should I say smirks? Well, fuck you!'

She was on her feet now and ready to leave. She took one last look around to make sure she hadn't left anything. She wanted to rush off, but hadn't quite finished with me. She hesitated as if being pulled by contrary forces.

'Aren't you frightened? Frightened of ending up alone. With nobody. Frightened of being isolated? I know I would be. I'd be terrified if I was struck dumb. To never speak to another human being until I died, that's the stuff of nightmares. Like being stranded on a beach that never ends. Or waking up to find your mouth sewn up. Not being able to reach out. Not being able to call for help. I'd be terrified, I tell you. My heart would just stop beating.'

She started breathing heavily, as if suffocating. She had to get away from me to somewhere she could breathe. Her face was pale and bleak. I smiled at her, hoping perhaps to reassure her. In that smile was all the love I had for her, for everybody. She saw it and it confused her. She thought I was depressed. Depressed people don't smile like that, with sudden warmth.

She shook her head and turned away. It was an ancient gesture, as if she'd done it many times before. Her hair looked greyer than I remembered, her body stiffer. There was an exhaustion in her no words could heal. With grim determination she headed for the door. She had a slight limp.

She didn't look back.

I didn't move. I sat in front of my empty coffee cup, wondering idly why I drank coffee in the city. Out in the field, I drank only tea. I watched the students coming and going. None took the slightest notice of me. My pickled-onion voice now had its say.

I understand why you said those things to me, Janet. You were trying to get a rise out of me, fair enough. But you are wrong about a lot of it too. I am not depressed. I'm light and I'm free. I can raise my face to the sun and feel the delight of it. I can go walking in the rain and hum. I can sit in exquisite twilight and watch the stars quietly emerge, or fade. I can hear the steady, joyful beating of my heart and know that all life is a blessing. I can dance with the shadows and flirt with the light. The possible destruction of my known world from nuclear war or environmental destruction no longer sits heavily upon me, and you can judge me for that if you wish. I could hold my hand up in front of my face but a bullet would pass right through it. I have not internalised that unfolding doom, even as it makes me sad. My silence is the lightest cloak.

I am not throwing a tantrum or a hissy fit, as Aria called it. I am calm, calmer than I've been for a very long time, yet nothing like a zombie. Zombies are not calm. I can read, and revel in the flow of words passing before my eyes. I can write as long as I stick to the facts. Words can't pin anything down; they only appear to do so. They pass through the world like shadows. I hope you'll eventually forgive me for no longer grasping for them.

I don't despise humanity, or feel superior to anybody, far from it. Rather I feel sad. Sad that we are killing everything around us. Sad in the face of greed and stupidity. People don't make me nauseous. I see people in all their beauty, and ugliness. I see people made luminous by light or locked in darkness, emerging from themselves or disappearing. I don't know why there has to be a moral to my life. I haven't lived my life to prove a point. Does a tree have a moral? Does a stone? Does the brief life of the Ephemeroptera? *The long life of a tuatara? Are human stories different in this respect? I don't know. I cannot just make up a moral where there is none. I am under no obligation to produce a moral. That would be ridiculous. A human life tells its own story. Take what you like from it. My life is not a cautionary tale or an inspirational one. There are no prizes for me in the lucky dip. I take what I get.*

I do, however, take to heart your accusation that I have copped out. Silence has never stopped any atrocity in its tracks. Only vociferous opposition can do that, powerful and passionately reasoned. My silence won't change anything, or subvert anything. I don't think it is particularly admirable. I'm not trying to be admirable. I don't want, or expect, anybody to emulate me. This isn't a place to stand, still less raise a flag. It is just the awkward place where I've landed. After living a lifetime in Balashikha with Olga, I have returned to this world emptied of words. I was in Charlie's, I opened my mouth but nothing came out. That was neither a virtue nor a fault; it is just what happened. Was it under my control? Could I snap out of it, as everybody is urging? Maybe, but that is not what is happening. Somehow it feels right and fitting, a right and fitting end, if you like. Somehow my whole life had been leading up to that moment, the moment in Charlie's when I'd opened my mouth to say something to Chad, something that would wake him up, and found my throat empty. It is not a pathology. There is no pill for it. You think it's my Great Refusal, and I'm tempted to do the same, but that's making too much of a myth out of it. If anything it is acceptance. I accept what is. I'm not making a big fuss about it; other people are making the fuss.

When I got up to leave the student café, I realised how tired I was, more than tired, world weary was the term. While still young of body, I felt ancient inside with all the weariness of an old soul. I found myself talking inside my head to you, my word bringer, and my voice was no longer a pickled onion. There was a softness in it. *Life is bigger than us, comrade, certainly bigger than me, for I'm nothing more than one of those particles in Aria's accelerator, a Higgs boson perhaps, more theoretical than real, nothing more than a few nanoseconds of miraculous existence and bedazzlement. In those few nanoseconds I pass through the birth and death of suns, the rise and fall of planets and the coming and going of the word. The Word. I am weary, but the life within me isn't, if you can understand that, if you're still there to understand it. The weary word can barely make it from one syllable to the next without falling into the dark spaces between. Janet wants me to stand up for the world, and she is right to do so, but you know as well as I do that the time for that, at least for me, has passed.*

There was more than weariness at work, however, as I passed from the student café into the afternoon light. Something I didn't want to face. If talking gives my words body, not talking makes me bodiless. I would slowly become invisible. People would be able to walk right through me as if I was nothing more substantial than a notions, a passing thought. So far, I'd felt that I could start talking again if I truly wanted to; if the occasion ever arose, the words would be there. You can't forget how to talk. Now I sensed that the distance between spoken words and myself had grown insurmountable, and that I would return to speech only at some terrible cost I could hardly imagine.

A bridge between the public and the private

In the winter our library becomes a source of warmth and security for the city's homeless and displaced. Quiet and respectful, not making eye contact, they shuffle in seeking the comfortable couches by the windows where they can doze and recover from the cold. They wear long, shapeless clothes of indeterminate colour they find at the Red Cross or City Mission shops and scarves wrapped around their faces. The men have unruly beards. As long as they don't make any fuss, however, the library staff tend to ignore them. Every so often, public-minded citizens make an effort to get rid of them, to keep the library as a sanctuary for actual readers, but run into the unanswerable question – where are they to go?

When it is too cold or wet to sit in the park I join them, finding a table where I can set up my notebook and enjoy wandering the aisles, enjoying the collective murmur of words from the shelves. That murmur sounds like the ocean, heard from a distance, rubbing against the shore, and I think of them like that, an ocean of words sighing as they rise and fall. Sometimes I'm quite focused, looking for a particular book, and sometimes I just dawdle along enjoying their presence.

During one particularly aimless ramble I met one of these homeless, known as Shirley, coming the other way, from the crime section, veering from one shelf to the opposite, pausing momentarily to peer at some volume as if she might indeed one day get around to reading it, forestalling any untoward attention from the vigilant librarians. Shirley is what is known as a 'character' for her ravaged appearance and sudden outbursts. Everybody knows Shirley and everybody avoids her. She has long, greasy grey hair and a face marked by years of suffering and abuse. Her eyes are a startling blue and as sharp as pieces of glass. Woe betide any of those public-minded citizens who are impaled on that blue gaze, for she doesn't hesitate to give them a piece of her mind, often random or obscure complaints.

Shirley doesn't lower her eyes as many of the homeless do when they confront those better off than themselves but will fix them with an accusing stare and begin to rumble in her chest as if rummaging around for words in a dank basement. She's on her best behaviour in the library, having on occasion been ejected by stern librarians for accosting innocent readers or scaring children. When she saw me coming, she swerved towards me and stood right in front of me, close enough for me to smell her, the smell of the unwashed, and see that her mouth was moving as if she were chewing on something. Close enough to become subject to that penetrating gaze.

'I know you,' she said, her voice so vocally fried it was leached of any timbre. 'You're the bloke who doesn't talk.'

I nodded.

She cackled as if that were a hell of a joke, and put her hand over her mouth the way a child would who's said something out of turn and looked around wide-eyed as if there were hostile ears everywhere. 'Your name is Zechariah, and you have been struck dumb by the Lord.' She lifted up her arms in supplication. 'Oh ye of little faith.'

I backed away and she followed. 'You must believe! Believe and you will talk again. The Lord will unlock your heart. Return to him and he will return to you.' Her voice rose and the librarian behind her desk looked in our direction. Shirley noticed too, and put her finger to her lips as if I were the one making the noise.

Later, I would look up Zechariah and discover that he was the father of

John the Baptist. The Gospel of St Luke told the story of how Zechariah didn't believe an angel of the Lord who told him that his wife, Elizabeth, would soon give birth to a son. They were too old, Zechariah said, and demanded a sign that the angel spoke the truth. For his lack of faith, his god struck him dumb and he could no longer pray. That was the only sign he was going to get. At the time, however, I could only stare at Shirley wondering what it was all about. I had become accustomed to mockery, but nothing like this.

'You'll get your sign all right,' Shirley said, and, making peculiar circular motions with her hands, pointed dramatically to a random book as if conjuring it out of the air. Then she turned and walked away with a distinctive, half-limping gait, looking back over her shoulder at me fearfully as if I might be coming after her.

When she had gone, I examined the book, *The Words* by Jean Paul Sartre. I took the book to a table and sampled various pages. The writer seemed to have grown tired and disillusioned with words. One sentence jumped out at me: 'I confused things with their names: that is belief.' I thought about that for a long time while the life of the library buzzed on around me. What did it mean to confuse things with their names, and is that what I had been doing all my life?

> 'I was the beginning, the middle and the end all rolled into one small boy, already old, already dead, here, in the shadows, between the stacks of plates higher than himself, and outside, very far away, in the cast and gloomy sunshine of glory. I was the particle at the beginning of its trajectory and the series of waves which flows back on it after it has struck the terminal buffer. Reassembled and compressed, one hand on my tomb and the other on my cradle, I felt brief and splendid, a flash of lightning swallowed up in darkness.'

I read and re-read that paragraph, thinking of the way we ping back and forward between our childhood and our present moment, and how we are held, wordless, between those polarities, 'a flash of lightning swallowed up in darkness.' Hadn't I too been 'reassembled and compressed' by my experiences in the Alps and my time in Balashikha? I knew from my discussions with Aria about the wave/particle duality at the quantum level where matter could not be pinned down by our words and by our either/or thinking, and that the polarity between mind and matter was similarly problematic.

'All children are mirrors of death,' Sartre wrote, and I felt that was true, particularly when our childhood becomes merely the images we have of it, flickering and discontinuous. There we find time bending back upon itself, the Pterodactyl world echoing into our present.

While reading and pondering, I was aware of Shirley hanging around behind me, not close enough to be intrusive but close nevertheless. There was a gleeful aspect in the way she was watching me as if anticipating some spectacle, that I might leap to my feet and shout something revelatory, or go mad there in the quiet sanity of the library, trapped between my being and nothingness. She was acting as if she knew me, that we shared some special, intimate knowledge. I didn't like that but I tried to ignore it.

'I invested myself with a holy silence,' Sartre wrote.

I did not think of my silence as holy in any way. I'd heard the expression 'the fool of god' or 'holy fool' but I did not think of myself in such exalted terms; I was no more than an ordinary fool, sans god. Sartre seemed to be seeking some grand, overall meaning, as if words contained their own redemption whereas I, sitting in the library, this mausoleum of books, was seeking nothing more than a resonance with my own experience. I knew that, underneath the skin of things, I was not alone.

Knowing that you would soon leave me and even writing would become impossible, I began to see a way forward from plant taxonomy to the purposeful recording of memories, experiences, opinions, and emotions. Sartre's autobiography revealed a distinction between narrative as a literary tool and narrative as a lived experience. I had no interest in literary tools but grappled with my lived experience. Reading Sartre threw me back to Hanmer and my earliest experiences. Those memories were, of themselves, a mirror. In that mirror I saw not just myself, but various selves at various stages, all of which I could lay claim to without slipping into fiction and literary devices, which I wanted to avoid like the plague.

I also saw that the 'me' who was sitting in the library reading, and the 'me' of the lived experience could enter into something of a co-creative relationship. Was it possible for me to go back in time and rescue my former self from the oblivion of childhood? This 'me,' this person sitting in the library, could then become a governing force within the writing, as I explored emotions, thoughts, intersectional identities, social roles, relationships in their temporal positions. I saw that this was, in essence, writing to the self, not just from the self. By writing to the self, the self knows itself, creates itself, frees itself. In this way I might make sense of the world and put me in sync with my authentic self.

This way I could avoid the temptations of fiction, with its devices and deceptions, and cleave directly to the truth of the matter. In doing so I would take care to avoid creating an ideal self rather than a real self. I could always sit there, in my library chair, and decide how to project myself to the world, fabricate a self rather than uncover a self, using the seductive excuse that by so doing I might stage the rebellion against the destructive social order I didn't have the courage for in my actual lived experience.

My true interest, and what was causing the blood to pump purposefully through my veins, was the kind of writing that became, through the process of disclosure and discovery, a meaning-making activity, one that entailed making sense of the world and the experiences I had endured within it. Through such an approach, the outlines of an identity might be perceived, and a bridge between the public and the private created, as Sartre was attempting to do.

If I could bring in not just my past self but my present, speechless self, sitting in the library now scribbling furiously in my notebook, I might capture how the sense of my experience of the present moment could convey, to my eager reader, the very quality of this life itself, enabling its usefulness regardless of surreal and imaginative fiction.

I faced an inchoate desire to abandon my science writing, my meticulous cataloguing, and write my own exquisite, wind-tunnelled book in which I might tell my story in the plainest language I could find, my own discovery and loss of words, the dissolving of my word cage. I was sure I would have no difficulty finding a language scarred enough by life for the job. The problem was readers might think I was writing fiction, and then where would we be? Lost among the mirrors. I wouldn't want my story to be mistaken for a novel, dismissed as a fantasy. I could avoid that trap by sticking closely to what actually happened to me.

Besides, I wouldn't have the skill to write such a fiction.

While I was thinking all this through, thinking about the division between the self and others, the limits of remembering and forgetting,

Shirley was still lurking behind me, and the other homeless on their couches were no longer dozing but appeared to be watching me with prurient interest, as if I were about to strip in public. Shirley had begun to do an exotic, seductive dance, weaving her arms in what she perhaps imagined were sinuous movements, and rotating her hips. This display was not too overt, but attracted the interest of the librarian, who came out from behind her desk and approached. The homeless laughed and nudged each other as Shirley was gently escorted to the door. Before meekly leaving, Shirley half-turned and shot me a knowing look.

The tongue set free

After Shirley went, I got up and headed for the autobiography section to return the Sartre, and it was there I found a treasure: all three volumes of Elias Canetti's autobiography, *The Tongue Set Free*, *The Torch in My Ear* and *The Play of the Eyes*. These titles alone excited me. It was love at first sight, even before I'd read the first sentence. Triumphantly, I bore my prize back to the desk. As soon as I began reading, I felt at home. This was quite different from Sartre, who made me feel displaced and whose natural habitat was alienation.

The Tongue Set Free begins with an arresting first memory, and a wonderfully arresting first sentence: 'My earliest memory is dipped in red.' I had to stop right there. I began to wonder if memories could be stained with colours and if so, what colours my memories might be.

Canetti relates how, as a child, he comes out of a door to find a red floor and a red staircase, and a man, smiling, coming towards him all friendly, who, after asking him to poke out his tongue, produces a jackknife, which he places against the boy's tongue, and says, in a cheery voice, 'Now we'll cut off his tongue.' The boy is too terrified to move. 'Not today, tomorrow,' the man says, putting away the knife and moving on.

Years later, Canetti realises that this was his nursemaid's lover, frightening him into silence about their rendezvous. Speech thus becomes the portal into the forbidden adult world. Say the wrong thing and lose your tongue.

I liked this more than Sartre, perhaps because Canetti writes like a nineteenth century novelist, that is, as if we had all the time in the world to read and ponder, time to allow sentences to unfold and thoughts and images to resonate in our minds.

Excited by my find, I took the books to the check-out desk and watched the librarian verify my library card. She didn't say anything and I guessed she knew I didn't speak. She was business-like, but not open and friendly. I think she thought I might be a homeless person too, but the homeless don't carry notebooks around or have library cards. Still, there was something not quite right about me, and she didn't want to meet my eye. Perhaps she thought I would never return the books.

As I headed for the door, planning to return to my cheap room, I saw, sitting among the homeless men, the old man with the quilted jacket I had seen at Charlie's. Was he homeless too? Dispassionately, he watched me leave the library.

I carried that look with me out into the street.

A vision marvellous to behold

It was while sitting in Hagley Park, with the sound of barking dogs and the voices of children pattering around me, that the outlines of a possible writing project came to me. I began to scribble furiously in my notebook. I couldn't talk, yet words could speak through me onto the pages of my notebook. That was the only conduit they had.

All I had to do was follow my development from Hanmer to the present day without any fictional tricks. Very straightforward. Some judicious editing was all I'd need.

When I was young, before I became a devotee of taxonomy, I thought it would be nice to write a novel. A celebration of the self. I soon gave up on the idea. Forget the self and study the world, I decided. Study the life you can scrape off a rock with a knife. Resist the lure of the word. Be as the fungus. Eschew fiction at all costs.

The word novel conjures up a more leisurely age; the leisure to create one, the leisure and the money to consume it, the concentration to encompass it, to enjoy the pleasure of its intricacies. I don't know if the novel is possible now. Brutal factors have intervened. Massive cultural dislocations and upheavals have taken place. Writing novels and reading them has become a privileged activity.

However, an honest report from experience – that was something else. I would incubate it most fastidiously as it grew into form. Fidelity to its movement would be my guiding principle. The vision I had of the work belonged, if anywhere, to the Platonic realm of forms. I knew I could never bring this vision into the world, since it was more in the nature of an enchanted intellectual entity, but it might give birth to itself on the page in what words I could summon for the task. Ordinary words. Perhaps this is why you came to me in the first place, preparing me for this very task from the moment I started feeling my way in the world with words. Or trying to.

Now I am rendered speechless that I might, paradoxically, undertake this report.

A boy and his dog.

That particular afternoon was warm and I decided to sleep on a park bench. My field work had accustomed me to sleeping rough. Sleeping under the stars had always been a pleasure. Lying quietly in my mountain jacket and leggings, watching the sky darken and shadows creep out from under everything, was to anticipate that pleasure. Now I could add the pleasure of contemplating my great vision. An open sky of words.

I had already started making notes on my early life in Hanmer, remembering things forgotten, such as how snow, when falling from the sky, looks black from underneath, and how Conical Hill became the dark forest of fairy-tales, complete with the brooding presence of a hybrid creature, half hawk half bull. I was of that age. The world curved into magic. Brightly coloured beings flew up from the pages of a book. Cowboys rode out of storm clouds. A girl in a pleated dress stood under a sycamore tree. She was dressed in the colours of autumn. The word bringer appeared out of the silence, bringing with him an ocean.

I wrote as much as I could as fast as I could, driven by the fear that the next morning I would wake up and I wouldn't have language, that written words would go the same way as speech, that my pen would hover above the page with nowhere to land, that my sentence would slip forever beyond my grasp, unfinished. I jotted everything down before it vanished. True details. I only wanted true details. The real thing. I was convinced that words were as real as things in themselves. All I had to do was tear off their masks. Let the real show through.

A gold-coloured labrador came running up to me and offered to lick my hand. I am not that keen on dog slobber and patted its head instead. A child's voice called and the dog raced away, running to a boy who was watching me. The elm tree under which he was standing strained delicately towards the lowering sky. He had a presence bigger than his body. I gave him a brief glance but couldn't tear myself away from my notes. True details, but how to cut the difference between memory and the imagination? There was a family story about how I once chased Frank down the main street of Hanmer with a garden fork. I seem to remember the incident, but am suspicious of the memory as I saw myself and Frank as if from the other side of the street, as if I was someone else watching us. Two kids running along, the older chasing the younger. That can't be right.

Perhaps this is a false memory created out of images I have formed from the story as told by my parents, who thought it was very amusing and liked to tell lots of people, so I must have heard it many times and put pictures to it. It might have happened, but I can't be sure I remember it. How many of my memories, I wondered, were similar constructions. Canetti didn't say anything about that.

Wrapped in these thoughts, I didn't notice that the little boy was now right in front of me, the dog beside him.

'Are you the man who doesn't talk?' the boy said. The dog looked at me encouragingly.

I nodded.

'Don't you have a tongue?'

I poked out my tongue to show him that I did, remembering the man who threatened to cut off the tongue of a little boy who might have seen too much. I put pictures to that too, but it didn't happen to me. It was someone else's memory.

He poked his tongue back at me. We understood each other perfectly.

'Don't you like talking?' the boy said.

I shook my head slowly.

'What does your mother say?'

Good question, what would my mother say if she were alive? She would probably shake her head just as I was doing. What could she say? Words fail me? That she had been afraid of this all along? That talking had been a struggle for me right from the start? 'Poor Michael finds it hard to hold onto the world,' she might have said. 'He took ages to learn how to talk and even then... even then he stuttered like a constipated chook.' Had Mum really said that, at some point, or had I just made it up because it was something she might have said? Because it sounded like her? Memory and the imagination doing a tango. The pen moving both ways on the page.

'Are you a freak? You must be. He must be,' the boy said to the dog. The dog didn't answer him either. 'Mum would whack me if I clammed up.'

I was beginning to see that writing things down as they happened, simply and chronologically, had pitfalls. Don't over think it, I instructed myself. Transcribe this conversation as it happened. My notes were just observations, not that different from my field notes; they were a different kind of field notes. The taxonomy of a life. Hours carefully catalogued. The mountainside on which I trod so carefully in search of a small bird was not made of rock and shale but memory; the empty city which I traversed with my childhood sweetheart was not of brick and glass but delicate shades of fancy. Unlikely creatures of the air, a strange boy on a logging track, another boy who flew down his grandparents' stairs, and who was offered scones and raspberry jam. Another boy whose mother turned into a pig and danced around the room with him as the saints came marching in. Another boy who trembled with the shadows on the path up Conical Hill.

I thought the boy now standing in front of me would get bored and run away. That didn't happen. He held onto the dog's collar and stared at me solemnly while the dog quivered with impatience. I guess he'd never met anyone who didn't talk, even when you got cheeky.

'Could you talk if you wanted to?'

I nodded very slowly, not quite sure what 'wanting' had to do with it. I didn't want anything at that moment but to scribble my thoughts down before they escaped on the run, or hid around the corner of the years. Maybe later I'd want something to eat. I had a corned-beef sandwich in my pack, which is why the dog was sniffing around it.

The boy nodded with me, as if he'd just attained great wisdom. 'Sometimes I have to bite my tongue. If I say the wrong thing...' He drew his hand across his throat. Say no more!

In the background, his friends were calling for him. Shadows were flying over the grass from fleeing clouds, heading west. The world was moving but the boy was struck still. He was fascinated by this guy who didn't talk, not because he couldn't, but because he didn't.

'I've gotta go now,' he said. His friends were still calling him. The dog was pulling him away. Shadows were racing over the grass in hot pursuit of the afternoon. We were caught in the heartless passage of time. He was reluctant to go. There was something here for him and he didn't know what it was. I didn't know either. I didn't know if I had anything to give him. We stared at each other. Suddenly he had nothing to say. He was momentarily caught in the web of my silence. An eddy in time. We reached an understanding. We were alike. The same things fascinated us.

Language often hides rather than tells, I thought. Show and tell are smoke and mirrors. That was why I felt so free and airy not having to talk. I didn't have to hide anything. Spaces opened up endless possibilities not concerned with expression. Things happening beyond the clutter of mind might show themselves the way the world showed itself to the receptive eye. Something of this touched the boy. He stood on the edge of all the possibilities of his life.

'I hope you find it,' the boy said obscurely, turning and running away, the dog bounding joyfully along beside him. They didn't look back. I watched as he joined a small group of other boys. The boy with the dog pointed at me and the others all turned to look at me.

I jotted some more in my notebook, a couple of sentences concerning my expeditions to the singing stones and a river that could carry the sky all the way to the sea.

I kept writing until the light gave out.

Hey, mutie!

The group of children edged closer. First, they went into a huddle, their heads together, talking in low voices, the dog waggling in and out between their legs, and having come to some decision, they began to work their way towards me, laughing and fooling around. As they got closer, I saw that some of them were older than the boy with the dog, young teenagers, and there was a girl among them, a tomboy-looking girl.

I had a book open on my lap and was contemplating a quote from Karl Jung. I had begun to seek out writers whose experiences reflected mine. They helped me feel part of something larger rather than an impossible outsider. Jung wrote: 'Solitude is for me a fount of healing which makes my life worth living. Talking is often a torment for me, and

I need many days of silence to recover from the futility of words.'

The futility of words. That was the heart of the matter. The word bringer's curse. I thought of all the useless words Aria and I had shouted at each other, and my futile encounters with Chad in the no-mans-land of Charlie's. I thought of the glossolalia that had poured from my mouth as Cargill and I fossicked for stale cream buns behind the Stevens sisters' café in Hanmer. I thought of how, in Balashikha, words had fallen away as Olga and I grew closer. How our love grew in the solitude of the empty city.

The truth bringers were having their tongues cut out, even as I sat there.

Something hit the back of my neck, light but insistent. I swung around to see the children, standing back a safe distance with sticks and little stones in their hands and nervous grins on their faces. They waited tensely to see what I would do. I guessed I'd been struck by a stick.

'Hey mutie, why don't you say something?' one of them called. He was the oldest and the meanest. That made him leader, at least for the moment.

'He's not a mutie, he's a mutant,' another said, and they all tittered at this witticism. The boy with the dog did not laugh. He looked ashamed of himself but couldn't turn away, couldn't break with the group. The dog looked confused.

'I think he's a bit daft,' the girl said, speaking with a cockney-infused London accent. She looked askance at me as if she'd seen specimens like me before. 'You never know what he's bloody thinkin',' she said.

That was true. People were afraid of me as if, like that character of Kafka's, I had turned into an oversized beetle. Humans talk so that they don't become frightened of each other.

I replied with my most gentle and disarming smile. It was not insincere. I didn't want to scare anybody. What chance did these children have, given the world they would be growing into? Maybe they would live long enough to see the world burn up right in front of their eyes as fires leapt from mind to mind, glaciers melted and seas rose.

They edged closer. I could see one was getting ready to throw another stone. It looked a little too big. I stood and faced them. They edged back. 'Mutie, mutie!' one of them chanted.

If I tried to walk away, they would follow me, grow bolder with their success and perhaps throw more stones or sticks. If I did nothing, they would also be encouraged to test their bravery. I pointed to my throat and shook my head. I looked at them with great sadness.

'Aw, come on, let's go,' the boy with the dog said. The dog barked approvingly. Maybe their parents had told them to be nice to disabled people.

'Let's have some fun with him,' the one with the stone said.

'Yeah, let's,' the oldest and meanest said, keen to re-establish his dominance.

I shook my head again, crossed my hands over my heart and pointed to the sky.

'What does that mean?' the one with the stone said uneasily.

'He's going to die,' the girl said. 'That's a bit spooky, init?'

Suddenly none of them wanted to throw stones at the dying mutie.

'Let's get out of here,' the boy with the dog said, starting to walk away, the dog only too happy to follow him. A couple of others drifted away.

The one with the stone and the eldest held their ground. There was an identical cruelty in their look. I locked eyes with them. I'd heard that you could stare some animals down. Maybe it was the same with these children.

'He's a half-wit,' the one with the stone said. 'He's boring.' But he didn't drop his stone.

The eldest had a stick and desired nothing more than to poke me with it. Maybe he could poke some words out of me. I locked eyes with him.

'We can get him any time,' the eldest said.

'He's always hanging around here,' the other said.

By common accord they moved away. The afternoon was getting on and the shadows were growing long.

That wasn't the end of them. In subsequent days they picked up my trail from time to time, when they had nothing better to do, and devised ways to torment me. I thought of picking up a stick and chasing them, but soon discarded the idea. There was nothing they would like better. Being soft and accepting was my best defence, although not a perfect one. I remained to them a constant temptation.

I came to dread the sound of their voices, voices filled with eagerness for wounding words, poking words, cutting words, jabbing words, jeering words, words like one of Topsell's monsters with teeth and claws and poisonous stings.

Baiting me became their favourite game.

It took them a long time to lose interest.

Hard etched and trippy

Now that I've stopped talking, my senses have sharpened. The visible world looks hard-etched and trippy, as if it's surrounded by a nimbus of energy. The sun hurts my eyes. The wind gets stuck in my teeth. The air rasps my skin. The blue of the sky is crackly. The stars called The Three Friends or Orion's Belt stand out like polished buttons on a black coat. I can see further than I used to. Into the spaces left behind after speech faded.

On Brighton Beach, looking east across the Pacific Ocean, my eye can follow the curvature of the world. When I leave Hagley Park to walk up Riccarton Road, going west, it's not long before the Southern Alps appear, glowing white, looking as if they're just a short stride away. Strength surges through me. My legs could eat up the miles between me and the alps, me and Balashikha.

When I read, the words jump out at me as if they were lying in wait. I absorb whole paragraphs at a glance.

If I talked, I would say everything at once.

My hearing has sharpened. I can hear far-off sounds as if they were close by, picking up conversations from the other side of a busy café. People's speech is full of flinty accents and scratching sibilants. I have to wear ear-plugs when close to loud traffic, a snarling motorbike or a grinding truck will rip through my head. At night, sitting in Hagley Park, I can hear the crash of waves on Brighton Beach, which should be impossible given that it's a good two hours walk away. A jet passing overhead will get half way to South America before its echo fades. When people speak to me, it's the sounds that come at me, intrusively loud and blatant, while meaning follows a little later. This pause between the sound and its meaning makes me seem a little slow on the uptake, a little slow to return my now practised nods, smiles, shrugs and shakes of the head.

Aromas have never been more present. The air is a medley of odours, not all of them pleasant. I can smell the scent of a rose from the other side of the park, or the stink of garbage streets away. In the street, I can smell a heavily perfumed woman before she comes into view. From as far away as the museum, I can smell food being cooked at the Gumption restaurant in the city centre. I can smell herbicide being sprayed in the gardens of Merivale a couple of kilometres away, and can even smell the difference between the ubiquitous Roundup and other acrid formulations. It takes a lot of time for the aftertaste in my mouth to subside. Once I smelled death and walked for five minutes before finding a dead cat discarded behind a fence.

I've become super sensitive to everything around me. My skin prickles in the morning air. Wind caresses my arms with moth wings. The sun slides over my body like silk. Everything I touch seems to contain, in its topography, a hidden landscape, sharp edges and deep furry hollows. The night sky is pure velvet. When I touch a leaf I can sense its life throbbing. It immediately connects me to all the other leaves and to the tree itself, and all the other trees and living things. Everything that pulses.

I am finding the city increasingly difficult to deal with. Everything is loud and jangly. Metal shrieks against metal, horns blare with industrial strength. Neon clashes with neon. People shout at each other across narrow spaces. Underneath it all, as if coming from the ground, there is a dark, grinding noise as if there were engines buried in the magma far below.

My life as a mutie

Increasingly I live in the park, the middle, as far away from these noises as possible. I didn't try to buy myself a new apartment. At first I tried renting. That didn't work. Other renters wanted to talk to me, find out who I was. It became uncomfortable. Then it was hotels. They were better. Nobody was too keen to engage me.

I became a homeless person, sleeping in different places, sometimes getting a hotel for the night, sometimes in a homeless shelter, sometimes in the park. I have my mountain back-pack, with two or three changes of clothes, my mountain wear and a toilet bag. The rest of my gear, tent and other necessities for doing field work I put in long-term storage.

I have plenty of money. The apartment sold for a high price and after Aria and I had split the money, I had enough to keep me going for many years as long as I didn't try to buy another apartment. I can stay at a swanky hotel if I want to, and sometimes do, for I discovered that when you have money you can find silence in a city. You can feel hermetically sealed in an expensive room, cut off from the blare and glare.

Wherever I sleep, I seek out a café that opens early, read the newspapers and drink coffee. I read the *International Herald Tribune*, which comes printed on wafer thin paper, *The Nation*, *New Scientist* and of course the *National Geographic*. Sometimes I buy *Newsweek* and *The Saturday Review*. I want to keep up with the world and what is happening in it. It is easy to serve myself a breakfast and point to the drink I want. I stay in the café until it fills up with chatterers and then move off to the park or a bench, maybe the library, which is always nice and quiet, and continue my research and writing. As my senses fill up with the world, my sense of self diminishes. I have less and less need for what is called a 'personality.' Without that personality, I can simply be myself. Along with personalities come complications. Not talking has stripped my life of those complications.

Sometimes I just sit in Hagley Park, beside the Avon, and watch bits and pieces flow past. I watch hundreds of lives flow past. I often think back to my childhood in Hanmer, the freedom I had to roam. From the age of three I was a free wanderer. Maybe my parents were neglectful or remiss in letting such a young child roam about, but I'm glad of it now, glad that I'd been able to get away from the need to talk because of my stutter. Glad to watch the play of light on river stones. Of Olga and our shared language, our wondrous privacy. Of the somewhat mysterious Mrs Rockwell and Topsell's *History of Four-Footed Beasts and Serpents*. I'm glad Mrs Rockwell showed me that book, for, looking back, I see that Topsell was, with his fantasy creatures, portraying human beings in their true state, their authentic, inner selves. Poring over Topsell had helped prepare me for the human world.

Sometimes I think of nothing much at all, not getting drawn into any particular memory or the emotions memories trigger, just floating, gossamer light, above the moving water, feeling the ebb and flow of the city around me – a restless, prickly creature.

On one occasion, while sitting beneath a very English beech tree with no one around, I found words, or at least sounds, beginning to bubble out of my mouth. It felt like the flowing Avon had caught up my tongue and was carrying it away. It felt a bit like talking in tongues, and I was reminded of Mrs Rockwell's solemn exploration of glossolalia. I had the uncanny sensation that I was trying to talk in some language left over from Babel and no longer spoken. I was the last living speaker of a forgotten language. The sensation passed, leaving me feeling peaceful, as if I had just said everything that I needed to say.

I usually get up from these meditations by the river feeling refreshed and needing to walk. I pass people, dog-walkers and joggers, and smile at them. Some smile back, others look puzzled, still others look wary. Some are used to me and give me a familiar nod. Some, who were frightened of me at first, have got used to me. Some people grin the way they do when they spot the village idiot. I am the mutie, the speechless guy. Ultimately harmless.

I like to pause and listen to an ancient Chinese man who squats on a little box and bows bent notes on a one-stringed instrument, playing with sensitivity and feeling, turning the air sad. He has a hat out on the ground in front of him, but since he tends to choose remote spots, he can't make much money. His playing is repetitive and melancholy. He doesn't look up or acknowledge anybody, even those who put something in his hat. His face is like a graven mask. When I sit in front of him and listen, time slows down. I always throw a few silver coins into his hat.

The town idiot

Not only do I have mocking children to contend with, it seems I now have imitators, followers who also wander about the park carrying their possessions in backpacks, scribbling in a notebooks and refusing to talk. They form a little cult of which I am the unwitting leader. I don't know how many there are, but I have seen two of them. One is a young man who started following me at a distance, doing what I do. If I sit on the river bank watching the river flow, he will do the same. If I sit on a park bench reading a book or writing he will do the same. He looks terribly intense and I avoid him whenever I can. He keeps his distance, but lurks just close enough for me to be aware of him. Another is a woman, maybe in her fifties, lean and angular, with a particularly rigid, fixed way of walking. She tends to avoid me, but once when passing by, walking in the other direction, she gave me a meaningful look, as rigid and fixed as her walk, as if we shared some profound understanding. I don't like the look of her and am glad she keeps out of my way. There are others, although some of them may be mockers.

Rather than being inconspicuous, which is my aim, I have attracted attention and am recognised wherever I go. After all, Christchurch is not such a big city, and I have become too much of a common sight, getting around with my backpack, nodding and smiling and scribbling. I am everybody's fool. Many people treat me as if I'm mentally deficient, which is natural enough. Others, who see me writing, realise that I'm not mentally deficient and conclude that instead I must be crazy.

One day I was sitting on my favourite park bench overlooking the river, envying its ever-placid movement, when two uniformed policemen approached me. One was middle-aged and tired. The other was young and officious. They stood on the path and observed me. I nodded to them courteously. They didn't nod back. I didn't know what to do and turned back to the river. All this will pass, the river murmured.

I tried not to feel afraid. I had committed no crime. I hadn't been doing anything to arouse suspicion, unless lying under a tree in the park on a hot day for several hours watching clouds come and go constitutes being a danger to the public. I had not drawn attention to myself with unruly behavior. I didn't drink or take illegal drugs.

I read somewhere that when confronted by the law, everybody feels like a criminal. I didn't want to feel like that. Not talking was not a chargeable offence.

They approached me and began asking questions. Who was I? Where did I live? Did I have a job? Did I sleep in the park? Why did I loiter around the park walkways children used going to or returning home from school? Was I harassing children? Could they inspect my backpack? Perhaps we should go to the station for a chat.

I suspected some zealous parent found my presence disturbing.

They were not happy with my silence. I pointed to my throat and waved my hand in front of my mouth. I wanted them to think I was suffering from a medical condition. They would understand that. They looked at each other. They were not impressed. The older one considered me with weary bewilderment. The younger one reminded me of the boy with the stick who wanted to prod me.

They watched me alertly as I dug unto my backpack and pulled out my documents. I showed them my documents, including a driver's license, my university staff card (out of date, but they didn't bother to check), my library card, my passport, and my bank book. Showing them my account balance did the trick. They raised their eyebrows at each other, walked off some distance and spoke in low voices.

The older one returned with some friendly advice. I shouldn't draw attention to myself. I should stay away from children. I shouldn't lie on the grass and stare up at the clouds. Since I had the money, I should find suitable lodgings. I couldn't live on park benches, even in the summer.

And, finally, they would be keeping an eye on me. Did I understand? I understood.

An instrument of subtle reception

Perhaps I will talk again; words may be lying in wait for me. I don't believe that I am special or strange in any way. My future is not set in stone. Sometimes I imagine I might fall in love again and rejoin the talking world. Love may only be a heartbeat away. Other times I imagine becoming a reclusive mountain man where the police would never bother me, driven to human habitation only by the need to buy food and supplies.

Since I stopped talking, I have become a listener, a watcher, a receiver. I see the human mind as an instrument of subtle reception rather than a factory for the creation of words and ideas. The mind receives signals from across the spectrum of matter and spirit, but does so imperfectly when we are constantly producing words. Increasingly, I see words as a screen hiding reality from us. Words in themselves are not real things, they merely pretend to be. They may trip images off in the mind, but they can't bring us to the substance of things. In their thrall we become creatures of oblivion.

I saw that my silence was my true and essential condition.

Reality has become debased into a worthless product of a degraded language, as Orwell foresaw. My speechless state suspends me, holds me in its gentle calm. Words pass by on slippered feet. When I look at them, they look the other way. They are ashamed of their treachery, their poverty, the compromises they have made. Their debasement.

I yearn to connect with that which lies beyond the haze of language.

Trickster time

Time is starting to play tricks with me. It is as if surrendering speech has freed me from the bonds of time, as if the grammar of language itself creates time. I saw a child enter the park from the west going home from school and leave the park aged and bent. I heard a song in the street that was popular in the 1920s called *Yes, We Have No Bananas*. I saw a woman bring a baby into the park and leave with a toddler, although she did not seem to change. I sat under an elm tree for a few hours, during which time its leaves turned yellow, dropped from the tree, fresh green leaves sprang from the branches and grew lush. I felt a wind that sprang from the other side of the world. I saw the world burn up, to cool down epochs later. I saw people dressed strangely, some in rags, wandering about looking lost in time, like extras who have wandered onto the wrong film set. In the middle of the night I saw a moa run down Cashel Street as if on stilts. When I lie and look up at the sky, I can easily believe it is the same sky my ancestors looked up at thousands of years ago.

The cycles of life turn, and I am at their still, voiceless centre.

My body seems to grow old and young depending on what I'm doing. Lying on my back staring up at the sky, I grow very old indeed, perhaps to the moment of dying, a lifetime behind me. When I wander as far as the Waimakariri River, and begin to follow its course back up into the mountains to my childhood home, I become young again, so young time hardly means anything to me at all.

Sometimes I think that I will wake one morning and find myself back in the empty, mirror-bound city of Balashikha, which will become my eternity. Olga will be there and we will be kindred spirits. We won't talk because we'll have no need to. Our eyes and hands will talk our love for us. We will linger on Lovers' Bridge with nowhere else to go, and watch the slow, silent water slip by. Balashikha may dissolve like a dream, but will always reconstitute itself on a clear day.

And sometimes I imagine waking up as a child again in our mountain village, a little person struggling with language, trying to attach words to things, stuttering in my efforts to engage with phonemes. Once more walking up the Hanmer River as if I could follow it to its source in the Hossack Saddle. Olga would be by my side, dark-haired and laughing. My twin. My soul.

The word bringer

You have put me on notice, Ariel. You, word bringer, will be leaving, and taking these words with you. You will become the word-taker. I will finish this report and put my pen and notebook aside forever. At that point my true journey will begin.

For the first time ever, you came to me in corporeal form, You assumed a body. That was unexpected. Maybe that was always in your power.

I was sitting on a park bench, thinking about this report, now nearly complete, when a man came up and sat down beside me. It was clearly deliberate, there were empty benches he could have chosen.

At first, I didn't look at him. Strangers who approach me are usually trouble.

Then I saw he was the old man with the straggly long hair and the quilted jacket I'd seen a couple of times in Charlie's, and in the library. Now I saw he was Ariel in disguise, my word bringer, my imaginary playmate, my shadow. Here before me in the flesh.

'You have fulfilled your duty,' he said.

What duty? I wasn't some soldier in the field.

He pointed to the notebook. 'You can burn it now, if you wish.'

I don't wish.

He laughed. 'Of course not. Everybody wants to leave something behind. To scratch their mark on stone. Words don't last in thin air.' He smiled. It was not condescending. His face glowed like the rising sun.

I wondered if he could be me. Me with another thirty or forty years etched on my face. Me after all is said and done.

I looked at him and you looked back at me. You were quite calm. We recognised each other. You were the ancient one. You were the secret self, hiding inside my name, inside my mother's dresser mirror. At the same time, you were Ariel, the demiurge who could turn words into flesh. And set them walking. Making their own way. Finding their own mountain, their own Balashikha.

You've put me on notice. These are to be my last words. Writing this report was little more than a subterfuge. I hadn't left words behind at all; I'd just driven them underground and they'd found their way onto the page. Now that loophole is closing.

'You are relieved.' You laughed. Perhaps the idea that a conscientious objector was some kind of soldier was amusing to you. I saw people shelling each other with words from their entrenched positions. Grief was never far away.

I felt dizzy, as if I was going to fall off the bench, into the soft grass, into the hard earth, though the earth, out into space, the void between stars. The earth hesitated in its orbit.

'I have business elsewhere. I must take my enchantments with me. They are not mine. They have to be returned. These last words I now pass over to you. They are all I have, and all I've ever had, and we will not mourn them. The last chapter of humankind is being written.'

We are on our feet facing each other, each the mirror of the other. It is a moment as solemn, joyful and bloody as birth. The world whirls around us in a blur. Syllables scatter like autumn leaves.

'Let's seal up the book,' you say.

And we do just that.

Together.

End

Mike Johnson –Publishing history

Novels

2020 – Driftdead, Lasavia Publising: Auckland

2016 – Zombie in a Spacesuit, Lasavia Publising: Auckland

2014 – Hold my Teeth While I Teach you to Dance: Lasavia Publishing Ltd: Auckland.

2011 – Travesty, Titus Books: Auckland.

2004 – Stench, Hazard Press: Christchurch. (Republished by Lasavia Publishing, 2016)

2001 – Counterpart, Harper Collins: Sydney. (Republished by Lasavia Publishing, 2021)

1996 – Dumb Show, Longacre Press: Dunedin. (Won the Buckland Memorial Literary Award for fiction in 1997. Republished by Lasavia Publishing, 2016)

1991 – Lethal Dose, Hard Echo Press: Auckland. (Republished by Lasavia Publishing, 2019)

1987 – Antibody Positive, Hard Echo Press: Auckland.

1986 – Lear: The Shakespeare Company Plays Lear at Babylon, Hard Echo Press: Auckland. (Shortlisted for the NZ Book Awards)

Short fiction

2023 – Afterworld, A novella. Lasavia Publishing: Auckland

2017 – Confessions of a Cockroach/Headstone, two novellas.

2016 – Back in the Day, short stories. Lasavia Publishing: Auckland

Lasavia Publishing: Auckland.

1991 – Foreigners, three novellas. Penguin Books: Auckland.

Poetry

2025 – Wheeling South, Lasavia Publishing: Auckland

2024 – The Nine Lives of Willa the cat, Lasavia Publishing: Auckland. (Ilustrated by Frances Ryder. To be published in November, 2024)

2024 – Love In The Age of Unreason, Lasavia Publishing: Auckland. (To be published in November, 2024)

2023 – Selected Poems, Mike Johnson, edited by Jack Ross, Lasavia Publishing: Auckland.

2023 – Sketches (Graphics by Leila Lees), Lasavia Publishing: Auckland.

2020 – The Raising Light Trilogy, Lasavia Publishing: Auckland.

2020 – The Raising Light Trilogy published as separate volumes: The Toy Box, Hide Your Eyes and Extinction Rebellion, Lasavia Publishing. Auckland.

2017 – Ladder with No Rungs, Lasavia Publishing: Auckland.

2016 – Two Lines and a Garden, Lasavia Publishing: Auckland.

2011 - To Beatrice Where We Crossed The Line, Second Avenue Press: Auckland. (Graphics by Simon Oosterdijk)

2009 – The vertical Harp, Titus Books: Auckland.

1996 – Treasure Hunt, Auckland University Press: Auckland.

1985 – Standing Wave, Hard Echo Press: Auckland.

1984 – From a Woman in Mt Eden Prison & Drawing Lessons, Hard Echo Press: Auckland.

1983 – The Palanquin Ropes, Voice Press: Wellington. (Co-winner of the John Cowie Reid Memorial Competition for a long poem or sequence of poems)

Non Fiction

2025 – Bob Dylan's Never Ending Tour: Volume I The Eighties and Ninties, Lasavia Publishing: Auckland.

2025 – Bob Dylan's Never Ending Tour: Volume II The New Millennium, Lasavia Publishing: Auckland.

2025 – Bob Dylan's Never Ending Tour: Volume III The Twenty-teens.

2014 – The Angel of Compassion, Lasavia Publishing Ltd: Auckland. (Shortlisted for the Aston Wylie Awards, manuscript section)

1973 – Dialogue, Whitcomb and Tombs: Christchurch: a text for senior English, (Co-author with A.T. Johnson).

Children

2019 – Flipperty Flupperty Flop (graphics by Daniela Gast), Lasavia Publishing: Auckland.

2016 – Kenni and the Roof Slide (Graphics by Jennifer Rackham), Lasavia Publishing: Auckland.

2015 – Taniwha (Graphics by Jennifer Rackham), Lasavia Publishing: Auckland. Bilingual: English and Te Reo.

About the Author

Mike Johnson, fiction writer and poet, is recognised as one of New Zealand's leading innovative writers. He lives on Waiheke Island and has taught creative writing at AUT University and the University of Auckland. In 2002 he received The University of Auckland's Literary Fellowship, having been Literary Fellow at Canterbury University in 1987. His first novel, Lear: the Shakespeare Company Plays Lear at Babylon was shortlisted for the New Zealand Book Awards in 1986, his novel Dumb Show won the Buckland Memorial Award for Literary Excellence in 1997, and he won the Frances Kean Award for his short story Magic Strings in 1999. His first book of poetry, The Palanquin Ropes (1983), was co-winner of the John Cowie Reid Memorial Competition. His non-fiction, Angel of Compassion, was shortlisted for the Ashton Wylie Award in 2014, and a poem from Vertical Harp: Selected poems of Li He (2006) was anthologised in the Essential New Zealand Poems: Facing the Empty Page (Random House, 2014). Critic Martin Edmond described the 2020 novel, Driftdead, as 'a masterpiece.' In 2025, Johnson published a three-volume musical study of Bob Dylan's Never Ending Tour.

Mike Johnson is the author of thirty-nine books, including eleven novels, seventeen books of poetry, four of shorter fiction, five non-fiction and three children's books.